SOUL REMAINS

TERRIBLY SERIOUS DAKNESS, BOOK TWO

SAM HOOKER

ISBN (print): 978-1-7329357-2-3
ISBN (ebook): 978-1-7329357-3-0
ISBN (mobi): 978-1-7329357-4-7
Illustration by Lian Croft
Cover design by Najla Qamber
Edited by Lindy Ryan
Interior Layout Design Rebecca Poole
Publication date April 23, 2019
Black Spot Books

DEDICATION

For Shelly, the Myrtle to my Sloot.

PREVIOUS WORKS BY SAM HOOKER

Peril in the Old Country (Terribly Serious Darkness, Book 1)
The Winter Riddle

CAST

- Sloot Peril, a late accountant and award-winning worrier.

- Roman Bloodfrenzy, Spymaster of Salzstadt for the Carpathian Intelligence service.

- Myrtle Pastry, Sloot's late girlfriend, who was in life possessed by a philosopher of no renown.

- Lord Constantin Hapsgalt, father of Willie and late Eye of the Serpent, who was skipped over for Soul of the Serpent by his son's untimely demise.

- Lord Wilhelm "Willie" Hapsgalt, the recently deceased Soul of the Serpents of the Earth and Sloot's employer.

- Mrs. Knife, a deranged lunatic who is as dangerous as she sounds. She became the Eye of the Serpent by murdering Willie.

- Gregor, a necromancer who's been up to no good for over a thousand years.

- Vlad Defenestratia the Invader, 37th of her name, ruler of Carpathia and the greatest warrior ever to have lived.

- Greta Urmacher, paramour of Vlad the Invader and wife of the late Willie Hapsgalt. It's complicated.

- Nicoleta Goremonger, a ghost, who was in life court wizard to Vlad the Invader. Her wardrobe could be seen from space.

- Dr. Arthur Widdershins, the aforementioned philosopher. You've never heard of him.

- Nan, Willie's late nanny, who was under the magically-induced impression that Willie was perpetually 6 years old.

- The Domnitor, long may he reign, despotic ruler of the Old Country.

- Winking Bob, proprietor of the Four Bells, queen of the black market, and "honest" businesswoman extraordinaire.

- Edmund, Bob's personal bodyguard and veritable dictionary of legal disclaimers.

- Flavia, Sloot's handler in Uncle, Salzstadt's rebranded Ministry of Truth.

- Grumley, a deceased fixer for the Serpents of the Earth.

- Sir Berthold Kriegstockente, a Keeper for the Skeleton Key Circle.

- Franka, apprentice to Sir Berthold.

- Hans Schweinegesicht, financier to Constantin's mother, the late Otthilda Hapsgalt.

- Geralt Schlangenkessel, financier to the late Constantin Hapsgalt.

- The Steward of the Skeleton Key Circle, of whom little is known beyond his position and expertise in the Book of Black Law.

- Agather, witch and proprietor of the Witchwood in the forests of Carpathia.

- Bartleby, a very old necromancer who insists that vampires are cool.

- Turk, proprietor and publican of Turk's.

- Barry and Gus, a pair of formerly living guards at the Old Country-Carpathian border.

- King Lilacs, ruler of the fairies.

- General Dandelion, leader of the fairy army.

- Sladia Peril, Sloot's mother.

- The Coolest, who require now introduction. They know everybody.

- Igor, a gremlin with aspirations.

And some other people as well, but there's not going to be a test or anything.

⅏⟶EVER HEREAFTER⟵⅏

I t was all grey. All of it. It occurred to Sloot that it hadn't always been grey—everything, that is—but in that moment, he couldn't conceive of what else it might have been.

Sloot panicked. At least that reflex was working as expected. He was lying in a grave. Well, *on* a grave would have been more accurate. If he were going for full marks, he'd have said *above*. He was hovering not quite far enough above a grave to trigger his standard-issue fear of heights, but even an inch of hover was enough to get the old hyperventilation reflex into gear. Until now, hovering hadn't been part of his repertoire.

He didn't hyperventilate, though. That would have required lungs. He couldn't recall exactly how long it had been since he'd had that bizarre conversation with Fairy Godmother—whatever her real name was—but it had been long enough for Sloot to have forgotten that he was dead.

"Dead," he said to himself, trying to wrap his mind around it. Sloot was dead, floating above a grave, bereft of lungs in an altogether grey landscape, and inexplicably craving a house in which he might wander indefinitely, moaning or rattling chains or something.

Sloot was a ghost. He'd schedule an exam with a physician at his earliest opportunity to confirm it, but only because that was what you did. Most of a physician's job was confirming the maladies people already knew they had. Without that they'd have precious little to say to anyone, aside from how to treat those maladies. Sloot was assuredly dubious that a cure for death was available to anyone, necromancers aside.

Sloot continued to panic. He lay there, staring up at the grey, silently pleading with his mind to grasp the enormity of it well enough to afford him the strength to sit up.

It wasn't working. His mind worked tirelessly at maintaining steadfast denial about the entire state of affairs, leaving him frozen in repose. After a while—which could have taken a few seconds or an eternity, Sloot couldn't tell—there was a lull in his panic. It didn't abate altogether, but it gave him just enough wiggle room to have a bit of a ponder.

"Why?" he pondered. Not *why* would he want to sit up at all, but *why* should he be in any hurry to get on with it? He was *dead*. If there was any benefit to having shuffled off the mortal coil, shouldn't it be that there was no longer a need to hurry? His time was his own! That hadn't been the case in a long, long time, not since he'd established his own rigorous sleeping schedule when he was four years old.

"Stay up as late as you want," his mother had said. Far from learned in the ways of the world, Sloot knew enough to be staunchly opposed to that sort of lackadaisical routine. That way led to hooliganism, he just knew it.

But now ... did the dead get to have jobs? He tried to amend the thought to *"must* the dead have jobs?" but he simply didn't have it in him. His body didn't get the work ethic in the divorce, it seemed.

How long had he been lying there? He wasn't sure. Time didn't really seem to pass here. Well, it did, but there was no way to know how much. He had no frame of reference, like riding in a coach with no windows on a very smooth road. And the horses were wearing wool slippers. It was a bad metaphor, but he didn't care to do any better.

No, he had a job. He was sure of it. As much as he tried to rationalize that people didn't keep turning up to work after they'd expired, he still felt the lingering dread that he was late for something, or that there was work left undone.

The distraction seemed to have helped. He'd forgotten to panic for long enough to feel up to sitting. He tried flexing his abdominal muscles in the standard practice associated with rising to a seated position, but it was no good. He lacked abdominal muscles.

Panic restored. It was comforting, in a uniquely Sloot Peril sort of way.

Eventually, though, he managed it. He discovered that there were ethereal equivalents to standard muscle movements. They weren't that different, really. Not in any way that Sloot wanted to consider at length, in any case. That way led nothing but more panic. Denial had been a favorite coping mechanism of Sloot's in life, and he was glad to see that it still worked in the afterlife.

Sloot sat up. No color but grey in any direction, which Sloot didn't find disagreeable, *per se*. What he remembered of colors he associated with extravagance.

It wasn't a very large graveyard, something Sloot felt was suspicious. Setting aside why graveyards would exist in the afterlife in the first place, and given the unfathomable number of people who'd died in the course of history, shouldn't there be millions of headstones there?

Sloot shook the thought from his mind, adding it to his growing list of things to ponder later. Or, preferably, not at all. His capacity for denial hadn't failed him yet, so there was hope.

The little graveyard sat atop a hill, which was one among a number of other hills, rolling, grassy, and grey. They seemed to stretch on forever in every direction. The only other things that he could see were the roof of a house and a dark forest beyond that. Fortunately, at least one of his preconceptions was fulfilled when he moved closer and found a large two-story house beneath the roof. The relief was nearly sufficient to make him forget he'd floated over the hills to it instead of walking, but that was not the sort of thing one forgot lightly.

The house was grey, which came as no surprise. It seemed familiar to him, though he was sure he'd never seen it before. It was as if a house he'd previously seen had a distant cousin he was meeting for the first time.

No, that wasn't it. It took a moment—which could have been ages, it was hard to tell—but he ultimately realized that he was *home*.

He went inside. More grey, from the high grey ceilings, down the grey paisley wallpaper to the grey wainscoting, and ending in the dark grey wood—or an ethereal approximation thereof—beneath his feet. The little entryway led into a long hall, which one might expect in a large house such as this one. However, Sloot had sworn off having expectations for the foreseeable future, given the way things were going.

He floated along the hallway, looking into the rooms on either side of it as he passed. They were mostly empty, though a few had bits of furniture in them. It was as though someone had moved into it from a much smaller place, and spread their furniture around as evenly as possible for the time being.

There was a large living room at the end of the hall. He hadn't expected to run into anyone there, much less someone he knew.

"You're noticing the grey thing," said Nicoleta. "Please tell me that you remember colors? No one else seems to."

Nicoleta had had a flair for color before she, along with most of the people who'd attended Willie and Greta's wedding, died in a maelstrom of goblins and shambling undead. She'd also had a firm grasp on the arcane workings of magic and could do some truly powerful things with it, but it had been her dazzling wardrobe that had really set her apart from run-of-the-mill wizards, whose robes were the amalgamated color of everything that had gotten on them since the last time they bothered to put on fresh ones. Most of it was soup.

"Sorry," said Sloot. "I remember that there was more than grey before … before…"

"Oh, no," came a pained wail from across the room, "not Sloot, too!"

"Oh," said Sloot, "sorry, I should go then?"

"No, no," said the voice that had wailed before, which he now recognized as belonging to Myrtle. "I'm just sad that you died, that's all."

Sloot blinked, or would have, if he had eyelids anymore. It's more accurate to say that his soul performed all of the expression of confusion that went along with a very slow and deliberate blink, and the netherworldly manifestation of his soul gave the appearance of having done so; however, the physical act of blinking never took place in the strictest sense. No eyes were moistened.

Explanations of the rote classification of metaphysical phenomena aside, Sloot was having trouble determining what Myrtle was trying to say. She'd been his girlfriend in life—he was fairly sure of it—so it stood to reason that she'd be happy they were both dead, so they could be together. Perhaps she'd not really been his girlfriend? He'd never had one before they'd done all of that kissing. He tried remembering whether Central Bureaucracy had a form that needed filling out, Declaration of Romantic Intent or somesuch, but he couldn't recall.

"That doesn't mean I'm not glad to see you," said Myrtle, as if reading his thoughts. She smiled in a way that would have warmed his heart, if he'd still had one.

Sloot took comfort in that, as well as some small measure of solace in his continued capacity to indulge in a bit of gut-wrenching worry. He considered that he no longer had guts to wrench, but tried to put the thought out of his mind. He'd need to curb the specificity of his inner monologue if he wanted to get anything done.

Oh, but that was worrisome. What was there to get done? His inner monologue returned to the matter of jobs, and whether the dead had them. He hoped so, lest his wealth of accounting knowledge go entirely to waste.

A very angry voice shouted a truly vile swear word from elsewhere in the house. In the direction from which he'd just come, in fact. It would be just Sloot's luck, only just given his own house, and already there was someone filthying it up with goblins.

"There's something familiar about this," said Sloot.

"It's just Constantin," said Nicoleta, referring to the elder Lord Hapsgalt, who had recently been perhaps the richest person alive, and head of a nefarious secret society known as the Serpents of the Earth. "He's been at it for a while."

"No, the house. I can't have been here before, can I? I've only just died."

"I was wondering the same thing," said a very tall and gangly ghost with a ridiculous recurved moustache, whom Sloot had never seen before.

"Sorry, have we met?"

"That's Arthur," said Myrtle.

"Arthur ... not the philosopher that you were possessed with? Or is it 'by'? Oh, bother. *Ahem.*" Sloot paused. "Not the philosopher who possessed you?"

"The very same!" said Arthur. "Don't worry, you'll get used to the Hereafter soon enough."

"Like you know," said Myrtle. "You may have been dead a long time, but you haven't been here any longer than the rest of us."

"I've been here longer than Sloot," said Arthur defensively. He may have technically been correct, but so was Myrtle. She'd witnessed the executions at the end of the Philosophers' Rebellion, one of whom had happened to be Arthur. Just as the guillotine was doing its job, the two of them made eye contact. Instead of moving on to the Hereafter, Arthur possessed Myrtle, who had been just a little girl at the time. It wasn't the worst fate that could befall an orphan, but she'd had trouble making friends after that. No one wants to talk to the five-year-old who won't shut up about existentialism.

"Why are you pronouncing 'Hereafter' like that?" asked Sloot. "All properly, I mean."

Arthur shrugged. "It didn't occur to me to do it otherwise. Surely you know about Eierunglück's Treatise on Instinctual Pronunciation."

"I do not," said Sloot, who was uncertain that he possessed any instincts at all, linguistic or otherwise.

"Well, it's mostly used for ostracizing foreigners," said Arthur, "but it's got some practical applications."

Constantin shouted more swear words from elsewhere in the oddly familiar house. Sloot cringed again, both for the goblins that were sure to result, and for his particular dislike of the swear word that literally meant the smell of rotting fruit, but was used by the wealthy as a pejorative for anyone who had little enough money that it could be easily counted.

"Relax," said Nicoleta, "there are no goblins in the Hereafter."

"Am I thinking out loud or something?" asked Sloot. "I've got some fretting to do about anatomy, perhaps I should leave the room."

"No, no," said Nicoleta. "We just know how you like to worry."

Sloot said nothing. Were he to have said something, he'd probably have denied that he *liked* to worry. It was just something that he did all the time. Worry was an old friend, as constant a companion as a hungry wolf who runs exactly as fast as he does.

Willie floated into the room, looking at once dapper and downtrodden. "Oh," he said, in a dejected sort of way.

Wilhelm Hapsgalt, son of Constantin Hapsgalt and heir to the Three Bells Shipping Company fortune, had been put to the business end of Mrs. Knife's ... knife, shortly after he'd done the very same thing to his father. He hadn't wanted to, of course. Willie was a gentle sort of idiot, having only found himself in possession of a great fortune and in the upper echelons of the Serpents of the Earth as an accident of birth. It was their gruesome traditions that had compelled Willie to fratricide.

"Something wrong, Willie?" asked Myrtle, seeming disinterested in the response.

"Yeah, I've seen this room before."

"And that's bad."

"It's all right, I guess. I was just hoping it'd be bigger."

"The room?"

"The house!" Willie rolled his eyes. "We all live here. It should be bigger, shouldn't it?"

Two things struck Sloot as funny. The first was the use of the word "live," which none of them were doing in the proper sense. The second was that Willie was right. Sloot knew it to be true. He definitely, well, *resided* there. It lacked any feeling of coziness or comfort that one would expect to find in a home, possibly due to the lack of covers having been knit for everything. Sloot had lived with his mother for a very long time.

"How much space do you need?" asked Nicoleta. "I'm not entirely sure that 'space' properly exists here."

"Finally," said Arthur, "a proper debate on existentialism! Do you know how long I've been waiting for one of you to join me on an intellectual level?"

"That's cute," said Nicoleta, who had less than zero respect for philosophy. Wizards considered it to be the lowest form of magic. They'd disavow it altogether, were it not for the fact that it does come with a few quasi-magical abilities. That was how Arthur had managed to possess Myrtle, after all.

"Where am I supposed to put my wardrobe?" asked Willie, who punctuated the question with a little huff. He'd tended to do that in life, when he'd been too long without a nap.

"You don't wear clothes in the Hereafter," said Nicoleta.

"Nonsense. Explain this cravat."

"It's a manifestation of your psyche," said Arthur.

"It's silk!"

Sloot looked down. He was wearing the same black wool ensemble he'd worn in life, only it was grey and translucent, like everything else. All the clothing he'd owned in life had looked very similar, as was proper. Fashion was a distraction. They'd taught him that in accounting school, along with a complete recounting of the unanimous agreement on the correct size, shape, and placement of leather elbow patches.

The outfit that Sloot wore now wasn't exactly what he'd been wearing when he died, but rather the average of every piece of clothing he'd ever owned in his life. It was the first pleasant thing he'd found about being dead, aside from Myrtle being there as well, though he didn't want to take joy in that.

"That's all the Hereafter is," said Nicoleta. "It's the amalgamation of every psyche within it manifested in a way that they can all sort of agree upon."

"That doesn't make the house any bigger," said Willie.

"It doesn't matter," said Myrtle through clenched teeth, "you haven't got any things!"

Willie's eyes went black. A pair of smoky, ethereal wings sprouted from between his shoulders. His forehead sprouted a pair of menacing, recurved horns to round out the look. The horns caught fire.

"All things shall be mine," said Willie, both in his regular tantrum voice and in a matter-of-fact one far deeper than the normal range of human speech. He gnashed his teeth, which were thrice as long as they'd been a moment ago, and razor sharp to boot.

Sloot was worried by this, but hardly surprised. Following the whole ritually-murdering-his-father-and-then-being-ritually-murdered-himself business, Willie was now presumably the Soul of the Serpent, one of two leaders of the shadowy secret society. The dead one. Mrs. Knife, having killed him, would be the Eye of the Serpent. The living one.

What Sloot didn't know about evil cults could fill several volumes of an encyclopedia. Or, quite possibly, it couldn't. He wouldn't know, would he? But it stood to reason that becoming the Soul of the Serpent might come with some bells and whistles that might, to the casual observer, come off as evil.

"By the Domnitor's eyes!" Sloot exclaimed, invoking the despotic ruler of the Old Country in the most potent exclamation he could muster. *Long may he reign,* he added silently.

"Sorry, what?" Willie was back to normal again.

"That was amazing!" said Nicoleta. "Can I do it?" She made a few faces that one might normally affect in the course of lifting heavy iron contraptions in gymnasiums, which exist only for the purpose of being lifted.

"I suppose not," she said, scanning everyone else's faces with a dejected smirk.

"Don't feel bad," said Willie. "Nobody can pull off the Cadbury Lad without practice. Took me years to make it look this effortless."

"Ah," said Sloot. "That would be the pose you're striking, then."

"No, the eyebrow raise! Honestly Sloot, it's like you don't even care about these things."

"A bit like that m'lord, yes."

There was a knock at the door.

"Just the one," noted Myrtle.

"One's all it takes," said Sloot, noticing how it had reverberated throughout the house.

9

"One of the servants will get it," said Willie, who hadn't opened a door himself in all the time that Sloot had known him. He wasn't altogether sure that Willie would know what to do with a doorknob if put to the task.

"I haven't seen any servants," said Myrtle.

"Oh," said Sloot.

"Oh, what?" asked Myrtle.

"I think that would be me." Sloot was referring to the tug he'd felt at Willie's suggestion, a gentle compulsion to do as he was told. But he hadn't been told, had he? He'd still been Willie's financier at the time of his death; perhaps he still technically worked for him.

Sloot couldn't suppress a little smile. He still had a job!

"I've heard about things like that," said Nicoleta. "Ancient kings would be buried with their servants, so they could be attended in the afterlife."

"But I don't want to be an ancient king!" Willie stamped his foot. "They had to stand still for portraits all the time, and I won't!"

There was a second knock at the door—one that implied there would be trouble if it had to repeat itself a third time.

"Hold your horses!" came a voice from the other room.

"Is that Nan?"

It most certainly was. She gave the top of Willie's head a kiss and a pat on her way past, and glared at Sloot.

"She was still working for Willie when she died as well," said Sloot. "But is she still under the spell that makes her believe Willie's a 6-year-old boy?"

"Powerful magic, that," said Nicoleta. "Must be a bit of necromancy, to follow her across the veil."

Necromancy. Magic having to do with the dead. Sloot remembered that from when he'd been alive. Roman had told him it had a lot to do with wizards who never took showers, owing to the fact that they'd just get dirty again in the course of rifling through fresh graves for finger bones and the like.

"Roman," said Sloot, to no one in particular.

"Still alive, I think," said Myrtle. Sloot took a measure of relief from that, even though it had been Roman—the Spymaster of Salzstadt for Carpathian Intelligence—who'd embroiled him in the harrowing chain of events that led to his untimely demise. While Sloot didn't believe there was such a thing as a timely demise, he hadn't yet finished paying into his retirement accounts. They'd be seized by the Ministry of Wealth upon his death since he had no heirs, and he didn't like to think that the Domnitor—long may he reign—would be disappointed in the amounts.

The door opened with a groan. There was no good reason for it that Sloot could see. After all, why would the ethereal representations of iron hinges need oiling? Probably something to do with the way that people who'd formerly been alive expected hinges to work.

The figure that entered was clad and hooded in a robe like the black ones everyone had been wearing at Willie and Greta's wedding. The hood provided an exceptional level of shadow over his face, which was probably one of those expensive-but-worth-it-for-making-ominous-entrances upgrades that tailors charge. All that could be seen of his face was a bulbous nose and a sideburns-and-connected-moustache arrangement that had gone out of fashion centuries ago.

"Well, I'm off," said Willie.

"What?" Nan balked. "Where are you going?"

"I must not be detained," said Willie, his voice and features going all malevolent again. He strode past the visitor and through the door without another word.

Before Sloot was able to wonder aloud—or quietly, for that matter—where Willie could possibly have been going, he accidentally committed eye contact with Nan. Her face had festooned itself with a half-crazed leer that demanded, simply, "Well?"

"Well, what?" asked Sloot in response.

"You know very well, well what!" Only one of Nan's fists were at her hips, her other hand having been called away for the urgent task of waggling a stern finger at Sloot. "You'd better get after him!"

⅏OLD BONES⅏

Sloot was utterly bereft of instincts with the singular exception of his flight response. He was sure he'd heard it called a "fight or flight response," but given that it had never called on him for the former, he assumed he'd heard wrong. In any case, he fled the house at Nan's insistence and found himself plodding along behind Willie. They were following a path that led into a dark and foreboding forest behind the house. He'd like to think that the path led *through* the forest to something else, but he was far too new to the afterlife to be sure.

"Er, pardon me, m'lord," called Sloot.

Willie turned. A forked tongue darted out from between his razor-sharp teeth. His glossy black eyes glared such malice into Sloot that he was certain it would have frozen his heart, if he still had one.

"I must not be detained," he boomed, with the same pair of voices he'd used before.

Sloot cringed. He was too fearful to do anything else, so he hoped it would be sufficient.

Willie's frightening visage vanished. "Oh, hi, Sloot," he said in the unaccompanied voice he'd used in life. His outfit had become an outdoorsy ensemble like the one he'd had tailored in homage to his hero, Sir Wallace Scoffington the explorer.

"Yes, hi," said Sloot. He continued to cringe, hoping perhaps that the shrinking pose would come off as a martial arts maneuver. "Er, would you mind telling me where you're going? Not that I'd dream of detaining you, of course."

"Oh. Um, well..." the pained expression on Willie's face conveyed to Sloot that he was thinking very hard about something. Sloot knew from experience that thinking was not Willie's forte.

"It's all right," ventured Sloot, "you can tell me."

"Oh, all right then," said Willie, "I've got to run and check on Dad's bones."

"You've got to check on your father's bones," repeated Sloot, while doing his level best to repress a shudder of revulsion.

"I thought 'Dad' and 'Father' meant the same thing."

"They do, I wasn't correcting you. I just meant ... really?"

"Well, yeah," jibed Willie, making a goofball smirk at Sloot that added a silent "duh."

"Okay," said Sloot, "good, good. Er, would you mind if I tagged along?"

Willie beamed. "That would be great! I've always wanted a sidekick. Where's yours?"

"Where's my ... oh."

Willie's outfit had changed again. He was wearing an opera ensemble, complete with a floor-length cape and burglar's mask like the ones criminals wore on the Ministry of Propaganda's posters.

Try as he might, Sloot couldn't even begin to fathom how to change his wardrobe. The clothes he was wearing, according to Nicoleta, were a projection of his psyche.

"Er, perhaps we should go incognito," he suggested.

"Incognito," said Willie, the pained expression of thought creeping back across his face.

"Less formal," said Sloot. "Perhaps try to blend in a bit, look inconspicuous?"

"Incon ... spacious?"

"This is an important mission," Sloot said, just above a whisper. "Shouldn't we avoid drawing attention to ourselves?"

"Of course," said Willie, suddenly wearing the sort of overcoat and tall boots one might wear on the fanciest fishing trip ever. "Now, then, where are we going?"

Death had definitely changed some things about Willie. He'd not been able to grow horns and wings and razor-sharp teeth in life. That was new. He'd had the attention span of a fish. That wasn't. It was a "worst of both worlds" outcome in Sloot's mind, but such is life—or the lack thereof—when one works for the vastly wealthy leaders of deeply sinister cults.

As time did not seem to pass in the Hereafter, Sloot wasn't sure how long it had taken him to remind Willie of his purpose and get them back on the road toward it. He was sure, however, that it had taken far longer than it should have done. They made their way through the path in the darkened wood, Sloot in his grey amalgamated ensemble, and Willie in a hunting jacket and matching hat.

From the outside the woods had seemed dark and ominous. From the inside they were also disturbingly quiet. Just when the stillness had become too much to bear, something made an impossibly deep grumbling sound. Something that presumably had teeth the size of broadswords and claws to match. The grumble implied that its throat was wide enough for Sloot to walk down it without stooping.

It was just enough to make Sloot long for the maddening silence to return. He looked around frantically as they continued to walk, but saw neither hide nor hair of any broadsword-toothed beast. After a while, he simply resolved never to think about it again. In his experience, that was the best thing to do.

"Ugh, this is boring," said Willie. "Where is my coach? Why is everything all grey?"

"Er, we're dead now, m'lord."

Willie turned around and demonstrated a confused expression that was far too strenuous to have been entirely natural. Willie knew all of the most fashionable walks, poses, dances, and even the most popular modes of tantrum. In Sloot's mind, it stood to reason that he'd be in the know on some couture facial expressions as well. This one was probably called something like the Contrite Starlet, or the Ambivalent Shrew.

"Are you sure?"

"Quite, I'm afraid."

"When did this happen?"

"Do you remember your wedding?"

"Of course I do," said Willie. He affected a look of realization, probably called the Staunch Hedgerow or somesuch nonsense. "Hey, I'm a married man!"

"Well, er, yes, technically. That is to say, right after the wedding we—"

"Where is my wife? Oh, and Sloot?"

"Yes, m'lord?"

"*Who* is my wife?"

"Ah," said Sloot, scrambling to compose a cohesive answer to all of the questions that had built up over the last … well, ever since Willie had gotten bored with walking.

"A married man should know that sort of thing, I think." Willie struck a dashing pose that Sloot felt should be reserved for advertising alcoholic beverages. He had no way of knowing that it was called the Once Upon a Thursday, and had been used twice for that very purpose.

Sloot racked his brain, grateful for the respite that Willie's infatuation with striking poses had bought him. He felt compelled to answer Willie, though he didn't feel particularly honor-bound to tell him the entirety of the truth. Greta was a friend of Sloot's, after all, and she'd been none too keen on being married to Willie. Still, nitwit that he was, Willie deserved some sort of answer.

"Her name is Greta, m'lord."

Willie continued staring off into space as though he hadn't heard what Sloot had said. All part of the pose, Sloot guessed. The affectation of staring off into the future, or the horizon, or whatever. It didn't matter, really.

The statement did eventually catch up to Willie, though. He shook his head. "Whose name is Greta?"

"Greta's, m'lord. Your—"

"Right, of course," snapped Willie with a dismissive wave. "It would be, wouldn't it? Aren't all Gretas named Greta?"

"Er, yes? Yes, m'lord." Sloot wore his most puzzled expression, which had no name of which he was aware.

Willie patted Sloot on the shoulder. "You're a decent fellow, Peril. I know you're trying to impress, but overstating the obvious isn't going to get you there, all right?"

"I appreciate the advice, m'lord."

Willie nodded. "It's this way."

As they continued down the path, Sloot waited for Willie to return to the uncomfortable subject of his nuptials, but it never came up. Either he'd forgotten the conversation entirely, or he'd felt the conversation had concluded in a satisfactory manner. Either way, Sloot was content to leave it alone.

They eventually came to a fork in the path. One way led further into the darkened wood, into very dark shadows that seemed far more foreboding than Sloot felt he had the fortitude to traverse. The other direction looked much the same, but was barred by a foreboding iron gate. It was twisted and spiked at the top, just the sort of thing that weird teenagers would draw on their bedroom walls, much to their parents' chagrin.

Two roads diverged in a haunted wood, one behind a scary-looking gate. It was simple odds, but Sloot had never been lucky.

"We're going that way, aren't we?" Sloot pointed toward the gate.

"How did you know?"

Sloot sighed. "I'm here."

Willie looked puzzled for a moment, but then tossed his head and gave a carefree chuckle, as though he'd just remembered that he was ridiculously wealthy. He gestured lazily toward the gate and it creaked open.

Down the path and into the distant shadows they went, eventually coming to a graveyard. It was the second one that he'd seen in the afterlife, which, at this point, was unremarkable. If there was one graveyard, there may as well be two.

"There's nobody else here," Sloot pondered aloud.

"No," said Willie, "just us and them."

"Them?" It was then that Sloot learned that the sensation of hairs standing on the back of one's neck was dependent on having neither.

"Them," Willie repeated. He pointed toward a sinister-looking mausoleum near the back of the graveyard. There was a dim grey light emanating from within it. Willie strode toward it.

"Wait!"

"What?"

"Who's in there?"

"Lots of people." Willie rolled his eyes. "That's what mausoleums are for, right?"

Sloot opened his mouth to ask more questions, but shut it when he considered that none of them could possibly result in an answer that would make him feel any better. He resigned himself to following Willie along the path toward possible doom, hoping that the dandy's demonic transformations came with strength beyond that of whatever horrors lurked in the crypt.

There was nothing. Well, not *nothing*. There were the standard accoutrements one would expect to find in a mausoleum: lots of marble, some long-dead flowers in marble vases … or, rather, the ethereal approximations thereof. The whole place was dimly illuminated, though Sloot couldn't tell from where.

"Hey!" shouted Willie. "What do you think you're doing?"

"Me? I was just—"

"Not you, them!" Willie pointed toward the altar on the back wall of the crypt. There were some old candlesticks that had fallen over, some quasi-religious-looking statues that made Sloot feel strangely uncomfortable, but no people.

"Oh, dear," moaned Sloot, more reverberantly than he'd intended. It felt strangely satisfying, moaning like that. The acoustics in the mausoleum were quite nice. Sloot felt as though this would be a perfectly nice spot to do a bit of haunting, if only it wasn't someone else's property. Wait, how did he know that? He wasn't sure how, but he was certain of the fact. Pity, it was just the sort of place that he'd love to moan and rattle a few chains at odd hours of the night.

"Hey you, stop that!" Willie was pushing against an invisible wall of some sort, straining under the effort. Curiosity got the better of Sloot, and he moved to place a hand against the wall himself.

He felt nothing. His hand passed right through it. He felt certain that Willie hadn't suddenly taken up pantomime, given how often he'd compared mimes to "clowns that don't know how to do balloon doggies or anything."

As Sloot watched Willie struggle with the non-existent wall, a shadow moved in the corner of his vision. He looked over at the altar and saw it again. The dim light was coming from the left side of the altar, at a jaunty angle suggesting that there was a space behind it.

"A secret passage," said Sloot. He'd just noticed that the altar wasn't quite centered on the wall, as though it had been moved a few feet to the right.

"Almost there," said Willie. His eyes had gone all black again, and there were lines of energy crackling beneath his palms, across the surface of the invisible wall.

"That looks dangerous," said Sloot, taking a step backward. "Are you sure that you should—"

There was a sound like glass breaking under water. Willie lurched forward a bit as the non-existent wall before him gave way, and there remained a sort of jagged hole in … Sloot wasn't sure in what. Space, probably, or maybe reality. But whatever it might have been, the other side of the hole was something Sloot hadn't seen in … well, since he died.

Colors. There were colors! Only faint ones, as it was nighttime on the other side of the jagged hole, but Sloot knew "not grey" when he saw it.

"Now then," said Willie, "time to put a stop to this."

"A stop to what?" asked Sloot. He hesitated in following Willie through the jagged hole, but felt obligated. He'd only come along so he could keep an eye on Willie. He didn't have any idea how he might have done much else, given that he was armed with nothing but a growing list of questions.

"You there," Willie shouted as he rounded to corner into the secret room behind the altar, "what do you think you're doing? When my father *oof*—"

Sloot ducked. He couldn't see anything coming his way, so he assumed he'd done it as a reflex. He'd liked to have taken a moment to ponder whether cowards might have instincts after all, but imminent danger was woefully effective at pulling him toward itself at the moment.

"That's the late Wilhelm Hapsgalt," said a tall man in a dark grey suit, who was pointing a wand at Willie. There were no sparks coming from the end of it, as Nicoleta's certainly would have done, but it was effective nonetheless in pinning Willie to the wall.

"There's another one!" The woman standing beside the tall man was tall as well, her long blonde hair woven into a pair of braids, the tips of which lightly brushed the tops of her ... well, Sloot had a girlfriend, didn't he? He wasn't about to carry on noticing the *attributes* of other women, regardless of how well their corsets brought their ampleness to bear. He wasn't sure whether "ampleness" was a word, but resolved then and there to never find out.

"Oh dear," said Sloot, studying the ceiling with singular focus. "Do forgive the intrusion, we were just *oof*—"

Sloot was pinned to the wall next to Willie. The woman was pointing her wand at him. Her other hand rested on the pommel of a longsword at her hip, in a casual way that said, "I know how to use this, and I'd be ever so grateful for a reason to prove it."

"I told you," she said to the tall man, "they make a handy distraction."

"Still," the tall man replied, "it's not proper for a lady—"

"To run around in the middle of the night, moving shuffled-off mortal coils from place to place, but you don't have anything to say about that, do you?"

"That's the job."

"A job which doesn't mandate a dress code, last time I checked."

"Can we talk about this later?"

"I don't want to talk about it at all!"

"Who are you?" This interjection from Sloot caused the two

ostensibly living people in the crypt to shift their icy glares from each other to him. It also caused Sloot to deeply regret having opened his mouth.

"Nice try, creature of evil," boomed the tall man in a practiced baritone.

"Hey," Sloot protested. He didn't feel evil, but the accusation raised an existential question—one he wasn't keen to ponder. Scary questions rarely had answers that were otherwise.

"They're from the Skeleton Key Circle," said Willie, in a rare fit of helpfulness.

"The what?"

"Silence, fruit of the grave!" The tall man's baritone verged on musical. If skulking around in crypts and threatening dead accountants didn't pan out, he'd likely do well in musical theatre.

"Fruit of the—" the woman closed her eyes and gave her head a quick shake. "Never mind. How do you know who we are?"

"Well, it's obvious, isn't it?" Willie rolled his eyes. "You're down here in the crypt with my father's bones. Who else would know where they were?"

Sloot had only been dead for … well, not long. He didn't pretend to understand the mysteries of the spheres, but he was baffled nonetheless by this sudden display of deductive reasoning by Willie. Perhaps the power imbued in him by the Serpents of the Earth balanced out some of his natural *innocence*, a word used in this case to indicate a complete lack of common sense as a result of monetary excess. In other words, Willie had been too rich in life to have been bothered with things like learning.

"This is bad," said the woman. "The Serpents are going after the Circle, I can feel it in my bones! We must—"

"We must honor our purpose," said the tall man. "We must show the Serpents that we can be trusted to do our duty in the face of trying times. The fate of fair-weather friends is just desserts."

"People are dying," the woman pleaded through clenched teeth. "The weather is foul and they aren't our friends anymore. We should snare these two in soul circles until we can figure out what to do with them!"

It should go without saying that Sloot had no idea what a soul circle was, but his mind had already taken it up and charged headlong into terrifying conjecture, like a star athlete with whatever thing the sport had put into contention. Usually a ball of some sort, he imagined. It should go without saying that Sloot was entirely at sea with sports metaphors, and deeply regretted having attempted one.

"The *Book of Black Law* clearly states that we cannot harm or hinder a member of their order," said the tall man with a patience that could have eroded marble. He lowered his wand, and Willie dropped away from the wall.

"My humblest apologies, Lord Hapsgalt," said the tall man with a solemn bow. He shot a look at the woman and jerked her head in Sloot's direction.

The woman rolled her eyes and lowered her wand. She didn't bow or apologize to Sloot, which was just as well. He doubted he could ever be comfortable on the receiving end of obeisance. He just hoped that they continued assuming he was a member of the Serpents, which he was not.

"No problem," said Willie. "Just leave my father's remains here with me, and we can forget about it."

"I'm afraid I can't do that."

"Oh, I know it's unusual," said Willie, who started digging through his pockets, "but I've got a note here that says it's all right this time. Oh, bother, what did I do with that note?"

"That's not the way this works," said the woman. She tightened her grip on her wand and spread her feet a bit wider. Sloot had seen Vlad do that before, right before she drew her sword and turned a number of people into a larger number of bits of people.

"She's right," said the tall man. "There's a form that must be delivered to the Steward of our order. We can only reveal Constantin's bones if—"

"Right, yes," snapped Willie, "only this time I have a note! It's from Mrs. Knife. She's very important, and so am I!"

"Then you'll have no problem filing the form with our Steward. I'm sorry, Lord Hapsgalt, but those must be my final words on the matter."

Since Sloot had known Willie, he'd only ever seen the little lord told "no" on a handful of occasions, and none of them ended with Willie not getting what he wanted. There was usually a tantrum involved, and the face that he was making was his standard prelude to one. However, at the point where the tears and the screaming at the top of his lungs usually started, his visage went all demonic again, with the black eyes, horns, wings, and teeth whose only purpose could have been turning people into meat confetti.

"I shall not be denied," said several octaves' worth of Willie's voice. "All things shall be mine, starting with this. Look upon me and despair!"

The tall man lowered his stance and the tip of his wand went up. "Forgive me, your lordship, but you leave me no choice." His wand made a series of quick flicking motions, and he recited a string of what Sloot could only assume were words.

There was a little ethereal *poof*, and Willie was gone.

"What did you do to Willie?" asked Sloot, though he was sure he didn't really want to know.

"This," said the tall man, turning his wand to Sloot. The same series of flicks, the same strange words, and a little yelp of panic from Sloot. Suddenly, he wasn't there anymore either.

Well, that was an assumption. As far as he knew, he could still be in the very same spot, bereft of all his senses. He could see nothing and no one, only an endless black void that stretched on forever in all directions. It reminded him of when he'd died the first time, before his conversation with Fairy Godmother had gotten underway.

"Hello?" he hazarded aloud. He heard himself say it, which he could have taken as a good sign, were he an optimist. He wasn't, though. Erring on the side of pessimism, he acknowledged that there was a distinct possibility that he'd heard his own voice repeated by some malevolent demon who wanted to lure him into a false sense of security, because it'd be easier to drag him into madness if he were reassured first.

⫷⫸BLOOD ECONOMY⫷⫸

Sloot didn't remember going to sleep, but he must have done so because he awoke atop his grave again. The one in the Hereafter, on the grey hill beneath the grey sky. In the brief calm of first waking, he wondered if there was a corresponding marker in a graveyard in Salzstadt. It might have been comforting to know there was some remembrance of him in the land of the living, but probably not enough to offset all the wretchedness that had befallen him since he died.

Sloot groaned. It soothed him, just the tiniest bit. The spiritual equivalent of stretching a sore muscle. He found himself thinking he could spend an entire night groaning, if only he had someplace to haunt.

Sloot shook his head, repulsed at the thought. Why did that seem so attractive to him? Why did he feel as though rattling a nice chain would soothe away all of his worries? He decided not to think about it. Repression had worked wonders for him in life. There was no sense in fixing what wasn't broken.

Sloot floated glumly down the hill and into the house through the front door.

"Well, it's about time," said the cloaked figure in the hallway. Sloot could tell by the moustaches that it was the same visitor who'd come along right before Sloot had followed Willie on his secret business.

"How can you tell?" asked Nicoleta. "Time doesn't seem to pass in the Hereafter. Do you get used to it?"

"Not really," admitted the moustaches under the visitor's hood. "The passage of time is not the forte of the dead. I just know that I've been kept waiting, and that sort of thing won't do." He turned to face Sloot. "Now then, boy, where is Lord Hapsgalt?"

Sloot wondered whether he qualified as a boy again due to his heretofore-brief tenure as a ghost. However, even if the epithet was intended to offend, Sloot lacked the sort of bluster that might have drawn a "now you see here" out of him.

"Er, I assumed he would have gotten back before I did."

"Back from where?"

"It was a cemetery," said Sloot. "In the real world."

"The Narrative," said the visitor with a chiding tone. "In the Hereafter, we refer to the land of the living as the Narrative."

"Oh," said Sloot. "That probably makes sense."

"Not really," said Nicoleta.

The visitor made an exasperated noise that requires a sharp exhalation in the real ... er, in the *Narrative*.

"You'll get it when you've been here a while," he said with a dismissive wave. "Not much changes in the Hereafter. The Narrative is the only show in town, when it comes right down to it. Only place worth haunting, anyway."

"Are there still colors there?" asked Nicoleta.

Sloot nodded. "There are."

A toothy grin stretched across Nicoleta's face from ear to ear.

"Enough of this prattle," snapped the visitor. "Is Lord Hapsgalt here or not?"

"Willie!" shouted Nicoleta. "Are you here? You have a visitor!"

"No need for that," said Nan, waggling a finger at Nicoleta as she walked into the room. "You still here, Grumley? I thought you'd left."

The visitor—Grumley—said he'd been sent by the Serpents of the Earth to get some preliminary business squared away, and he needed to speak with Lord Hapsgalt very urgently.

"I'm sure the old goat's rattling around here somewhere," said Nan. "You can go and fetch him, Peril. I'll just be hiding in the basement."

"I need to speak to the *younger* Lord Hapsgalt," said Grumley.

"And what could you need to say to him that's so important? He's only six years old!"

Grumley fixed Nan with an incredulous look. "What? Who's only six years old? Wait, no, never mind. Look, I need to speak with Wilhelm Hapsgalt. He's the Soul of the Serpent, perhaps you've heard of him?"

"Finally," boomed a voice from the next room that grew louder as it approached. "It's about time we got down to business!"

In life, Constantin didn't simply walk into the room, he conquered it. He'd been an impressive figure, hale and ruddy in a way that other men envied until the moment of his death. Strange then that he was now in a wheelchair and appeared as fragile as an antique tea set.

"Hello, Lord Constantin. Listen, I need to speak to the Soul of the Serpent, but he's obviously not here. When he returns, would you please—"

"Hogwash," said Constantin. "I'm right here!"

"Er, hang on a minute," said Grumley. He held his hands out and a scroll appeared in them. Sloot made a mental note to ask for lessons. Very handy, being able to call up documents so easily.

"We have you down as a Shade, Constantin." Grumley said. He dropped his hands and the scroll faded away, probably filed neatly away in whatever drawer it was supposed to reside. Sloot hoped.

"There's been a mistake," said Constantin. "I was properly murdered by my son, who is now the Eye of the Serpent, making me the Soul. That would make my mother, Otthilda Hapsgalt, the most recent Shade."

"The Serpents do not make mistakes," said Grumley. "Your son is the Soul, and Mrs. Knife is the Eye of the Serpent."

If anger is the stormy sea of the emotional spectrum, then the tantrum is the unspeakable behemoth that should be sleeping at the bottom of it. Constantin unleashed his inner child, who had grown up with as many silver spoons as it could fit in its mouth, and had never once quietly accepted a limitation. His eyes went black and his voice did the same low-register rumble that Willie's had before. The behemoth, it seemed, had awoken before naptime was up.

"Who would deny me," Constantin snarled, "you? You haven't got the—"

Constantin was still shouting, but suddenly he was doing it in silence.

"I have, in fact." Grumley was holding a single finger up toward Constantin. It was the "shush" finger, not the lascivious one that was tantamount to waving goblins in. "Now, is Lord Hapsgalt's financier here, at least?"

"Yes," said Sloot, surprising himself at his lack of hesitation in answering. *That settles it,* he supposed to himself. Nothing as trivial as death could release him from his duty.

"Good," said Grumley. "Let's sit you down with Schweinegesicht and Schlangenkessel. We need to get you up to speed."

There is a common misconception among the living that death is the end of it. Go vigorously onto the business end of a sword, wear the colors of a west-end boulderchuck team into an east-end pub, or simply hang around long enough for your organs to start switching off, and that's the end of the line.

On the contrary, there is such a thing as death for the dead. No one is really sure how long it takes, but eventually, each and every ghost withers away and ceases to be.

"Well, that's not exactly true," said Hans Schweinegesicht, financier to Constantin's mother, the late Otthilda Hapsgalt. Sloot had seen portly men with upturned noses in life, but none were so intrinsically porcine as Hans. He looked as though he'd stood up from the slop trough on his hind legs, put on a suit, and sallied forth in pursuit of an accounting degree.

"Isn't it?" asked Geralt Schlangenkessel, financier to the late Constantin Hapsgalt. He looked a lot like Sloot, who recognized him as a fellow worrier right off the bat. A lot of them ended up in the accounting profession, owing to its steady pay and low-risk lifestyle. (Financiers to leaders of sinister cults aside, of course.)

Hans shook his head, his meaty jowls swaying in an off-putting way. "Of course not. I mean, ghosts wither away, but that's no more the end than the first death was!"

"Oh," said Geralt, "I didn't know. I've only been dead since Lord Wilhelm's wedding."

"Ah," said Hans. "The Fall of Salzstadt! Terrible tragedy."

"The what?" Geralt and Sloot exclaimed in unison.

"The Fall of Salzstadt," repeated Hans with a partially exasperated air. It had a giddy undertone that said *hooray, I never get to do exasperated*! "Everyone's talking about it, you must have heard."

"Nonsense," said Geralt. "I know things got a bit messy, but fallen? Salzstadt? It's simply not possible. The Domnitor wouldn't hear of it, long may he reign."

"Long may he reign," echoed Sloot. "Hear, hear!" Even in death, and despite secretly having been a Carpathian his entire life, Sloot Peril was a true salt of the Old Country, through and through. He wasn't about to sit there and listen to such seditious talk.

"Long may he reign," said Hans, but with a bored sort of obeisance that revealed his heart wasn't in it. It was the reflexive response of having said it countless times during life, unlike Sloot, who still felt a swell of pride every time. It was perhaps more like a swell of subservience that had been ground into his psyche by draconian propaganda over the course of his cut-short life, but Sloot didn't have the wherewithal to tell the difference.

"Look, I hate to be the bearer of bad news," Hans continued, his toothy grin betraying his glee, "but the news is everywhere! Besides, what do you care? You both lost your lives in the cathedral. Your head popped off, didn't it, Peril?"

"Did it?"

"That's what I heard."

Geralt squirmed with indignation. "That's beside the point. I was a loyal and true salt my whole life! It's not like that changes just because I was trampled by a horde of the walking dead."

"No." Hans sighed. "Our old loyalties follow us into death, hence we all still work for one Hapsgalt or another."

"Then my faith remains in mighty Salzstadt! I'll not hear any more seditious talk about it falling."

"But it's not disloyal to face facts. Salzstadt has fallen! The dead walk the streets, and every building is positively crawling with goblins. It's an unmitigated disaster."

"That can't be true," said Geralt.

"You sound like them," said Hans.

"Who?"

"The people still living in Salzstadt. They're going about their daily lives as if nothing had happened, even though they're rubbing elbows with the walking dead every day at the market."

"If the people of Salzstadt are going about their daily lives," said Geralt, "then Salzstadt hasn't fallen. Think of St. Bertha and her mighty broom! The city has crushed the goblins before, and they'll do it again. The walking dead, too. I'm sure the Domnitor has a plan, long may he reign."

"Long may he reign," Sloot repeated.

"Fine," said Hans. "Long may he reign. Can we get on with it?"

"It should probably wait until after supper at this point, shouldn't it?"

Hans' eyebrows twisted in on themselves as he looked askance at Geralt.

"Do try to keep up," he said. "I know you're only recently dead, but … well, are you even hungry?"

Like misplaced luggage that had finally been delivered to its owner, Geralt's face revealed he'd only just realized: the dead don't eat food.

"Toffee," he moaned.

"Never again, I'm afraid."

Sloot didn't have any specific affinity for food, though he'd become rather fond of Carpathian breakfast toward the end of his life. That was doubly problematic. Not only would he never eat it again, it was treason for a citizen of Salzstadt to enjoy Carpathian anything.

While the recently deceased fretted over their gastronomic losses, Hans caught Sloot up on the only economy that really mattered in the Hereafter, and its precious currency: blood.

"There's vital energy in blood," said Hans. "The more you have, the longer you live—or rather *last*—in the Hereafter. Pool up enough of the stuff, and you could effectively be dead forever."

"The elder Lord Hapsgalt pooled up loads of it while he was the Eye," said Geralt. "I imagine he's set for several millennia."

"And the younger Lord Hapsgalt?" asked Hans.

"What about him?"

"Well, he's been a member of the Order for most of his life. Surely he's pooled up some blood for his own security."

"I doubt it," said Sloot. "Needles make him squeamish." *As well they should*, he added silently. In Sloot's estimation, anything designed to sneak sips of blood out of a perfectly good body couldn't be trusted.

"Not his own," said Geralt. He thrust his eyebrows toward the ceiling and leaned toward Sloot, the universal signal to infer with gusto.

"What, you mean *murder*?"

"Usually, yes," said Hans. "Oh, you've got fellows like Lawrence the Bleeder who was so gentle when he crept in through his victims' windows that most of them thought they'd simply come down with a mild case of anemia. But he was an artist, you see? Most don't have that sort of time. A brutal stabbing, then send in a blood wizard to collect the red kroovy. Easy peasy."

Sloot was of two minds about this, the first of which he considered the normal and proper reaction to having heard such a gruesome scheme. The horror! The rampant villainy! What sort of a world did he live in, where people would murder each other for the sake of staying dead a little longer?

His other mind was surprised only at the first one, for having allowed itself to be shocked by this. After everything he'd learned about the Serpents of the Earth while he was alive, how could he be so naive as to not see this sort of thing coming? Honestly, it was like being shocked to learn that the milkman didn't pay his cows. Sloot prided himself on being thrifty in all things, and here he was throwing shock around like it grew on trees.

Just as he was coming to grips with all of it, a third mind floated in behind the other two. If he'd managed to leave any worries behind when he died, this would fill in the gaps and then some. He realized that he hadn't pooled up any vitality, either.

"He'll have his allowance," said Geralt. "I know I was counting on that to pad the elder Lord Hapsgalt's retirement fund, but now he's not the Soul, is he?"

"Allowance?"

"Think of it like a mutual fund," said Hans. "A bit of the blood that results from the Order's basic murder rate will go straight to the Soul."

"That's diabolical!"

"Yes, and it's automatic. You can get Wilhelm's wizard to cast ... oh, I don't know the name of it. They have a spell that will fetch the current rate for your ledgers."

"He's supposed to have a wizard?"

Hans and Geralt exchanged looks that asked, "How did this idiot's lord become the Soul?" and replied, "Your guess is as good as mine."

"Well, how long can one reasonably expect to, er, remain dead without any ... income?" asked Sloot.

"He's asking about himself," said Geralt.

"Oh," said Hans. It was the long, downward "oh" that ends in a silent "you poor fool."

"Well, I wouldn't worry about it," he continued. "You'll draw a bit from the Order's basic murder rate just for being a member, that's something."

"I don't think so," said Sloot. "I was never actually inducted."

"Oh."

A long, uncomfortable silence settled in like a just-divorced uncle who hadn't seen why he should spring for an attorney. They could safely assume it would linger through the holidays.

The passage of time is a lot more subtle in the Hereafter than in the Narrative. There's no sun to cycle through the sky, no nights through which to sleep, and not a single clock that Sloot had noticed thus far.

His mother's watch! He reached into his pocket and fished it out, but it wasn't ticking. He pushed the button on the top, but the face didn't open. It was just the memory of the watch, after all, not the thing itself. That was probably beneath his rotting bones in the ruins of the cathedral, beneath the shambling remains of the walking dead.

"So that's it then," said Sloot after an indeterminate amount of time. "I'll be a ghost until I'm nothing."

"Well, not *nothing*," said Hans. "Not necessarily."

"Something else, then?"

"Well, there's considerable debate on the topic. Especially among the philosophers."

As if things weren't already bad enough, thought Sloot. He knew it was coming. It was only a matter of time before—

"Did someone say *philosophy?*" Arthur appeared in the doorway, his moustaches standing on end.

Oh, no, thought Sloot. "Please, nobody say any—"

"Hans was just telling us that no one knows whether ghosts are really gone after we fade away."

Arthur's eyes were wild, like a lion who hadn't eaten in a week. Geralt must have resembled a porterhouse.

"Portnoy the Sacrilegious once chained himself to the doors of the cathedral to prove the impossibility of life after death! He was wrong, obviously, but his arguments are sound if applied to life after death *after death*."

"Well said, Arthur," Sloot blurted. "I think that's all that anyone can—"

"Malarky," said Hans. "You're saying there's nothing beyond the Hereafter, based on a theory that there is no Hereafter?"

"I've still got a few more questions—" Sloot began.

"It's not that simple!" Arthur was pacing around the room and gesticulating wildly. Myrtle had always refused to indulge him in that while he had her possessed. "It makes sense in light of his Treatise on Bedtime Disobedience—which he wrote when he was eight—but only if you understand the finer points of Mauler's Unticking Clock. I can solve this in … seventeen moves!"

"I'm sure you can," said Sloot, "but I really need to ask Hans about—"

"I studied Mauler in college," said Geralt. "The Unticking Clock is a metaphor for the struggle between hunger and apathy. I hardly think it applies—"

"That's where you're wrong!"

Sloot wandered off. He could never stomach philosophy for this very reason. Even if you didn't know anything about Nutter's Hungry Clock or whatever, you could join in the conversation with your angriest voice. Philosophy, as far as Sloot could tell, was the art of determining who could have the loudest opinion while not doing anything useful.

He wandered through the corridors of the house, unable to shake the feeling of familiarity he kept getting from it. It was unnerving, like a stranger who walks across a crowded room to reassure you that he has no intention of stabbing you.

He'd never been there before, but he definitely had. Sloot was sure it had something to do with the way the Hereafter works. It's the collective consciousness. Everyone sort of throws their ideas on how everything should look into a hat, and the hat does its best to make everyone happy.

Sloot wondered if anyone was ever happy with the results. It was like how camels were created, only they were trying for a horse.

Sloot walked past a closed door and heard faint weeping coming from it. From *behind* it, presumably, but then he'd met a sentient door once. He hesitated, and then knocked.

"Yes?"

"Er, sorry," said Sloot. "Just … is everything all right?"

The door opened abruptly. Nicoleta was standing there with a stiff upper lip, still as drab and grey as everything else.

"It's just … I don't know what to do," she said. Her stiff upper lip started trembling, her face contorted into dramatics, and she fell to the floor in a sobbing heap.

"There, there," said Sloot, in his best approximation of a comforting tone. His hands went out to comfort her, but he didn't want to be too familiar. He just sort of patted the air around her, as though he were comforting the giant invisible bubble inside of which she wept.

"Magic doesn't work here," she managed between sobs. "I remember all of the incantations, all of the hand-waves and wrist-flicks. I mean, I figured I couldn't do the ones that need a wand, or a cauldron, or animal bits, but a glittering butterfly doesn't need any of that. *Troloch!*" She made a one-hand wavy motion with a wiggling pinky. "See? Nothing!"

Thump.

"That wasn't nothing," said Sloot, who shivered for coming so dangerously close to having used a double-negative. He trusted that Nicoleta understood the context.

"That wasn't me."

"Are you sure?"

"Fairly sure," said Nicoleta. "I've tried casting that spell dozens of times since I got here, and it's never gone *thump* before."

She'd stopped crying, at least. That was something. Between unexplained *thumps* and having to comfort a crying person, Sloot wasn't sure which was more terrifying.

Thump. Thump.

"Probably just someone walking around in another part of the house," said Sloot.

"Think again."

"What? Oh." Sloot remembered that he hadn't taken a single step since he'd died. He had the feet for it, but he wasn't using them. They just sort of hung there, like a ballerina in mid-jump, while he floated around like a proper ghost. Hopefully there was a rational explanation for the *thump* sounds, and he'd be able to tell the story later and everyone would have a good laugh. He'd think of a more rugged metaphor for his feet than the ballerina one.

⊱⊰ THE CIRCLE ⊱⊰

Y ou can't make me." The ground shook a bit when Willie spoke. That was a chilling touch, really added an edge to the whole demonic-voice-and-monstrous-visage bit.

Willie's shouting had drawn Sloot into the spare room where a magic circle had been drawn on the floor. Grumley had sent a wizard over to do it, claiming it would help with Willie's episodes.

"That's quite enough of that," said Nan. "You put your proper face back on this instant."

"You can't make me do that, either!" Willie snarled and growled, his forked tongue lashing out from between his long, sharp teeth.

"That's it," said Nan, her fingers clenching into fists and relaxing again. "Your proper face had better be back on by the time I count to three, or there will be no story time for you, do you understand?"

"I demand a story! You wouldn't dare!"

"One."

There was no air in the Hereafter, so it was just empty space in the room that took on a certain onerous thickness. It was no longer the free-wheeling, happy-go-lucky space in which a carefree ghost might float idly, casually wiling away a sliver of eternity. It had tension now. Tension that you didn't linger in, and you'd think twice about slouching or shuffling your feet through it. Sloot floated backward a couple of paces.

Unbeknownst to Sloot, Nan was invoking a kind of magic older and deeper than anything in a wizard's book. It was motherly magic, the sort that transcends time, cultures, even death. At that precise moment, it appeared to have given Willie pause.

"Two."

"Ugh, fine," said Willie. His smoky wings and horns evaporated, and his eyes returned to their normal, guileless grey. "But I don't want to sit in the circle anymore! It's boring and it feels funny."

Sloot was grateful for the circle, even if he didn't fully trust Grumley. Willie's outbursts had become unpredictable of late, and Sloot found himself longing for the days when he could see them coming. Being made to wait until the end of a meal for dessert was sure to bring one on, or challenging his expertise in footwear.

"You're supposed to sit in the circle when things start shaking," said Nan. "That's what Mr. Grumley said, and he wouldn't have said without a reason."

"But—"

"Rhymes with 'shut,' which is what your mouth needs to do, young man!" Nan's fists were on her hips.

Willie crossed his arms and huffed. The ground started shaking again, a bit more violently than it had before.

"You see? Shaking! You're supposed to get in the circle when the shaking starts. Now march, young man, and not another word!"

The end of her sentence grabbed the protests out of Willie's open mouth and had them standing in the naughty corner before Willie knew what was happening.

"March!"

It was more of a sulking float than a march, but it was in the direction of the circle, so Nan didn't bemoan the specifics.

"You've certainly got a way with him," said Sloot, once they'd left the room.

"Got to take a firm hand with willful lads like him," said Nan. "It's getting harder, now that I don't have dessert to bribe him with."

Sloot nodded, suppressing a wince at the preposition with which she'd ended her sentence.

"It's especially bad when he won't sit in the circle," Nan continued. "Mr. Grumley seemed to think he'd only need a few moments here and there, but I swear he's been in it for hours at a time! It feels like hours, at least."

Sloot nodded. "Perhaps they drew one of the sigils around the circle upside-down or something?"

"All's I know is that I've never gotten to two before. I don't know why they didn't make it 'count to five,' give us a bit more to work with."

That was troubling. As far as Sloot was aware, Nan had believed Willie to be six years old for more than thirty years. In all that time, he'd never once tried to test Nan beyond "one." Why start now? There was the off chance that death had somehow emboldened him, but that was doubtful. Boldness required effort, and Willie avoided that sort of thing at all cost.

He must have noticed that he was more powerful now. The great leathery wings should have tipped him off, even if the bonus octaves in his voice had somehow escaped his attention. Then again, this was Willie Hapsgalt. He was as likely as not to have noticed by now that he was dead.

It had to be the power. Willie was the Soul of the Serpent, and there were blood wizards feeding him murder victims. Sloot shuddered. He knew that nothing good could come of blood magic, and he now had the misbehavior of children—or near enough to it—to count as evidence.

"Have you got a minute?"

There were no chirping birds in the Hereafter, but Sloot felt as though he could almost remember what they sounded like when Myrtle spoke. She motioned to him from the hallway, which was enticing and scary in equal measure. Being beckoned into a dark hallway by a comely ghost tended to have that effect on people.

"Er, pardon me, Nan."

"Shh!" Nan was wearing her brooding face. It's always a bad idea to interrupt a gran in the middle of a brood. Sloot reflexively hunched his shoulders in preparation to creep out of the room before remembering that ghosts float silently. As silently as the grave, in fact, which was dreadfully predictable as similes went.

"What is it?"

"I don't know," said Myrtle. "Not exactly. It's just ... something is off." She opened her mouth as though to say something further, then didn't. She nodded her head toward the hallway behind her, and then floated off in that direction. Sloot followed.

"Everything's off," said Sloot. "I blame our collective loss of life. I know I haven't been quite right since I woke up here."

Myrtle fidgeted. "Well, there's that, but it's something more for me. Everyone else seems to have certain compulsions. Things left undone, you know?"

Sloot shrugged. "I don't think I have any compulsions. Nothing beyond putting figures into Willie's ledgers. Oh, I could spend eternity settling up columns of ... oh, wait. I see."

"Right, like that. And what about haunting?"

"Now that you mention it, I could go for a good haunting. Rattle some chains, find a spot in a nice hallway and freeze the air. Oh, my. Why does that sound so pleasant?"

"Nicoleta said the same thing," said Myrtle. "About the haunting, I mean. She's not interested in ledgers as far as I could tell."

"Well, what's unusual about that? I liked accounting when I was alive. It makes sense that I'd want to keep doing it."

"Why do you still work for Willie, then?"

"Because ..." Sloot had been so sure that some sensible answer would follow that single word out of his mouth that he didn't close it. "Well, *because*. I've never quit a job, you know. There was the counting house, then I was promoted to Willie's financier, and then, well ... death."

"Willie's still got a lot of ledgers that need tending then, does he?"

"Not as such, but it would hardly be polite to quit."

"My point is that you were working for Willie when you died, and you're still working for him. I think that's a sort of standard ghostly compulsion."

"No it isn't," said Sloot. "It's just good manners."

"Well, what about me? I'm not compelled to do anything at all."

"You were independently wealthy when you died. You weren't doing much of anything, were you?"

"Careful."

"Sorry," said Sloot, silently chiding himself. He'd worked around the wealthy before. He knew better than to point their idleness out to them.

"I had a big house. Shouldn't I want to go haunt it?"

Yes, Sloot thought, *you should.* His mind turned to his old apartment, the one Mrs. Knife had burned to the ground when she almost killed him the first time. He'd thought about that quite a bit, in fact. He fervently wished it was still there so that he could go and haunt it. It had been *his* for a long time, and now ... what? The butcher who owned the building would just rent it out to some other pasty bachelor with little ambition?

"I see your point," said Sloot. "Perhaps you were more, I dunno, *fulfilled* than the rest of us when you died. No unfinished business?"

"Maybe."

Sloot was completely out of his depth when it came to comparative weirdness. In his experience, things were normal or they weren't. You start letting people stand around between the two, and they'll find the spot that's just weird enough to be cool. From there, it's a slippery slope to masters degrees in the arts, and suddenly you live with your parents again.

Sloot knew that wasn't cool. His mother had told him so.

"Why don't you ask Arthur about it? This sounds like existentialism. Or post-existentialism, perhaps."

"I'd rather not, thanks." That made sense. Arthur had been inside Myrtle's head for most of her life. She was probably grateful for the separation.

Sloot was starting to consider what possession must be like when he felt an insistent itching just behind his ear. No, not itching. *Tugging.* Perhaps both? He'd never gone fishing while he was still alive because he was afraid of worms. No, not afraid, but he was sure that he couldn't trust them. In any case, the thought occurred to him that the sensation might be like what a hooked fish felt upon being reeled into a boat.

"Sloot? What's happening?" Myrtle's voice was far away, indistinct.

That's what you get for trusting worms, Sloot silently chided the metaphorical fish, just before he found himself elsewhere.

"Wait!" shouted Myrtle, suddenly much closer than she'd been a moment ago, and far more *real* as well.

"There you are," said Roman.

"Roman?" said Sloot and Myrtle in unison.

"Myrtle?" said Roman, a look of utter confusion twisting his neck as though he owed it money. "You're alive?"

Sloot looked down. He was still grey and translucent. Myrtle, on the other hand, was opaque and rosy-cheeked. She was *alive*.

The vast majority of moments come to pass in a very rote, predictable way. That's why cause-and-effect was invented. Eat questionable meat sold from a cart in an unfamiliar city, spend the following day earnestly wishing you hadn't. Cause and effect. Predictable.

Then there are moments in the minority, like this one. It hadn't been so long ago that Myrtle had met a grisly end at Gregor's hand, yet she appeared to be as alive as whatever rodents they're putting in cart meat these days had been at some point, presumably. That was unexpected, though not in quite the same way that Sloot couldn't have predicted seeing his severed and preserved head hanging from Roman's belt.

"Roman, is that—"

"Well, you'd know, wouldn't you?"

"It is, isn't it?" Sloot groaned, or rather *moaned*. The echo was reverberant in a way that only the dead could manage, one of many natural traits that made them the pinnacle of evolution when it came to things like haunting.

"Winking Bob put me in touch with her guy," said Roman with a grin. "Top notch attention to detail, don't you think?"

Myrtle stared at her hands, which started to shake. "How is this possible?"

In his horror over finding a primary bit of his mortal coil repurposed as fashion, Sloot had entirely neglected Myrtle's apparent resurrection. Some boyfriend he was turning out to be. Even with his dearth of experience in the role, he knew this was the sort of thing he was duty-bound to notice.

"Oh, dear!" Sloot exclaimed, rather louder than he'd intended. "Overcompensation" was a particularly offensive word among accountants.

"But I ... I don't ... am I *alive?*" Myrtle stared at her hands as though they were a pair of trembling sausages that had fallen off a cart and attached themselves to her wrists.

"Probably not," said Roman. He poked her shoulder with his finger. "Solid, though. And not bursting into flames, so you're not a vampire. That's lucky."

For reasons unknown to anyone who knows anything about the economy of blood or the way that death works, vampires have long enjoyed literary infamy as powerful, romantic figures who live forever and know how to brood better than anyone. Nothing could be farther from the truth.

Blood is a precious commodity to everyone in the Hereafter, and anyone with the common sense of a broken clock—which is right twice a day—does everything in their power to conserve as much as possible. That's why ghosts don't bother with corporeal forms. Sure, they don't get to get drunk or wear fashionable shoes, but they get to be ghosts for a very long time.

Vampires, on the other hand, are doing it all wrong. They've got all the maintenance and upkeep associated with a regular living body, plus things like super strength and seeing at night and turning into bats that really throw their blood mileage for a loop. Also, they don't breathe or sleep or eat proper food, so their only means of replenishing the vital energy in their blood is to eat someone and stuff themselves full of more blood.

The vital energy in a pint of blood can keep a ghost going for years, or give a vampire a couple of days, during which he might wander into some sunlight and burn himself to a crisp of gristle. There used to be a Carpathian food cart that specialized in that sort of thing, but in terms of preference, catching vampirism from questionable cuisine was a distant second to botulism.

"I was in the Hereafter a moment ago," said Myrtle. "I was talking to Sloot, and when he started to slide away, I followed him. Followed? I suppose that's right."

"You're definitely dead, then," said Roman. "Unless you're a necromancer. Read any books bound in human flesh lately?"

"Not that I'm aware."

"Probably wouldn't matter." Roman squinted as he studied Myrtle more closely than standard propriety would allow. "I imagine vampirism is easier to catch than necromancy. Got to learn the spells and whatnot to be a necromancer."

"Is this supposed to be comforting?" asked Myrtle.

"Not specifically, but good on you if it is."

"Well, it's not."

Roman shrugged. "I was just trying to help. I figured the truth would be more comforting than anything else. You'll probably feel better once you know what's going on."

"Could be." Myrtle paused, her face going all contemplative. "Hang on, I think I can—"

Myrtle disappeared abruptly, leaving nothing behind but potential panache. No puff of smoke or anything. She could learn a thing or two from Nicoleta about making an exit that leaves an impression.

"Where did she go?" Sloot wondered aloud.

"Hard to say," Roman replied. "Her kind come and go as they please, very hard to track."

"Her kind?"

"Leave it," said Roman. "That's where you and Myrtle differ. I doubt the truth holds any capacity to make you feel better."

Roman was right about that. For most people, the truth is a light that shines on the dark and scary unknown. It robs the unknown of its power to inspire fear. It's different for worriers, who staunchly believe that what they don't know can't hurt them—*yet*. To them, the world is a horrible place, teeming with things lining up to do them harm. If they're still sticking to the shadows, there's something holding them back from using their sharp teeth or writhing tentacles or biting social commentary to pull their legs off, or whatever. It's not until they've stepped into the light that things start to hurt.

Sloot remembered then that he was upset with Roman.

"You've shrunk my head and put it on your belt!"

"And you recognized it straight away."

"Of course, I recognized it! It's *my* head!"

"We got lucky on that," said Roman, admiring Sloot's shrunken head as though it were a bottle of wine so expensive that you were expected to read the label and nod with approval. Sloot missed wine, even though he'd never liked it. He'd only ever drunk the stuff that you gulped as quickly as possible so you could avoid tasting it.

"Lucky?"

"It landed right next to me when it popped off."

"Popped?"

"Afraid so. Tends to happen when you're at the bottom of a fray like that. I managed to scoop it up before any of the undead got hungry."

"*Hungry?*"

"I honestly can't tell," said Roman, "but are you doing your usual flustered bit, or are you having trouble hearing me?"

"It's not a bit!" Sloot was offended. He'd never *acted* flustered in his life, or after it.

"All right, all right," said Roman, showing Sloot his palms in a placating gesture. "Morbid, I know, but it's the easiest way to summon you."

"I'd rather you didn't."

"Is that any way to talk to an old friend? Besides, death doesn't release you from service to Carpathian Intelligence."

"That makes sense," said Sloot with a sigh. "I still work for Willie, too."

"I figured as much. Not much has changed, then, aside from the dead milling about in Salzstadt."

"So it's true. Salzstadt has fallen!"

"I wouldn't say that," said Roman. "I mean, it probably would have, if it were anywhere else, but these salts have something that regular people don't."

"Right you are," said Sloot, swelling with patriotism.

"Denial."

"What?"

"Overflowing with it, each and every salt in the city. I learned the hard way that you don't talk about the walking dead in Salzstadt."

"The hard way?"

"Yep," said Roman. "Publican overheard me, took my beer away. I had to find a new place to drink."

Had Sloot not been born in Salzstadt and raised in the traditions of the Old Country, he might have balked at the depth of denial playing out on the cobbled streets of the city. But knowing what he knew, it seemed about right. The Domnitor, long may he reign, would never truck with widespread panic. Order was essential. It was the bedrock upon which a functioning society erected everything from the courts that provided laws, to the universities that provided knowledge, to the abandoned sewer tunnels where black marketeers offered special prices on brass knuckles on the first Thursday of every month.

"Of course, the Domnitor's fled," said Roman, as he turned down Grocers Row. A gran carrying groceries nodded primly to the desiccated husk of a city watchman, who gave a guttural groan in response.

"That's not possible," said Sloot, floating along behind him. "The Domnitor, long may he reign, would never abandon his people in a time of crisis!"

"Suit yourself."

"You're serious!"

"I go in for whimsy every now and again, but not this time. Mrs. Knife has taken up residence in the palace."

Sloot turned to look to the east. The palace on the hill looked like it always had, flags fluttering in the breeze and everything. He'd thought for a moment that Mrs. Knife would have put her own up in their stead, but that would just be asking for trouble. She was power hungry, but she was subtle about it.

Plus, Sloot knew what flag makers charged in Salzstadt. Given the recent population shift that everyone was ignoring, "an arm and a leg" might be a more apt metaphor than ever.

"I can't believe it," said Sloot.

"He's in Stagralla."

"What, ruling in exile?"

"*In absentia* is more like it. Nobody really knows he's gone. The ministries are carrying on as they always have, squashing things like questions and unsanctioned long lunches."

It would have been unusual indeed for the city to have slipped into utter chaos in the simple absence of its prepubescent dictator, even in the wake of an undead horde. Sloot imagined that Uncle—the cleverly re-branded Ministry of Truth—would have stepped in to ensure that order was maintained in the city at all costs.

They had, and they'd done a good job. Were it not for the fact that ghosts can't smell anything—which, as it turned out, was the deepest question Willie had ever pondered while he was alive—Sloot would have noted that the lingering stench of rot was the only real difference on the streets of Salzstadt. Sure, Vlad the Invader had cut a bloody swath through the streets on the day of Willie and Greta's wedding, but cleaning that up had taken little more than the following day. Even government janitorial workers were eager to get on with pretending it had never happened.

"Where are we going, anyway?" There was something dreadfully familiar about the street they were walking down. Sloot had been there before, he was sure of it. The greasy feel of it stuck to him the way a sock would stick to the bottom of his foot, once it had found the single wet spot on the kitchen floor.

"To a meeting," said Roman. "Only we've not been invited, so you'll need to keep quiet."

"Oh," said Sloot. He began to worry. Well, *began* is the wrong word. Better to say that he added this to an already impressive array of other worries that he was juggling. It was just the sort of thing that would happen to a clown who already had a couple of swords in the air with his pins, and had just actively thought *well, at least none of this stuff is on fire.*

Roman ducked into a doorway, waited a moment until he was sure no one was looking, and started working at the lock in the door with a pair of metal hooks.

"What are you doing?"

"What does it look like I'm doing? Just keep an eye out for danger."

"Look out!"

"What? Where?" Roman stood up abruptly, the tools disappearing into his pockets. He started up a tuneless whistle, the sort that only guilty people perform when they're trying to look casual.

"You," hissed Sloot. "Stop that! That door is locked for a reason!"

"Oh, come on." Roman shook his head and got back to work at the lock.

"This is dangerous," said Sloot. "What if we're caught?"

"They'll probably kill you," Roman mumbled. Sloot knew derision when he heard it. He was about to give Roman a few stern words about etiquette when he realized where they were.

"Wait a minute," said Sloot.

"Almost there."

"Aren't we close to the Domnitor's castle, long may he reign?"

The door gave a *click*. Roman turned the handle and it opened.

"Ludicrously close," he replied. "Haven't you ever been inside it?"

Had this been one of the proper doors that led into the castle, it would have been far too well guarded for Roman to have gotten so close. But what sort of spy needed proper doors? Of course, there would be secret entrances. Some ancestor of the present Domnitor, long ere he reigned, would have wanted to disguise himself and do things that were … *undonmitorial*. He'd have needed to get out of the castle and back in again without anyone having known, and clever arrangements of doors and tunnels were the traditional means of doing so.

"I doubt if the present Domnitor even knows about this one," said Roman. He plodded along the dark and cobwebbed hallway, taking very little care to tread silently. It was apparent that no one had come this way in a very long time.

"Long may he reign," added Sloot.

"If you insist. It's just us down here, you know."

On the one hand, the Ministry of Propaganda had done a bang-up job of convincing Sloot—and all of his countrymen and countrywomen—that

Uncle was always listening. He was sure that he was never truly alone. Apart from polite, following the rules was pure self-preservation.

On the other hand, what was the point of living within shouting distance of another human being if you were going to chuck the rules out the window the second it became convenient? Sloot had no need of the threat of interrogation to convince him that respectful formality needed heeding, even when he thought he could get away with breaching it. *Especially* then.

In any case, he decided it was pointless to argue with Roman. Sloot may have been Carpathian on his mother's side, but Roman was a proper Carpathian. They didn't show the same deference to Vlad the Invader that the good folk of the Old Country showed to the Domnitor, long may he reign. They were less sophisticated in Carpathia.

The dusty old hallway wound its way around corners and bends, crossing an old sewer tunnel at one point, until at last they came to a door. Roman gave a complicated knock that sounded a lot like the cadence of poetry that had no respect for words like "pentameter" or "iambic," traditionally performed by college freshmen who knew everything.

"It'll be a minute," said Roman. He was right. The sound of very heavy furniture moving over a stone floor emanated from beyond the door. Eventually, it opened.

"What kept you?" asked Greta.

⇒⊱THAT'S NO DAMSEL⊰⇐

It was clear that Greta had never seen a ghost before. Or, if she had, it had been a very long time. Or, if it hadn't, she'd managed to convince herself it hadn't been what she thought. She'd been born and raised in Salzstadt, so she was very well-versed in the practice of denial. That sort of thing comes in handy when living under the constant scrutiny of a draconian regime.

"You're really a ghost!" Greta pointed at Sloot with a rigid and trembling hand, her eyes wide with exaggerated shock.

Roman rolled his eyes. "Calm yourself. There are no extra points for theatrics."

"Sorry," she said, drawing her outstretched hand back in to fidget with the other. "I just didn't know that ghosts were real."

"As real as you and me," said Sloot. "Especially me, as it were."

Greta had obviously spent a great deal of time in the lavishly appointed apartment. There was paper everywhere, most of it covered with drawings of bits of clockwork. At least Sloot thought it was clockwork. As far as he knew, it might have been nothing more than clever groups of squiggles that were specifically designed to confuse particularly talented accountants.

"And what is that?" Greta was leering at Roman's belt the same way that children consider new vegetables, alongside their parents' insistence that it's good for them. "It looks like ... Sloot."

"That's because it *is* Sloot," said Roman.

"Well, that's just—hang on. Before I say something offensive, is hanging the shrunken heads of your friends from your belt a cherished Carpathian custom that just hasn't made it this far south?"

"No, it's—"

"Then it's horrible! I can't imagine that Sloot, may he rest in peace, approved of this before you went ahead and did it?"

"Thanks," said Sloot, "but you don't have to do that."

"Do what?"

"The 'rest in peace' thing."

"Oh. I thought I was being polite."

"I know you intended it that way but, well … I'm not, am I? Resting, I mean. In peace or otherwise. I'm every bit as busy in the Hereafter as I ever was in life, and that's without being summoned up by my own head."

Roman rolled his eyes and sighed. "It was the best way to talk to you."

"I didn't mean to offend," said Greta, "I meant for it to come off more like 'good luck,' or 'happy trails' or something. I imagine you'd like to rest in peace, right?"

Sloot thought back to the argument with which Arthur had waylaid Hans and Geralt. If he was right, then once Sloot came to the end of his afterlife, that was it. The end, curtain down, nothing but oblivion—which was, in fact, nothing. If that was what awaited him across the metaphor of "resting in peace"—or, rather, didn't—he wanted nothing to do with it.

"Let's worry about that later," said Roman.

"Er … okay," said Greta. Sloot knew that "er." It was the beginning of a question that was destined to be the first of many but elected to slip away for a nap rather than go to all the trouble.

"I saw your signal in the window last night," said Roman. "You got something for me?"

There was a candle on the windowsill that had burned down to a stub. *Probably the signal,* Sloot thought, the extent of his deductive powers reached.

"I do," said Greta. "It's big, and I'm not sure what to do about it."

"Sounds juicy," said Roman. He grinned and rubbed his hands together. "Start by telling me everything you know."

"Mrs. Knife is going to—"

"No, no," said Roman, "not like that! You've built it up too much to blurt, but not big enough for the reveal."

"What?"

"Lead us into it," said Roman. "Give it a bit of theatrics."

"Oh, *now* he's interested in theatrics."

"Yeah, give it some panache!"

"Ugh, fine," Greta sighed. She cleared her throat. "There I was, minding my own business, when all of a sudden … uh … Mrs. Knife is going to kidnap the Domnitor."

"Long may he reign," said Sloot. He gasped.

"You call that panache?"

Greta pinched the bridge of her nose. "I call it big news! Can we please focus on more important matters than my delivery?"

"I suppose so," said Roman with a derisive snort that was incredulous at her indifference. "How's she going to manage it? The Domnitor's in exile in Stagralla."

"Long may he reign."

"You don't have to do it every time, Sloot."

"But I *can*, right?"

"I suppose so."

"Old habits and all," said Sloot with a shrug.

"In the name of all the swear words there are, could you two please focus for a moment?" Greta was staring wide-eyed at the floor, fingers at her temples. Sloot's mother used to do the same, right before shouting at him to stop re-checking his math homework and go play outside. His subsequent requests for the school to remain open on the weekends had done nothing to help his popularity with the other children.

"Sorry," said Roman. "You were saying?"

"I don't know how she's going to manage it," said Greta, "but it's going to be soon."

"Oh, no!" said Sloot. "She's not going to kill him, is she?"

"Quite the opposite."

"She's going to ... give birth to him?"

"Not the literal opposite!" She stared wide-eyed at the floor again. "She wants to bring him back here and make everyone think things are back to normal. She means to make a puppet of him."

Sloot and Roman exchanged a horrified glance.

"Not a literal puppet," said Greta through clenched teeth, with eyes to match. "Look, the economy has been doing very poorly since the fall of Salzstadt. The undead walking the streets, goblins infesting everything, the Domnitor in exile—"

"Long may he reign."

"Sloot!"

"Sorry." He said it, but he wasn't.

"It makes sense," said Roman. "Well done, Greta. Did they give you anything else to go on?"

"She's meeting later today with someone called 'the Steward.' I think it might be related."

"Do you know where they're meeting?"

"I wrote myself a note yesterday. Hang on."

Had Sloot never seen Greta's shop, he'd have wondered how she could have found anything among the tottering piles of ... things. He'd love to have been more specific, but Greta hadn't grouped her piles in any order that he could discern. He supposed that there could be a world in which dirty laundry, sketches of clocks, and empty bottles of schnapps should be grouped together, but he wouldn't want to live there.

"Here it is," she mumbled, flopping a heap of papers onto a table that was already piled haphazardly with papers, candlesticks, and mouldering dishes. She rifled through the heap and withdrew a page covered in squiggles so agitated that they seemed annoyed to have been written.

"Mrs. Knife said they were going somewhere called 'The Cross.' Does that mean anything to you?"

"It does," Roman nodded. "You're sure that's what that says?"

"I should, I wrote it."

"Doesn't look like any sort of writing I've ever seen."

"It's a code." Greta grinned at her own cleverness. "It's based on the Salzstadt Mechanical Engineers Guild notation for timing gear ratios. My own design."

"Why not just write it down properly? Wait, you've been talking to Mrs. Knife!"

Greta made an "I'm actively suppressing a swear word" face.

"I haven't had time to read him in on things," said Roman.

"Apparently not. I'm Mrs. Knife's hostage," she said to a spot of air where Sloot may or may not have been standing.

"What? That's awful! Roman, we should rescue her!"

"Sloot, don't—"

"Ugh, here we go again!" Greta threw her hands up in disgust, sending stacks of paper to their new careers as carpet liners. "Even in death, men always think that women need rescuing! Just a helpless damsel in distress, am I?"

"Er, sorry," said Sloot. He'd have shuffled his feet if they were touching the floor. "It's just—I only—you just said you were Mrs. Knife's hostage!"

"And there's no way that I could rescue myself, is there?"

"Well, technically, that would be escaping, but you haven't—"

"Sloot, please—" Roman started.

"There's a tunnel to freedom behind my armoire! You just walked through it, or rode in your shrunken head, or whatever. Do you think the presence of bosoms upon my person precludes my capacity to reach obvious conclusions?"

Sloot said nothing. A woman had just said "bosoms" in his presence! He quietly performed the spiritual equivalent of hyperventilation, which he found vastly more unnerving than the real thing.

"Greta is remaining in custody of her own accord," said Roman. "She's been able to do a great deal of snooping to provide me with critical information."

Greta's mouth-agape stare at Roman overflowed with disbelief. Her head shook once.

"Unbelievable," she said. "Do you need me here for this conversation, or shall I go cross-stitch a pillow? I know, I could gaze out the window and pine for Vlad."

"Sorry," said Roman.

"So sorry," said Sloot.

"Never mind," said Greta. "The meeting is this evening. Also, there's something else, and it doesn't make any sense."

"Do tell," said Roman.

"I overheard Gregor talking about the ransom demands they're sending north to Vlad. They want to exchange me for directions to Carpathia."

"You're right," said Sloot. "That doesn't make sense. 'Go north.' That's your directions. Er, *direction*."

"Especially not for Gregor," Roman added. "He's *from* Carpathia. Well, he's from the land where Carpathia now stands."

At the fall of Salzstadt, Gregor revealed that he had long ago been the wizard Ashkar, who'd laid a curse on the Carpathian army over a hundred years before. If he wasn't lying, as wizards are famous for doing, he was over a thousand years old. He'd have been born before the nation of Carpathia had been formed, when it was all roving bands of cannibals up there. If you read the official Old Country textbooks that were approved by the Ministry of Propaganda, you knew that everyone beyond the borders of the Old Country practiced some degree of cannibalism. That's foreigners for you.

"So, what's really going on?"

"I don't know," said Roman. "We'd better go, Sloot. Got to find an entrance to the Cross, and that could take hours."

"Greta should come with us. I know, and I'm sorry, but you can't possibly think you're safe here! What if they move you to another room, or things change and they decide you're better off dead?"

"That's a risk worth taking," said Greta.

That was a phrase that Sloot had heard a few times in his life. It hadn't made sense when he'd been alive, and dying hadn't shed any light on it.

"Does Vlad know?"

"Of course not," said Greta. "If she knew, she'd insist that I escape so she could attack the city again."

"Oh." Sloot had been there when Vlad attacked Salzstadt the last time. He'd seen firsthand the devastation that had resulted. He'd been a part of it, in fact. According to Roman, his head had popped off.

"None of us like it," said Roman, "but there's nothing to be done about it now. The best thing we can do is get to the Cross and listen in on Mrs. Knife's secret meeting."

With that, Roman walked back into the tunnel. Sloot was compelled to follow him, thanks perhaps to some instinctual urge to keep up with his head. It didn't make any sense, really. What did he need with his head? His apparition still had the semblance of one, was that not good enough?

They took pains to make sure no one saw them emerging from the door at the other end, and then made haste away from it. It was more likely they were making haste toward somewhere else, but Sloot didn't know where that might be, so he made do with what he had.

The subject of the walking dead in the city was emphatically never remarked upon by polite society, though it hadn't been overlooked entirely. Here and there, a few subtle and forward-thinking entrepreneurs were providing services that catered to the city's newest demographic. There were all manner of adhesive applicationists peddling everything from glues to splints to giant staples. Bits falling off the walking dead is an inevitability, and quite often the "bits" should really have been referred to using words more befitting their size and importance. An arm on the cobbles, for example, is rather more serious an occurrence than the phrase "you've lost a bit" is equipped to manage.

Then there were the cosmetics. Some of the shambling abominations were in less advanced stages of decay and were far from coming to grips with their own conditions. This had given rise to all manner of tonics, preservatives, lipsticks, powders, and even a few re-purposed salves intended for use in animal husbandry becoming available from carts and wagons on every street.

They had trouble selling to the real rotters, though. The modern parlance of the times had been given phrases like "there's only so much lipstick you can put on a corpse" and "there's no comb-over for a missing head."

The city's middling perfumeries had gotten in on the action as well. Melvin Eierschneider, for one, discovered that while no living woman wanted to wear any scent from his latest collection—owing, no doubt, to his thrifty decision to make use of several hundred gallons of vinegar he'd bought at a deep discount—the walking dead were somewhat less discerning. Whether their noses had rotted off or *eau d' vinegar et moss* was still better than the stench of rotting flesh, Melvin cared little. People were buying.

"I remember this," said Sloot. Roman had just come to the door that led to the black market. "I never did get that belt."

"You sound sadder about that than you should," said Roman. "Not like a belt would help you now."

He was right, of course, but Sloot had always wanted one. A nice leather belt. You couldn't get them in the city without spending a fortune. If you were going to work for a treasonous cause, you'd best keep your pants up. There was nothing like leather for it.

Not much had changed in the black market since the last time Sloot had been there. A few of the stalls had cleared out their older product lines in favor of newer ones related to the dead. They seemed evenly divided between products for the dead and products to defend against them. Some of the options were more practical, like swords for taking off heads. Others were the sorts of things you'd expect to see in a den of thieving opportunists, like undead insurance.

"No need to worry about getting your brains gnawed upon as you walk down the streets," proclaimed a hawker wearing a barbute, "we've got you covered!"

"How do they manage that?" asked Sloot.

"Gregry's been selling helmets down here for as long as I can remember," Roman answered. "Now he's selling insurance policies at triple the price of a helmet, including the helmet in the price, and requiring the rubes to wear them or the insurance is void. He appreciates a good trend. He's old school, Gregry."

They sauntered on in silence.

"Roman?"

"Yes?"

"Do you think Mrs. Knife is really going to kidnap the Domnitor, long may he reign?"

"Not if I can help it."

Sloot grinned.

"If we can kidnap him first, it might turn things around for us."

"What? You can't be serious!"

"I'm completely serious. And you owe your loyalty to Carpathia now, don't you forget it! Blood and honor!"

"Blood and honor," Sloot muttered in the way a child would begrudgingly agree to wash up before supper. Sloot enjoyed being a loyal salt of Salzstadt the way children enjoyed being grubby.

The usual complement of unaffiliated cutpurses and stick-up men were plying their trades among the crowds. Sloot was hard-pressed to think of the patrons who made it past them to give their money to the insurance salesmen as "savvy," but he supposed that limitations of intellect were a spectrum. There was a rube for every crook, and the black market was a finely tuned ecosystem. So long as everyone stayed in their lanes, everyone could earn an honest day's pay. Well, a day's pay, anyway.

The key to answering any question is knowing where to look. If the question has anything to do with a destination in the sewers beneath Salzstadt, it's a good idea to start by looking for a wall. Namely, the one in the black market that's being held up by the unnervingly pale sewerists who are leaning against it. Sloot got the impression that they might have been trying to push it over, given the intensity they employed to the task of leaning.

"This needs to be handled delicately," said Roman.

"If you say so," said Sloot. If progress was the output of a well-oiled machine, everything in this part of the market was covered in a layer of rust. Sloot couldn't imagine that anything more subtle than a librarian's warhammer would turn the wheels of business, so he trusted Roman to get the job done.

Sloot had little experience dealing with criminal types. Just making eye contact with people here gave him the visceral urge to hand over his wallet and run.

"Sewerists talk to each other, see? Got to have something to do while they wait for their next fare. We need discretion, or else there could be trouble."

Discretion! Finally, something Sloot knew a thing or two about. He'd spent his life managing the finances of the insanely wealthy. It was impolite to talk about money no matter who you were, but if you were really *somebody*, your accountant wouldn't dream of talking to anybody about your finances. Certainly not *you*. There was only one problem.

"We don't really have time for discretion," said Sloot. In aristocratic finance, "discretion" generally meant hoping that one's client's life ran out before their money did. It was really the most polite way to avoid distasteful conversations.

"No, we don't," Roman agreed. His eyes had taken up a squint as they scanned the line of leaning sewerists. "That one, over there."

"What, the sewerist wearing the derby that he obviously, er, encountered in the line of duty?"

"That would be the one. He knows how to keep a secret."

"How can you tell?"

"It's a gift," said Roman with a smug shrug. He dusted off his jacket, straightened his lapels, and affected a straightened posture that wouldn't have looked natural even if goose-stepping were still popular.

"Pardon me," Roman said to the sewerist he'd indicated to Sloot before. "I was wondering if—"

"Down there, if you please, sir." The sewerist pointed to the other end of the wall, where one of his contemporaries waved and flashed the brownest smile that Sloot had ever seen in an approximation of charm. At least Sloot hoped he was going for charm. In the wrong light, it had all the hallmarks of malice.

"All right, but if I could just—"

"Oh, but we've got to have rules, sir," said the sewerist, who smelled as though he took his job very seriously, indeed. "This is the Old Country after all, isn't it? You know how goblins feel about cutting in lines, sir."

"Right you are," said Roman, "but I'm not here to hire a sewerist. I'm here for you in particular."

The man's eyes narrowed, as well they should. Anonymity was a sort of professional courtesy that everyone in or adjacent to the criminal underworld afforded everyone else. The nerve, wanting to speak to a private citizen without an appointment! What's next? Names on mailboxes, so everyone knows where you live?

"Look, I don't know who you are, but—"

"It's about the money your auntie left you," said Roman. "Is there somewhere we can talk in private?"

"Oh, there must be some mistake! I don't have an auntie that I know of." The man's eyes were opened very wide, in the obvious performance of the third most popular gesture meaning "please keep your voice down, you idiot," behind a finger to the lips and a hand cutting across the throat. Those two were often skipped when subtlety was desired.

"Oh, no mistake," said Roman. "I'd be happy to help you carry it home, though you can just as easily—"

"Let's talk in private, shall we?" He practically jumped away from his place on the wall and shooed Roman into an alcove behind a cart where vials of blood were selling like, well, vials of blood. They were always a top seller in the black market, and comparing their demand to anything else would be anticlimactic.

"What are you trying to do," the man spat in an urgent whisper, "take away all of my friends?"

"What? I thought inheriting wealth would make you *more* friends, if anything."

"Sure," said the man, "until you've loaned them money. Then they'll never talk to you again."

"Right, sorry."

"Never mind. How much did she leave me?"

"I must have been really convincing, to hoodwink you too."

"What?"

"You don't have an auntie!"

"What? I mean, I know, but … then why would you do that?"

"I need to get to the Cross in a hurry," said Roman. "You know where it is, and you look like the sort of fellow who can keep a secret."

"What makes you think I know how to get there?"

"I'm an excellent judge of character, mister …"

"It's Milos. Wait a minute, you didn't know my name, but you know I don't have an auntie?"

"Correct," said Roman. "Look, I don't have time to get into all of that now. If you can get me to the southern point of the Cross within the hour and keep it under your hat, I'll pay you five times your going rate."

Milos narrowed his eyes again and gripped his lapels in his grubby hands as he regarded Roman. He had the look of a man who knew that he didn't know what was going on, and that was something. Your average streetwise type also wouldn't have known what was going on in this sort of situation, but he wouldn't have known it. Being just smart enough to know that you're not very smart puts you miles ahead of most people.

"Eight times," said Milos, after he'd leered at Roman for what he felt had been long enough to get him squirming. "And when you're done, you come back to the lineup and clear up this 'auntie' business."

"You drive a hard bargain, Milos. Shall we?"

⊰⊱SKELETON KEY CIRCLE⊰⊱

The Serpents of the Earth had members all over the world, none of whom were eager to advertise it. It wasn't something that went over well in polite company. "I truck with people who wear black robes, hoard other people's blood, and toy with the fates of nations. Oh, and our mascot is a snake. I think everyone can agree there's nothing sinister about that." Very few people would want to be friends with anyone who talked like that, not even the Serpents of the Earth in most cases.

This is why they've gone to great pains to keep their identities a secret, silver snake rings notwithstanding. In some cases, they even need to remain anonymous with each other. This is why they've made places like the Cross.

The Cross is a collection of four tiny rooms, each only large enough for one person. Or, in this case, one person and one ghost of an accountant-turned-spy.

"There are three other rooms," Roman whispered into Sloot's shrunken head's shrunken ear. The most unnerving part was that Sloot heard him particularly well. "Their entrances are all over the city, hidden to protect the identities of those summoned to meetings. At the appointed time, the magic candles in each room will alight, and everyone will be able to hear each other."

"Who will be able to hear each other?"

"Mrs. Knife will be in one of the rooms, and the other two are the reason I brought you along. You see, I have a hunch."

"I've never noticed it," said Sloot.

"No, an *intuition*. You're dead, see?"

"Well intuited."

"Very funny. See, the dead can perceive things the living cannot. I'm told the magic enchanting these candles is necromantic, so you may be able to follow the links between them."

"Er, okay," said Sloot. "Then you want me to … what, follow the links?"

"Precisely," whispered Roman. "I've been gathering intelligence about this meeting for a couple of days now, and Greta overhearing that Mrs. Knife is attending made it really interesting. If this meeting is what I think it is, it could be the break we need!"

"To do what, exactly?"

"To crush the Serpents of the Earth! You do remember the plan, don't you?"

It would take a lot more than vacating his corporeal form to make Sloot forget that the Serpents of the Earth were dangerous. But in the moment, he felt that he never properly considered the fact that they have necromancers on staff, which meant they could probably do very nasty things to the dead.

Before he had a chance to settle into a proper fit of fretting, a flame burst from the tip of the lone black candle in the room. Roman was startled by it, his bug eyes going even wider than usual. He used two fingers of his right hand to point to the eyes of Sloot's shrunken head, then waved the gruesome souvenir around the room as if he were providing the worst tour ever.

"What?" whispered Sloot.

Roman gave a sharp intake of breath through clenched teeth. He held one finger against Sloot's shrunken lips as if to shush him.

Sloot looked around the room. He could see the candle, the flame, and Roman, panicking as quietly as possible.

"Who's there?" came a voice in a sort of dull, reversed echo. It sounded like a murderer who'd gotten drunk in the future, and was speaking through a bucket. To be more precise, she will have gotten drunk in the future; however, she won't. It's just a metaphor.

In the end, it didn't matter how much the metaphorical murderer from the future will have had to drink, or how much of life Sloot might eventually forget in death. He would have recognized Mrs. Knife's voice anywhere. It had a tinny rage to it, even when she was in a good mood. Not that Sloot could remember ever having seen Mrs. Knife in a good mood.

"The Steward of the Circle," came another, equally future-bucket-distorted voice. This one belonged to a man, Sloot was fairly certain. "I believe that Constantin's keeper is with us as well."

"I am," came a third voice. It was unmistakably a woman, and Sloot thought she sounded familiar.

"On to business, then." Mrs. Knife had a way of making even the most perfunctory of statements sound like a threat. "We're still sorting through the remains from the incident. As soon as we've been able to determine which belonged to the elder and younger Lords Hapsgalt, we'll deliver them to you in the usual way."

"Go, go!" Roman mouthed to Sloot.

Go where? Sloot wondered. Then it seemed that whatever magic was at work in the Cross answered him. There were three very faint lines emanating from the candle's flame, ethereal things, reaching through the walls. Perhaps the other ends were attached to the other rooms of the Cross?

"I already have the elder Lord Hapsgalt's remains," said the unidentified woman's voice. It matched Mrs. Knife's tone in terms of confidence, if not malice.

"What? How? You have violated protocol by trespassing into our affairs!"

Roman was shaking with an urgent frustration that was starting to cause Sloot more trepidation than the fear he was presently staring down: moving through walls. It would make sense that he'd be able to do so, but a lifetime of having had a face with a very tender nose on the front of it simply couldn't get behind the idea.

"I did not trespass," said the woman. "Upon Constantin's demise, his remains came to me by means of an enchantment. That had been arranged long ago, by my predecessor. Lord Hapsgalt was well aware."

"I was never informed of this. I must insist that you return them at once!"

"That would be a clear violation of protocol," said the man. The Steward, he'd called himself.

As dearly as Sloot would have loved to pluck up his nerve and get on with it, he simply couldn't think of a way to get himself to take the first step. So he resolved to act without thinking, which has far more to do with fooling one's self than bravery. It's what we use when we try to catch pots of boiling water that are falling from the stove, or tell our significant others how their posteriors *really* look in those pants. That was what Sloot was thinking—or, rather, *wasn't*—when he picked a line and walked through the wall to follow it.

"I am the Eye of the Serpent!" Mrs. Knife was clearly unaccustomed to having her orders questioned. "The Circle works for me. Now, do as you're told!"

"The Circle serves the Serpents of the Earth," said the Steward, "but we do not take orders from you. The Book of Black Law specifically states—"

"Don't quote the Book to me, Steward."

It was nauseating, walking through solid walls. Sloot was thankful he didn't have guts, else he'd be hurling their contents at the experience. Then again, scientific curiosity would have a field day with where said contents would end up. If he happened to be passing through a brick wall, would they supplement the mortar? Sloot wondered about that as fiercely as possible. He wanted to avoid concentrating on what he was doing at all costs. He continued following the line, which had led him through several city blocks already.

"The elder Lord Hapsgalt's remains are being cared for in the traditional way," said the woman. Her voice was calm in the way that a hungry tiger watches a zookeeper's hands at feeding time.

"And how is that, exactly?" Mrs. Knife spat. "The Skeleton Key Circle has been acting without oversight for far too long, if you ask me."

The Skeleton Key Circle! Had Sloot heard that correctly? The people with whom he and Willie had tousled in the secret room beneath the crypt—isn't that who they said they were?

"That's the entire point of our organization," said the Steward, "to act without oversight. The founders of the Serpents of the Earth—"

"Another subject upon which I need no education from you!" Sloot had heard Mrs. Knife this agitated before. She'd been stabbing him at the time. He shuddered, which resulted in some bizarre psychic reverberations. He wished he could have resolved never to do that again, but he knew himself too well.

There was no way to know which of the other rooms in the Cross he was heading toward. He could still hear the entire conversation because he was on the line. A familiar bit of panic latched onto him as he realized he might end up face-to-face with Mrs. Knife at any moment. Fate and circumstance were not muscles, though he'd certainly have a go at flexing them both if it would have helped.

"The new keeper awaits the remains of the new Soul," said the Steward. "They should have been delivered by now, but you say that there have been extenuating circumstances. When may we expect delivery?"

"You may not."

"I beg your pardon?"

"As well you should," said Mrs. Knife. "Make no mistake, if I could look you in the eye, I'd have the point of my knife wiggling around in your liver."

"You do not threaten the Steward," said the woman. Unlike Mrs. Knife, her voice was not rising. All the same, it did seem to be strapping on its helmet and inching toward its sword.

"Mark my words, your days are numbered." Mrs. Knife chuckled. It was the sort of chuckle that you'd expect from a meat cart vendor who'd just served last Thursday's souvlaki to his brother-in-law, the one who was always telling his wife she could do better.

"You have no authority in this matter," replied the Steward with all the furor and intensity of his father after binging on dinner at Snugglewatch, probably.

"That's where you're wrong," Mrs. Knife practically sang. Sloot could hear her smiling. "There's a passage in the Book of Black Law that allows me to dissolve the Skeleton Key Circle and take possession of all the Souls' remains."

"That's preposterous," said the Steward.

"No argument there," said Mrs. Knife, "it was my lawyers who found the loophole. All I need is the agreement of the current Soul, and he wouldn't dream of disagreeing with me. I spent his entire life ensuring that the mere whisper of my name would terrify him."

Not just him, Sloot thought. He was sure that Mrs. Knife had applied some of the same treatment to him. If she hadn't, he'd shown real initiative in picking it up himself.

"I believe I know the loophole of which you speak," said the Steward. "Fortunately, until his remains are in the custody of his proper keeper, his word is not sufficient to shape the Black Law."

"That's what you think," Mrs. Knife growled.

"That's what I know!" The Steward had finally had enough, it seemed. He'd started using his I-really-must-insist tone of voice. "It is my job to know the Book of Black Law, namely as it pertains to the Skeleton Key Circle, backward and forward! Until Wilhelm's remains are in the custody of their keeper, he may be unduly influenced by whomsoever possesses them, so he cannot apply his voice to the Black Law. Without his agreement, you cannot change the Black Law, Madam Eye."

"We'll just see about that."

"You'll see that I'm right." The Steward's voice gave no indication that he harbored any doubt. "Deliver the Soul's remains to us, and there's nothing I can do to stop you from burning the entire Book. Until then, I'll not sit here and be insulted by a would-be tyrant. Good day."

"Listen to me very carefully, you little—"

"I said good day!"

The line disappeared. Sloot began to panic. Not that he wasn't panicking before, of course. Sloot was an accomplished panicker. It would be more accurate to say that he opened a new line of panic to add to his already impressive portfolio, and fretted over the increased workload.

What to do? He was in the middle of an abandoned tenement building, or at least he hoped it was abandoned. There were a few people sleeping in it, and he hoped they were homeless. It was not something he wished upon people in general, but he couldn't bear the thought that they were paying to be there.

He resolved to continue along his present trajectory, at least for a little while longer. If he were close, perhaps he'd stumble into another chamber of the Cross before its occupant left.

It wasn't the first time Sloot had secretly wished he wasn't so smart. There had been the time in grade school when he'd been beaten up for answering all of his teacher's questions with such zeal that the rest of his class felt they'd been made to look bad. Afterward, in the recess yard, a few of them had decided to teach him a few things that he didn't know, namely about the taste of dirt and how the wind might be driven from his lungs by a well-placed fist.

This time was far less painful in the physical sense, but Sloot had a feeling it would be far more troublesome in the long run. He'd hoped to eventually find a room like the one where he'd stood with Roman, only it would be empty. Curses, rotten luck, back to the business of death and eternity, then.

Fortunately, or unfortunately, depending on whose side you were on, Sloot did indeed find such a room. Unfortunately—from his point of view—there was a person in it. To his further chagrin and misfortune, he recognized her as the tall woman from the secret room beneath the crypt. The one who had pinned him to the wall with her wand.

In a welcome break from Sloot's standard rate of misfortune, he'd emerged from the wall just as she was trying to light a candle of the normal variety. It was totally dark in the room. She hadn't seen him! Acting on a cowardly impulse that came across very much like cat-like reflexes if you'd never met Sloot, he dodged quickly upward into the corner behind her.

Her sparker set the candle alight, and she stood there for a moment as the flame cast a warm glow about the little room. It was exactly the same as the one where he'd just been with Roman, down to the slightly askew stone walls and rough-planked table with one leg slightly shorter than the others, so it wobbled a bit when she picked her satchel up for a moment.

She sighed. Sloot was nearly in fits over the possibility of her whirling around too quickly and discovering him, but he couldn't help catching a whiff of sorrow coming from her. As if on cue, her shoulders lifted twice in a little sob. She suppressed it with a sniff, shook her head, and squared her shoulders.

"He's gone, and that's that," she murmured. "It's up to me now."

To Sloot's chagrin, he found her sorrow intoxicating. He felt drawn to it, in a way that he found deeply troubling. What sort of person could possibly find amusement in another person's misery? Aside from the obvious, like people who brag to hungover people that they never get hangovers. He didn't want to find her melancholy so scintillating, but he did. He'd have had a long think about why that was later, had he not been the sort of person who bottled up his uncomfortable feelings and vowed never to look directly at them. You know, a normal person.

Sloot managed to stay behind her as she made her way through the door and out into the very shadowy daylight. Sloot followed her and found himself on a little walkway beneath a bridge that ran across the river.

For lack of a better idea, he continued to follow her. He started out keeping his distance, even going so far as to find places—flower shops, hat shops, and other shops as well—where he could duck in and be inconspicuous. He eventually recalled that the good people of Salzstadt were observing the practice of ignoring the dead, and that he was probably calling more attention to himself by going through the motions of subterfuge. Since no one was gawking or screaming at him, he decided to abandon the pretense and simply keep up. It wasn't until she was within a block of the black market that he felt a familiar tug behind his ear, and turned to meet it.

"So," said Roman, "what'd you find out?"

"Less than I could have," said Sloot. He didn't want to be involved at all, but since his preferences on the matter seemed to count for nothing, he'd have settled for doing a good job. "I think she was headed for the black market. She was nearly there when you summoned me."

"Following the woman, eh?" Roman wiggled his eyebrows in that way that respectable people don't. The way that they teach creepy uncles to do, presumably at beer-swilling camp. "What did she look like?"

"Yes," said Myrtle, "do tell." She was wearing the sort of expression that amused girlfriends do not.

"Myrtle! When did you get here? Where are we?"

"We're in an alley." Roman's tone was definitely sarcastic, as was his sweeping gesture to draw Sloot's attention to the piles of garbage, leaky rain gutters, and other standard accoutrements that one might expect to find in such a place.

"I just picked one of the lines and followed," said Sloot. "I didn't know it was hers!"

"It doesn't matter," said Myrtle. "I've come to bring you home."

"Home?"

"To the Hereafter. Things have … escalated. You're supposed to step in."

❧❧PUPPIES MOST VILE❧❧

B eing dead was … well, fine, really.

No, not fine. It just *was*. Sloot's general opinion of this, the next phase of existence, wasn't really something he cared to pick apart. At best, he no longer had to worry about the effects of fatty foods on his digestion. At worst, he was no closer to being free of the tribulations of his earthly affairs than he'd been before his head was repurposed in the name of fashion.

He'd been told more than once that the affairs of the living were no longer his concern, that he had to deal with the affairs of the dead. That would have been fine if the affairs of the dead weren't determined to intersect with the affairs of the living at every opportunity.

Myrtle had seemed anxious to get Sloot back to the Hereafter. It undoubtedly meant there was trouble, or at least he hoped it did. Otherwise, his probably-girlfriend was merely casually anxious for him to depart the land of the living.

"Things are getting bad," said Myrtle, making Sloot feel better and worse at the same time. "If you could just do something about Constantin, Nan could probably get Willie back into the circle."

"Constantin." Knowing that he didn't have to deal with Willie gave Sloot a measure of relief. It was an unusual sensation, and he wasn't sure it could be relied upon. His suspicion turned out to be well-founded.

"He's gotten wind that Nan is here, and he's hunting for her. She's hiding from him, and Willie won't listen to anyone else."

"Oh," said Sloot. When he'd first met Constantin, the old man had specifically forbidden Sloot from allowing Nan to have anything to do with Willie. He'd unwittingly sworn on salt and spit—which was a big deal in the Old Country—to hire her if she cleared the house of goblins, which she did. Of all the things that could have followed Sloot into the grave, he'd never thought that answering for that would have been among them.

"Well, he's just an old codger now, isn't he?" Sloot was trying to convince himself as much as anyone else. "No Soul powers or anything. He's just a lot of hot air."

"In theory," said Myrtle. "He still gives me the creeps, though."

This is ridiculous, Sloot thought. He believed in respecting one's elders, but only to the extent that the Ministry of Etiquette and Guillotines allowed.

Around fifty years before Sloot had been born, Sir Stellan Hosenfurcht had been named the youngest Minister of Etiquette and Guillotines in the history of the Old Country. Finding it impossible to get anything done for all of the old obstructionists in Central Bureaucracy, he pushed legislation that made deference to one's elders a felony. It was summarily overturned upon his untimely demise at the hands of the Salzstadt Council of Elders which, strangely enough, no one saw coming. However, Sir Stellan's zeal for the project had fast-tracked it through the lines at Central Bureaucracy—no one saw that coming, either—and the Ministry of Propaganda had so thoroughly postered the city with warnings to "Tell Grandpa Where He Can Shove It" that even now, nearly a century later, some of them were still up. No one really knew what the rules were anymore, but it would certainly never occur to a true salt of the Old Country to be more polite to anyone than the law required.

Of course, no one wanted to cross the elderly. The lessons learned from Sir Stellan were that age and treachery always overcome youth and enthusiasm, and that a bureaucracy at rest will not put up with some young upstart trying to rush things along.

None of this, of course, gave Sloot any indication as to how he might rein Constantin in. He needed to think of something. It wasn't as though Willie was going to begin spontaneously listening to him. Sloot was still *the help*, after all.

Sloot said a swear word under his breath. The one that isn't grammatically correct in any context, and is most often repeated at least a dozen times while failing to regain one's footing on a slippery kitchen floor.

How was he supposed to get Constantin under control? Try as he might, he was unable to even consider striding up to Constantin in a non-deferential manner, and starting a sentence to the tune of, "Now you listen to me, you peer or lesser sort of person!"

He'd worked for Constantin at the Three Bells. That is to say, his supervisor's manager's director's board of director's managing partners' oversight committee's chairman worked for Constantin's undersecretary, but the result was ultimately the same. When Sloot had been promoted to Willie's financier, he never officially left Constantin's employ. Now that he was dead and those sorts of loyalties had become permanent, he was no more capable of dressing the old man down than dressing him up, ghosts' lack of physical appendages considered.

"I saw her!" boomed Constantin's voice from within the house. "That harpy! That coddler! Bring her to me so I can thrash her within an inch of her life!"

Sloot was able to disobey that on the grounds that Nan was already dead. Oh, sweet technicality! He'd have given it a big, wet kiss if he didn't most likely have a girlfriend.

"Coming, m'lord!" Sloot floated quickly through the dusty corridors of the house, attempting to sidestep the confusing reality that dust exists in the Hereafter. A severe dose of good old-fashioned Old Country denial was just the thing for it. He was eager to find Constantin and placate him. He grimaced at that eagerness, not that it slowed him down.

There was a worrisome darkness in the corridor that must have been half cat, in that it couldn't make up its mind whether it wanted to be inside the house. It kept nearly casting the house into total darkness, then bringing the lights up again.

Worry. That was familiar, if unsettling. Sloot was just starting to settle into some proper fretting over how the cat darkness thing could go horribly, horribly wrong when the voices joined in.

Whispers, sobbing, maniacal cackling. It was a cacophony that couldn't decide where it was going, but it had enough funding to hire one of everything, just so they had it. The screeching was the worst, though Sloot had to admit that it did the most to set the mood.

He finally found Constantin sitting in the parlor, wearing his pajamas. Retirement seemed to be setting in.

"I saw her!" Constantin repeated. Echoes are very soothing to the dead, even though this one seemed to agitate him intensely.

"Who did you see, m'lord?"

"That woman! Willie's old nanny. I saw her here, with my own two eyes!"

"Well, that's disturbing."

"She's coddling Willie, I just know it! He's going to be the Soul of the Serpent one day, you know."

A gout of flames shot down the hallway just outside the parlor. Its timing insinuated it was making a little money on the side, punctuating the rants of cranky old ghosts.

"What was that?" demanded Constantin.

"Er, I believe it was Willie, m'lord."

"Willie? What's he doing?"

"Well ... venting, I suppose?"

"Good! Good for the constitution. Hapsgalt men can eat coal peppers right off the vine, you know."

Coal peppers were one of the first forays into evil produce. A grocer in Kaldakos was convinced by a book that was far smarter than he to flip through its pages. Upon realizing his folly, he closed it quickly enough that only the shadow of the corrupt spirit trapped in the book made its way into him. Once they'd gotten cozy together in the grocer's mind, they cooked up the idea to craft a murderously hot pepper that would kill anyone who ate it. It met with some success, but only after it was rebranded as a tool for fraternity hazing. Sloot had never tried one, so he had no grounds upon which he might have disputed Constantin's claim.

The air, or whatever they had in the Hereafter that passed for it, trembled. A low rumble passed through the room, like the sound that might be made by the growling bellies of several million hungry spiders. The lights were starting to fade again. It was an ominous sort of darkness. Not the cool, clean sort of darkness that was good for sleep, but the oily sort that lurked at front doors and threatened to sell you things.

"Have Grumley come in here," said Constantin with a dismissive wave. "He'll sort out that noise in the walls. Rattling pipes, is it?"

"Er, that's one possibility," Sloot replied, giving satisfaction to neither lies nor truth. He seized the opportunity to leave the parlor and hoped that Constantin would fail to remember about Nan for a while.

Sloot went searching for Willie, figuring that following the ghastliest phenomena in the place would get him there eventually.

The Hereafter doesn't seem creepy enough on its own, Sloot imagined Willie saying to himself. *I know, let's get the floor undulating. That'll add just the right amount of menace to the place.*

He wasn't in the room with the circle that served to contain his power, though that wouldn't have been hard to guess. He wasn't in the room where all of the furniture was screaming, either. That one was particularly unnerving, so much so that Sloot barely noticed the difference in tone between screaming leather and screaming velvet. Leather was a bit more warbly.

The undulating black roots spilling out ankle-deep from the end of the hall should have been obvious. Sloot reluctantly followed them and found Willie's head lurking in the formal dining room. The rest of him was there as well, but the distinction was noteworthy.

"Oh, hi Sloot." Willie's head rested on a silver platter. There was probably a metaphor there, or at least a pun.

"M-m'lord?"

"Yes?"

"You seem to be a bit ..."

"Debonaire? More than a bit, I imagine. I got good marks in that at school, you know."

"I'm sure," said Sloot, "but I was going to remark upon your, er, decorum."

"My what?"

"Your ... decentralization."

"I can make up words too, Sloot."

"I beg your pardon, m'lord, but ... well, your head's off."

"You noticed that too, did you? Horribly inconvenient. I've tried telling my body to get with the program, but it doesn't seem to want to have anything to do with me."

"I see."

"I just wish I knew what it was doing over there. What *I* was doing over there."

Willie's body would have been entirely unrecognizable if it hadn't been alone in the room with his head. It was wearing a tattered shroud in lieu of anything remotely fashionable, and if it was striking any pose that might have been intentional, it must have been called something like the Certain Violent Intent, or the Your Grave Needs A Good Spitting Upon.

"I'm not going to hurt us, am I?" Willie sounded truly worried for the first time since he'd realized he couldn't smell his perfume collection anymore, or find it.

"You've removed your own head," said Sloot. "I'd imagine that if you were going to do worse than that, you'd've done so already."

"That sounds reasonable. All the same, what am I *doing* over there?"

"If I had to guess," said Sloot, who abhorred guessing for the implied risk involved, "I'd say you're working some sort of black magic."

"Hmmm," said Willie, in an approximation of thoughtfulness. "That would explain the tortured moaning that's coming from that melting wall over there."

Sloot tittered nervously and nodded. "Wouldn't it just?"

They watched for a while as Willie's body committed whatever atrocities it was up to. Sloot, at least, was racking his brain for a way to stop it, but coming up empty. He didn't realize how badly the attempt was going until he found himself glancing over to Willie, in case he'd perhaps thought of something.

"Do you think you might go sit in the circle for a bit, m'lord?"

"Probably a good idea, but all of my sitting bits are otherwise engaged at the moment."

"Ah."

"It's a strange sort of dance, isn't it?"

"I don't think it's dancing, m'lord." If he were being completely honest, Sloot was no authority on the matter, having never danced a step in his life. That was just the sort of thing that led to wearing tight pants, and poor circulation would kill you. Hardly a factor now, but if *that* was dancing, he wanted no part of it.

"Looks like necromancy," said Nicoleta.

"When did you get here?"

"I never left," Nicoleta snapped. "While you were out gallivanting across the Narrative, *Mr. Peril*, I was here trying to help Willie! Never mind that I didn't succeed. Anyway, the best I can tell is that his body's up to some sort of death magic. Necromancy."

"I'd prefer if that were dancing," said Sloot, feeling more than a bit abashed. His divided loyalties meant he was attending to each of them poorly, and he hated doing a bad job.

"Necromancers go in for that sort of stuff," said Nicoleta, pointing at Willie's body with disdain. "Big gestures, hands clawing at the heavens. Show-offs, the lot of them. I'm sure he'd rather be on a cliff overlooking the sea during a thunderstorm."

"I find it hard to believe that Willie's body is a necromancer when his head's not looking."

"Of all the things that have happened since you died, *that's* where your suspension of disbelief hits a wall?"

She had him there.

"You're a wizard," said Willie, "go over there and tell him—me—to stop doing that. If I come over here and put my head back on, we can try some of that 'forgive and forget' business that I'm told poors are fond of."

"I am a wizard," said Nicoleta, with a note of praise to Willie for having noticed. "But my spells still aren't working. Besides, it looks like all of your talking and reasoning bits are on your platter. If you can't get your body on board, I've got nothing."

"Never fear!" shouted a voice from behind Sloot, close enough that a whisper would have gotten the job done. "Reason and logic shall prevail!"

Sloot yelped and wheeled on Arthur with a haunted look.

"Was that entirely necessary?" Sloot's voice had gone shrill and warbling in alarm.

"Oh, good," groaned Nicoleta. "Arthur's here."

"Oh, good," beamed Willie, "Arthur's here!"

"As always, there's a logical explanation for what's going on here. There's no need to go ascribing everything that happens to *magic*, no matter how strange it may seem."

"It's summoning something," said Nicoleta. "That was clearly the 'come hither' gesture it just did with Willie's left hand."

"It didn't look very welcoming to me," said Willie's head.

"That's because you're not an unnameable terror from the void beyond the stars. Or an imp. But you use the right hand for them."

"Why is he summoning an unnameable terror from the void beyond the stars?" asked Sloot, throwing in some nervous fidgeting in case his voice didn't adequately convey his terror.

"Ahem," said Willie.

"Sorry, m'lord. Why is m'lord's body summoning an unnameable terror from the void beyond the stars?"

"Clearly, we're all suffering from Chestinger's Communal Hallucination," said Arthur. "What sorts of mushrooms have we all been eating?"

"No kinds," said Nicoleta. "We're dead."

"Well, you can only catch communal hallucinations from eating the wrong sorts of mushrooms, so we must have done."

"Or it's not a hallucination."

"There's no time for you to question my expertise!"

"We really need to stop this before Willie fin—er, *m'lord's body* finishes summoning what ever it's … summoning."

When surrounded by the trappings of incalculable evil—such as writhing masses of shadow tentacles wriggling across the floors of one's home—it's often difficult to decide how one should feel when said incalculable evil starts to leave. If decided in a committee, there would undoubtedly be a split between the optimistic "hooray and good riddance to it" types, and the "but where is it going now" types who consider themselves pragmatists, not pessimists. A true pessimist wouldn't turn up for a committee meeting, because what's the point?

"Well, that's a relief," said Sloot, who'd never been accused of optimism in his life.

"Don't relax just yet," said Nicoleta, taking a far more Sloot-typical position. "I'm not sure what the disembodied—wait, no, headless body of Willie—could want with writhing tentacles of dark energy. But whatever it is, it can't be good."

"Good," said Arthur with a derisive snort. "No such thing! Evil either. If you'd done your reading, you'd know that Professor Calbage of Wilcestermount-Upon-Shatserbury-Adjacent-The-Sea has a seventeen-point treatise that firmly eschews the notion—"

"I've been to Wilcestermount-Upon-Shatserbury-Adjacent-The-Sea," said Willie's head. "But don't tell anybody. I had a phase in my twenties, experimented with community theatre."

"Er…" Sloot pointed to the melting wall behind Willie's body, which had nearly melted entirely. All of the tentacles of evil—or whatever analog Professor Calbage's treatise would acknowledge—were slithering off into the darkness beyond it. A pair of glowing eyes fumed within the darkness.

"Eyes that glow in the dark don't growl, do they?" Sloot had surmised, accurately, that there was more to whatever lurked beyond the melting wall. Probably teeth. And if Willie could be decapitated, then perhaps teeth from within melting walls could threaten a ghost.

As the last of the tentacles slithered into the blackness beyond the wall, Sloot considered running away. He dismissed the thought without much ado, on account of the way his luck tended to go. There hadn't been a coin minted that, when tossed, would fall the way Sloot called it. He'd be better off wagering on standing there and being devoured by whatever malevolence was assembling itself in the shadows. It seemed like a sure bet, but Sloot had a way of bucking the odds.

Perhaps it helped. Perhaps not. What emerged from the black maw in the wall was no ferocious beast.

"It's a puppy," said Nicoleta, her voice tinged with appropriate confusion and disbelief.

"Well, that makes perfect sense," said Arthur.

"It does?" asked Sloot.

"I wouldn't expect you to understand," Arthur retorted, his nose turning upward severely enough that he'd have drowned, had it been raining. "Communal hallucinations often cloud the minds of those experiencing them. You don't even remember eating the mushrooms."

Willie's body made its way over to the dining table. He didn't so much set his head back atop his shoulders as reabsorb it and waver for a moment.

"Well, that's a relief," said Willie. He patted down the front of himself, most likely assuring that he was dressed appropriately for the occasion, but he also could have been looking for his keys, which he did not have. The trousers of his tuxedo were far too tight to have accommodated them.

"Er," began Sloot, as was his fashion, "do you know anything about the puppy, m'lord?"

"Oh, I nearly forgot! Where is my head these days?" He looked around at all of them with a gleeful sneer of self-amusement. "Well, no, actually. Didn't one of you get him for me? Is it my birthday?"

"Hard to say," said Nicoleta. "But ... weren't you paying attention?"

"I have people for that. Sloot! Pay the woman."

"Your body just summoned the puppy. All of the tentacles? The melting wall? Surely, you must remember some of it."

"I'm pretty sure I'm the boss," said Willie from beneath smarmy eyebrows, "let's leave the 'musts' to me, shall we?"

Nothing. That would do it. In the absence of any possible logical response, Sloot had historically managed some very positive results from saying nothing at all. In his experience, logic was a moving target. If you just stood still long enough, it would eventually fall into place.

"I know what's going on here," said Willie, alongside the spiritual equivalent of snapping his fingers. "This is another one of Nipsy's classic pranks!"

"I highly doubt that, m'lord."

"Oh. Right." Willie giggled, then straightened up and started shouting in an amused sort of way. "I suppose this all just sort of came together naturally, and there's no one hiding ... under ... here!"

He was right. No one had been hiding underneath the table, where his head had rested while his body had been about the business of conjuring evil puppies. Sloot had to hand it to Willie: if all of this *had* been some sort of elaborate prank, under the table would have been the best hiding place available.

Willie spent several minutes refusing to allow anything as pedestrian as the earnest insistence of everyone else in the room to convince him that his old friend Nipsy wasn't somehow at the bottom of this. The puppy, in the meantime, confounded Sloot by engaging in the full gamut of standard puppy behavior. It yipped. It chased its tail. It tilted its head and looked at him with big puppy eyes. Never once did it waver in its commitment to the role, though Sloot didn't doubt for a second that it would have preferred terrorizing a countryside or lurking under a child's bed. It was, in a word, terrifying.

And adorable. Two words.

"Fine," said Willie after failing to discover Nipsy's hiding place. "If he won't come out and own up to it, I'll name the puppy Nipsy, and he'll be my new best friend. Do you hear that, Nipsy?"

Nipsy barked. The puppy, that is. Willie's eyes darted around the room as if chasing a mosquito.

"Fine!" he said again, and this time stamped his foot. "Come on, new Nipsy, we've got some secret business that we can't tell Sloot about."

"Sorry, m'lord?" asked Sloot. Willie came no closer to answering than increasing the pace at which he floated from the room. Nipsy yipped and went chasing after him.

"That can't be good," said Arthur.

"I thought there was no such thing as good," Nicoleta mocked.

"You leave the philosophy to me," Arthur barked, clearly ill at ease with having his expertise questioned.

"It's an evil puppy," said Sloot. "It doesn't seem evil, but it is, right?"

"It seems that way," said Nicoleta. "Willie was failing to contain all of the dark power being fed to him. I think his body just sort of ... puppied it."

"Weird that his body was able to do that," said Sloot.

"Not really," said Arthur.

"I'd always heard that magic was done in the mind," said Sloot. "And by wizards."

"Not a good idea to go imposing rules on magic," said Nicoleta. "It'll fight you on that, leak out through the seams."

"No, no," said Arthur. "We'll be here all day if you just keep guessing! It's obvious that Willie's body had all the power, and he needed to be free of his head's nonsensical blabbering to get anything done."

"That makes a lot of sense, despite being completely ridiculous." Nicoleta stared off into empty space, of which the Hereafter had quite a lot.

"Myrtle would certainly agree with me," said Arthur. "I taught her everything she knows! Where is she, anyway?"

"Gone," said Sloot. He wasn't sure how he knew, but there wasn't a doubt in his mind. Perhaps they shared some sort of link, having to do with the love that they'd so briefly shared before they were crushed beneath a dust-up between a congress of goblins and a horde of the walking dead.

Well, *he'd* been crushed. She'd had her neck snapped by Gregor. No matter, the important thing was that they'd loved each other. Whisking the details of whose violent death was more gruesome than whose distracted from the point. Sloot's love for Myrtle seemed to be pointing him toward her, so he let it lead the way.

"I'll just clean all of this up then, shall I?" Nicoleta had a firm grasp of sarcasm and spared no opportunity to remind everyone.

"Find Nan," said Sloot, then added, "er, please and thank you. Have her find Willie and put him in the circle. I'm afraid it'll be more than a puppy next time!"

Sloot followed his heart, which led him out the front door and into the hills. When did she leave the house? Sloot imagined that she must have had important business, to leave him to his own devices when every inch of the house was positively wriggling with malevolent darkness. She must have known he'd be safe, or that Willie's shenanigans couldn't possibly make everyone in the house any more dead than they already were.

Myrtle *was* dead, wasn't she? Of course, she was. He'd seen her die, and she'd been all spectral in the Hereafter before the incident—maybe it was just a fluke? Lots of dead people wanted back into the Narrative. Perhaps Myrtle had a special knack for it.

On Sloot went, over the grey hills that surrounded the house, until his path led into the darkened wood where he'd followed Willie to the crypt. He reckoned that a darkened wood was probably the only sort he was likely to encounter in the Hereafter. Sunny glades where the bunnies befriended the deer were unlikely in this sinister landscape—unless, of course, the bunnies were part of a cult that needed to sacrifice a deer to open up a portal into the nether reaches of some unpronounceable demon dimension, where they could rule as gods and sup on the souls of those who had been truly naughty in life.

It was that sort of charging headlong into baseless worry that would have killed Sloot due to heart strain within a few years, had his head not popped off when it did. Nevertheless, he was overcome with relief to discover there were no bunnies within the darkened wood. The innumerable spiders skittering across every surface in the place made short work of said relief, but still, bunny-free.

"It looks lost," whispered several thousand tiny voices in unison.

"I'm not lost," said Sloot in his highest falsetto. He cleared his throat and tried to calm himself back down to tenor. "I know exactly where I am."

"Then it's either very brave," whispered the multitude of spiders, "or very stupid. Or both."

"It's certainly not the first one," said Sloot. He'd learned a long time ago that pretending to be brave when you were afraid, despite the well-intentioned advice offered by dads everywhere, tended to earn you nothing but more of a bully's spit in your ear. "What are you going to do to me?"

"Don't worry about it," whispered the spiders, who had obviously never met a worrier before. They erupted into a frenzy. Most of them jumped up and down, which made a sound like an avalanche on the side of a molehill. The rest of them leapt all around him, spinning silvery strands of webbing into a diabolical sort of prison.

"Oh no," Sloot whimpered. He'd never been particularly afraid of spiders, preferring to think that he feared all things equally. Under the circumstances, that was likely to change.

"Oh yes," whispered the spiders, "do stay here with us. Forever. We insist!"

The prospect of forever suddenly seemed a lot longer than it had before. An eternity of keeping Constantin from learning that Nan was living in his house and coddling his son—who was the Soul of the Serpent in his stead—seemed downright pleasant when weighed against an eternity in the presence of more spiders than even he could count.

That would be the fear talking. Sloot was an accountant. He knew perfectly well that a precise number of spiders existed there, but this was one occasion upon which he felt that a solid, rational number might be far more unnerving. Innumerable it was, then.

He couldn't move. There was a logical part of his mind screaming at him that he was a ghost, and he could float unhindered through the cocoon they were weaving around him. Sloot trucked with logic as a rule. Unfortunately, fear wasn't logical, and the fearful part of his mind was screaming far louder at him that he was in grave danger, and how was he going to spend eternity in a spider web? They wouldn't know where to forward his mail!

While his inability to move was mostly thanks to fear, it owed partial credit to the Agreement.

When the first ghosts awoke in the Hereafter, they were just floating around in a void. Having recently been living people with physics and everything, it was disorienting. The first thing that they did was to agree on some ground rules, literally including the establishment of the ground. They agreed not to go around floating through each other, retaining some symbolic semblance of the physical world they'd left behind, because it was comforting and familiar.

When Sloot died, he'd been granted a set of new instincts, like the urge to haunt things and make the sound of rattling chains, especially when in close proximity to a bedroom. The Agreement was a part of the package deal. He knew that he could break the Agreement and simply walk out of the webs that had been woven around him, but he dared not. Somehow, staying right where he was for whatever span of eternity lay before him seemed preferable to breaking the Agreement.

No, not preferable. Definitely easier, though. He assumed that breaking the Agreement would land him in some very serious trouble that would involve a lot of bureaucracy to clear up. While he was intrigued by the prospect of visiting whatever bureaucracy the Hereafter had to offer, he didn't want to risk finding out that there wasn't one. He didn't know what that sort of disappointment would do to him.

The spiders continued their weaving, chittering excitedly among themselves as they worked. Sloot couldn't hear what they were whispering anymore, not that he lamented that fact.

So, this was eternity, then. Were there others? Kindred spirits, no pun intended, who'd been so foolish as to traipse heedlessly into the spiders' web? Quite the menagerie they'd make.

Some time passed. Sloot spent a good deal of it amassing a feeling of resentment for the earlier ghosts, for not coming up with some way to mark the passage of time. He'd never thought much about the sound of his heart beating in his ears, as it was usually most prominent during his reaction to terror. But standing there, imprisoned by spiders for the first little bit of the rest of eternity, he felt the accompaniment could have served as his ticking clock. At least he'd have a way to count eternity.

More time passed. If he had to guess, he'd say he'd been there for several ... time. Time? What did you call them, the bits that were marked out on the edge of the ... round thing ... little arms in the middle ... time circle? He had a firm grasp on the words when he was in the Narrative, but he simply couldn't seem to summon them in the Hereafter.

"Sloot? Is that you?"

Myrtle! It was Myrtle! Sloot couldn't decide whether he was relieved that he was about to be rescued after so many long ... time? Whatever. There was also the matter of being rescued by one's girlfriend. In the great sagas, the muscular heroes were always rescuing the scantily clad damsels from imminent danger, not the other way around! Not that Sloot was particularly muscular or, in fact, muscular at all. If anything, the ghostly apparition that was his soul's projection of itself might have been a touch scrawnier than he'd actually been in life. Given Sloot's borderline contagious low self-esteem, that made quite a bit of sense.

"Er, yes," he admitted.

"Why don't you come out of there?"

"I'm not sure I can."

"He can't! He can't!" chanted the spiders. "He's our prisoner for eternity, a victim of our terrible webs!"

"All right, you've had your fun," Myrtle conceded in a sing-songy way. "Sloot, please come out of there. We have things to do."

"No," hissed the spiders, suddenly petulant. "He's our victim, we found him fair and square!"

"I really don't think I can," said Sloot, his voice quavering a bit. "I'm all bound up."

"Oh, for ... ugh!" In her frustration, Myrtle said a swear word that could have curdled a glass of milk at ten paces. "It's just their silly little game, Sloot! They can't hurt you. Just close your eyes and follow the sound of my voice!"

Sloot did as he was told. As off-putting as he found showing even the slightest shred of bravery, he could no more have refused to obey Myrtle than use his own webs to ensnare all of the spiders and say, "There, that's how *that* feels, you jerks!"

"That's better," said Myrtle.

Sloot opened his eyes. Myrtle was smiling at him, and there was a cocoon of webs behind him that matched his height.

The spiders were swarming in their direction. He shuddered.

"Naughty, naughty," whispered the spiders. "What shall we do with it now?" They descended into excited whispering among themselves, from which the occasional word was distinguishable. "Devour" came up a few times, though not quite as often as a word that Sloot would have needed special exercises to pronounce, but that he understood to mean "very nearly touching the tip of his nose, making it itch like mad."

The spiders abruptly ceased their joyful sussurus when Myrtle spoke a word, though "word" might have been a generous description. It seemed more accurate to Sloot to say that she left a flaming bag of excess consonants on a doorstep and ran away.

It was quiet.

"You've got a knack for getting into trouble," said Myrtle.

"What are you doing here?"

"Saving you from spiders, obviously. Please pay attention, darling."

The spiders were going out of their way to clear a space for Myrtle.

"It seems like they're afraid of you."

"To be honest, I'm not sure what that word meant. Worked, though."

"You mean that audible lurch that silenced the spiders?"

"That's the one. I'd never heard it before, but somehow I knew it would make the spiders behave."

"What's it mean?" asked Sloot.

Myrtle shrugged.

"It's our middle name," whispered the spiders.

"So all of you have the same middle name."

"Of course we do. Our mothers hatched thousands of us at a time. I'm sure human mothers have the time to give their children different middle names, but how else do you strike fear into thousands of young without using their middle names? A proper telling-off for tracking mud across the web would take the better part of a week!"

Everyone knows that middle names are a hex that mothers place on their children to keep them in line, it had just never occurred to Sloot that it applied to spiders as well. It wouldn't, though—Sloot wasn't anybody's mother.

The spiders dispersed, apparently knowing that their little game had come to an end for good and all. They swarmed back toward their little copse of trees, presumably in search of some other incredibly morbid means of passing eternity.

"Can we go for a walk?" asked Myrtle. "Unless you've got business you need to finish up here."

✻ WITCHERY ✻

Sloot was endlessly pleased to have left the spiders' den. He only wished he felt sure that it had entirely left him. He was sure that there was a cobweb in his hair, and no amount of ruffling it with his hands was going to get it out.

"For the last time," said Myrtle, "they never actually touched you!"

"It feels like they did."

"We're ghosts. The spiders, too. There's no touching with ghosts."

"There's a spider under my collar, I just know it."

"Just try not to think about it. What were you doing in there, anyway?"

"Looking for you," said Sloot.

Myrtle stopped floating along the path and looked at him. She smiled in that radiant way that Sloot had always liked. It raised his confidence to the level of an acne-afflicted teenager, which he'd never managed to attain when he *was* one. He felt as though he could conquer the world, or maybe ask if he could walk her home from school.

"You're very sweet," said Myrtle. "I'm sorry that I ran off, I just needed to be alone for a while. A lot on my mind, you know."

"I know." As little as Sloot had wanted to die in the first place, the idea of being shoved back into a pile of flesh, blood, bones, and who-but-doctors knows what else—gristle, cockles, and earwax was probably most of it—was utterly repellent. Who would want to go back to putting food in one end, only to wait until it came out the other? Being a ghost was far less off-putting when you thought in terms of biology.

It couldn't have been easy for Myrtle. Though a gentleman avoids fully considering the endgame of a lady's digestive process, he could consider the whole "returning to the flesh" business in the abstract and sympathize.

"I don't even know how it happened," said Myrtle. "We were talking, and you started to leave in the middle of it. 'Oh, no you don't,' I thought to myself. I sort of ... I don't know, stepped into it with you, and *poof*."

"Poof?"

"Metaphorically speaking."

"Ah."

"We were in the Narrative, only you were still a ghost, and I was all elbows and earlobes."

"I noticed."

"It was weird." Myrtle wrinkled her nose and shivered. "It wasn't like I remembered it at all. It was ... I dunno, *thicker*. Like I was driving myself around in a lump of clay."

"Maybe it was an aberration."

"Is that like an abomination?" Myrtle looked wounded.

"No," Sloot hastened, "like a fluke. Energies of the universe getting crossed up, something like that. Have you tried it again?"

"Yes. I went all fleshy again."

They floated along a while in silence, which is not simply to say that they didn't speak. There were no ghosts of birds chirping, no ghost of wind blowing the ghosts of leaves around. No footsteps, no crickets. Sloot affected the noise of clearing his throat just to make sure his hearing hadn't quit.

"Yes?"

"Oh," said Sloot. "Nothing. Sorry."

"The Quietus," said Myrtle. "Strange, isn't it?"

Sloot nodded, banking on the possibility that the question had been a non sequitur. He didn't disagree, primarily because he wasn't absolutely positive what the Quietus *was*. If he was picking it up correctly from context, it was the absolute silence. It was unnerving, just like Mrs. Knife's steely gaze or Vlad the Invader's muscular chin.

He was soon back to thinking about Myrtle in the flesh, and that sent Sloot's train of thought off into mournfulness. It's just the sort of thing that ghosts are inclined to do, yearn for the things they loved most in life. For Sloot, the first things to come to mind were cracking open a brand new ledger and feeling Myrtle's lips smile as he kissed them. The fact that she could find herself in a bodily way and he could not was disconcerting.

She was fully capable of putting him in situations where he could feel as clumsy and inadequate as he liked. Sloot, on the other hand—titan of insufficiency that he was—could not rise to the occasion.

"I wish there was a way," Sloot sighed.

"There is," said Myrtle.

"What, to give us both bodies?"

Given the absolute dearth of color in the Hereafter, it is not possible for a ghost to blush. However, the grin-and-wiggle maneuver that Myrtle executed left no doubt in Sloot's mind that that was exactly what she was doing.

"That's not what I meant," she replied, "though I like where I think you're going with it."

Sloot felt as though he was blushing as well. He was also absolutely certain that the spiders had invented some form of ghostly substantiation, and were crawling around in his shoes, which he wasn't actually wearing. He tried not to think about it.

"I think I know how to find out what's happening," said Myrtle, "but I'm not going to like it."

"Probably not," ventured Sloot. "It's been a while since I've liked anything. Part of being dead, I believe."

"It's not just a feeling. I know it to be true."

Sloot cocked his head and narrowed his eyes. "I never pegged you for a worrier. Oh dear, I used to be so good at recognizing one of my own."

"No, no," said Myrtle, "I mean it's inevitable. Truly, properly inevitable. I've known for a while now that I'm not going to like it, and I've only just seen that we're going to go."

"What do you mean, 'seen?' And where are we going?"

"I can't really explain the former," said Myrtle, "but maybe Agather can."

"Agather? From the Witchwood in Carpathia?" They'd gone there together once in life, and Myrtle had bought a broom. Sloot had a proper hyperventilation fit over that. In the Old Country, brooms were only for married people. That was a possibility that he'd been ill-equipped to consider at the time, to say nothing of the legal implications.

"That's right," said Myrtle. "That's where we're going."

❧⚶❧⚶❧⚶❧⚶

It was the first time Sloot had been to the Narrative without having been summoned by means of his shrunken head.

"It's around here somewhere," said Myrtle, who was looking as lovely as ever in her human skin. That was just the sort of compliment which, in the Narrative, would ensure a first date was never followed by a second. Even though he was armed with an abundance of context, Sloot predictably elected not to risk it.

"I really thought we were in the Old Country Hereafter," said Sloot.

"It's just the Hereafter," Myrtle replied. "It's not attached to the land of the living in terms of physical space."

"That's awful! What does that mean for taxes? Oh dear, that's going to keep me up at night."

"Have you been sleeping? I haven't." Myrtle groaned to the tune of "great, one more dead people thing I'm not doing correctly."

"Just a figure of speech," said Sloot.

"I thought you hated figures of speech."

"I did," said Sloot. He was an accountant, after all. Figures of speech were a lot like estimates in that they were imprecise. Why estimate when you can add a column of numbers? And why start using figures of speech now? "Nerves, I suppose."

"Well, that much hasn't changed. Oh! I think it's this way."

Carpathia hadn't changed much, which made sense. Sloot hadn't been dead for long. The countryside was still full of crags, the shadow of Ulfhaven loomed on the horizon, the forests were dark and foreboding, and Sloot couldn't shake the lingering fear that cannibals were lurking around every corner. At least they'd get nothing from him now.

"I think we're getting close," Sloot kept saying, as though he were able to tell one tree from another or, if he were being frank, from a bush.

Eventually, he said it enough times to become right. Past yet another tree—which looked exactly the same as all the rest to Sloot—was the Witchwood. Agather was stirring her cauldron over a big fire pit, as likely making stew as anything else. Then again, anything in a cauldron could be stew, if you were brave enough.

"Ow!" said Myrtle, her hand flying to her face.

"Oh no," said Sloot, "was it a bear? I've heard the outdoors is silly with bears."

"No, I think I just walked into a wall."

"Well, I don't see any—" Sloot put a hand forward and it met with resistance. It wasn't a wall made of bricks or wood or stone. It wasn't properly a wall at all. There was nothing there. No, not *nothing*. Something that was barely more than nothing, which didn't want him to pass. It wasn't exactly stopping him, more like firmly insisting that this wasn't the sort of place where the dead were welcome. Sloot was disappointed to find that sort of bigotry in this modern era.

"Hold yer horses," said Agather, "I'll be along directly."

She gave her cauldron one more big stir. A forceful one. Not a great big sloshing affair, just one that had authority. "You've been stirred," it said to the contents of the cauldron, "and there'll be answers owed if there are any burned bits at the bottom, are we clear?"

"That's that, then," said Agather. She hiked up her skirts a bit to keep them out of the mud and waddled in Sloot and Myrtle's direction. "Speak to me, spirits. I ain't got all day. The living got priority, ye know."

"Hello, Agather," said Myrtle. "Do you remember me?"

Agather squinted. "From the Old Country," she said. "Gretchen, wasn't it? I can't remember yer name, lad. Probably Hans. Ye look like a Hans."

"It's Peril. Sloot Peril."

"Peril? Are ye sure? Don't sound like an Old Country name. Sounds Carpathian."

"It's a long st—"

"And ye, Gretchen," said Agather, who seemed to have time for a long story, though not the patience. "I suppose that broom met with more goblins than it could handle on its own."

"It was a necromancer," said Myrtle, gnashing her teeth in a way that Sloot found both alluring and scary. "And it's Myrtle, thank you."

"Important things, names," said Agather with a smile whose teeth were partially in attendance. "Best to hear them from the source to make sure ye've got them right, makes curses a lot easier to manage when spirits get out of hand."

Sloot whimpered. Agather nodded in satisfaction.

"Necromancy," Agather spat. "Worst kind of magic. Oh, where are me manners? I'll summon ye in, just a moment."

Agather hiked and waddled to the shack at the edge of the clearing. It was ancient and overgrown, the sort of place you don't simply walk into. It swallows you up, or in this case, it swallowed Agather up. It reluctantly reproduced her a few minutes later bearing a wand, a bell, and what appeared to be a rug from a harem.

"Not the sort of thing I usually leave lying around," said Agather. "Wand magic stuff. Clashes with the rest of the decor."

Sloot was no aesthetic by any means, especially now that he had no earthly possessions, but even he felt Agather was playing fast and loose with the term "decor." Most of what wasn't just piles of dead leaves was either host to a pile of dead leaves or several layers of cobwebs atop piles of dead leaves.

Agather used a very old and dangerous-looking broom to clear a spot on the ground. To be clear, she didn't do any sweeping. She brandished the broom in a severe sort of way and the leaves and twigs found other places to lie.

Nothing was as purple as that rug. Had that not been the case, Sloot might have remarked upon the silver stars that seemed to dance around the silver circle embroidered into it. He didn't though, because of how vastly purple it was.

"All right then," said Agather, holding the wand and the bell aloft, "in ye go." She struck the bell with the wand. The barrier that had previously kept him at bay gave Sloot a sort of "all right, but I've got my eye on you" and relented. All at once, Sloot was standing on more purple than ever should have been allowed to exist in one place.

"What about me?" asked Myrtle, still on the outside of the barrier.

"Odd," said Agather. "Let's try that again." She struck the bell with the wand a second time, and the entire world seemed to vibrate around Sloot. The chirping of the birds went all thick, as though they were chirping through soup. When things calmed down after a few seconds, he was still alone on the purple. Er, on the *rug*.

"Still nothing?" asked Agather.

"I'm afraid not," said Myrtle, still as not-inside-the-Witchwood as ever.

"Hang on," said Agather. She squinted and waggled a finger at Sloot. "There's something different about ye."

"Well, I'm dead." That was a guess. Sloot hated guessing, but it was too purple to think straight in that moment.

"That's it," said Agather with a snap of her fingers, which then transitioned to waggling at Myrtle. "Ye ain't dead!"

"But I *am* dead," insisted Myrtle. "Killed by a necromancer."

"Okay," said Agather, "but you've got … whatchacallems. Limbs and hair and such."

"Not in the Hereafter," said Myrtle. "I'm a ghost there."

"Everybody's a ghost there, even the living if they're stupid enough to go and visit."

"So I'm still alive?"

"Not if ye was killed, ye ain't! Give me a minute, I've got to fetch me other rug."

Moments later, Agather had a very red rug on the ground next to the purple one. It was crawling with black shapes, most of which made Sloot very glad he didn't have dreams anymore. Several of them were snakes who looked like they were plotting to ask him for a loan.

"That doesn't look like such a good idea," said Sloot.

"Yeah," said Myrtle. "I could just stay over here, if you don't mind speaking up a bit."

"Oh, it looks scary," said Agather, "but only because it's an infernal thing that drives mortals to madness if they look directly at it. Don't worry, Mr. Peril, ye don't count as mortal anymore."

"But what about me? Am I still mortal? I've already looked at it!"

"Ye ain't vomiting fire and trying to claw yer eyes from yer head, so I'm going to say no, yer not."

"You're not mortal, then?" Sloot asked Agather.

"Not exactly," she replied, "but that's beside the point. It's my Witchwood, see?"

Agather produced a black recurved horn from within a leather satchel. It looked sinister. Agather's broom, which was resting against the trunk of a nearby tree, bristled.

"Before you—" Myrtle began, overestimating the value that witches place on other people's feelings regarding their plans. Agather blew a long, low note that caused all of the light in the Witchwood to dim while the air reverberated. When it finished, there was something standing on the carpet. It was Myrtle-shaped, but the lava-red eyes and razor-sharp teeth were decidedly someone else's.

"I thought as much," said Agather. "Yer a demon."

"That's ridiculous," said Myrtle in three voices at once, the lowest of which would have been a welcome addition to any church choir, certain complications aside. "Oh dear, why do I sound like that?"

"A witch need not repeat herself," said Agather. "Perks of the job. I'd show ye a mirror, but the only one I've got would trap ye for eternity."

"What is she going on about?" Myrtle wheeled on Sloot quickly enough to startle him, though in her present state, a lazy, sauntering circle would have managed that.

Sloot said nothing. What could he say? The woman he loved had gone from undead possession, skipped right past death itself, and moved onto demonry. Demonism? One of those should be correct. Sloot focused on the grammar, which helped keep him from screaming aloud. Demonicity?

"It's true, isn't it?" Myrtle's volcanic eyes went wider as she looked at her hands, whose fingers were now twice as long as they'd been previously and ended in pointies. "How did this happen?"

"Happen? Demons is demons," said Agather. "Ye mean yer whole life, ye didn't know ye was one?"

"I wasn't!" Myrtle thundered, her scaly wings flapping with agitation. "I was possessed by a ghost for most of my life, he'd have known about it. Right?"

"What sort of a ghost?" asked Agather.

"A philosopher."

"Then yer right. Philosophers never hold back when they have a tidbit of information worth spewing to the wind."

Myrtle started weeping in little wracked sobs. Sloot's first thought was to go and comfort her, though it was swiftly followed up by a severe panic that warned against it. Her tears were probably sulfuric acid or something. Plus, there was the matter of his soul. Didn't demons eat those? He was sure he'd read that.

Oh, show a little backbone, Sloot's thoughts said to his panic in a surprising turn of events. And why shouldn't he? This was still Myrtle, after all. She may be the visual embodiment of all his teenage fears surrounding encounters with the opposite sex—which had followed him well into his thirties—but there had been something real between them, hadn't there? She'd been his girlfriend! Hadn't she been a demon the whole time? What had really changed?

"I was right," said Myrtle. She sniffled.

"About what?" asked Sloot.

"I knew I wasn't going to like it."

"Oh."

"So that's it, then?"

"Not quite," said Agather. "I'll have to hex ye before I can let ye out, I'm afeared."

"Hang on a minute," growled Myrtle, who was more than a bit menacing with all of her demonic accoutrements bristling.

"Ye seem nice enough," said Agather, "but yer a demon all the same. It's standard witchery, hexing demons so they can't go all 'bathe in the blood of the innocent' in me territory."

"I'm not going to—"

"That's right, yer not." Agather wiggled her wand about in the air, then flicked it in Myrtle's direction. Myrtle went limp and collapsed.

"Oh dear," said Sloot, who didn't normally approve of that sort of outburst, but felt it warranted given the circumstances.

Myrtle gave a little groan, and then stood up. It would be rather more accurate to say that Myrtle *tried* to stand up, given that she failed spectacularly.

"What's going on?" Myrtle roared. "What've you done to the world? It's all spinny!"

"That'll be the hex," said Agather. "Yer allowed to come visit, but yer inner ear will wait for ye outside."

"You'll pay for this, witch!"

"There it is," said Agather. "Nice as ye may be, yer still a demon."

"Oh," said Myrtle. "I really didn't mean to say that."

"I know, dearie. Ye'll forgive a witch her precautions."

"I suppose so."

"Now, if there'll be nothing else?"

"Nicoleta," said Sloot.

"Who?"

"Nicoleta Goremonger. She was Vlad's court wizard before she died."

"Oh, *that* Nicoleta! Met her before, very nice, if not a bit hard on the eyes."

"That would be her," said Sloot. Nicoleta's colorful attire had given him headaches more than once. "She can't do any magic now that she's dead."

"Well, of course she can't."

"Oh."

Agather had said it with such authority that it didn't occur to Sloot to question the matter any further. At least he could tell Nicoleta he'd tried.

"The magic of the living don't work in the Hereafter," said Agather. "Witchery does to a point, but it's not the fancy book magic that wizards get up to. It's much older."

"I see," said Sloot.

"She'll need to learn something else, like necromancy."

"I thought you said necromancy was foul!"

"Oh, it is," said Agather, "for the living, anyway. Controlling the forces that lie beyond the veil is an abomination! Unless, of course, yer already dead. In that case, yer playing in yer own sandbox, see?"

"Oddly enough, I do," said Sloot. He didn't tend to understand magic talk or want to do so. He was a mathematician, and mathematics were about as far removed from magic as thoughts of live centipedes in your mouth were from a good night's sleep.

"We only know the one necromancer," said Myrtle, who'd stopped trying to get up and curled into a ball on the rug. "We're not calling him."

"It's not Bartleby, is it?" asked Agather.

"Gregor," said Sloot, "though he's gone by other names."

Agather waddled over to a tree that had a great hollow in it. She gave the tree a solid kick. It grumbled at her.

"Go ask Bartleby if he's ever gone by 'Gregor,'" she shouted into its big knothole. "There's a nice pile of gizzards in it for ye."

The tree shook disconcertingly and was still.

"That could take a while," said Agather. "I'll send him yer way if he's not yer Gregor."

"I'm not sure how to tell you where we live," said Sloot. "Well, not live. *Reside*."

"I know yer names," said Agather. "That's all a witch needs to find the dead."

❧ PUB RULES ❧

The return trip to the Hereafter didn't take long enough to be awkward. One of the benefits of being a ghost was being able to put yourself back in your grave without a whole lot of fuss. That's how Sloot would have seen it if he were an optimist, but alas.

"I've never seen grey sparkles before," said Nicoleta. Fortunately for Sloot, she'd been in the parlor when Sloot and Myrtle had returned to the house. She was lying on the sofa, watching tiny grey explosions of light dance among black clouds that rolled across the ceiling.

"Willie's still not in the circle, I assume." Myrtle spoke eagerly to Nicoleta, apparently keen on avoiding eye contact with Sloot. To be fair, anyone would have done. His gaze had a haggard sort of fear to it, the sort that cowards wear to dinner when the entree might be seafood with the heads still on.

"No," Nicoleta replied, then pointed up at the ceiling, "but it's pretty. I just wish they were purple. Not that I remember purple. I remember *liking* purple, and something tells me it would go well with the sparkles."

Sloot felt as though he might be ill, thinking of the violently purple rug to which Agather had subjected him. "I've had my fill of purple."

"That's because you're boring." There wasn't a hint of malice in Nicoleta's delivery. It was cheerily casual, the way she might have told him the time, the absence of the concept of time in the Hereafter notwithstanding.

There was a knock at the door.

"Am I supposed to get that?" asked Sloot. "I'm still unclear."

Nicoleta sat up, an eager smile crossing her face. "Don't. Let's just see what happens."

No one moved. The knock came again.

"I think I should get it," said Sloot.

"What sort of compulsion is it?" asked Nicoleta.

"Pardon?"

"Is it the resistible sort?"

"I don't know that I've ever felt a resistible compulsion."

Nicoleta sent a puzzled look to Myrtle, who countered with a shrug. They waited in silence until most normal people would assume whoever had knocked had given up. Then their assumptions about human behavior were challenged by a third knock.

"I should really go answer the door," said Sloot, his voice starting to waver with nerves.

"The best case scenario," said Nicoleta, "is that you're welcoming the walking dead into our house."

"The walking dead are the only people in the house," Sloot replied. "And Nipsy, of course. And Myrtle."

"And Myrtle?"

"She's a demon."

"Oh, thanks for that!" Myrtle spat.

"I'm sorry?"

"You should be! Giving away a lady's secrets like that. I'm just wrapping my head around it myself, and here you're telling everyone as though it were yours to tell!"

"Sorry," said Sloot, "I only thought—"

"No, you didn't."

"You're a demon?" Nicoleta looked more fascinated than alarmed, though that was usually the case.

"According to Agather," said Myrtle.

"From the Witchwood? How is she?"

There was a fourth knock at the door, not that Sloot was keeping count. Not that Sloot was fooling anyone. Of course, he was keeping count.

Sloot whimpered.

"Oh, go and answer it then," said Nicoleta. "We gals need to talk! Far more interesting than teasing you, although that was fun. Now, shoo!"

Sloot practically sprinted for the door. His running form was no less embarrassing now, even though he only had the psychic impressions of spindly limbs to hurl spasmodically forward. Watching Sloot run reminded one of juvenile octopuses having a slap fight.

"It's about time," said Grumley. "Not your fault, I presume. Snared up in more of Lord Hapsgalt's manifestations, I'm sure."

Sloot simply nodded. When facing the equally terrifying options of not correcting a false presumption or admitting to dereliction of duty, it seemed the sensible thing to do.

Nipsy padded into the room and gave a *yip*. It looked at Grumley in a way that was nothing short of adorable, but then Nipsy was a very small puppy. That was the only sort of look at its disposal.

"And now there's a puppy?" Grumley's eyebrows were raised in question, as though they were trying to get as far from his nose as possible. It was an awful nose, gnarled and bulbous. One for which his parents should have apologized.

"Willie's named it Nipsy," said Sloot.

"Not after the late Minister of Interrogation, I hope."

"After a friend from his hunting club."

"That's good," said Grumley. "The late Minister wouldn't have approved. He was furious with the Ministry of Propaganda's rebranding, you know. What was it they call it now?"

"Uncle."

"Uncle. Ha! No, no, Nipsy hated that. Where's the puppy gotten off to, then?"

Sloot turned. Nipsy had vanished. He had the common sense to be afraid of the thing, born of dark magic as it was, and it terrified Sloot to know that it could be watching him from the shadows, waiting for its opportunity to strike.

"I couldn't say for sure," said Sloot with a shiver. "It's probably around here somewhere, unfortunately."

"Couldn't say for sure? Egads, man! I was sure you'd have all of this well in hand!"

Sloot fidgeted. He was unaccustomed to being dressed down for doing his job improperly, and a lifetime in the Old Country had left him permanently paranoid with regard to swearing. He wasn't sure where "egads" lay on the profanity spectrum. Probably closer to "oh, dear me" than the one that sounds like the feeling of a hangover on a hot, humid day.

"I don't have to impress upon you how important it is to rein in the Soul, do I?"

"It would be ... bad," Sloot hazarded. "Disastrous, in fact, if he were to ..."

"Not to be dramatic, but basically all of the worst parts of chapter 314 of the Book of Black Law. You know the one."

"Supposing the specifics had slipped my mind?"

"You should find a way to refresh your memory. You've still got contacts in the Order on the other side, I'm sure."

"Okay," said Sloot, who didn't. He'd never actually joined the Serpents of the Earth, a fact which Grumley had clearly forgotten.

"I'll leave you to it," said Grumley. "Let me know when you've gotten rid of the puppy, will you?"

"Gotten rid of? Er, yes, of course." Atop everything else piled on Sloot, he was now expected to kill a puppy!

It wasn't a real puppy, of course, rather a puppy-shaped manifestation of dark forces, resulting from too much blood energy having been fed to the Soul of the Serpent. Still, it was a puppy. Even with the extenuating circumstances, killing a puppy was hard to contemplate. Just the thought of it was making the room go dark, though that might have been something else, because a belfry's worth of spectral bats also fluttered in through the front door and disappeared into the clouds on the ceiling.

"Good evening," said the gaunt, creepy figure that had mysteriously appeared in the doorway. "I have arrived. Vhich one of you is Sloot?"

"Ugh," said Grumley. "Don't invite him in. Vampires are ridiculous, you'll never get him to leave."

"I'm not a vampire," said the mysterious visitor. "Thanks, though. Vampires are cool."

Grumley rolled his eyes and drew up his hood. "I've got to go, Peril. Do get a handle on things around here, will you?"

"Er, yes, fine."

Grumley left, smirking at the mysterious visitor like one would do at a forty-year-old son who was still living at home.

"So you are Sloot?"

"What? No. Well, yes, but ... can I help you?"

"I am Bartleby," said ... Bartleby. He moved his head back and to the left, throwing a one-eyebrow-raised look at Sloot. A bolt of lightning crackled across the sky behind him.

"Cool, right?"

"Er, yes," said Sloot. "A bit scary, if that's what you were going for."

"I vas!" Bartleby could scarcely contain his delight. "Agather asked me to look in on your friend, may I come in?"

"Sure, why don't—"

"No, vait!" Bartleby drew back into a mysterious and menacing pose. "Vhat I meant to say vas *you vill invite me in!*" He wiggled his fingers in a complicated sort of way, leading Sloot to wonder whether he'd had an extra knuckle or two installed.

"What's that?"

"It is a beguiling charm," said Bartleby. "Are you not compelled to let me in?"

"I mean, I was going to."

"Oh. But you're not ... you know ... bent to my vill?"

"Your will?"

"Never mind. Maybe since you vere already going to."

"Er, all right."

Bartleby floated into the room, his massive black cape billowing slowly in a wind that wasn't there. Sloot's coat did a version of the same thing, but it was far less impressive.

"A nice place you've got here," said Bartleby, his gaze transfixed on the cloudy ceiling. "There are powerful spirits here, yes?"

"That's true," said Sloot. "Lord Hapsgalt, anyway. The younger one."

"I didn't know there vas a younger one."

"It wasn't important until the Fall of Salzstadt."

"I heard about that. I'd like to talk with him later, if that's all right."

"I don't see why not."

Sloot led Bartleby through the corridors to the parlor, where Myrtle and Nicoleta were engrossed in conversation.

"Er, ladies—"

"Sloot, look out!" shouted Myrtle, pointing behind him. "Vampire!"

Bartleby melted into a big, fangy grin.

"This is Bartleby," said Sloot. "Agather sent him."

"Oh," said Myrtle. "You're the necromancer?"

"I am," said Bartleby. "You're the demon?"

"Sloot! Really!" Myrtle was on her feet, hands firmly on her hips. "You're telling everyone who walks through the door now?"

"What? No!"

"Agather told me," said Bartleby. "You really didn't know that you vere a demon your whole life?"

"I don't think I was."

"You didn't think you were a demon at all," said Sloot, "until we went to see Agather."

"Thank you for that," said Myrtle with a scowl. Realizing what he'd said, Sloot was suddenly very thankful for his complete lack of blood. At the very least, it would have run cold, but given that he'd just angered a demon, "the very least" was probably too much to hope for. She'd probably boil it, or turn it into seawater, or something.

"Unusual," said Bartleby, "but not impossible. Vhen did you die?"

"At the Fall of Salzstadt," Myrtle replied.

"There vas a lot of veird magic flying around that day. I vish I'd been there! But alas, I vas in a crypt in Nordheim at the time."

"Am I missing something?" asked Nicoleta. "Why is Agather sending us necromancers?"

"Your magic doesn't vork anymore, does it?"

"That's none of your business."

"Don't vorry, it happens to everybody. Living vizardry doesn't vork in the Hereafter."

"Why didn't they tell me that at the University?"

"Marketing," said Bartleby with a shrug. "If vord of that got around, it might hurt enrollments."

"I have to ask," said Myrtle, "why do you look so much like a vampire?"

"Vampires are cool," said Bartleby. He did the crazy stare thing again.

"We've heard otherwise," said Sloot.

Bartleby shook his head in slow disapproval. "No accounting for taste."

There was, though. Sloot has taken courses, though he really couldn't grasp more than the basic concept without a deeper understanding of fashion.

"So, you can help me get my magic back?"

"Not exactly, but I can teach you some necromancy. It's like vizardry, only ... vell, *dead*."

"How do you know Agather?" asked Sloot. "Pop in on her carpet, did you?"

"No, I just valked into the Vitchvood."

"So you're alive."

"I vas—" Bartleby drew in a breath as to say something else, then stopped to squint at the ceiling. "It's complicated. Do you know many necromancers?"

"Only Gregor," Myrtle growled.

"Ha! That old stick in the mud. I vas vondering why the Slithering Shades asked if I vas using his name."

"You know him?"

"Ve both served the same master," said Bartleby, "but that vas years ago. Centuries, in fact. No one has seen *him* in a few plagues."

"Sloot," said Nicoleta, "where are you going?"

Sloot's inherent sense of discomfort had been subconsciously driving him toward the door. He didn't notice it himself until he was nearly past it.

"Er, it's Willie," said Sloot. "I've got to get this business with his powers sorted out."

"Better you than me," said Nicoleta. "I wouldn't even know where to start."

Yes. Well, thought Sloot.

"Vhen in doubt," said Bartleby, "start at the pub."

"I don't think there are any pubs in the Hereafter," said Myrtle.

"Of course there are! Do you think I vould spend so much time hanging around here if there vere no pubs? I'm obsessed vith the dead, but I still have a life."

According to Bartleby, finding a pub in the Hereafter was easy. All you had to do was dwell on your feelings of dissatisfaction with the world and your place in it, and wish desperately to escape.

꘎꘎꘎꘎꘎꘎꘎

"Well, that was easy," said Sloot.

Turk's was a dark, grey place, but in a dingier way than the rest of the Hereafter. It was worn, dirty, and overgrown in a way that gave Sloot the impression that it had always been there. It looked old enough to have been visited by the first people ever to have died, whose first thoughts upon seeing it must have been "wow, I wonder how long this place has been here?"

He went inside. There was no smoking in the Hereafter, owning only to the absence of anything to smoke. There were no smells either, but be that as it may, the distinct impression that the room had been used as an ashtray for centuries nearly knocked Sloot flat. He started coughing.

His coughing drew stares. Not new ones, mind you, but the faces of patrons that appeared to have been staring off into space for years directed themselves toward Sloot.

"Don't get much of that anymore," said the man behind the bar, presumably Turk. "You must be new."

"How—" Sloot coughed, sputtered, and did his best to find his composure. "How is this hap—*cough, hack*—pening?"

The room darkened slightly. A faint rumbling sound emanated from everywhere at once. A look of alarm clambered onto Turk's face, giving a much needed but unwanted break to the bored one that had undoubtedly been on duty for far longer than Sloot could reckon.

"Whatever do you mean?" blurted Turk loudly, as if for the benefit of someone listening in. "There's certainly nothing unusual happening here, lad! Why don't you come and have a drink, then?"

"A drink?" Sloot sat on the barstool that Turk had offered him. He was puzzled but intrigued, and that was new for him. He'd always been risk averse in a way that called upon him to mistrust anything he knew nothing about. The only good surprises were the ones he'd taken great pains to plan for himself.

"A drink," Turk confirmed. "You know, beer in a mug? That sort of thing. You're an odd duck, pretending not to know about drinks."

"No, I know about drinks, I just didn't think you could get them here."

"Here? You mean Turk's?"

"No, I meant the Here—"

"—we go again with your odd duckery!" Turk interrupted. "You can't fool me, you know."

"I can't," said Sloot flatly, unsure himself whether it was a question.

"You obviously know about drinks," Turk continued, holding a mug under a tap. "You wouldn't have walked into a pub if you didn't, and that's exactly what this is. A perfectly normal pub."

Turk appeared to have finished pouring the drink, but the mug that he set in front of Sloot was empty.

"Yes," said Sloot. "I, er … well, I do know about drinks."

"I can see that you're still a bit out of sorts," said Turk with a sympathetic nod. "Why don't you tell me what's bothering you while you enjoy that perfectly standard drink?"

"Because I can't," said Sloot, as plainly as he could.

"Ah," said Turk, who was using a towel to rub down a bit of the bar as though something had spilled upon it, "you're one of them *glass half empty* types, aren't you?"

"In most cases, yes," said Sloot, "but this particular glass happens to ... be ... entirely ..."

Sloot allowed his sentence to end unfinished, in response to the wide-eyed look that he was getting from Turk. The big man had his hands on the bar and was leaning toward Sloot pointedly, in a joint effort with his expression to insist that Sloot not finish that particular thought.

"Yeah," growled Turk, just above a whisper, "there are lots of places in these parts where someone might wax literal about the nature of things, and that's all fine and dandy. But those places aren't pubs, see?"

"Right," said Sloot, who was still as confused as ever.

"Pubs get a bit of extra scrutiny, see? What with all the booze flowing freely and good folk tying one on, it stands to reason that if anyone were going to commit any serious breaches of the Agreement, this would be a likely scene of the crime."

Sloot nodded. From what he knew of the Agreement, it was basically a sort of collective consciousness that brought order to the Hereafter where the laws of physics apparently didn't apply outside the Narrative. The most troubling part of this new line of inquiry was the "who" of it. Specifically, who was keeping their eye on pubs to make sure that no breaches of the Agreement occurred?

"So, logically," Turk continued, "if we all want to continue sitting on marginally comfortable stools and wiling away the time like we did before ... well, you know."

Turk made a sickly sound in his throat and held a fist over his head, as though he were playing two roles upon the gallows simultaneously.

Sloot nodded.

"Right," said Turk with a wink. "If we all want to keep ourselves on our stools, it behooves us to be *glass half full* types. Or, given that I just handed you that one, you should presently be a *glass entirely full* type. I'd ask you if you understand, but there's obviously no need. You look like the intelligent type."

Sloot glanced around the room. To his chagrin, Turk's weren't the only eyes upon him. In his naiveté, he'd become the center of attention for the entire place. Every eye was upon him, giving him a very stern "if you mess this up for us, I'll bring whatever unpleasantness to bear that I'm able."

Having already had far more unpleasantness leveled at him than he knew what to do with, Sloot latched onto the affectation of agreeableness for dear life, or whatever he had that passed for it.

"Go on, then." Turk's eyes were darting down to Sloot's obviously-not-actually-empty mug and back up to him.

"Yes," said Sloot, "of course. I mean, that's why I've come here, right?"

Every head in the room nodded.

"Right then," said Sloot, raising the definitely-full-of-beer mug to his lips. "Er, cheers?"

"Cheers," said the rest of the room in unison. They all tipped their mugs back, and so did Sloot. It was still empty, but much to Sloot's surprise, the taste of beer insinuated its way into his mouth.

Such is the power of the Agreement, thought Sloot. As he contemplated the considerable attraction of conformity, a feeling of unease washed over him. It didn't take long to sort out what had caused it. When he looked up, he noticed that every weathered old face in the pub was looking at him expectantly.

He looked down at his mug again, and sure enough, it appeared half full. He took another sip and made the traditional "ahhh" sound in the back of his throat.

The tension went out of the place. The patrons went back to whatever it was that they hadn't been doing before, and Turk gave him a nod of approval.

"So," said Turk, using a rag to wipe another spot on the counter that Sloot silently Agreed needed it, "what's on your mind, mate?"

Somehow, Sloot managed to maintain a placid exterior. His mind, on the other hand, was bouncing around with glee. Idle chitchat! In a pub! He'd spent time in pubs before, of course, but he'd never considered himself a "guy" in a pub. He'd always ordered his beers—one for himself, one to put under the stool for the goblins—cleaned off his stool, tightened the screws that attached the legs, decided he didn't like that one, tried again with another stool, gotten it right with the third one, and ultimately be left alone to enjoy one of his drinks in the relative ostracism of his own company. He couldn't recall ever having been asked anything by a bartender not having to do with the transaction at hand, much less being referred to as "mate."

Sloot's voice only cracked mildly as he responded as casually as possible. "Oh, you know how it is."

Turk grinned with the satisfaction of a pupil well taught. "Do I ever, mate. Do I ever."

Unfortunately for Sloot, Turk didn't have any advice relevant to one's employer's influx of dark energy being so high that it manifested in puppies that were probably just biding their time before chewing everyone's throats out, or ruining the furniture or something. He stumbled a bit as he left the pub, that being the sort of thing that one was expected to do.

❧⟶INNER PEACE❧⟶

When Sloot returned from Turk's, he found everyone in the sitting room. Sitting. It was just the sort of orderliness that he'd always wanted, but it was so out of character for this lot that it made him nervous.

At least Willie and Bartleby were sitting on the floor. Mild defiance of the sofas was a far sight from bodies going rogue from their heads and summoning puppies, but it wasn't nothing. According to Nicoleta's expression, they'd been at it long enough to go into debt with her patience.

"According to Bartleby, it's called 'meditation,'" she whispered, an irritated edge to her voice. "I'm not sure they've even started yet."

"Meditation," as it turned out, was a fancy way of saying "sit there with your eyes closed and don't think about anything," which was a lot harder than it sounded. Especially for Willie.

"And it's … helping?" Sloot whispered hopefully.

"Well, Willie hasn't made any more puppies or anything," whispered Nicoleta. "Can you do something to get him into the circle? Bartleby's supposed to be teaching me necromancy, not babysitting Willie."

Willie opened his eyes and sighed. "Look, you've tried your best," he groaned, "but you've overlooked one very important thing. It's *boring*."

"It's not boring," said Bartleby, "it's stillness. As still and qviet as the grave. Vicked cool, meditation." He had his legs folded up with each foot atop of the other leg's knee. It looked horribly painful to Sloot, but the necromancer seemed relaxed in spite of it. It was how Sloot must have looked to everyone else at University when final exams for mathematics came around. No one else had an incurable smile that day. No one had invited him out for commiseratory drinks afterward, either.

"You're wrong about that," said Willie. "This is boring. Believe me, I know."

"How do you know?"

"It gives me the same feeling I get when other people are talking. You know, all antsy, like … what, don't they know *I* could be talking to *them?*"

"You're not doing it right," said Bartleby. "You must learn to control your restless mind. Make it still."

"No, it's right where it's always been. Now, what sort of tricks do you do?"

It turned out that the only way to get Willie to sit down with Bartleby had been to tell him that the spooky stranger could work strange and wondrous magic.

"There are no tricks in magic."

"The man who came to my birthday party did tricks, and he said they were magic." Willie was wearing his suspicious face. He usually trotted it out in response to assurances that he'd like whatever came before dessert.

"Tricks are for amateurs and prestidigitators," Bartleby insisted.

"So you're not a magician." Willie's eyes and mouth scrunched with indignation, fixing Bartleby with an I'm-mad-*and*-disappointed glare.

"Of course not," said Bartleby, still not opening his eyes. "I am a necromancer, a master of the forces of life and death! Vell, death anyvay."

"I was told they were two sides of the same coin," said Nicoleta.

"I vouldn't know about that. I'll leave such platitudes to the philosophers."

"What? How dare you, sir?"

"Arthur? How did you get here so fast?" Sloot wanted to be

impressed, but the fact that this couldn't possibly end well got him no farther than surprised, with a side of chagrin.

"Duty calls," Arthur seethed. "I'll not sit idly by while those untrained in thinking go around assigning work to philosophers. You'll leave nothing to us, sir! We will keep our own counsel on what is to be pondered!"

Sloot was surprised that Arthur knew the meaning of the word "duty," given his violent opposition to doing anything that resembled work. He assumed the philosopher was employing some form of irony that he didn't understand.

"I vasn't trying to start a fight," said Bartleby, not opening his eyes. "Take a seat, vhy don't you? Ve vere just contemplating the universe."

"Maybe you were," said Willie, who was trying to uncross his legs. Success eluded him with impressive deftness. "Sloot, this is more boring than the circle! At least Nan tells me stories when I'm sitting in the circle."

"Sorry, Willie. Ow."

"Oh, don't be such a baby. I barely touched you."

"You didn't touch me at all," said Sloot. His eyes were shut tight as he attempted to ride out something approximating a headache. "It was—ow—something else entirely. Don't worry about it."

"Who's worried? I'm just bored."

"Philosophy's not supposed to be boring," Arthur groused. "This creepy vagrant's doing it wrong!"

"I didn't say I vas *doing philosophy*," said Bartleby. "I'm teaching Villie how to meditate. You should join us."

"I know all of the meditations I need," said Arthur with a scoff and a snort. "Wagstaff the Blithe wrote an entire book of them from his barstool, and none of them involve throwing in with vampires, afflicting credentialed thinkers with nonsense, or sitting on the floor!"

Bartleby sighed and opened his eyes. He made a very slow, deliberate production of standing up. It made sense to Sloot that coming up from that sort of position would take a while.

"It's a different sort of meditation." Bartleby smiled, baring his unnaturally white and pointy teeth, and speaking with a level of patience that appeared to catch Arthur off-guard. That made sense too. Arthur had a way of putting people off and was not often approached with civility. He eyed Bartleby with suspicion.

"What would the world need with a different sort of meditation? How much whiskey is involved in this sort?"

"Vell, none, but—"

"Worthless!"

"Hardly. Besides, how much vhiskey have you gotten into since you came to the Hereafter?"

"Don't you try to ply me with logic! When was the last time your clothing bothered with inseams, hmm?"

"I learned the secrets of meditation in the monastery at Blasigtopp," said Bartleby. "Everyone there vore robes."

"Good for you," said Arthur with a sneer. "Found a whole commune of hippies who found that disdain for bathing was easier than the practice of it, did you?"

"You don't have to join us if you don't vant to."

"I don't," said Arthur.

"Oh, I don't want to either," said Willie, perking up at the notion that participation was optional.

"Oh, er, well," sputtered Sloot, "I'm sorry, m'lord, but I'm afraid you must."

"But that's not fair!"

"Don't listen to him," Arthur counseled Willie. "You're your own man, aren't you?"

"I think so. Can I go be my own man, Sloot?"

"Don't ask him! The inherent dignity of every man demands he be allowed to set the course of his own destiny! You see? Wagstaff's Forty-Third Meditation clearly states that—"

"But Willie has to learn to control his power," said Sloot, who was no more comfortable interrupting people now than he was the first time he'd tried it.

"Stop telling Willie what to do," said Arthur. "Did you hear me say 'set the course of his own destiny,' or do I need to berate you with Haversham's Anonymous Retort to Tyranny?"

"I'd really rather you didn't," said Sloot.

"What about women?" asked Willie.

"What *about* them?"

"Do they get to inherit destiny too?"

"*Inherent*," Arthur over-enunciated. "I don't know, Wagstaff didn't have a meditation for women. Terrified of them. Perfectly rational stance, if you ask me."

"There is no difference betveen men and vomen," said Bartleby. "Not vhen it comes to meditation, anyvay."

"Whose side are you on?" asked Arthur, his hands setting up a threatening pose on his hips.

Bartleby grabbed the edge of his cloak and used it to cover the lower half of his face. The movement was swift and fluid in a way that only could have been managed if he'd practiced it thousands of times in a mirror.

"Never reveal vhat side you're on! It keeps them guessing."

That made little sense to Sloot. "You prefer that your allies don't know you're on their side."

"Obviously," Bartleby warbled mysteriously.

"That seems like it could be confusing."

Bartleby dropped his cape and shrugged. "That's the price of embodying the mysteries of the arcane."

"What sort of philosophy is that?" Arthur demanded, his fists slowly rising above his waist in anticipation of a debate.

"I don't know that it is a philosophy," Bartleby mused. "If it is, it's a mysterious one."

"I don't think I need any kind of philosophy," said Willie. "Can I go and play now?"

"You must learn to control your power, Willie," said Sloot.

"I cannot be controlled," said Willie, his eyes gone black again. Scorpions started pouring from the folds of his clothing and skittering across the floor.

"That's the spirit," said Arthur with a wicked grin. "Give 'em hell, Willie!"

"I could," said Willie. He seemed delighted at the realization.

"Vicked!" Bartleby was grinning from ear to ear, his sharp teeth gleaming in the gloom.

"We should really do something," said Nicoleta.

"Ow," said Sloot. His headache was getting worse. "Shouldn't *he* do something? Find his center, perhaps?"

"I could as easily find yours," Willie growled.

"That's not nice," said Nicoleta. "What's happened to Nan? Isn't it time for your nap?"

An argument of typical proportions started up around the subject of Willie's naptime, but Sloot was too busy doubling over in pain to make it out. More like doubling inside-out, really. It was a lot like the sensation he'd felt when Roman had summoned him, only with eyefuls of molten lead thrown in.

"Would you please let me do it properly?" asked Roman. His voice had the sort of croak to it that would naturally accompany a stiletto heel to the windpipe.

"I need to be sure," said a voice Sloot had heard before. He worked on focusing his vision despite the blinding pain and recognized the woman holding his shrunken head.

"I know you," said Sloot. "You're in that Skeleton Key Circle."

"Quiet!" She snapped. "You know too much about that which you scarcely understand!"

"Sorry," said Sloot. "Wait, is that even possible?"

"Would you mind not vexing her?" Roman's tongue lolled as he drew in a ragged breath.

"Sorry. What do you want?"

"Answers," she demanded. "Who do you work for?"

"That's a complicated question," said Sloot.

"For the Serpents of the Earth?"

"Sort of. Technically. Again, it's complicated. Ow."

"I knew it," said the woman. "Time to end this."

"Wait!" said Sloot. "I just work for Willie, not Mrs. Knife!"

"Willie? You mean Wilhelm? Hapsgalt?"

"No one calls him that," said Sloot, "except Nan, when he's being naughty."

The woman's eyes darted from Sloot to Roman and back again. She considered her options for a moment and removed her boot from Roman's throat. Roman gasped and coughed, which was what was expected of him, given the circumstances.

"Talk," said the woman. Her voice was starting to fade, as though she were speaking through mud. The pair of them were going dark.

"Sloot? Is that you?" A voice that sounded like Myrtle's echoed faintly to him from another direction.

"You're losing him," said Roman, through the mud. "Give it here."

"Sloot," echoed Myrtle, "what's happening? I can almost—"

"There," said Roman, suddenly very clear and distinct. He was holding Sloot's head with one hand and gingerly checking his throat for blood with the other. They appeared to be in a sewer tunnel in the Narrative, possibly close to the black market.

"My headache's gone," said Sloot. "Where's Myrtle?"

"Who?" asked the woman.

"His girlfriend," said Roman. "Sorry, lover boy, haven't seen her."

"But I just—"

"It's not too late for me to kill your friend here," said the woman. In one of her hands was a sword pointed at Roman, and in the other, a wand pointed at Sloot. "No more distractions, tell me what you know. You! Not a word."

Roman nodded to Sloot, and he recounted the events that took place on the day that they went to the Cross to listen in on the meeting.

"The fourth door should have been guarded," said the woman.

"Right you are," said Roman. "Simple matter of making two guards each think the other was on duty."

"And how did you find the door?"

"A gentleman doesn't reveal all of his secrets."

"A lady could reveal a gentleman's entrails."

"No need for that," said Roman. "For now, let's just say I've got friends in low places. We can share contacts if we can agree to work together, Franka."

"You know my name? All the more reason I should empty your belly of guts."

"I know a lot more than that," said Roman, "and I'm going to need my guts where they are if I'm going to help you get Willie's remains."

"Even if you could hand them to me, I can't accept them. I don't even know who his Keeper should be."

The Skeleton Key Circle is a uniquely complex entity that was created by the people who wrote the Book of Black Law centuries ago. The Serpents of the Earth knew the sort of deviants who were likely to join shadowy cults bent on world domination, and were smart enough to devise a means of keeping their members honest. Well, honest-*ish*. With each other, anyway.

When the Eye of the Serpent passes away and becomes the Soul of the Serpent, their mortal remains become a thing of power. Sloot pleaded with Franka to skip past the specifics of what a wizard might do with putrefying bits of evil cult leader, and she ultimately relented because it's hard enough to beat a living person until they stop crying, to say nothing of ghosts.

The Steward of the Circle interacts with the Eye of the Serpent on behalf of the Circle's Keepers, each of whom are responsible for the remains of six Souls. They keep specially coded journals that record where a Soul's remains are being kept at any given time. Each Keeper is responsible for training his or her replacement before they die.

"When Sir Berthold died," said Franka, "he left me his estate and everything in it. Most importantly, his journal. The only entry I've made pertains to the current resting place of his—my—sixth and final charge, Constantin Hapsgalt."

"Not Sir Berthold Kriegstockente?" asked Roman. "Didn't he just die a few days ago?"

"The same," said Franka, nearly in a whisper. She shed a single tear at the mention of his name.

"So I don't suppose that the Souls' remains are kept in their graves," said Sloot, trying to change the subject.

"That would be clever," said Franka. "Unlikely, but clever. No one who knew what they were doing would think to look there, but it's still too obvious. They'd know about the decoy graves as well, but there are too many to watch all the time."

"Is that where your Souls' remains are?" asked Roman.

"Don't trouble yourself with that." Franka waved her sword casually in Roman's direction, implying that it would be no trouble for her to see to all of Roman's dissection needs if he persisted. He did not.

"And you don't know the identity of the next Keeper," said Sloot.

"That's the Steward's business," said Franka, putting her sword and wand away. "I just want to get Willie's remains to him. He can sort it out from there."

"Not to pry," said Roman, "but how is it you managed to recover Constantin's remains, but not Willie's? They were on top of each other when they died, you know."

Franka gave Roman a withering look. A squinting, sneering, disposing-of-your-corpse-is-going-to-be-a-lot-of-work sort of look. An I-*just*-put-my-sword-away sort of look.

"I know," said Roman, showing her his palms in a placating let's-not-jump-to-murder-straight-away sort of gesture, "but we're going to have to share some information if we've any chance of working together to steal Willie's remains!"

"You're probably right," said Franka, who was probably only partially disappointed that slitting Roman's throat was a bad idea. At least she wouldn't have to tidy up. "Sir Berthold had cast a spell on Constantin a long time ago. When he died, the spell transported him to ... someplace."

"Good enough," said Roman.

"Er, sorry," said Sloot, "but do we really need to *steal* Willie's remains? The Steward made it sound like there was a legal means of getting it done. Perhaps we could, you know, wait it out?"

"Come on, Sloot," said Roman. "Do you really think that Mrs. Knife will—"

Roman probably continued speaking, but Sloot was no longer there to hear it. Instead, he found himself back in the Hereafter. More specifically, he was in the library with Nicoleta, Bartleby, and—to his gentle elation—Myrtle. She and Bartleby both had their hands outstretched in an incantational sort of way, as though they'd worked together to bring him home.

"Are you all right?" she asked, her eyes wide with concern. "I heard you calling out before, but I couldn't reach you."

"I'm dead," said Sloot. "Past that, I'm all right, I suppose."

"So nothing gruesome befell you," said Bartleby, somewhat crestfallen.

"Not really. Sort of. I was summoned poorly, and that hurt."

"Oh?" Bartleby perked up a bit.

"Give them a moment," said Nicoleta. "Can we please get back to the Shroud of Silent Screams?"

"I nearly forgot," said Bartleby. "You're not viggling your fingers enough."

"They've been at this for a while," said Myrtle. "Nicoleta's a quick study though, finally starting to get some of her power back."

Whatever Nicoleta had been doing wrong before, Sloot wished she'd kept it up. He hated rooting for his comrades' failure, but the Shroud of Silent Screams was a truly dreadful thing to behold. The only nice thing that Sloot could think to say about it was that the name was accurate. The shroud—or, in this case, the lace doily covering the coffee table—rose up and looked as though it were covering a face that was screaming in silent agony.

"Vonderful!"

"Hardly the word I'd use," said Nicoleta, "but it's nice to be able to bend something to my will again." She was still wiggling her fingers like mad, prompting the horrid thing to roam about the room, trying in vain to outrun whatever it was that was causing it such anguish.

"At least it's quiet," said Sloot. Okay, two nice things.

"That's the Shroud of Silent Screams," said Bartleby. "Ve'll move on to the Screaming Shroud next. You have to valk before you crawl, you know."

SAM HOOKER

"And what's all of this … for?" asked Myrtle.

"It's cool," said Bartleby. He furrowed his brow in a "duh" sort of way.

"It's practice," said Nicoleta. "Bartleby's right, knowing wizardry is helpful, but necromancy is very different. I imagine I'll have to learn a bunch of basic spells like these before he's able to teach me anything really powerful."

"Er, right," said Bartleby. "Poverful."

"Can we talk?" Myrtle hadn't really meant it as a question, given the way she was leading Sloot away by the hand. She led him through the corridors of the house, up the stairs, past Constantin's bedroom—where he sounded to be berating the bed for just lying there—and into her own bedroom where she closed the door behind them.

It was the second time that Sloot had been in a girl's bedroom. Same girl, different bedroom. This time, he was even less sure what might happen next. He was a ghost now, and she was a demon. He wasn't even sure if they were still … compatible. In a more-than-friends sense, that is.

Myrtle sighed and then lunged at him. To say that Sloot was caught off guard would imply that nature had seen fit to equip him with any defenses whatsoever. Better, then, to say that he was merely caught. While shocking, it was not unpleasant. Just as he had begun assessing all of the feelings that were upon him, Myrtle started weeping. Sloot chucked what little he had worked out and started over.

"What's wrong?" That seemed like a reasonable place to begin.

"Oh, what isn't wrong?" Myrtle wailed ceiling-ward. She broke away from Sloot's embrace and started floating around the room. "I'm not dead, I'm not alive. I'm not compelled to haunt things or serve those whom I served in life. Agather says I'm a demon, but what does that mean?"

Sloot had thought that bit was self-evident. Then again, perhaps Myrtle hadn't seen her own leathery wings when they went to the Witchwood.

"I think," said Sloot, who'd hoped that starting a sentence that way would coax some grain of wisdom forth from deep within his subconscious. He hadn't done any wisdom in a while and thought perhaps he was due. The whole thing ultimately called him to question whether the dead even have a subconscious.

"Yes?"

"Oh, that failed spectacularly," said Sloot. "I'm more confused about my own state now. Sorry."

"I'd have found that charming once," said Myrtle.

"When we were alive, you mean?"

"Yes, in fact."

"Oh."

"What?"

"I didn't know," said Sloot. "It turns out I was worse at this in life than I'd previously realized."

They stood there in silence until Myrtle burst into a fit of laughter. She doubled over on the floor. Sloot continued standing, his awkwardness the only apparent fixed point in a roiling sea of confusion and insanity. It was the closest to normal Sloot had felt since he'd told his mother he'd gotten promoted at work.

"Dear Sloot," Myrtle gasped, wiping a tear from her eye. "Thank you for that, I really needed it."

"For what? Are you sure it was me?"

She kissed him on the lips, then threw her arms around him and started sobbing again.

"Oh dear," said Sloot. He scrambled desperately for another awkward confession that he could lob toward her. He felt sure that they would move closer to a reasonable conversation if they just kept pushing through the insanity than if they were to turn back.

"You'll still tell me the truth, right?" she asked, her eyes imploring his for reassurance. "Death hasn't granted you the ability to lie with a straight face, has it? You certainly couldn't manage it in life."

"I don't—I think—I'm terrified right now. No, not that—not terrified—it's just—well, it's like, when a man and a woman love each other, there could be kissing. And if you don't—"

She kissed him again. Hard. Sloot gave a little whimper that didn't know what feeling it was trying to represent, but it wasn't the cold grip of fear that was holding him in place. That much, he knew for sure.

"I love you, too," said Myrtle.

"You won't believe what's going on down there," said Arthur. He strode into the room with utter disregard for the significance of having had to open the door to manage it.

"For the last time," shouted Myrtle, "you can't keep invading my privacy like this! It was bad enough having you inside my head for most of my life."

"What privacy? Sloot's here."

"Er, yes," said Sloot. "Hello."

"Fine," said Myrtle, "*our* privacy. Now if you'll just—"

"I guess it makes sense he could fool Willie," said Arthur. "Imbeciles, the pair of them. At least Willie doesn't pretend to know things about philosophy. It's a good thing I was there to set the record straight."

"If you don't get out of here this instant, I'll—"

"What do you mean, 'set the record straight?'" asked Sloot.

"Don't you encourage him!"

"Sorry," said Sloot, "it's just that—"

"I told him, 'sitting on the floor isn't philosophy, no matter how funny you fold your legs up.' I didn't even have to prove the point, he did it for me."

"Did what? How?"

There was a howl from outside the house. It filled Sloot with a sense of foreboding, like the opening profanity on Swearing Day at the Salzstadt Broom Carnival.

"Oh, no," said Sloot. He left the room at what passed for a sprint, when all you had to work with was left feet and elbows. Down the stairs, through the corridor, and out onto the lawn he ran, arriving just in time to see what looked like the shadow of a three-headed wolf baying at the moon. The moon seemed nervous.

"That's Nipsy," said Nan, pointing at the wolf monster.

"What?" balked Sloot. "No, that can't be right. Nipsy's just a puppy!"

"Puppies grow up."

Sloot couldn't deny that she was right about that, though he couldn't remember ever having seen a puppy that had sprouted extra heads on the way to adulthood. Then again, he'd avoided dogs as much as possible. He'd always been suspicious that their reputations as homework gourmets were the result of fabricated excuses, but all the same, it didn't seem worth the risk.

"I told you," chided Nan, "you never should have let Willie have that puppy."

"You never said that."

"I shouldn't've had to! You know what he's like. Who do you think has to clean up after it?"

"You, I presume?"

"Not anymore," said Nan. "This is the last straw. It was your idea, you can clean up after it."

"This wasn't my idea!"

"Oh, that's convenient, isn't it? Doesn't matter, your problem now. No givin' it back, neither!" And with that, Nan stormed off into the house.

"What do you suppose we should do about it?" asked Myrtle.

"How would I know?"

One of the heads breathed a gout of something very much like fire. A second head snapped at the first in admonition, and the third head gave a bark of warning that seemed to say "don't make me separate you two." The next thing Sloot knew, all three of Nipsy's heads were growling with their toothy mouths open. One by one, they all turned to focus on him.

That drew the natural reaction from Sloot that it would have drawn from anyone under the circumstances, but it's hardly worth mentioning. "Sloot was afraid" was almost as important to state for the record as "fire is hot," or "bricks are bad for the face," or "stay out of Granny's reach when she's gotten into the schnapps and is swinging a sock with a brick in it."

Sloot was afraid, to be sure, but he also felt oddly comforted. Since he'd awoken in the Hereafter, precious little had credibly threatened his continued existence. He was quite overdue by his own reckoning, and there was something reassuring about not having lost his place in the natural order of things.

All three heads stopped growling at once, and their six ears perked up. Sloot heard a faint howl in the distance, far higher in pitch than the ones that Nipsy had been making before. Nipsy turned suddenly, and one of the heads answered the howl as the whole monstrosity bounded off into the forest.

"Well," said Myrtle, "that can't be good."

Sloot shook his head and indulged in an all-too-familiar sinking feeling. If the natural order of the universe had taught him nothing else, he knew that no matter how far Nipsy roamed, it—he?—would ultimately be Sloot's problem to solve. But before he had a chance to ponder what he might do about it, he felt a familiar tugging from behind his ear.

"You shouldn't disappear like that," Roman said. They were standing in the dark, in the tunnel that led into Greta's chamber.

"Sorry," said Sloot, then cursed himself for apologizing, then decided not to make a fuss about it. He followed up on that by seriously considering dressing Roman down for summoning him uninvited so often, but found that he lacked the will. Whether that was due to some loyalty to Carpathian Intelligence he'd carried with him to the grave, or just because he was Sloot Peril, he'd probably never figure out.

The subject needed changing. "Where's Franka?"

"She wouldn't say. Big surprise. Forget about her for now, we need to check on Greta."

"We?"

"Fine, *you* need to check on Greta."

"I thought that was what you meant."

Sloot recognized the dank, cobwebbed hallway in which they were standing, and that depressed him. It was the secret passage into the Domnitor's castle, long may he reign, the one that ended behind Greta's armoire. That wasn't the depressing part—Sloot quite liked Greta, actually—he just hated that his afterlife consisted of myriad opportunities to say things like "oh, I remember this awful place."

"You're catching on." Roman beamed with pride. "She hasn't made a report in a while, and she won't answer the armoire. I'm worried that something's happened."

"I know my place in the pecking order," said Sloot, "but couldn't you handle it? I've really got a lot going on in the Hereafter right now, and I'd—"

"This is more important," said Roman. "You took up your mother's position, remember? That duty comes before all else."

"They *all* come before all else."

"Yeah, well, this one in particular."

Sloot knew futility when he saw it, and arguing the point any further definitely qualified. Sloot floated through the armoire and into the room, which was entirely empty.

"It's empty," he said, sticking his head back into the tunnel.

"That can't be good," said Roman. "She may still be in the castle somewhere. Have a look around, and come find me when you've got something."

"Come and find you? I wouldn't have the faintest—"

"There's a pub around the corner from the library. Take your time."

⁂ GOBLIN ANTHROPOLOGY ⁂

The Domnitor's castle—long may he reign—was a grand, luxurious place, just as Sloot had always dreamed it would be. Some of the grandeur of the place had been lessened by the goblins, who were even now amusing themselves with choruses of rude noises that wouldn't have been possible without ingesting massive quantities of spoiled meat. Despite Sloot's best efforts to avoid learning anything about goblin culture—if one could call it that—he'd heard of their tradition of gathering around a pile of meat that had sat out for several days to spoil, so that they could increase their status within the congress (that being the name for a group of goblins) by defiling their guts in amusing ways. They referred to the tradition as being "in session."

Sloot had never dreamed he'd see a congress in session up close, though he'd had frequent nightmares about it. At least death had robbed him of his sense of smell. If the cacophony of flatulence was any indication, the grand ballroom must have smelled like an abattoir on a particularly warm day.

Then there were the chandeliers. Great, delicate crystal affairs, wrought by the nimble hands of expert craftsmen a hundred years prior. Priceless and irreplaceable. Had Sloot been the sort to look on the bright sides of things, he'd have counted himself lucky to have shown up when he did. After all, it was only a moment later that the two teams of goblins who were swinging the chandeliers toward each other finally succeeded in making them collide with sufficient force to send them crashing to the ground.

He floated on through the deserted-but-for-the-congress-of-goblins-infesting-it palace, sulking at the twisted remains of suits of armor, shredded paintings and tapestries, and a grand piano that looked as though it had ended its days as a sled upon the grand staircase. He worked hard at resisting the urge to have a long, ghostly moan in sympathy for the sorrow that the Domnitor, long may he reign, would no doubt feel upon his eventual triumphant return.

There was a part of Sloot that wanted to keep looking around the upper floors of the castle, but the Ministry of Etiquette and Guillotines had taken a clear position on that sort of thing. While snooping on his friends and family was just good patriotism, snooping on the Domnitor—long may he reign—or his agents was tantamount to spying. That was just the sort of heresy that made you no better than the standard Carpathian savage. Sloot's status as a spy for Carpathian Intelligence made a conundrum of the whole thing, so he decided to give it a miss.

The goblins eventually noticed Sloot. Once they'd figured out he wasn't a threat, they made a game of jumping through him, or worse, standing within him and making rancid-meat-induced noises. An anthropologist specializing in goblin studies would have taken that as a great honor, given that the goblins were attributing their great works to him. Sloot, however, was merely mortified.

Most anthropologists studying goblins were really just stacks of goblins in human clothes, anyway.

Sloot managed to elude the maelstrom of goblins that were following him around by taking a detour through the scullery. There was nothing shiny or pointy within to pique the goblins' interest, and the cleaning supplies powerful enough to be any fun had already been drunk by the goblins who were sleeping it off on the floor.

Eventually, Sloot found the steel-gated entrance to the dungeons and reasoned that if he were going to find Greta anywhere, that would be the place. It took him a moment to work up the nerve to float through the bars, wishing he'd had a key so he wouldn't have to break any rules. Any *more* rules, that is. He was fairly certain he lacked permission to be in the castle at all, to say nothing of ransacking his way through locked gates like a filthy Carpath—

Sloot really needed to stop saying things like that. Or thinking them. His mother was Carpathian, after all, not to mention—well, that was enough acceptance for one day.

The staircase leading down to the dungeon kept itself within traditional standards. It was dark, it was damp, and Sloot had no reason to believe that it wasn't both cold and musty as well. The occasional rattle of a chain sounded faintly in the distance. The whole affair would certainly fetch full marks if the marshal were inspecting it that day.

Floor covered in straw, check. Sparse torchlight, check. A bit light on rats, perhaps, but Sloot supposed it was better than the alternative. He eventually found Greta in a little cell, slumped in a corner with manacles on her wrists.

"Sloot?"

"How long have you been down here?" Sloot asked.

"Sloot, don't—"

Unfortunately for Sloot, he did. Had Greta been quicker, she'd have warned him about the spell that Gregor had cast on a lantern near the cell, to trap any ghosts that tried to walk past it.

"Ugh, sorry," she groaned.

"Quite all right," said Sloot. "I'll just … no, I suppose not. But perhaps I could … hmm, not that either."

"At least there's a bit more light now," said Greta, "and someone to talk to."

Sloot was imprisoned in a battered tin lantern that looked like the ones atop Salzstadt's ubiquitous gas lamps.

"There's a hefty fine for stealing these," said Sloot with uncharacteristic anger. "You point me to the hooligan that made off with this, and mark my words, I'll ask him to turn himself in!"

"Stern words. It's not painful or anything, is it?"

"What, the lantern? No, ghosts don't do pain. Well, not usually."

"You're like a little grey flame in there."

"Really? I'm afraid of fire."

"Of course you are. Listen, I don't know how long we have before they come back, but I've got to tell you something important."

"*Tsk, tsk, tsk,*" came a sharp clucking of a disapproving tongue from somewhere in the darkness. "It's that sort of naughtiness that got you locked down here in the first place."

Sloot knew that voice, that menacing tone of malice and disapproval. He groaned aloud.

"The feeling is mutual, Peril. I was hoping for the valet. What's his name? Roland?"

"It's Roman," Greta snarled.

"Either way, he's made of meat," said Mrs. Knife. She drew her wicked blade from the sheath at her waist. A single ray of light that shouldn't have been there caught the gleaming steel as it sliced through the air. If she'd set that up on purpose, it'd had the desired effect. Sloot was terrified.

"You don't scare me," said Greta, who consisted entirely of the sorts of things that Mrs. Knife's blade was designed to menace.

"Yes, I do," said Mrs. Knife. "You're only experimenting with bravado because you think I need you to deal with Vlad the Invader."

"Of course you do! Why else would I still be alive?"

"Because you make it *easier* to deal with her," said Mrs. Knife. "But you should know that I've no intention of returning you unharmed, no matter what I might tell her."

"That's dishonest," said Sloot, who was instantly sorry he'd reminded Mrs. Knife that he was there.

"Oh, I beg to differ," said Mrs. Knife. "Playing nice never got me anywhere, never earned me any respect. To be fair, I never really gave it a chance. Fear was always more expedient. Take your Domnitor, for example."

"Long may he reign," said Greta and Sloot together. Force of habit.

"See? That's what I'm talking about. Expedient. Why should I bother threatening all of the simpletons in this accursed country into obeying me, when that boy's already done the work?"

"So, you're really going to do it," said Sloot. "You're going to kidnap the Domnitor, long may he reign!"

"Not exactly," said Mrs. Knife. "I'm going to liberate him. Restore him to his throne."

"You're—really?"

"No, not really. I'm going to kidnap him and restore him to his throne."

Sloot was silent, the way that lamps tended to be. He was either utterly perplexed or getting into character.

"He'll be her puppet," said Greta.

"There will be a lot of intellect gone to waste when I slit your throat."

"How're you going to do it?"

"I have my Serpents watching his Stagrallan villa as we speak, and a Three Bells ship with diplomatic papers fully provisioned in the harbor. As soon as his guard is down, he'll be whisked away before anyone's the wiser."

"It doesn't make sense," said Sloot.

"It makes perfect sense, dimwit."

"No, it's—if your big scheme is kidnapping the Domnitor—long may he reign—from Stagralla, why do you need directions to Carpathia?"

Among the questions that Sloot regretted asking the most—and there were more than a few—that one yielded as much regret as any three of them combined. The look on Mrs. Knife's face as she trudged into the light could most readily be described as "haunted rage," which struck Sloot as an excellent name for a fragrance. Her phantasmal stare seethed with the hunger for revenge that cats bear for every human who's never fed them, and most of the ones who have.

"What did you say?"

"Er, never mind," said Sloot.

Mrs. Knife always looked like she was just barely hanging onto her mask of sanity. Unbeknownst to Sloot, that was crucial to maintaining her status as a villain. If she were to let fly with a stark raving tirade in the wrong company, she could find herself downgraded to lunatic in a hurry. Villains get lots of perks that lunatics don't, like lairs, henchmen, and discount magazine subscriptions. It was a good thing for her, then, that the right people weren't watching when she started stabbing at the empty air.

"How much do you know, wretched ghost?" Her voice dropped into a gravelly croak and her eyes flitted around as though chasing a fly. She stabbed after it again and again.

"Nothing! I swear!" Sloot panicked. Mrs. Knife had stabbed him once before, and she was known to be the sort of villain who got what she wanted at any cost. Even if what she wanted was to stab a ghost to death. Until he was absolutely certain that she couldn't manage it, Sloot resolved to panic on the side of caution.

"Keeping us in the Dark, eh? Clever, clever little man. But not clever enough. Ha!" She lunged at the darkness, knife first.

"Ahh!" shouted Sloot. "Please, I don't know anything! I'd tell you if I did!"

"This is some rescue," said Greta.

"You did!" shouted Mrs. Knife, her eyes wide and unblinking, as though she'd been possessed by a fish. She stabbed between the bars of the cell and started slashing at the air, still several feet from Greta. "You knew, didn't you, little man? Tell me!"

"I don't know! I don't know!"

"Leave him alone, you hag!" Greta leaned forward as far as she could, undeterred by Mrs. Knife's slashing. Whether she knew the range of Mrs. Knife's arm or simply hadn't developed a proper sense of fear for sharp steel on the move, Sloot couldn't tell. He was grateful in either case, as her courage had made the slashing stop.

Mrs. Knife froze. She blinked, finally, and looked around as if trying to remember where she was. Her eyes narrowed and locked on Greta.

"Not long now," Mrs. Knife said through a clenched grin. She gripped the knife firmly, holding it inches from her own face, pointed at Greta's. "Your precious Vlad will watch you die. Count on it!"

She turned and walked away, sheathing her knife as she went. Her footsteps faded away, and then silence took a turn at running the conversation for a bit. It was a thick sort of silence, one that had no respect for personal space. It got right in Sloot's face and dared him to say something. Sloot, who had never risen to a dare in his life, remained silent.

Greta remained in her defiant pose long after Mrs. Knife had left, perhaps to ensure that she was really gone before she sagged to the rotten-straw-covered stone floor to consider the psychopath's threat.

"That was unusual," she said after a while, at which point the thick silence slunk off into the shadows, with an urgency that implied it was late for ruining another conversation.

"Right," said Sloot. "It definitely stood apart from her usual death threats. You're taking it rather well." *So am I*, though Sloot, who generally responded to threats of any sort with all-out panic. He was panicking, to be sure, but perhaps only half-out.

"She's going to kill me or she isn't," said Greta. "Crying out about it won't change the outcome."

That was a lot for Sloot to take in. While his ideas about the operations of the world around him were challenged on a fairly regular basis, the concept of panic and worry being utterly useless hit particularly close to home. Perhaps now, more than ever, he desperately wished for a long soak in a hot tub.

"Her little meltdown," Greta continued, "what do you think she meant about 'the Dark?'"

"Er, well, it's dark in here."

"Yes, but that's not what she said. She said 'the Dark,' like ... *proper* dark."

"The *Dark*," said Sloot, as properly as possible. "Nope, doesn't ring any bells. What are you doing?"

"Looking," said Greta.

"Looking," Sloot repeated.

"For some Dark," said Greta, pronouncing the word very properly again. "Mrs. Knife is the Eye of the Serpent now. They're involved in all sorts of evil, I imagine."

"I try not to."

"Imagine?"

"Generally, yes."

"That's sort of ... sad."

"Oh, I dunno," Sloot shrugged. "I think it's cozy, living with the world the way it is. No surprises."

"What about that?"

"What about what?"

"That bit over there." Greta was pointing to a particularly dark corner near the ceiling. Sloot wasn't exactly sure what he was looking at, or for, but he had to agree that it was particularly dark.

"I don't recall her having stabbed in that direction," said Sloot.

"Perhaps not," said Greta. "You were right about the other thing, though."

"I was?"

"Directions to Carpathia. You go far enough to the north, and there you are. There's a road from the northern gate of Salzstadt that leads right to it."

Sloot remembered all too well. It didn't matter that he was a Carpathian himself, or that he'd been there, sat at Vlad the Invader's table as her guest, and had his first kiss there. A lifetime of having been professionally fear-mongered by the Ministry of Propaganda left him quivering at the very mention of the cannibal-ridden vortex of depravity to the north. Even in this mouldering dungeon, he found himself giving thanks for the Domnitors that came before the current one, long may he reign, for having built the great wall at Salzstadt's northern border.

"Ow."

"Hmmm?"

"Nothing. Well, not nothing. Probably someone trying to summon me, but they can't pull me out of this lamp."

"Spirits trapped in lamps." Greta scoffed. "Gregor's work, I'm sure. He's an odd duck."

"I can't argue with that. We've got our own necromancer now, though."

"What? You can't trust necromancers, Sloot! What were you thinking?"

"It sounded reasonable when Agather suggested it."

"Agather … from the Witchwood?"

Sloot nodded. Then he remembered he was just a grey flame in a lamp and said "yes."

"So a witch told you to cozy up to a necromancer, and you thought it sounded reasonable."

"At the time," Sloot squirmed. "It was for Nicoleta, mostly. Living people's magic doesn't work for her now."

"Hmmm. Well, you've got me there."

That was the last thing that Sloot wanted. Winning arguments was not his forte, and he didn't love the idea of learning how to deal with the responsibilities that went with being right. He countered with the classic Coward's Defense and said nothing at all.

Time passed, as it was wont to do. Nothing changed, really. Greta maintained the look of grim focus she generally always had, aside from when she and Vlad were making eyes at each other. She'd get all smoldery, and Vlad's gaze would become infinitesimally less aggressive. If that wasn't love …

"Ugh," said Sloot, after what seemed like an eternity, "how long have we been here?"

"I don't know," said Greta. "I haven't slept, so it's not been a whole day."

"Really? I thought it had been weeks." Though time seemed to pass at its normal rate in the Narrative, there were no windows or clocks in the dungeon.

"It's maddening," said Greta. "I've never been without a clock in my life. I've never had to guess at the time before."

"I don't sleep," said Sloot. "It's impossible to tell time when you're dead."

Greta made a thinking face.

"That makes sense," she said after a while. "You don't have a heartbeat, do you?"

"I mean, that's … personal."

"Oh, come off it. Of course, you don't have a heartbeat. If your body doesn't tick or sleep—"

"Or exist, for that matter."

"Right, that. Well, you've got no means of reference, do you? You'd need a heart for that."

Sloot knew that Greta was talking about the blood-pushing organ that resides in the chest, but he couldn't help thinking of it through the lens of the most despicable profession: poetry. He had a heart in that sense, lamentable though it was. Even the dead could love, it seemed.

But what about demons? He and Myrtle hadn't really sorted out where they stood since the fall of Salzstadt, and he'd assumed up to that point that she felt the same as she'd done in life. But did she?

It was a good thing that Arthur wasn't around, because that particular ponderance led him down an existential rabbit hole he'd certainly have avoided, had he seen it coming. *Did* he feel the same way about Myrtle as he'd felt in life? He thought so. He certainly still loved her, but so many other experiences were pale by comparison, now that he was dead. What if his heart —metaphoric as it now was—simply wasn't in it anymore when it came to balancing ledgers, properly knotting shoelaces, or Myrtle?

"There you are," said Myrtle, who was suddenly standing in the cell.

"Myrtle!" exclaimed Greta. "I thought you were dead! How did you get in here?"

"I followed Sloot," she said. "It's easier when he's thinking about me, which was very sweet, by the way. Where is he?"

"Here," said Sloot's lamp.

"So, you've got special powers now?" Greta's expression implied that she wouldn't be put off.

"I died," said Myrtle, "but I'm a demon, not a ghost. Not sure how it happened, but I promise I'm not evil or anything."

"As far as you know," said Greta.

"What's that supposed to mean?"

"Well, you wouldn't really know, would you? I mean, you may not be feeling evil at the moment, but how many stories have been written about nice demons who come up from sulphuric pits to grant wishes?"

"None that I know of."

"Precisely. You're probably being honest, but people don't usually trade their souls to your sort in exchange for soup kitchens or hospitals, you know."

"I suppose not," said Myrtle. "I should probably do some research after I rescue the two of you, just to make sure I'm not going to start demanding sacrifices or anything."

"Oh, I'm not going with you," said Greta.

"Of course you are," said Myrtle.

"Mrs. Knife just promised to kill you, no matter what!" Sloot was aghast. A ghost aghast. He'd have been more entertained by the word-play, had he been the sort of person who trucked with entertainment.

"Yeah, but she hasn't yet, has she?"

"Well, no, but—"

"Look, the more time she has to kidnap the Domnitor, long may he—" Greta said a swear word. There was a faint "pop" and the sound of scuffling feet. "I've got to stop saying that! Anyway, it would be bad if she succeeded. I've got to stay here and do my part to stop her."

"What, from inside this prison cell?" asked Myrtle.

"Oh, what," Greta spat, "you too? Just because I'm a woman in a prison cell, I'm some helpless damsel who needs to sell her soul to a demon to be rescued?"

"No souls," said Myrtle, "I just—"

"That's what you say now," said Greta. "You're all the same, all of you! I've worked with some of the most intricate machinery the world has ever seen, and you think that a pair of manacles and a rusty gate can keep me wilting like a delicate flower in the dark, until a big strong man or an unwitting denizen of evil—no offense—comes to whisk me away?"

"None taken," said Myrtle, with a smirk. She snapped her fingers and the lamp burst in a shower of bright yellow sparks.

"Come on, Sloot," said Myrtle, as she began pulling them back into the Hereafter.

"Wait!" said Sloot. "We can't just leave Greta here to die!"

"She's stated her position," said Myrtle. "What would you have me do, kidnap her?"

"Well, if you put it that way—"

"Looks like you'll be the only damsel I rescue today."

ꜱ⸎RESCUES AND ABDUCTIONS⸎ꜱ

"Try it vithout the exuberance," said Bartleby.

"I thought you'd know me better than that by now," said Nicoleta.

"I never said it vould be easy. Thunder doesn't rumble ominously over sunny meadows, you know."

The balcony was the only part of the house not presently flooded by the thick black sludge that was pouring out of Willie. It seemed that while Sloot had been away Willie had been left unattended, and this was the result. Constantin had spotted Nan in a hallway and given chase. While they were playing hide-and-seek, Sloot could only imagine all of the sitting in the circle that Willie wasn't doing. He may have burned off a bit of his power with a one-man-child fashion show, as he seemed to be the only one among them whose outfits kept changing.

"A fine mess, Peril," Grumley chided. "I don't know where it is you keep gallivanting off to, but you have responsibilities!"

"Keep it down, vould you? Ve're trying to make thunder over here."

"We've got bigger problems at the moment," said Myrtle. "I've run this a hundred ways in my head, and I can't find a way out of it. If Greta doesn't escape, Mrs. Knife is definitely going to kill her."

It turns out that demons are not all the same, despite what the League of Casual Racists would have everyone believe. Each one has a special power and purpose. Some are very grand, which is very irksome to blockage demons, who spend the vast majority of eternity wedged in the plumbing.

Myrtle, as it turned out, was a causality demon. Her special power was a lot like seeing into the future, but it was far from a clear picture. She wasn't able to make predictions with any certainty until events took root in the present. For instance, she'd have had no way of knowing that Mrs. Knife was going to kill Greta before Greta had refused to leave. That act of defiance set several eventualities into motion, one of which would eventually become the future, then the present, and then the past.

"I haven't quite figured out which one is which," said Myrtle. "You'd think becoming a demon would have come with a manual or something."

"Irrelevant," said Grumley. "For the last time, you are no longer alive. You've crossed into the Hereafter. The affairs of the living are no longer your concern!"

"Tell that to Willie," said Nicoleta, who was working very hard to grimace, but could only manage it in an adorable way. "He's been droning on about 'woe unto the mortals' all day. Or night. Whatever it is right now."

"Concentrate," said Bartleby. "Let the ambivalence flow through you like ... *vhatever*. Veren't you ever a teenager? Vhat kind of poetry vas in your private journal?"

"That's none of your business, Dad! Oh, that was embarrassing."

"Not exactly the reaction I vas looking for, but you're starting to tap into some serious darkness."

"Can't you do that somewhere else?" shouted Grumley.

"No," growled Bartleby, suddenly shrouded in black smoke. A bolt of lightning sizzled through the air, casting ominous shadows across his gaunt face.

"Oh, well done," said Nicoleta. "Do you think I could do flowers instead of smoke?"

"There are no flowers in necromancy. Vell, dead ones are probably okay."

"It's a start."

"You're not leaving me much choice here, Peril," said Grumley. "The order has sent me to ensure that things are running smoothly. You've been charged with managing Lord Hapsgalt's affairs, and look! Just look at what's going on in there! If you're not able to get this under control straight away, I'm going to have to relieve you of your post!"

Sloot smiled.

"And given all that you know about the Serpents of the Earth," Grumley continued, "you'll have to be remanded to the Well of the Void, where your soul can play out the depths of its worst torments until eternity comes to a close."

"Oh," said Sloot, his smile quickly turning to a frown. "And how long will that take?"

"Eternity is a very long time," said Grumley. "Leave it at that." Grumley nodded, and then disappeared in a puff of black smoke.

"Vicked," said Bartleby. "I've never seen the smoke exit done vithout the bats before. Simple, but elegant. I'll have to try it sometime."

"I like the bats," said Nicoleta.

"I do, too. Never mind. Vait a minute, are you vearing any eyeliner?"

"I didn't know ghosts *could* wear eyeliner!" Nicoleta's face was engulfed in a gleeful, open-mouthed grin.

"You're not going to be doing any necromancy vith all of that smiling. Vhat did I tell you about raising eyebrows?"

Nicoleta sighed. "One at a time."

"And eyes opened vide?"

"One at a time."

"It takes practice," said Bartleby, patting Nicoleta on the shoulder. "You'll get there."

Meanwhile, Sloot was quietly spiraling into a panic.

"I know that look!" Arthur shouted, jumping up from his recumbent position on the balcony's railing. "You're having a crisis! Which sort is it, existential? Moral? Is it full-on melancholy, or is it a simple conundrum?"

"Melancholy!" shouted Bartleby. "That's the vord I've been looking for."

"Sure," said Nicoleta, "when I was a teenager. But that was just an affectation! I've seen enough of the world to know there's beauty in it, regardless of how dark and drab things may seem."

"Unchecked optimism!" Arthur was shaking with rabid glee. "How dare you bandy that about without fear of reprisal, while I still draw breath?"

"You're not breathing," said Myrtle.

"And you! What have I told you about the wanton use of literal interpretation? Honestly, it's as if—"

"Shut up!" shouted Myrtle in an impossibly low octave, her scaly wings suddenly appearing from between her shoulders. "The philosophical ramifications of any state or series of events are secondary to the consequences they bear in any real sense!"

No one moved. The wings folded themselves down into nothingness. Myrtle took in a breath and gave an enormous sigh of relief.

"Vicked," said Bartleby, admiration gushing from him without restraint.

"I can't tell you how long I've been holding that in," said Myrtle.

"What about the Domnitor," asked Sloot, "long may he reign?"

"I'm sure he's embroiled in a crisis of his own," said Arthur. "It's not every day the proletariat rises up and throws off the yoke of oppression, sending you running for exile with your tail between your legs!"

"The proletariat didn't do anything," said Sloot. "It was the walking dead."

"There it is, the people's curse." Arthur folded his arms and shook his head, frowning with all the condescension he could muster, which was quite a lot. "The aristocracy has you believing that you're powerless against them."

Arthur had a series of arguments that he insisted were incontrovertible proof of the power of the proletariat. Unfortunately, their validity lay in the willingness of the proletariat to sit through all seven hours of his lecture without stopping for lunch; therefore, if Arthur's arguments were valid, the people's only obstacle to overcoming the aristocracy was their affinity for lunch.

"This is all beside the point," said Sloot. "We have to stop Mrs. Knife from kidnapping the Domnitor, long may he reign!"

"That's a good idea," said Nicoleta.

"Really?" asked Sloot. "I didn't think you were a supporter."

"We should tell Vlad, so she can kidnap him instead!"

"Heresy!" Sloot shouted, his voice cracking ever so briefly into the soprano.

"It isn't," said Myrtle. "Not anymore. Actually, it never was for her. She's from Carpathia."

Nicoleta grinned and nodded. "Patriotic of me, in fact."

"But you can't," cried Sloot. "We can't! Set aside kidnapping being wrong, this is the *Domnitor* we're talking about! Long may he reign."

"She's got a point," said Myrtle. "He'd be much safer with Vlad, don't you think?"

To Sloot's horror, he found himself agreeing with that. Vlad was the finest warrior the world had ever seen. If she could be convinced to protect the Domnitor, long may he reign, there could be no safer place for him. Then again, Sloot knew Vlad's temper. Convincing her to protect the Domnitor, long may he reign, would be a lot easier if Greta was around to keep Vlad's rage from boiling over.

That was it! A reason to rescue Greta, against her will if necessary! Even Roman would see the sense that.

※　※　※　※

"Out of the question," said Roman. Sloot had expected nothing less, of course. He'd have been suspicious had Roman said "good idea, Sloot," and steered them down the path of some sensible scheme that was sure to end well for everyone.

"Why not?"

Roman leaned back on his bar stool, looked from Sloot to Myrtle, and sighed.

"Look, aside from my complete and unwavering support for Greta making her own choices—regardless of how stupid they may seem to me—we can't take the risk of going after her now."

"What risk?" asked Myrtle. "I know exactly where she is! I pop into the dungeon, break the manacles and teleport her away before she has a chance to say anything about it."

"Oh, there's solidarity for you." Roman was being sarcastic. It was obvious enough that even Sloot didn't have to wonder.

"I'm sorry," said Myrtle in a disingenuous pout, matching Roman's sarcasm pound for pound, "I forgot that all women were a sisterhood, and that I should champion her decisions whether I agree with them or not."

"You did before," said Roman, "when you rescued Sloot. You said so yourself!"

"Things have changed since then!"

"Right you are!" Roman looked around, suddenly very conscious of the fact that their conversation had risen in volume. They'd become the focus of all eyes in the bar. He scowled and gave the other patrons an agitated wave that said "mind your business, or would you have me in yours as well?"

Roman sat down and repeated himself at a properly conspiratorial volume. "Right you are. Things have changed. We don't know if Greta is still in the dungeon. Mrs. Knife is bound to have noticed that Sloot has escaped, so she's probably lain a trap for us, just in case."

"We have to tell Vlad," said Sloot.

"We *can't* tell Vlad," Roman hissed. "If she learns the severity of the situation now, she won't hesitate to storm the gates of Salzstadt again, charge right up to the castle, and all but guarantee that Greta's head bids her body a bitter farewell before Vlad gets within a hundred feet of rescuing her.

"Well, then she can't kidnap…" Sloot looked left and right as inconspicuously as possible, which was intensely suspicious, " … *you know who*."

Roman's face broke into a mocking sneer, and he hummed four quick bursts to the tune of "long may he reign."

"I can't possibly have to remind you again that death does not excuse you from your duty to Carpathian Intelligence."

Sloot sighed. He could think of further arguments, but at the end of the day—which was happening at that very moment, if you wanted to be literal about it—he was going to do his duty. Arguments were uncomfortable business, and he'd just be doing it for sport. Sloot Peril had proven, time and again, that he was no athlete.

Myrtle sighed. "Of course, you're right. I suppose I'm just mad at myself for not dragging Greta out of there when I had the chance. Even if she was still mad at me about it, she'd be safe."

Roman nodded. He raised his glass. "To Greta."

"To Greta." Myrtle and Roman drank. Sloot made a mental note to pop into Turk's again, as soon as he had a moment.

Sloot looked around. It was the first time he'd seen the walking dead in a pub in the Narrative, and it was more than a bit disconcerting. It wasn't that they were crawling with grave beetles, though that did prompt him to wonder how they'd gotten there. Hadn't the walking dead never been buried? Neither was it that bits would occasionally fall off of them, or that the ones whose jaws had fallen off tended to moan incoherently. It was the fact that they weren't drinking.

"The bartender still charges them a two-drink minimum," said Roman. "He told me the goblins don't like them, so they give the place a wide berth. It's a win-win situation."

"You'd think that all of the living folks wouldn't want to hang around with the undead," said Myrtle. She was putting away the booze with alarming speed, but it didn't seem to affect her. Demonic powers, Sloot guessed.

Roman said a swear word, one that Sloot knew this time. It compared a person to the skin that grows on mayonnaise if it's left in the sun too long.

"What?"

"Vampires," said Roman. "Don't look, maybe they won't come—hello, boys, what can I do for you?"

"Ve vant to drink your blood!" said the tall, pale one with the widow's peak and the high collar.

"I'm sure you do," said Myrtle, "but you won't. Trust me."

Sloot was momentarily impressed with Myrtle's bravado, then

realized she'd probably just seen no futures in which that came to pass. It was still more bravado than he'd ever shown, but that wasn't a very high bar.

"How dare you speak to us like that!" The other tall, pale one with the widow's peak and the high collar made his cape do a billowing flourish maneuver. It was undoubtedly intended to impress, but failed miserably. Sloot didn't need Willie to tell him that it was a churlish maneuver, one that certainly wouldn't be making the scene this season, or any other for that matter.

"I'm just stating facts," said Myrtle. "You're going to think it over for a minute, then come up with a thinly veiled attempt to salvage your pride before you bolt for the door. Go on, we'll wait."

"Foolish mortal! You would threaten the princes of the night, the spawn of blackness, the—"

The first tall, pale one with the widow's peak and the high collar whispered something to the second. His eyes went wide with alarm. He was looking at Roman and Myrtle with the panicked suspicion that the elderly cast on anything less than thirty years old.

"Really? Vhich one?"

The first vampire shrugged.

"One of you is a demon?"

Roman grinned. Myrtle maintained the uncomfortably severe sort of eye contact that tradesmen think will get them somewhere with the ladies.

"Ve, er," the vampires exchanged nervous glances. "Ve really prefer virgins."

"So, you'll be drinking each others' blood tonight, then?" Roman's grin changed keys.

"Ve're going to let you off vith a varning this time," said the first vampire as they backed toward the door.

"There's a good lad," said Roman.

"Demon powers are fun," said Myrtle, once they'd bolted through the door and into the night. "Vampires. Pfft. Honestly, what does Bartleby see in them?"

"No idea," said Sloot.

"How'd you become a demon, anyway?" asked Roman.

"No idea. I thought I was just dead, like everyone else. Maybe something to do with Arthur? A body dies, one ghost comes out? Maybe when two souls came out of me, they didn't know what to do with the second one."

"Anything's possible, I suppose," said Roman. He took a sip of his drink. "All right, let's make a plan. I want to inform Vlad about the Domnitor thing as soon as possible."

"Long may he reign," said Sloot, limply observing tradition in lieu of defending the Old Country against his best friends, the heretics.

"Sloot has to do it," said Myrtle.

"What? Why me?"

"Sorry, darling, not sure why yet, but I've foreseen that it's the best move."

Myrtle batted her eyelashes in a way that Sloot found at once adorable and frightening. Par for the course, he supposed, if you're dating a demon. As dearly as he'd love to have resisted, he knew it would only be a matter of time before he relented and agreed to float all the way to Carpathia on his own. He may as well get started.

⋙⋗CASTLE ON THE BORDER⋖⋘

Ulfhaven, the capital of Carpathia, was a long walk from Salzstadt. Sloot had made the trip on horseback a couple of times, and it hadn't been his idea then, either. At least he'd had company on those occasions. And a horse. And a body.

At the moment, there were scarcely any signs of life at all, not that he brought anything to the table in that regard. It was the middle of the night. There was only about half the moon showing, and it kept disappearing behind the clouds.

"Fine!" Sloot shouted at it. "I don't need your help to see where I'm going anyway!" It wasn't just the passive aggression talking. Ghosts can see just fine in perfect darkness, one of the few perks. The more interesting point there was that Sloot, in his frustration, had managed to engage in a bit of aggression. Sure, it was the passive variety. Yes, it was directed at the moon. We all have to crawl before we walk.

"Hey, wossat?"

Sloot froze. He was too far from both Salzstadt and Ulfhaven to reasonably flee in panic to either, so the phrase "middle of nowhere" came to mind.

"It's a ghost," said a voice employing a nonchalance that implied Sloot wasn't the first ghost the speaker had seen. He looked around and saw a few heads poking out from behind a suspicious-looking pile of boulders. He couldn't quite place what it was about them that looked so suspicious, but they did. It was undeniable.

"Er, hello," said Sloot.

"State your business!" said one of the heads.

"Just—nothing. Thank you." Sloot had been on the verge of reflexively telling the truth. The truth was one of his favorite things, after all, along with hospital corners on his bed sheets, perfectly balanced ledgers, and mystery novels approved by the Ministry of Propaganda. (There were two. The Domnitor—long may he reign—was the protagonist in both, and he rooted out heresy with the help of his talking dog, Justice.)

Sloot decided to keep his mouth shut. The truth, in this case, was that he was going to Carpathia to conspire with Vlad the Invader about kidnapping the Domnitor—long may he reign—from his summer-vil-la-in-exile in Stagralla. He'd have to see what was beneath those heads to have a chance at guessing how they'd react to that information. It wasn't as though they could kill him or anything, but conflict avoidance was among Sloot's favorite things.

"So, you just thought you'd stroll out to the border on a lark? Nothing better to do? Hang on a minute. Come on, Gus."

Two of the heads moved out from behind the pile of rocks and shambled in Sloot's direction. They were dead, or at least did an excellent job of imitating the telltale shamble.

"Now then," said the rotting husk of what had recently been a person, "who were you shouting at?"

"Oh," said Sloot, "no one. Forget it."

"Hey, you're on our land! I'll decide who forgets what around here, ain't that right, Gus?"

Gus nodded. He was dead as well, and in an advanced state of decay that had mostly skeletonized him from the neck up.

"Gus agrees."

"I gathered that from the nod."

"Don't be clever." He shoved a finger in Sloot's face. "Gus lost his vocal cords to a pack of dogs before he woke up and realized they were at him. He's understandably sensitive about it, and doesn't appreciate you being glib about his personal tragedy."

Gus shook his head.

"I'm terribly sorry," said Sloot. "I haven't been dead that long myself, it's all a bit bewildering."

"You got that right. Now, no more stalling. Who were you yelling at, and what are you doing out here?"

"I was yelling at … it's embarrassing."

"Tell me anyway."

"I don't want to!" Sloot stamped his foot in defiance. The maneuver qualified at once as both cowardly and brave. It was the sort of paradox that had always made him uncomfortable.

"Look, you may think that being a ghost means we can't hurt you, but you don't know that for sure. Am I right?"

Gus cracked his knuckles for emphasis, leaving one of his pinky fingers hanging at a weird angle. Sloot guessed that if Gus hadn't been wearing gloves, that pinky would be on the ground at his feet. Regardless, Sloot had to admit that he didn't, in fact, know for sure that he was beyond harm. Plus, he really was very fond of telling the truth.

Sloot sighed. "I was yelling at the moon."

Silence. The two rotting corpses looked at each other for a moment, and then back at Sloot.

"You're right, that is embarrassing."

Sloot shrugged.

"Well, it's not a crime, anyway. Now, what are you doing here?"

"Out for a walk," said Sloot. It was the truth, just not all of it.

"That just seems coincidental."

Had the phrase "it's a free country" not been explicitly censored in the strongest possible terms by the Ministry of Etiquette and Guillotines, Sloot certainly would have employed it as a non-sequitur just then. Of course, it would have been doubly bad had he done, given the Ministry's strict ban on the use of non-sequiturs without a license.

"Look, I've got to get going."

"What's the matter? Your leisurely stroll going to get cold?"

"No, it's just—"

"I knew it. You're thinking of haunting our castle."

"What?"

"Don't bother denying it! There's not another castle for at least fifty miles. What else would a ghost be doing out here, shouting at the moon?"

"I can't think of a single thing," said Sloot, "but—"

"Look, all I can do is ask you not to. We've just got it set up the way we like it, and if you start haunting it now, all that work will have gone to waste."

"What castle?"

The two corpses looked at each other, and then sagged with relief.

"You're a good sport. *What castle?* Ha!"

Gus nodded, presumably in approval.

"Er, thanks," said Sloot.

"I'm Barry, by the way. This is Gus."

Gus waved, his pinky flapping haphazardly about.

"Peril," said Sloot. "Sloot Peril. At least I was, before the Fall of Salzstadt."

"I think we get to keep our names," Barry whispered, adding a conspiratorial wink.

"Oh, okay," said Sloot. He made a mental note to refrain from metaphor for the remainder of the conversation.

There were about a dozen corpses milling about the pile of boulders. It had been hard to see from his vantage, but when Sloot accepted their invitation into the castle—contingent upon his promise not to haunt it—he could see that that was exactly what it was: a pile of boulders. It lacked the grandeur of other castles Sloot had seen, but he couldn't remember any specific statutes mandating levels of grandeur as a prerequisite for use of the term *castle*. Plus, Barry and the other corpses liked it fine, so who was Sloot to argue?

Behind the castle was a very large, perfectly circular ring of stones. There was a single stone in the center that was roughly square. It lacked the haphazardly-piled charm of the castle—such as it was—and was far too symmetrical in Sloot's opinion to be up to any good.

Barry had been personally disemboweled by Vlad at the siege that preceded the fall of Salzstadt, and was all too eager to show Sloot the seeping wounds beneath his tunic. What was left of his guts was being held in place by a series of cleverly employed belts, a couple of which were leather. Sloot momentarily considered them with envy before coming to his senses.

It was a good thing that Sloot hadn't mentioned he was heading to Carpathia, since Barry's company was there on Mrs. Knife's orders. The castle was their outpost, and they were there to secure the border against invasions by foreign hordes.

"Done a fine job so far," said Barry. "Not a single cannibal has made it past us."

"Well done," said Sloot.

"Peril," said Barry, listening to himself carefully recite Sloot's surname. "What sort of name is that? It sounds Carpathian."

"I get that a lot."

"You don't have papers, I presume?"

"Nor a hand with which I might pass them to you."

"Right," said Barry. He shrugged. "I guess you're all right, as long as you promise you're not here to haunt the castle."

"I promise."

"Fine. Off you go, then. You headed east? West? South?"

"Er, north, actually. Thought I'd see what the cannibals look like, now that I'm no longer an entree."

"Good luck with that," said Barry. "There *is* no more north."

"There's—what?"

"You saw yourself, didn't you?"

Sloot was confused, though that was nothing new. Little had entirely made sense since his head popped off.

"Maybe ghosts don't see as well as we do," Barry said to Gus. Gus shrugged. "There's nothing beyond the border anymore."

"Not until you get to Ulfhaven," said Sloot. "I'd imagine," he hastened to add.

"No, not nothing, *nothing*. At all."

"What?"

They walked back to the road, Sloot and Barry and Gus, and all the rest of their comrades as well. Not much passed for entertainment on the frontier, it seemed, not even among the recently deceased. Sloot peered north into Carpathia as intently as possible. To be sure, there was little more than dirt and scraggly brush, but it was more than *nothing*.

"You see?" asked Barry.

"I do," said Sloot, but without conviction. What was he missing?

"That's what I mean," said Barry. "Nothing."

"I just ... well, I'd ... look, if there were nothing—*nothing*—there, then I wouldn't be able to do this, would I?"

Sloot took a few steps forward, then turned to look at the shambling horde under Barry's able command. All of them were staring at him in shocked silence.

"What?" asked Sloot, becoming very nervous. Well, *more* nervous. "It's not dangerous, is it? Walk over, you'll see—"

"Are you still there, Sloot? Can you hear me?"

"I am, and I can! What's the matter? Look, if you'd just walk—"

"It must've got him," said another of the corpses, a big one that had started to bloat.

"What must've got him?" asked Barry.

"Dunno," said big-and-bloaty. "Whatever's on the other side of nothing."

"Can't you hear me?" asked Sloot. No reaction. He walked back over to them, and as soon as he got close, they all shambled back a bit.

"You're alive!" shouted Barry.

"Am not."

"Well, I mean, you're not—you're still dead!"

That much was true.

"You couldn't hear me when I was standing over there?"

"You disappeared when you walked through the shimmering wall."

Sloot turned to look behind him. No shimmer, just dirt and scraggly Carpathian brush.

"You can't see past the border," said Sloot.

"There's nothing there."

"Yes, there is! It's Carpathia!"

Try as they might, none of the undead were able to shamble their way across the border. They just sort of stood there, right at the edge, as though taking a single step forward were as mind-boggling as differential equations; or, rather, something that Sloot would find difficult. Like tennis.

He hopped back and forth across the border a few times for their benefit, hoping to convince them that reality hadn't abruptly decided to stop at the Carpathian border. In the end, he was unable to make them see beyond the border by any means available to him. Despite his utter aversion to the thought of helping Roman's plan come to fruition, he bid the border corpses farewell and continued north into Carpathia. He made it a few feet before he felt an uncomfortable tug behind his ear, and suddenly found himself in a familiar elsewhere.

❧❧THE HANDLER❧❧

S loot! How long has it been?" Flavia was as radiant as the first time
he'd met her, when she'd compelled him into service as a double
agent for Uncle.

Actually, she was more than just *radiant as ever*. She didn't appear
to have changed in the slightest since the last time he saw her. She
was wearing the same white dress and sitting in the same chair. Sloot
was sure that she'd have had to leave the room from time to time to
deal with the standard labors of eating, sleeping, reciting the Loyalist
Oath before the Old Country flag—compulsory human behaviors.
Then again, when compared with all of the other oddities he'd experienced in the latter part of his life—and since—would it really be
so odd to learn that Flavia was some sort of automaton in service to
Uncle?

Sloot had never had a proper uncle, so when the Ministry of
Propaganda had rebranded the Ministry of Truth as "Uncle," he'd been
eager to go along with it. It was only now that he started to question
who might have been sending him birthday cards "from Uncle." Had the
other children been getting them as well?

"I have no idea," Sloot replied. He put a mental pin in his reverie,
promising himself that he'd come back to it just as soon as a little portion of eternity became available.

"I'd heard that the passage of time is difficult for the dead," said

Flavia. "Probably a coping mechanism. Eternity is a very long time, you know."

"So I've been told." *Threatened* was more like it, but most things told to Sloot were delivered as threats these days. That's how it seemed to him, anyway.

"Well then," said Flavia, leaning forward across the table in a way that made her seem genuinely interested in whatever he had to say, "what can I do for you?"

"Sorry?"

"For what?"

"Oh, sorry," said Sloot, "that wasn't an apology. *That* was, I suppose. For the confusion."

"Are you confused?"

"Usually."

"No need to apologize for that," said Flavia. "The intelligence business can be confusing."

"Right. Sorry. Er."

Flavia smiled at Sloot, who was starting to float a bit off-kilter to the left. He hadn't realized that he'd been concentrating, ever so slightly, on keeping himself upright ever since he'd become a ghost. He suddenly became very disconcerted that she could put him so at ease that he'd start to fail at the basic tenets of apparition. She couldn't have drugged him, could she? If anyone had such a thing as ghost drugs, it would be Uncle.

"By the first 'sorry,' I meant 'what?'"

"Oh, I see! Although now I'm confused."

"Oh, dear."

"Do you mean to say that you don't know why you came to see me?"

"I do."

"Oh, good."

"No," said Sloot, "I do mean to say that I don't know why I'm here."

"Just a moment," said Flavia. She snapped her fingers and a hairy pile of muscles in a guard uniform entered the room. It handed Flavia a piece of paper and left.

"Oh, dear," said Flavia, reading over the paper.

"What's the matter?"

"Sloot," said Flavia with the sort of "I'm not mad" softness one uses to ask a child where the cookies have gone, "is there something you'd like to tell me?"

"Nothing comes to mind," said Sloot, who felt queasy at the lie despite his lack of guts. In truth, his mind was reeling with heresies he'd been party to, plots that had ensnared him, and terrible secrets that could bring scandal to the wealthiest of Salzstadt's citizens, to say nothing of the fact that he hadn't brushed his teeth in ... well, he didn't know how long it had been, but he was off the state-mandated schedule, that was certain.

"This says you made at least a dozen trips across the Carpathian border in less than an hour. Is that true?"

"Oh, that!"

"So it *is* true." Flavia frowned in a not-mad-just-disappointed way.

"Well, yes," said Sloot, "but there were circumstances!"

"Oh, good," said Flavia, leaning back in her chair and letting out a huge sigh of relief. She smiled. "For a minute there, I was worried that it had something to do with the plot to kidnap the Domnitor, long may he reign!"

"What? Oh, that's ... what?" Sloot was as skilled at bluffing as philosophers were at earning an income.

"You're not surprised that we know about that, are you?"

"Know about? Yes, well I ... that is to say ... you know. Of course, you know! Yes, right. I knew you would. You know?"

Flavia laughed. It was cheery and bright, shining on Sloot so that he might bask in its warmth. Had it not been so entirely captivating, Sloot might have wondered if Flavia had spent countless hours learning the craft of disarming hapless interrogation subjects with seemingly simple mannerisms, and worming her way into their confidence.

"Oh, Sloot, how I've missed your wit and charm. It's a shame you're dead." She winked and smiled.

Flattery! And flirting, to boot! Wasn't it? Like most men, Sloot was never sure when he was the target of a flirtation. He'd nearly botched things with Myrtle over his inability to see the roaring infernos that she'd lit to serve as subtle hints that she liked him.

Myrtle! Sloot looked down. How could he be so brazen? There he was, a ghost in love with a demon who may or may not have been his girlfriend this whole time, and what was he doing? Flirting! Well, not flirting himself, per se, but wantonly permitting another woman to ravish him with words that may or may not have the capacity to be interpreted as innuendos, or worse!

"I didn't know ghosts could blush," said Flavia, in a very proud-of-herself manner. "But I digress. You were just going to tell me about your little trips to Carpathia."

"Right," said Sloot, "those. Well, there would have just been the one, but the walking dead soldiers at the border were confused."

"I see," said Flavia.

"They didn't think there was anything on the other side of the border," Sloot continued, "so I was trying to show them. That's all."

"Do we know about any border guards?" asked Flavia, apparently of the air. A moment later, the same guard walked in, handed Flavia another piece of paper, flexed its chin, and left.

"No," said Flavia. She may have just read the entire contents of the paper. Sloot couldn't be sure.

"Well they're there," said Sloot, thankful for the change of subject. "They've built a castle."

"A castle? How do we not know about a castle within our borders?" Flavia's constant cheeriness listed sharply toward irritation.

"Well, not a *castle*, exactly. They call it that, but it's little more than a bunch of rocks piled up."

"How much more?"

"Well, it's a pile of rocks that they've collectively agreed to refer to as a castle. So more in name, I suppose."

"They didn't say who they worked for?"

Barry had told Sloot they were there on Mrs. Knife's orders. Sloot had taken that to mean that they worked for the government, but now realized that that couldn't have been the case. So Mrs. Knife's takeover of the Domnitor's palace, long may he reign, didn't mean she was in charge of the government! A drop of good news in a bucket of feculent disaster!

Since Gregor possessed the blood star, he had dominion over the walking dead. Was it he who'd sent them to the border, then? Why? Was he expecting a war with Carpathia?

"They mentioned Mrs. Knife," offered Sloot.

"That could mean a lot of things," said Flavia. "Probably something to do with the Serpents of the Earth. You're still in with them, aren't you?"

"Not entirely," said Sloot, trying to sound more upset about it than he was.

"Right, I suppose we'll just have to keep an eye on it. Now then, what were you doing in Carpathia?"

"Oh, right," said Sloot. "I was worried we'd forget to bring that up again! Well, there are plots afoot, aren't there?"

"Always," said Flavia. "Was it something to do with the plot to kidnap the Domnitor, long may he reign?"

"Long may he reign. Right! Yes. I was trying to sort out whether the Carpathians had wind of it." It was close to the truth, but it earned him a spiritual ulcer nonetheless. He'd actually been on his way to *give* the Carpathians wind of it, truth be told, which he'd prefer it wasn't.

"That's probably a good idea," said Flavia. "Good to keep up with all of the villains when heresy rears its ugly head. But is that really the truth, Sloot?"

In Sloot's experience, questions like that weren't asked in the absence of suspicion. This was why he didn't like to lie! Perhaps his old friend ignorance could be of assistance.

"Of course it is," he said, summoning all of his willpower to keep his voice from wavering.

"I want to believe you," said Flavia, "it's just that we know you're still working with Carpathian Intelligence."

"A double agent! That was always my value to Uncle, wasn't it?"

"Well, yes, but you haven't disclosed your relationship with ... what was her name? Meryl?"

"Myrtle," said Sloot, before he could stop himself.

"Right, Myrtle! Sorry about that. She's in Carpathian Intelligence too, isn't she?"

"She is," said Sloot. It felt a bit like he was betraying her, but Flavia already knew about it, didn't she?

"You really need to report this sort of thing," said Flavia. "When we hear about it through gossip, it's ... unsettling."

"Unsettling?"

"It gives the impression that you're trying to hide it from us. You wouldn't do that, would you?"

"No, of course not!" Sloot was more sure than ever that he should have filled out some form or another, declaring officially that Myrtle was his girlfriend. He loved filling out forms, especially new and exotic ones that he'd never had occasion to fill out before. He imagined that sort of form might bear a foil stamp. He liked those best.

"All right," said Flavia. "I believe you. But there's something else, and you're not going to like it."

"Go on. I'm used to it."

"It's about kidnapping the Domnitor."

"Long may he reign," said Sloot. "What about it?"

"We're going to need your help with it."

"Happy to help," said Sloot. "Anything to keep him safe! I'm a true salt after all, happy to prove—"

"That is to say we need your help kidnapping him."

It was a good thing that Sloot was already dead, because that was just the sort of talk that would have given him a heart attack. To his credit, he still tried his best to have one there on the spot.

"You ... you want ... you want ..."

"I know it's shocking," said Flavia, "but we're left with little choice."

"That's not true," Sloot pleaded. "You have infinite choice! You're Uncle! You can do anything you want, up to and including leaving the Domnitor—long may he reign— well enough alone!"

"*We're* Uncle," said Flavia, motioning to herself and to Sloot. "*Our* mission is to root out heresy and unrest wherever we find it, and there's enough going on in the Domnitor's own castle at the moment to keep all of us busy for the rest of our careers. Trust me, our experts have been over this every conceivable way, and they've come to the same conclusion every time. Unless we can put the Domnitor back on the throne, we have no chance of taking the city back from the Serpents of the Earth."

"Oh," said Sloot. "You want to put him back on the throne?"

"Well, yes," said Flavia, in a tone that suggested there was more to it than that. She opened her mouth again to say more, then apparently thought better of it and closed her mouth again.

Sloot thought. He was good at thinking. A bit too good, sometimes. At least he thought so, particularly when he arrived at answers that were scary enough to make him wish he hadn't. Thought, that is.

"This is a *coup d'etat*!"

"That's one way of looking at it," said Flavia.

"Yes? And?"

"And what?"

"What's another way of looking at it?"

"We'll just leave that up to the Ministry of Propaganda," said Flavia. "They're awfully good at coming up with answers to questions like that."

"I'm sorry," said Sloot, "but I don't think that I can be a part of this."

"I can see how you might feel that way," said Flavia. She was using a very warm smile, one that made Sloot very much want to trust her in all things forever. "But those are your orders."

"What are you going to do with him?"

"I've already told you. We're going to put him back on the throne."

"I'm confused," said Sloot.

"We've lost confidence in his ability to rule, but he's been the figurehead for the government for so long that he's indispensable. If we're going to take over ruling the Old Country, we'll need him sitting on the throne. Smile and wave, that sort of thing."

"He'll be your puppet."

"I like to think of it more as a mascot. That's more cheery, isn't it?"

It was, but not enough to change Sloot's mind. What he said next surprised him.

"I'm sorry," said Sloot, "but you'll have to count me out."

Who was this brave and principled Sloot Peril? He'd never pushed back against demands before, and he was less comfortable in that moment than he'd been when he'd worn shoes that were three sizes too small for an entire year. They were a gift.

"I was hoping it wouldn't come to this," said Flavia, smirking in disappointment. "If you refuse to help, we'll have to punish Myrtle."

"What? You wouldn't!"

"We would. We wouldn't like it, I promise; but we would. And I know what you're thinking, but it won't help."

Sloot stared blankly at her. If she knew what he was thinking, he was farther behind than he thought.

"About Myrtle being a demon," said Flavia.

"What? How do you know about that?"

Flavia smiled and stifled a giggle as best she could.

"How do you think we got our reputation for knowing everything? Oh, Sloot! We do laugh together, don't we?"

"You can't kill her," said Sloot. He hoped he was right.

"True enough," said Flavia, causing Sloot to sigh with relief, "but we can do far, far worse." Sloot gasped his sigh back in.

Sloot tried another bit of deduction, the last time having worked out well. "You've got demons on the payroll."

"Worse. We've got lawyers."

"Lawyers?"

"Lawyers. They've got more red tape than they know what to do with, and believe me, they know how to use it! We'll get her pitched off whatever assignment she's currently on and have her working at an office so far beneath Infernal Bureaucracy that she'll be chained to her desk for the eternity. Quite possibly literally."

Sloot said nothing, just soaked up the familiar feeling of being entirely helpless and at the mercy of bullies.

"If it makes you feel any better," said Flavia, "very few people will know what's actually happened. Your average salt will go back to believing that the Domnitor reigns in Salzstadt, and they'll appreciate that the dead are in the ground where they belong. I know you're going to do the right thing, Sloot, I just know it. Think it over, but don't take too long."

⋙ᴖBUREAUCRATIC HORRORᴖ⋘

The Old Country is a cold place. It's not so cold as Nordheim, where there's been snow on the ground for so long that the Vikings who live there have furious debates over the existence of dirt beneath it; however, the answer to "should I bring a sweater just in case?" is always a resounding "yes."

Until recently, the elderly salts who lived in the capital would unequivocally condemn the cold as a deliberate assault on their old bones. Until recently.

Since the Fall of Salzstadt, the dead hadn't been going into the ground where they belonged. Thus the air in the city had a higher concentration of effluvium, thanks to the rotting of the proletariat. That meant that if the air were warmer, the city would stink more. This presented a conundrum for the elderly in the city, as acknowledging an upside to the cold specifically violated several bylaws that the Salzstadt Chamber of Curmudgeons held dear. As luck would have it, the unspoken agreement to pay no attention to the walking dead had gone into effect immediately following the Fall. That meant they'd be breaking more than just rules if they brought the matter up. They'd be breaking tradition. The elderly would ignore their own legs being on fire if tradition demanded it. Henceforth, the Chamber could—nay, *should*—leave any discussion on the matter off of their agenda until further notice.

There were more goblins around since the Fall as well, though that had no olfactory effect. Scientists have long been baffled by the phenomenon known as Boolean Olfactoration of Goblins (BOoG), whose summary theory states that one goblin can pollute the atmosphere to the same effect as any larger number. Scientists who are interested in the phenomenon—colloquially referred to as BOoGers—have come to the Old Country from all over the world to study it.

Sloot reflexively hunched his shoulders against the cold as he left his meeting with Flavia through the particularly unremarkable door. Uncle's contractors had obviously put a lot of effort into making sure that it was completely unremarkable in every way. No further description is available, due to the excellent work that said contractors performed.

"What are you still doing here?" Myrtle asked.

"Myrtle! I—nothing!" Salzstadt was a big city, and the chances of running into any given person by chance were so astronomical as to be suspicious. The Ministry of Propaganda was very clear about that in their posters, which encouraged citizens involved in such coincidences to submit themselves to the Ministry of Conversation. Just to be on the safe side.

"You're being cagey," said Myrtle. She turned her face a bit, but kept her eyes on him. A classic sign of suspicion. "Did you just come out of the Inquisitorial Complex?"

On the off chance that it has been undersold to this point, Sloot Peril was no good at lying. He was only marginally better at keeping secrets, which was unusual, because secrets are nothing more than truths that dally in the darkness and ask their keepers to lie on their behalf. He hadn't told Myrtle that he'd been recruited into Uncle, and every passing moment made the lie seem all the more enormous and damaging. That meant that that particular moment, more so than any other up to that point, would have been the worst possible time to tell her.

"I—" Sloot began, having no idea where he'd end up.

"No, that's ridiculous," said Myrtle. "But what are you doing here? You should be halfway to Carpathia by now!"

"I just—"

"I felt you thinking about me, which was very sweet by the way, but then I figured out you were in the city."

"Well, I—"

"I tried teleporting to where you were, but I met with some resistance. I ended up standing in front of an unmarked door, which was weird. I have no way of knowing what's behind it, obviously."

"Obviously," said Sloot. Unbeknownst to the good folk of Salzstadt, dozens of nondescript doors in the city led into the ministries of Conversation, Information Defense, Scrutiny, and about a dozen others that could have you out of your home in the middle of the night, and under a very bright light in your pajamas before you could say "hang on a minute."

"Don't tell me you're scared," said Myrtle. "You're a ghost, remember? Nothing out there can hurt you."

"It's not that," said Sloot, then instantly wishing he hadn't. It would have been very convenient to have heard a bit of reassurance and been sent on his way again, perhaps even adding in a quick trip across the veil so they could have a kiss for good luck.

"What, then?"

"It's just ... Willie."

"What about Willie?"

"He's right over there." Sloot pointed at the specter of Willie, who was walking into some government building or another. The only people who would know what went on inside it were the people whose jobs provided them desks there. Even then, if you asked one of them, they'd probably say it was their first day and they weren't really qualified to answer that sort of question.

But the mystery of what might or might not be happening inside the building—or what Willie might be doing there—would have been eclipsed entirely in the mind of any bystanding statistician. As previously mentioned, chance encounters in Salzstadt were almost unheard of. Two within as many minutes were almost certainly a conspiracy.

"That's odd," said Myrtle. "What's Willie doing, going into government buildings?"

"I have no idea," said Sloot. *It's a convenient distraction, though.* "Should we follow him?"

"It's risky," said Myrtle. She was right. You didn't want to wander into the wrong government building unprepared. There were places like the Department of Conversions, where anyone guilty of any misdemeanor infraction against the Domnitor—long may he reign—could bypass the hassle of a trial and simply submit themselves for ten years in a labor camp in exchange for a clear record, no questions asked.

It should be emphasized that *not a single question* will be asked. The second a person walks in, they're seized by guards and processed. They'll find themselves performing some task integral to the production of root vegetables within the hour. The Department of Conversions should win the award for most efficient department every year, but the honor usually goes to Central Bureaucracy, where it takes forever to do just about anything; however, the lawyers who run the place won't be outdone by some jumped-up human cattle processors. It's surprisingly easy to threaten award committees with a lifetime of courtroom battles.

It should be noted that the aforementioned reference to "threatening award committees" has been stricken from the official record, and any further references to it will most likely land the referrer in a position to report themselves to the Department of Conversions. You have been threatened. Er, *warned*.

"He's been so volatile of late," said Sloot. "He could hurt someone if we don't keep an eye on him."

"I suppose," said Myrtle with a shrug. "I'm not picking up on any potential futures in which walking through that door gets us any more dead than we already are."

"Are you? Er, technically?"

"What, dead? Well, I died. I think that counts."

They walked as casually toward the door as a demon and a ghost could manage in broad daylight. Fortune favored them in the form of a pair of recently deceased old men. They'd collided with each other in a race to secure the last copy of the newspaper, and landed in a literal heap of limbs. They were shouting at each other about whose leg was whose, and each of them still had an arm firmly gripping the last copy of the Salzstadt Courier.

Sloot shook his head. He was glad for the distraction, but the Herald was the clearly superior periodical. They printed it on thicker paper, which meant additional uses in unmentionable capacities. He'd always felt bad for anyone he saw on their way into the lavatory with a copy of the Courier under their arm.

They wandered casually past the quarrel and its audience with no further scrutiny. Myrtle pulled the door open, wincing very mildly in anticipation of whatever unspeakable bureaucratic horror might be waiting within to ask her for permits within an inch of her life.

"Oh my," said Myrtle. Sloot caught a glimpse over her shoulder of a dozen or so men kneeling before Willie. He'd liked to have known what was going on, and had been on the verge of asking Myrtle what she thought that might have been, when he felt a familiar tug from behind his ear and was no longer there.

꙲ᛞ꙲ᛞ꙲ᛞ꙲ᛞ

"It's been a long time, Mr. Peril. Edmund?"

"Lengths of time having transpired between meetings which may or may not have occurred in the past, and any meeting which may or may not be happening at the present time, shall in no way be used to establish, in any legal sense, intentional associations between any parties who may or may not be in attendance."

Winking Bob cleared her throat.

"Furthermore," Edmund continued, "uses or alleged uses of any and all words, including but not limited to 'meetings, 'occurred,' 'attendance,' or 'time' shall not constitute an admission of guilt or acknowledgment of same."

"Thank you," said Winking Bob. "Now then, Mr. Peril, it seems as though you've been a busy little bee since you shuffled off the mortal coil. I'm curious to know, whose side are you actually on?"

If the option had been available, Sloot would have elected to plant himself firmly on the side that rejected the concept of sides altogether; however, he was as uncomfortable with the minor paradox that would have been created by that as he was with just about everything else he'd been up to since correcting Vasily Pritygud's disastrous financial report. So, at the very least, he could take some solace in the fact that he didn't have to think too hard about that. He'd have done it, too—taken solace, that is—if he weren't morally opposed to optimism.

"Cat got your tongue?"

"Altogether possible," said Sloot. "Roman's got the rest of my head, but I can't be sure that every little bit is still in it."

"Clever," said Bob with a wink. A little too on-the-nose for Sloot's taste, but then he wasn't really calling the shots. "You didn't answer my question."

Sloot had always chafed at that particular phrase. No, in fact, he hadn't! Was it outrageous to think that a "please" was in order? He'd never actually say that to a person, of course. Not because it wasn't the sort of thing said outside a retirement home, but because it sounded dangerously like standing his ground.

"My loyalty to the Domnitor is unwavering," said Sloot. "Long may he reign."

"Long may he reign!" Bob laughed. Sloot didn't care for her sarcastic tone, though to be fair, he hadn't really liked anything about his day thus far.

"You really are something, Peril," she continued. That's just the sort of thing that people say when they don't want to say anything in particular, but don't want anyone else in the room to be the one talking. "You were on your way to Carpathia when you got picked up by Uncle, and you've been doing the bidding of the Serpents of the Earth since before you died. Well, trying, anyway. But not very hard."

"I'd be doing a better job," said Sloot, suddenly feeling as though he might be the sort of person who stood up for himself, "if I didn't keep getting summoned by one person or another without notice."

"Use of the word 'person' by unrepresented parties present at meetings which may or may not be underway shall not be construed to represent any specific person, persons, person-like objects, or future or former persons who may or may not find themselves under indictment at any future juncture."

"Thank you, Edmund. Look, I'm going to come right out with it, because I have some people waiting to sell me a very large quantity of blood." She paused. "Or do I?"

Edmund drew in a breath. Sloot waved his hands madly.

"I waive my recollection of having heard anything from anyone, and if there was anything to be heard, I disavow ever having had ears."

"You should have been a lawyer," said Bob. Despite her approving tone, Sloot had a hard time thinking of it as a compliment. "I need you to tell me what you know, Peril. If you don't, I'll have to use this."

Sloot Peril was an accountant. As such, he'd have been hard-pressed to remember every document he'd ever seen in his life, or subsequent to it. This one, though, was special. He'd signed it himself the first time he'd met Winking Bob, as part of a negotiation to get him into Carpathia. He'd even memorized the contents, which had been quite easy, since it was a blank piece of paper.

Bob had a collection of papers exactly like it, most of which bore signatures of people far more powerful, impressive, and alive than Sloot was at the moment. At her convenience, she had confessions to just about anything she could concoct.

"Is that really necessary?" asked Sloot. "Or ... wait, is that even a credible threat? I'm dead! What can you do, have me posthumously thrown into the salt mines?"

"Apparently, you haven't been dead long enough to learn just how dire a threat that really is. No matter. No, Mr. Peril, while I could employ this document to your great detriment in a number of ways, whether you're alive or not, that's not its true value. Do you honestly not grasp the significance of a document signed by the financier of a Hapsgalt?"

Money is just bits of metal and paper, if you're being literal with wanton abandon. While Sloot appreciated literal interpretations of just about everything in nearly every context, he understood what Bob was getting at: money, metaphorically speaking, is power. Furthermore, having insanely immeasurable piles of power available means that one is able to hire someone else to manage said power for one, while one indulges in more amusing pursuits. Case in point, Sloot had managed Willie's finances while Willie had done little but be seen wearing fashion that had yet to trickle down to the unwashed masses and, in most cases, never would.

"I don't suppose it's worth pointing out that a dead man's signature is worth very little," said Sloot.

"It is not," said Bob. "In fact, I'd go so far as to say it's completely worthless, insofar as ghosts are ill-equipped at performing signatures. That's why whatever I write atop your signature will be easy to pass off as having been executed before your untimely demise. In fact, it will be far more believable than the truth."

"I'm confused."

"I'm not surprised."

"What is it you want from me, exactly? Am I to provide you with some incentive to put my signature back into your safe? I'm short on funds at the moment."

"No, no, I don't need any money. Well, not the sort to be had from anyone less than princes, anyway."

"So, you've already decided to use it? Have you called me here to gloat?"

"Colder."

Sloot went silent. He hated guessing, which was a standard trope with accountants.

"You're no fun," said Bob with the affectation of pouting disappointment. "I want information, Peril. Information is power, you know."

"I thought money was power."

"It is. Lots of things are power. Raw sewage can be power, if you've got a long enough hose and can point the nozzle at the right people."

"What sort of information?"

"The kidnapping," said Bob.

"The *alleged* kidnapping," said Edmund.

"Yes, the alleged kidnapping of the Domnitor."

"Long may he reign," said Sloot.

Bob rolled her eyes and chuckled. "If you say so."

"If you are *alleged* to have said so, at this or any future point in time, which may or may not—"

"Are you representing Mr. Peril now, Edmund?"

"Sorry. Habit."

"Well," said Bob with a sigh, "we very nearly got there on glib repartee alone, but such is life." She winced. "Sorry. Tell me everything you know about the plot to kidnap the Domnitor."

"Long may he reign."

"Stop that!"

"Habit. Look, all I know is that ... wait, what happens when I tell you everything I know?"

"Nothing."

"Nothing?"

"Nothing," Bob repeated. "Specifically, the paper bearing your signature doesn't turn up in the Counting House of the Three Bells Shipping Company, on the supervisors desk, attached to the uncorrected version of the report written by Vasily Pritygud, advising that the Hapsgalt fortune—which, officially, is now part of the Three Bells Trust—should be counted at the earliest convenience of the head financier."

"What? Why? That's just mean! You'd stand to gain nothing!"

"You really don't understand how evil works, do you?"

"The use of the word 'evil' in this context," Edmund droned, "is set forth in an uncopyrighted and non-specific context to illustrate the intent of certain threats, or innuendos alluding to the delivery of such."

"I got that," said Sloot. "I don't think that any lawyers within earshot would try to use that, of all things, as leverage in court."

Edmund turned to look at Winking Bob. "You were right, He really doesn't understand how evil works."

"I forge your approval of that report," said Bob, "and financial markets will crumble under the uncertainty associated with the outcome. Sure, the end result will show that you were wrong, but that will take months."

Vasily was wrong, Sloot fumed silently. He'd never so much as misbalanced a column in his life.

"By the time it gets sorted out, the economy will be in flames."

"Figuratively speaking," Edmund offered.

"Tell that to the grocers," said Bob. "I'll never understand the unwashed masses' affinity for throwing flaming cabbages, but at the first sign of trouble, the price of cabbage goes through the roof. Fiscal chaos brings out the worst in people. Anyway, once they figure it all out, the first thing to happen will be the posthumous revocation of your credentials. Your name will be chiseled into the stone of the Wall of Heretics next to Jerry the Newsboy."

Jerry the Newsboy, according to the official record, had said a swear word—the one that the elderly insist is shouted at least three times in every song written more recently than their fiftieth birthday—in reference to the Domnitor's mother, long may her son reign. As to the question of whether it was true, well ... his name was on the wall, wasn't it?

"And to top it all off," Bob continued, "since I control the timing, I'll make a fortune."

"How's that?"

"I own all of the cabbage farms in the Old Country."

The shame! It didn't matter that he'd never get an accounting job in the Old Country again, of course. But to see his name on the wall, and to go down in history as the worst accountant the world has ever seen? He simply couldn't let that happen.

"You'd really send the economy into ruin for cabbage prices?"

"Not for that alone," said Bob. "I've got other interests that align as well, but that's none of your concern."

"Fine," said Sloot. "There's a plot to kidnap the Domnitor, long may he reign, from his home in exile in Stagralla. There, I've tattled. Would you like to gloat now, or wait until I leave?"

"Easy, Peril. It's good you've decided to cooperate, I knew you were a smart man. Now, tell me everything you know."

"Er, well, I have."

Silence.

"Is that how you thank me for saying you're smart?"

"It's how I tell the truth."

"Do you think you're the first person to try and bluff their way out of my debt? Come now, Peril. If we're going to insult each other, I'll have you crying in minutes."

"Look, I understand that it's not a lot—"

"It's nothing! You've told me literally nothing, Peril. You've barely regurgitated what I told you!"

"You didn't know he was in Stagralla."

"If I didn't know where the Domnitor was—don't you dare—I wouldn't be who I am today. I've known the Domnitor's whereabouts—I'm warning you—since before he was born. You know something I don't, whether you know it or not."

Long may he reign, Sloot thought to himself. *Long may he reign.*

⚡☞ DATING ☜⚡

It was a long time before Winking Bob was satisfied that Sloot was telling the truth about knowing next to nothing. Well, *satisfied* is probably the wrong word. A long time before she'd decided to accept disappointment, then.

Probably. Even setting aside that Sloot could perceive the passage of time in the Narrative, there were no windows in Bob's black market meeting rooms. No clocks either.

However long it had been, and to whatever degree Bob had reconciled acceptance and disappointment, she eventually dismissed Sloot. He went home to the Hereafter, and that's when things got really weird; or, rather, they didn't. Whatever Sloot had expected to see oozing, writhing, or exploding from the house as a result of Willie's latest failure to control himself, it simply wasn't there.

Typical, Sloot thought. He hadn't been looking forward to dealing with a new and terrifying manifestation of evil, but he'd have been comforted by the predictability. If human beings were creatures of habit, Sloot Peril had been the clock by which everyone else could measure their routines. An anthropologist would describe the Sloot as a pale mammal who panicked at the thought of being removed from the rut it had painstakingly worn for itself throughout the course of its life.

"What's going on here?" asked Sloot, who was partially relieved upon entering the house to find Willie pinned into a corner near the ceiling, spitting fire and shadow and smoke from his razor-sharp, bestial maw. Nicoleta's hands were contorted with the magical effort of keeping him there. Bartleby was standing with his back to hers, hands similarly contorted, pinning Nan in an opposite corner.

"Hello, Sloot," said Nicoleta without looking up. "Be a dear and see what's keeping Myrtle, would you?"

"You turn him loose!" shouted Nan. She was holding a broom, which was an odd thing for a ghost to be doing, and brandishing it at Bartleby.

"It's for his own good," said Bartleby. "You have to have noticed that Villie isn't himself at the moment."

"You're scaring him! He's only a six-year-old boy!"

"Vhat?"

"It's a long story," said Sloot, leaving off the part that he had no idea how it came to pass, and hoped that he could rely on the urgency of the situation to prevent him being asked to speak any further on the topic.

"She's working on the circle," said Nicoleta, with a measure of urgency.

"Right," said Sloot. He floated hurriedly away.

"Keep it down in there!" Constantin had wheeled himself into the hallway. There was plenty of room to go around him, but even in his withered state he cast an imposing figure that Sloot could not bring himself to ignore.

"Er, sorry, Lord Hapsgalt," he said, bowing several times in rapid succession, in an apparent attempt to toady as efficiently as possible. "Just dealing with some … noise."

"I'll say," said Constantin. "I can barely hear the Quietus over that racket!"

"No one can *hear* the Quietus," Sloot couldn't stop himself from saying. "Er, present company excluded, of course."

Constantin smirked. "Exceptional hearing in Hapsgalt men," he said. "I once bagged a lion on the veldt in the middle of a moonless night because I could hear its whiskers twitching. Thought it was going to eat *me*, the bugger! It came down to fisticuffs in the end. I pulled off one of its haunches and beat it to death! Ruined the pelt, of course, but it's kill or be killed in the wild. That reminds me of my first romance. Tough as nails, she was, living in a cave north of—"

"Sloot!" shouted Nicoleta. "I can't hold out much longer!"

"The nerve!" shouted Constantin. "Why I ought to—"

"I'll deal with it, m'lord!" Sloot closed his eyes and floated as swiftly past Constantin as he could. The fact that the old man continued to rail on in the absence of an audience did surprisingly little to quell Sloot's queasiness.

"Sloot!" shouted Myrtle, who was adding an extra layer of runes to the outside of the circle. "Where did you go? What happened?"

"Later," said Sloot, who was less relieved for the excuse to avoid an uncomfortable conversation now, and more nauseated at the prospect of having to have it eventually. "Nicoleta's having trouble with Willie, she asked me to come and find you."

"Just finishing up," said Myrtle. She drew a sigil with her finger that resembled two lawyers fighting to the death over nothing at all. So, two lawyers.

"Where did you learn how to do that?"

"Later," said Myrtle, the same look of uncomfortable relief washing over her as well. "Can you lure Willie in here?"

"I'm not sure I'm suited to it." Sloot had never been fishing, but he was familiar with the concept, and he knew what happened to the worms.

"Come on," said Myrtle, "he listens to you! Just talk about something he likes."

"He likes money," said Sloot, "but I'm not supposed to bring that up around him." In life, Willie's family had amassed the sort of wealth that didn't need to be counted, and as such were offended when conversations about finances turned serious. People in his position didn't want to know anything about interest rates, they just wanted to know that they couldn't make it to the bottom of their piles of money if they tried.

The last time Sloot had tried to talk to Willie about money, the estate had just been burgled. He'd had to stop talking about what Willie could and could not "afford" so that he could explain what "afford" meant. Roman had staved off the resulting tantrum, but only just. Sloot had resolved then and there to refrain from ever broaching the subject with Willie again.

"Try fashion!" Myrtle was having to shout over the rumbling sound that was overtaking the house. She sounded desperate and frustrated, a combination of emotions that Sloot had first experienced at the hands of his elementary school soccer coach, who'd nearly had a nervous breakdown over his failure to explain the concept of sport to young Sloot. In the end, Sloot had been allowed to take extra math courses instead of playing outside during recess. All involved were pleased with that outcome.

"I don't know anything about fashion."

There was a scream from the other room. It sounded like Nicoleta.

"Just do it!" Myrtle shouted, her eyes starting to glow.

"Oh my," shouted Sloot, "would you look at the double-stitching on this waistcoat!"

The walls started to boil. Grasping hands reached out from them. Sloot recoiled from the dragon that stormed into the room. It had three heads, each of them Willie's.

"Show unto me the waistcoat," said two of the dragon's heads, while the third scorched the ceiling with a gout of flame. "My darkness is eternal, and I shall not be denied!"

"Very good, m'lord," said Sloot from beneath a well-formed cower. "We can have it here in a moment. Would you like to tell me about your favorite sock-and-shoe combinations while we wait?"

"But yea, did the words of thy voice sing to me from yonder room," said all three of Willie's heads. "Lo did they beckon, for the waistcoat was thine to behold, and thou didst call its stitching good!"

Myrtle mouthed a word to Sloot that was either "stall" or a particularly nasty swear word that implied shared ownership of one's livestock with an uncle who wasn't quite right in the head. She appeared to have noticed a rune that wasn't quite right, and was frantically making it look less like a fox who'd been accused of embezzlement and more like a fox who'd been served the wrong breakfast.

"Quite right, m'lord, quite right," said Sloot. "Only I found a flaw under the armpit and sent it away to be corrected. I wouldn't want to ... offend thine ... eyes! With its ... blasphemy?"

"Thou servest me well, lowly drudge," Willie growled. He gnashed his teeth and flapped his wings. "Lo! I shall await in this place the return of the waistcoat which is prophesied! Now, cower thee in despair as I recite unto thee my commandments on clothing the foot! Never shalt thou commit the heinous blasphemy of open-toed sandals! And thrice be my condemnation upon the head of he whose depravity weareth such with sock or stocking, no matter the season! And in the months of snow upon the ground, though loafers lie in temptation upon the shoe racks of summer, wear them not upon pain of—"

There was a whooshing sound, accompanied by the screaming of a multitude of tortured souls as Willie was pulled into the circle by a shimmering vortex. He coughed.

"Hey, no fair!" said Willie. He scanned the edge of the circle, and then stamped his foot in frustration. "It's almost like you don't want me to leave the circle."

"Aha!" shouted Constantin. Nan went shooting past the door in the hallway, and Constantin went wheeling after her. "I've got you now, you filthy coddler!" He followed that with several slurs that would prompt anyone younger to cringe and point out that he was from a different time.

"You nearly killed me," said Nicoleta, who'd have been sweating if the dead could manage that sort of thing.

"You're already dead," said Willie. Nicoleta's inner turmoil was apparent from the quivering, pained expression on her face. Being casually corrected by an utter nitwit was not the sort of thing she had to cope with on a regular basis, and the effort was a strain on what little strength remained in her at that moment. Were she still alive, a long hot bath would have been the preferred remedy.

"That was far too close," said Myrtle. She didn't quite shout, but she got as close to it as one reasonably might without being shushed in polite company.

"Yes, it was," said Grumley, who seemed to have snuck into the room when no one was looking. "Fine bit of work there, Peril, managing Lord Hapsgalt all by yourself while your staff did their little bit!"

"Our little bit?" Nicoleta balked.

"His staff?" Myrtle did as well. They both floated there with their hands at their hips and mouths open, aghast at the rather severe devaluation of their contributions to the derring-do. Or, to put it another way, their having handled it entirely.

"Thanks, but—" Sloot began.

"But nothing," said Grumley. "I had you pegged as a slouch, Peril. I was here to relieve you of your post, but this changes things a bit."

"A bit?"

"A bit," said Grumley, with the sort of edge in his voice that made it plain he doesn't like repeating himself. "Look, I can't simply clear the slate because you've had one good day. Consistency, Peril! That's what we're looking for."

"Who's that?" asked Willie.

"That'll be Mr. Grumley, m'lord," Sloot explained.

"Just Grumley," said Grumley. "We didn't do 'misters' in my day. That's new, and I'm not one for things that are new."

"It's not that new," said Willie. He leaned against the invisible barrier that the circle now maintained. His sleeve caught fire, but he didn't seem to notice.

"Oh, sure," said Grumley, "not to you hip young people. Pity you weren't around for the Renaissance, or you'd know better. Everyone was a duke, a knight of the realm, at least three Orders of the Something-or-Other, and a notary to boot. Did away with all of that during the Tidy Reformation, didn't we?"

Sloot nodded. Having studied history with fanatic devotion, he knew that the Old Country has gone through a Renaissance, an Enlightenment, roughly a dozen Reformations, and a single Dark Age that started right after the Later Antiquity, and is due to end any day now.

"'Sirs' and 'madams' is where that all got started," Grumley huffed. "Mark my words, it's only a matter of time before you can't say hello to someone in under half an hour without offending them."

"Oh dear," said Sloot.

"It vasn't that bad," said Bartleby, who'd come in with Nicoleta. "The vitch burnings, now those vere bad."

"Serves 'em right," Grumley spat. "Anyone goes around wearing that much black is up to no good."

"Hear, hear," said Willie. "What's wrong with a splash of color, unless you're going to one of the fancy parties where everyone in the Serpents is wearing all black, and they bring in the ladies wearing all white, and then there's chanting, and then you never see them again?"

"Ooo, sounds vicked," said Bartleby.

"That's enough, Lord Hapsgalt," said Grumley, as politely as possible. "We are standing among the uninitiated, you know."

"What? I don't think so."

Grumley was right, of course. He and Willie were the only two people in the room who were members of the Serpents of the Earth, as far as Sloot was aware. Bartleby wasn't wearing one of their silver rings, two snakes coiled around a black stone, but it was the Hereafter, after all. Maybe necromancers had to remove their jewelry before they crossed over.

"There's a place for you, of course," said Grumley, turning to look at Sloot.

"For me?"

"If you play your cards right," said Grumley, mistaking Sloot's revulsion at the thought of taking on additional loyalties for the excitement he'd expected. "But you're going to have to keep a firmer hand on things around here."

"Er, okay."

"You're a capable young ghost, Peril. And you seem to have hired some decent servants here. You just may prove yourself yet."

"Now just hang on a minute," said Myrtle, who'd technically been a servant of the household at one point in her life, but was now a demon capable of making bargains where souls were the currency. Being called a servant by a ghost who probably amounted to a month's salary was sure to rankle.

"An excellent point," said Willie, who was now wearing a top hat with a crown in place of the hat band. "Have one of the servants stand in the circle for me, would you? I've got dinner reservations."

"You've got to stay in the circle, m'lord." Sloot smiled and bowed, hoping that Willie wouldn't break through the circle's barrier and devour him, or something worse. It could definitely be something worse. He could give Sloot additional duties, perhaps delivering in-depth evaluations of haircuts to people he had to see every day.

"But what about my dinner reservations?"

"The dead don't dine," said Grumley. "Take my word for it. I haven't done since I keeled over in my soup."

"You were poisoned?" asked Sloot.

"Stabbed," said Grumley. "Although now that you mention it, I don't know for certain that I *wasn't* poisoned. The knife may simply have beaten it to the punch. Well, that'll haunt me for a while."

"Sorry."

"No matter. Keep up the good work, Peril." And with that, Grumley disappeared in a puff of smoke.

"You've got some nerve, Peril!" Nicoleta's hands were still on her hips.

"I honestly don't think that's true," he replied. Sloot had once tried to work up the nerve to tell his mother that the other boys were being mean to him at school. He was very fond of tattling, thanks to a series of puppet shows put on by the Ministry of Propaganda. They insisted that tattling was the most fun a young person could have, but in this case, he'd decided against it. His mother was Sladia Peril, after all. She'd have made him stand up for himself, or worse: gone to school and stood up for him. That was just the sort of thing that parents went in for, protecting their children from harm to the severe detriment of their standing in the social hierarchy. The bottom tier of said hierarchy was composed entirely of mama's boys, kids who read for pleasure during recess, and that one weird kid who ate his own boogers.

Sloot didn't need any further social ostracism. Even the booger kid would've stopped talking to him.

"It's not important," said Myrtle. "Sloot's in enough trouble with Mister Grum— with *Grumley*. Let him have this one."

"Oh, fine," said Nicoleta. "But it's the principle of the matter, you know?"

"I know," said Sloot. "I'm terribly sorry."

"You'll find a way to make it up to me," said Nicoleta. No, not said. Directed.

"Yes ma'am," said Sloot.

Without another word, Myrtle took Sloot by the hand and led him from the room. She didn't have to say anything, of course. Sloot was less of a "what's going on here" sort of person, and more of an "excuse me, I'm terribly sorry" sort, who'd apologize for having left his foot where you wanted to step.

"Start talking," said Myrtle. She wheeled on him as soon as they were alone, hands on her hips.

"I'm sorry, I ... what? I'm, I'm, I'm—no, that's not it—you see, when it comes down to ... oh, dear—"

Myrtle sighed aloud. Her arms crossed in front of her, and she looked at him with a combination of annoyance, pity, and affection that was generally reserved for adorable wittle puppy-wuppies who'd just savaged an expensive shoe. He was making the eyes and everything.

"Your adorable befuddlement won't get you out of it this time," said Myrtle, her expression twisting to remain as mad at him as she could. "Every time I turn around, you're gone! Where have you been disappearing to?"

Sloot groaned. It bought him enough time to fight the urge to correct her grammar. Whether she knew the rule about ending sentences with prepositions or not, now wasn't the time to bring it up. Sure, it might make for a welcome distraction, but in the end it would just make her angrier.

"Roman's got my head," said Sloot, reaching for the easy truth to get him going.

"I know about that," said Myrtle, "but there's more, isn't there?"

Sloot nodded.

"Don't think," said Myrtle, "just blurt it out. What's the worst of it? What are you afraid to tell me?"

Sloot whimpered.

"You're thinking! What did I tell you? Just blurt, you fool!"

"I'm working for Uncle!" Sloot cried, his eyes shut as though he were preparing for a run through a haunted house at a carnival. It was braver than it sounded, given that the one time that very thing had happened before, a nine-year-old Sloot had run into a wall and knocked himself out.

"You're joking." Myrtle's eyes went wide.

"When have I ever?"

Myrtle gasped. "You're working for Uncle!"

"Keep your voice down!"

"You *would* say that. How long have you been living a double life?"

To Sloot's great detriment, he paused. By itself, that might have gone unnoticed; however, never having been one to quit while he was ahead, Sloot also broke eye contact with Myrtle and looked at the floor.

"Wait a minute," said Myrtle, who didn't have to be a prescient demon to have seen that Sloot had more to confess. "Sloot?"

"Er, hello," said Sloot.

"There's *more*?"

"Winking Bob," said Sloot. He'd never told her about the paper he'd had to sign for her, the one that got the Carpathian expedition rolling. It had been far more trouble than it had been worth, especially in hindsight.

"Ironic, that," said Myrtle, after Sloot had finished explaining.

"How's that?"

"I orchestrated the burgling of Whitewood to get out from under Winking Bob's thumb. If I hadn't, you'd never have needed to bargain with her, and you wouldn't be under her thumb now."

Sloot said nothing. He'd gotten special permission to skip literature classes and take more mathematics, so he was entirely unqualified to judge what was irony and what wasn't.

"I'm sorry about that," she said.

"No, I am," said Sloot, whose prowess with accepting apologies was non-existent. He had one of those faces that could take the apology right out of your mouth, turn it into an argument, and lose to it in seconds.

"It doesn't matter now. We've got to find a way to get you free of some of your fetters."

"Fetters?"

"If I'm all caught up," said Myrtle, "you're an intelligence agent on both sides of the cold war between the Old Country and Carpathia. You're being drawn into competing plots by Uncle, Winking Bob, Mrs. Knife, and Roman to kidnap the Domnitor, long may he reign, to whom you're still loyal thanks to a lifetime of propaganda. Your girlfriend is a demon, your employer is an uncontrollable vessel of dark magic, and if you're unable to control his power—having no means of doing so, of course—you'll be thrown into the Well of the Void to be tortured for an eternity. And to top it all off, you're grinning like an idiot! How can you be so amused by all of this?"

"So ... you *are* my girlfriend?" Ghosts do not blush, but that didn't stop Sloot's cheeks from becoming a more pronounced shade of translucent grey. He grinned from ear to ear, which was exhausting, unfamiliar as he was with the maneuver.

"Well, yes," said Myrtle. She clasped her hands in front of her. Her head shrank down into her shoulders, and she stared at the floor where her foot was idly drawing a shape. It's worth noting that said shape, when drawn in blood on the flank of a bovine sacrifice to the Arch-Demon of the Hell of Ritual Boredom—whose name consisted entirely of consonants, and qualified as a swear word in every language—would cause everyone who looked upon it to descend into a cackling madness from which there was no return. Those sorts of things come naturally to demons, who are no more capable of performing any truly random act than they are of drinking holy water and not spending the following century with a hangover.

"I just didn't know if you still wanted me to be," Myrtle continued. "You know, since I'm a demon now and all."

"I'm a ghost," said Sloot. "I didn't know ghosts got to have girl-friends. I thought maybe that was just for the living."

"Of course you do! At least, I think so. Being in a couple isn't a gov-ernment appointment or anything. No forms to fill out."

"Oh, dear," said Sloot.

"What is it?"

"Uncle! They know about you! They know you're a demon!"

"I wouldn't worry about that," said Myrtle. "I can do a lot more to the living than they can do to me! Er, not that I *would*, of course. I'm not an *evil* demon. I don't think."

"Is there another kind?"

Myrtle's brow furrowed into a very hurt expression. "You think I'm evil?"

"No! Er, probably not. Right?"

"Is that why you're avoiding the question?"

"Sorry, what question?"

"Do you want me to be your girlfriend or not?"

"I thought that went without saying," said Sloot.

"Well, it doesn't!"

"Oh. Well, then. Yes, please. I want you to be my girlfriend."

It may have been the scariest thing he'd ever said in his life, or whatever. Sloot wasn't one for taking risks, and although he had every reason to believe that it would go well, he still harbored more than a reasonable measure of apprehension. Fortunately, she started grinning as well, and threw her arms around him. They floated there, hugging and grinning like a couple of teenagers, one of whom was dead, and the other a demon. It was still very nice.

"Thanks for that," said Sloot. "While we were talking about our relationship, I'd forgotten that dark shadows loom over me from every direction, and that I'm an inch away from utter calamity and ruin every which way I turn."

"Ever the romantic," said Myrtle, rolling her eyes in a way that was only annoyed in the way that kittens feign annoyance for bits of string being dragged across the floor.

"Sorry," said Sloot, predictably. "Hopefully it'll be a while before I'm remanded to the Well of the Void for an eternity of anguish."

"Not much better."

"Sorry."

"It's fine," said Myrtle. "You do have a lot on your mind."

"There has to be a way out of it. Hasn't there?"

"Oh, yes," said Myrtle with surprising assurance. She looked more surprised than he did, her eyes going wide after she'd said it.

"Myrtle?"

"Amazing," said Myrtle, breathlessly.

"What is it?"

"I can tell you how to fix it!"

Sloot had never stared directly at optimism before, but this time he was sorely tempted. "Which part?"

"All of it," said Myrtle, who seemed as incredulous as Sloot. "I think I get it now."

"At least one of us does." Sloot had yet to completely wrap his head around the concept of death, and had not entirely given up on the hope that it could all be cleared up by a good night's sleep.

"I'm a causality demon," said Myrtle. "I can see multiple possible futures hanging off the ends of things that happen. Even something that seems insignificant now can lead to something big later on."

"I think I understand," said Sloot. "So what did you see? Did I turn to the left in a way that will ultimately restore the Domnitor to the throne, long may he reign?" Sloot didn't need logic to know that everything would be all right as soon as the Domnitor was in charge of everything again. Long may he reign.

"Not exactly," said Myrtle. She went quiet, her eyes scanning the room as though she were reading billboards that weren't there. "Oh, dear."

"What is it? Is the Domnitor in danger, long may he reign?"

"Forget about the Domnitor for a minute," said Myrtle. She may as well have asked him to stop breathing, which was a poor metaphor, given the circumstances. "This goes beyond my regular powers. It's a bigger one."

"How many powers do you get?"

Myrtle thought for a moment. "Eight hundred and nineteen, but this is bigger than almost all of them. It's more than reading causality from passing events. I can see into the future! More than that, I can give you the answers you need. I can tell you how to fix all of this. It's guaranteed!"

Optimism shook the foundations of the house. The floors positively thrummed with hope and relief. Sloot didn't see any reason why he shouldn't—

"But there's a price."

All right, *now* he saw it.

"There always is," said Sloot. Dread loomed at his heels, but he still wasn't ready to give up on optimism yet.

"You'll have to give me your soul."

Sloot's optimism made a weak pop before it fizzled. He could briefly feel the warmth that it had left, but it dissipated quickly. It was colder now than it ever had been before.

"What?"

"That's it, just your soul."

"I'm your boyfriend! Aren't I? I thought that you being my girlfriend implied that, though perhaps I'm wrong about that."

"No, no, you're definitely my boyfriend," said Myrtle, with a hint of a smile that would have been adorable outside the present context. "It's just ... there are rules."

"Demon rules?"

Myrtle nodded. "I can't use my really big power for free. The rules are pretty clear on this, actually."

"But this is my life we're talking about! Well, existence, I mean."

"Shh!"

"Are you doing existentialism in here?" asked Arthur, his head poking in from around the corner.

"No!" shouted Sloot and Myrtle in unison.

"Are you sure? It really seemed like there was about to be a conversation about the ephemeral nature of existence in here."

"Only insofar as it pertains to the role of manual labor in industrialized society," said Sloot.

"Oh," said Arthur, wrinkling his nose. "Carry on." He floated away, as far from talk of manual labor as his disembodied spirit would take him.

"That was good thinking," said Myrtle.

"Thanks," said Sloot, who was hoping he'd have one more moment of inspiration in him. With his continued existence on the line, he hated to think he'd spent his one on getting out of a conversation with Arthur. That was just the sort of thing over which he'd agonize in the Well of the Void for the better portion of eternity.

"Talk to me," said Myrtle.

"What?"

"Talk to me, I said."

"I know what you said, but about what?"

"I don't know," said Myrtle. She fidgeted. "You're my boyfriend now. That just seems like the sort of thing I'm supposed to say to you."

"Oh," said Sloot. It did nothing to abate his bewilderment at the concept.

"Are you upset?" she asked.

"Er, probably," said Sloot. "I usually am."

"I mean, particularly. Just now."

"Do I seem upset? Particularly?"

"A bit more than usual, yes."

"Oh, well I can't imagine why," said Sloot in a tone so sarcastic it hurt his own feelings. "I'm sorry, I guess I really am upset."

"What for?"

"You're demanding my soul in exchange for the answers to my problems! I thought that since you were my girlfriend, you might just help me out. I'd certainly do your taxes without charging you."

"I told you, the rules are clear on this sort of thing," said Myrtle. "I have to trade for your soul."

Sloot gave Myrtle and imploring look. He searched the deep, grey pools of her eyes for pity, or compassion, or even some hint that she was playing a cruel joke, and would laugh at any moment and say she'd only been kidding. But nothing like that was in there. Not one iota of humor about it, only the steadfast sort of determination that Sloot applied to the practice of accounting. No room for frivolity there.

"Oh," said Sloot. If the word had been a handshake, it could have cost him an unopposed election.

"Talk to me," she said again. That was when he saw it.

"You really don't know why that's upsetting, do you?"

"Why what's upsetting?"

"You're demanding my soul!"

"I'm not *demanding* anything," said Myrtle. "It's just the rules, that's all. A full causality workup costs one soul."

Sloot sighed. He chalked it up to demonic nature. Some sort of wall in the mind that kept their hearts out of their business acumen.

"All right, then."

"I'm sorry?"

"My soul. You can have it."

"Brilliant! I'll pop over to the Narrative and get it all sorted out. I'll come and find you when I'm ready. Bye, darling!"

She gave him a peck on the cheek and disappeared in a gout of flame. Sloot put a lot of work into ignoring all of the thoughts that probably should have been running through his head at the moment, electing to wonder instead whether he did gouts of flame or puffs of smoke when he disappeared from places.

No. It was no good. Sloot was a worrier at heart, and he'd just pledged his immortal soul to his demonic girlfriend in exchange for a chance at evading the annihilation that stalked him from the gathering shadows. "Do I look cool when I disappear?" simply wouldn't be sufficient to stave off the ponderance that his real problems demanded.

He floated off in search of a bed. He hadn't slept since he died, but he didn't imagine that the Hereafter would be so intentionally cruel as to deny him a good lie down.

⇒⊱⇝ETERNAL BOREDOM⇜⊰⇐

The dead do not sleep, exceptions being made for ancient horrors dwelling in blackened voids beyond the stars. But the ultimate destruction of the universe and all who dwell within it is a subject for another time. Suffice it to say that neither Sloot nor any of his contemporaries in the Hereafter needed sleep. Nevertheless, there were beds in the Hereafter. The house was silly with them, in fact.

The problem was that none of them seemed to belong to Sloot.

One might suppose that he could have simply lied down in any of them, but keep in mind that this was Sloot Gefahr Peril. The concept of ownership was very important to Sloot, and abiding by it was the best defense in the war on awkwardness. Imagine if someone were to walk in on him and say "hey, what are you doing in my bed?" While there were undoubtedly people in the world who could simply explain that it was a misunderstanding and have a good laugh about it, none of them were Sloot Peril.

He might've been able to have a conversation about it when they'd all just arrived, but that was a long time ago now. Probably. Though he didn't know precisely how long it had been, it had certainly been long enough that he was now afraid to ask.

In lieu of a lie-down, Sloot opted instead to go for a nice walk. He was nearly dissuaded by an inner voice that said "but what if somebody needs me here?"

Nice try, Sloot thought in retort. At this point, he was acquainted with as many people who could summon him at will as not, so his presence or absence was neither here nor there, no pun intended. Sloot was always eager to avoid inner monologue, as he could never say for sure with whom he was speaking. His own conscience, presumably, but his girlfriend had been possessed for most of her life, hadn't she? What if he was too, and his possessor was just more subtle about it?

Not worth the risk, he thought. He'd nearly made it to the front door before he was distracted by a pitiful moaning from the other end of the house. He shook his head and resolved to ignore it, or at least thought that he had. After a brief interlude, during which his memory went all fuzzy, he found himself standing inches from the circle and staring into Willie's eyes.

"That's it," said Willie, "just a bit closer."

"Oh, no you don't!" Nan grabbed Sloot by the ear, gave it a firm twist, and walked him back half a dozen paces.

"Ow!" he said. It hadn't actually hurt, but he instinctively went along with the Agreement.

"You can play with Willie if you want," said Nan, madly waggling a finger at Sloot, "but you need to keep an arm's length from the circle. My wittle Willikins has been a very naughty boy."

"Have not," said Willie. His serpentine eyes glowed and pulsed. All six of them.

"Don't you start!" said Nan, rounding on Willie so quickly that the waggle she'd started with Sloot moved on to him without missing a beat. "You tried to eat Mr. Bartleby!"

"No, I didn't."

"He vasn't going to manage it," said Bartleby. He and Nicoleta were in the adjoining room, playing with little wisps of darkness. They chased each other across the floor, pausing occasionally to lurch into the shapes of strange sigils that Sloot wasn't able to read. Nevertheless, he got the feeling that they were saying hurtful things about him.

"Oh, yeah?" said Willie. He puffed up his chest and his eyes burst into flame. "I could devour you any time I want, foolish mortal! You weren't supposed to jump out of the way."

"You'd rather I stood still and vaited for you to devour me?"

Willie's snake eyes caught fire as they darted back and forth. His expression went incredulous. "Yes, I thought that was obvious. Whatever, you're boring me with your mortal foolishness. I want to talk to Sloot now."

"Bevare, Mr. Peril," said Bartleby, using his cape to cover the bottom half of his face for dramatic effect. "Villie is trying to devour people today."

"So I've heard," said Sloot.

"Don't listen to him," said Willie. "Listen to me! I'm your employer, after all. I insist that you come inside the circle at once."

To Sloot's abject horror, he didn't hesitate to obey. He was within an inch of the circle when Nan grasped him firmly by the ear and yanked hard.

"Ow!" said Sloot. "Couldn't you grab my shoulders or something?"

"Not how it's done," said Nan. "If you'd been caring for children as long as I have, you'd know that there's nothing for it like a good twist of the ear."

"How old do you think I am?"

Nan scoffed. "Too old to be best friends with a six-year-old, if you ask me."

"I'm not—"

"Sloot," said Willie in an especially sibilant voice. It echoed in a sickly sweet sort of way, as though it had been spoken by a dozen snakes in unison.

"Yes, m'lord?"

"Come here," Willie demanded.

"Yes, m'lord. Ow!"

"I can do this all day," said Nan.

"She's here somewhere!" Constantin was shouting from the hallway. "I just heard her, I know I did!"

"Got to run," said Nan, turning to flee in the other direction. "Stay out of the circle!"

"Don't listen to her," said Willie. "Come in here at once, or I will visit such nightmares upon you as to make you beg for the sweet release from death!"

That was lucky, thought Sloot. The "or" gave him a choice, and inflicting nightmares upon someone as congenitally fearful as Sloot was about as effective as hurling thimblefuls of water into the ocean.

"I'll take my chances out here, m'lord."

Willie collapsed to the floor in a heap. Sloot had seen some of Willie's worst tantrums begin with this maneuver, and feared that they were in for a big one.

"It's so *boring* in the circle," Willie moaned. "They don't give you chocolates or clowns to make you balloon animals or *anything*!"

"That sounds dreadful, m'lord."

"It is! You have to *do* something about it! I swear on my life that if I don't get a birthday party in the next five minutes, I'm going to hold my breath until I die!"

"You're already dead, m'lord."

"I don't follow," said Willie, suddenly very deadpan. He stood up.

"That is to say ... well, you cannot die, m'lord."

"Says who?" Willie put his hands on his hips and tapped his cloven hoof agitatedly on the ground. Sparks danced across the floor. "It's just typical, you know? People always love telling their extremely wealthy betters what they can and can't do. Makes me sick, I don't mind telling you. Who do they think they are, real people?"

"Vhat?" Bartleby looked truly perplexed.

"Don't ... mind ... him," said Nicoleta slowly, without taking her eyes off of her little wisps of darkness.

"Oh, yes you will," said Constantin, who'd wheeled his way into the room. "He's a Hapsgalt, by gum! What's more, he's the son of the Soul of the Serpent, and next in line for that!"

"I thought Villie *vas* the Soul," said Bartleby.

"That's just the kind of dim-witted lack of vision I'd expect from a man in that much eyeliner," said Constantin. "Have you ever killed a man, sir?"

"Never had to," said Bartleby with a shrug. "Plenty of dead ones just lying around."

"Dad, make Sloot come over here and release me from the circle!"

"That's enough simpering out of you. You're a Hapsgalt! Be a man, do it yourself!"

The floor rumbled. The new sigils that Myrtle had placed around the outer edge of the circle glowed in a way that made them seem perturbed. Willie snarled from several different mouths at once, which was probably a very normal thing for a shapeless horror from the Void Whence Nightmares Come, but that didn't make it any less unnerving.

"Sloot," several of the mouths barked in unison.

"Yes, m'lord?" would have been the cool, collected sort of thing that Sloot would later fantasize about having said, but did not. He settled instead for screaming several octaves higher than he'd ever been able to do with the limitations of mortal vocal cords, and curled up into a little ball on the floor.

"You've been very naughty, Sloot." A pair of glowing eyes glowered at him from among the many mouths.

"S-s-sorry, m'lord!" he managed to squeak.

"That's more like it," said Constantin.

"Vicked," said Bartleby, eyes going all moony at Willie.

"Just when I'd gotten the hang of these," said Nicoleta. She waved her hand and the little wisps of shadow slinked off to join up with larger shadows elsewhere in the room. If Sloot had been less sufficiently terrified at the moment, he'd have had a good worry about whether they could come after him later, when no one else was looking.

"You vere doing great," said Bartleby. "Vhy did you stop?"

"Why did I stop plinking out *Maris Had a Little Goblin* while you were gawking over *Wicked Willie*, the Maestro of Darkness?"

"Now hang on a minute," said Willie and Bartleby in unison. Sloot knew what was coming next: an argument. They usually made him uncomfortable, but the distraction was well-timed. All he wanted was a quick lie-down to decide which of the dozen or so things in his worry queue would get first crack at sending him into hysterics.

That was ridiculous, of course. Sloot's spiritual ulcer was wide enough for all of his woes to link arms and dance through full can-can, with room besides for a buffet table. The can-can was hungry work. Still, the only thing worse for the nerves than dwelling on his problems was avoiding them, so Sloot took advantage of the argument that had broken out and slipped out of the house.

He just wanted a nice lie-down. The only place he managed to find any peace and quiet was in the graveyard up the hill from the house.

There was something off about the graves. He hadn't noticed it at first. The realization started as a salesman lurking in a corner, creeping ever closer, waiting for just the right moment to swoop in and sell you on a new set of kitchen knives.

There's nothing on them, Sloot realized. What's more, they all appeared to be the same age. Hardly shocking, as things don't really get older in the Hereafter, but it made one thing clear: this graveyard wasn't like the ones in the Narrative. There was something else going on.

Sloot was tired. Not physically, more like mental exhaustion. He'd felt a certain degree of that his entire life, and supposed that he felt honor-bound to continue the tradition afterward. All he really wanted was a nice lie-down. Just a little one so he could catalog all of his woes and give each a proper fretting as befitting its severity.

They were just headstones. No mounds of dirt or anything. They probably counted as symbolism, though Sloot couldn't say for sure. He'd deftly avoided arts classes during his education. Unlike the beds in the house, he instinctively knew which of the graves was his. He made a beeline for it and laid himself down.

It was quite nice. It was quiet, and that was most of it. The eerie-looking clouds that formed the sky of the Hereafter floated in sinister patterns overhead, no doubt drawing out sigils that would curdle milk, or ruin crops, or put children of a mind to try their hands at graffiti; but aside from their obvious malevolent intent, it was ... lovely. Peaceful. He hadn't felt that relaxed since ... since ...

"Don't over think it," said a voice.

Sloot shot up to a seated position and looked around, but saw no one.

"I didn't mean to startle you," said the voice again, but from where,

Sloot couldn't have said. "I just wanted to check in and see how you were doing."

The voice was familiar. Not just "didn't we meet at a party last June?" familiar. It was deeper than that. It was like one of his oldest memories had come back to give him a good haunting, and in one very specific sense, that was true.

"Fairy Godmother?"

"I still wish there was a better name for it," she said, "but yes."

It was his first posthumous memory. They'd spoken while he was a nascent ghost, just starting to come to grips with his timely demise. Most people would have said *untimely*, but Sloot couldn't imagine a more auspicious opportunity to expire than beneath an undead-versus-goblins brawl. Frankly, if that didn't qualify, nothing would. If all deaths were considered untimely, the word would cease to have any meaning. Accountants didn't truck with waste, and that included adjectives.

"So, how's it going?"

"Oh, fine," Sloot lied. It wasn't a real lie, just the inconsequential sort you used in response to this sort of passing conversation. It was a polite lie. You didn't want to unload on people, or they'd be sorry they asked and avoid you in the future.

"Hmmm," said Fairy Godmother. "That doesn't seem right."

"Doesn't it?"

"Not at all. You've got quite a lot of confluences."

"Oh," said Sloot, looking sheepish. "I thought that had cleared up. I don't have a body anymore."

"No, *confluences*. They're like the shadows of interactions with outside influences."

Sloot didn't cast a shadow anymore, he was sure of it. The last time he was in the Narrative, he'd checked. He opened his mouth to say so, and Fairy Godmother graciously interrupted before he had a chance to embarrass himself further.

"Your dealings with other people," she said. "That Myrtle, for instance. I can tell you're quite fond of her."

Sloot grinned.

"I hate to tell you this, but I think you ought to know."

Sloot's heart sank. "Yes?"

"Oh, I suppose I should just come out with it. No sense in delaying bad news, right? Yank off the bandage, get it over with?"

"Er, right," said Sloot. That was irony. He knew it in the bones he no longer had.

"All right. Here goes, then. Myrtle is … oh, bother. This is so difficult! It's just that I know how much you like her!"

"Please," said Sloot, "it'll be all right, just come out and say it!"

"Very well," said Fairy Godmother. She cleared her throat dramatically, which seemed unnecessary. "Myrtle Pastry is a demon."

"Yes, and?"

"What? What *and*? You don't mean to tell me you knew already?"

"Well, yes," said Sloot. This was unsettling territory for him. He'd grown quite accustomed to being the last to know about things, and didn't see why he should have to give that up now. They'd want him to set trends next. Trend-setting was best left to people in the arts, or perhaps their publicists, if they didn't have the time.

"Oh," said Fairy Godmother with a mix of surprise and concern. "And how long have you known?"

"I couldn't tell you," said Sloot. "A while."

"Sorry," said Fairy Godmother, "I forgot about the time thing. It's just … well … you *know* about it?"

"Yes."

"And you're all right with it?"

Sloot shrugged. "I fell in love with Myrtle while we were both still alive. I mean, they say you can't take it with you, but love's not really an 'it,' is it? Not in that sort of way."

"I suppose not," said Fairy Godmother. "I just … well, call me old-fashioned, but I just don't get it."

"Get what?"

"Well, the two of you. A ghost and a demon. It's just not natural! You should be with someone more like you!"

"Oh, we've got loads in common," said Sloot. "We've got all the same friends, we live together, very fond of kissing—"

"But wouldn't you rather be with a nice dead girl?"

Sloot sighed the way he usually did when things turned awkward. He was sure she meant well, but that was the problem. No one in the history of etiquette has ever said "I'm sure she meant well" in response to something having gone well. "Meaning well" was something that people started out with on the way to disaster.

"I'd rather be with Myrtle," said Sloot, his voice quavering. As much as it galled him to disagree with anyone about anything under any circumstances, he was in love with Myrtle, and that was that.

"Well, that's love for you," said Fairy Godmother. There was a soft breeze for just a moment, its timing fitting rather well with the timing for a disappointed sigh. "Just be careful, will you?"

"Always."

"I worry about you, you know." She meant it. Sloot could tell. His mother had never worried about him, he was fairly certain. So strong was Sladia Peril's belief in her son being made of sterner stuff that she must have thought him invincible. If Sloot's utter trouncing at the hands of a pair of ten-year-old bullies on his thirtieth birthday hadn't convinced her otherwise, then her belief in Sloot was matched only by her powers of denial, which she'd swear up and down that she didn't have.

"Er, thanks," said Sloot. "I should be going, I think."

"I'll be here if you need me. Bring a sweater, it might be cold out!"

"I'm a ghost, Fairy Godmother."

"Oh, right. Silly me."

Sloot left the graveyard and wandered back down the hill toward the house. He'd only just begun to fret over what other people might think about him consorting with demons when he saw Myrtle, floating serenely in the shade of a tree with her feet up. He needn't have remarked upon the shade bit, of course, seeing as the entirety of the Hereafter seemed to have been built in the shade, but retracting a passing thought seemed excessive. Plus, Myrtle was smiling at him.

Sloot smiled back. She gave him a kiss on the cheek.

"Thanks for that," she said.

"You're thanking me for letting you kiss me? Oh, dear. Was I supposed to be thanking you for that this whole time? I told you, I'm new at kissing. I don't know all of the rules!"

Myrtle chuckled, and the corners of her mouth curled up when she smiled. "No, silly! You stood up for me with your Fairy Godmother, didn't you?"

Sloot's smile returned. He nodded, then his face made all of the necessary preparations to ask her how she'd known about that.

"Demon powers," she said. "I'm getting quite good at reading causation. I was all but certain you'd have that conversation, you know."

"I know," said Sloot, who knew nothing of the sort. He did know that responding to a sentence that ended with "you know" by saying anything to the contrary was an invitation to an argument. He knew anecdotally that lovers quarreled, but he sought to avoid it anyway.

"I thought you'd be more impressed," said Myrtle. She frowned slightly, in a way that was more curious than angry or disappointed.

"Oh, I am," Sloot hastened to declare. "I didn't know you even knew about Fairy Godmother."

"I didn't," said Myrtle. "At least not before certain signs indicated that you'd be talking to her."

"Certain signs?"

"It's all very intuitive. It started with Willie trying to convince me to let him out of the circle."

"That's a favorite game of his lately. How did he know I'd be in the graveyard?"

"He didn't. Not exactly. He simply occupied the space in time that led me to the inevitable conclusion that that's where you'd be."

"Ah."

"Oh, dear," said Myrtle. "That didn't make sense at all, did it?"

No, thought Sloot, *it didn't*. He couldn't very well say that, though. Myrtle was his girlfriend! If he were a good boyfriend, he'd say something encouraging.

"You pronounced it beautifully," he blurted, then winced. He half expected her to roll her eyes in disgust and break things off with him right then and there.

Instead, she smiled. It was the sort of smile that embodied all of the best parts of a warm spring day, the sun flagrantly dappling gold across green fields from its pompous perch in the cloudless blue sky. Or something like that. It had given Sloot the keen sense of grey clouds over a darkening field of grey, where neither bird chirped nor soft breeze tickled. There may have been a grey sun behind the clouds, though.

Being dead is harder on romantic poets than it is on most people, or at least it should be; but despite all the bleakness that the long, grey Hereafter has to offer, poets are irrepressible in their knack for finding silver linings, bright sides, that sort of thing. It's irritating to anyone doing their best to wallow in a long stretch of dismal silence. That's why poets and stoics don't mix.

"You're not very good at lying," said Myrtle with a giggle. "I love that about you."

"Thank you," said Sloot.

"There you go again. Why is your awkwardness so adorable?"

Sloot started to panic.

"It was a rhetorical question," said Myrtle in a soothing tone.

Sloot relaxed, but only a bit. He made it a point never to relax completely. That was when they got you.

"I've got some good news," Myrtle continued. "I've figured out the first step in solving your problems!"

"Oh," said Sloot. "That's good."

"I definitely thought you'd be more excited this time," said Myrtle. She was less amused and more disappointed this time.

"I am," said Sloot, "it's just ... well, it's the price."

"The price?"

"My soul," said Sloot. "It's all I have left, really."

Myrtle didn't react. She was clearly waiting for him to explain why that was problematic. This resulted in an exemplary display of one of life's—poor turn of phrase—most disheartening outcomes, as both of their expressions turned slowly from expectant to defeated.

"Honestly," said Myrtle, "I don't understand what the big deal about souls is. It's not like you're using it."

"I'm not?"

"No one does. It's just an ornament, really. It's only there to make you feel special for having it. It's like a spleen, only it makes you feel special for having it."

"That doesn't make any sense," said Sloot. "If that's true, why are the poets always going on about the immortal soul?"

"Do you want to talk about sense or poetry?"

She had him there. You couldn't find a poet alive—sorry—who'd stand idly by while reason and logic were applied to their work. On the contrary, they'd most likely throw themselves on the floor and perform an eloquent tantrum about immortal essence withering on a vine, and other, more tragic metaphors as well, prompting any stoics in the room to casually start inching toward the door.

"I think it's mostly demonic tradition," said Myrtle. "I have to have your soul in exchange for using my power on your behalf."

A thought occurred to Sloot. He could ask her to bend the rules, just this once.

"All right then," said Sloot, "go ahead and take it."

Not likely! *Bending* the rules, in Sloot's opinion, was no different from breaking them. In fact, simply saying "bending" in lieu of having the fortitude to come right out and say it was the height of shame. Best to simply get on with it, then, which was what he did.

"Oh, not yet," said Myrtle. "You hang onto it for now, enjoy the spoils, and I will come collect it at a very dramatic moment. After the job's done."

"Okay," said Sloot. On the bright side, had he chosen to look there, Sloot would have considered it better to give his soul over to Myrtle than let Grumley cast it into the Well of the Void for eternity. Probably. In retrospect, he only had Grumley's word that it was an awful place where he'd be tortured for an eternity. He'd never seen it. If Myrtle was right, and it was just an ornamental sort of thing, perhaps the Well of the Void was more of a lost-and-found than an eternal swear-word-starting-with-an-H. A crevice between the sofa cushions of eternity.

ꕫ⟶WHAT DWELLS IN THE DARK⟵ꕫ

I t isn't nonsense," said Nicoleta. "It's just not very important, that's all."

"Then vhy to ve have to be here?" asked Bartleby. He had the pained look of a six-year-old who'd sat through thirty minutes of church, and was breathing in sighs to match. Willie used to do the same when he had to stand still for portraits.

"Myrtle seems to think there's something here that will get Sloot out from under his woes," said Nicoleta.

"And vhat might that be?"

"She didn't say," said Nicoleta with a shrug. "Why don't you ask her?"

"Never qvestion a demon," said Bartleby. "It never ends vell. I don't suppose she mentioned vhy I have to be here?"

"You're the only person at liberty to turn the pages. Roman's always mysteriously unavailable when this sort of thing comes up."

It hadn't been that long ago—well, probably not, anyway—that Sloot and Myrtle had happened upon Willie walking into what looked like a government building. The people inside had bowed before him, and then … well, Sloot wasn't really sure what had happened next. He'd been summoned away by Winking Bob, much to his chagrin.

It turned out that the building was the headquarters of the Royal Astronomical Society. It also turned out that astronomy, in Nicoleta's opinion, was about as useful as a book on democracy in the Domnitor's library, long may he reign.

"I mean, it serves a purpose," she said, "but astrology is where the real power lies."

"That's not what I've heard," said Sloot.

"Oh. Is that not what you've heard?"

"Er," said Sloot, weighing his response with care. Her words implied that they were having an open discussion among peers, but her tone suggested that the two of them had just entered a cage that only one of them was destined to leave. He could nearly hear the shouts of the old men shaking fistfuls of cash, mostly in her direction.

"I've heard that you can just round down all of your sums and keep the change," she said.

"Now hold on just a minute—"

"Well, that's what I've heard!" It was more than an interruption. It was a dare. *Let's offer up our expertise on each other's field,* it spat. *That's a really good idea that's sure to maintain our friendship well into the next couple of minutes.*

"So what's the purpose of astronomy?"

Nicoleta smirked. "It's the basis of astrology," she said. "The positions of the planets, the stars, their trajectories through the heavens, all of it's important. It's just *boring*. Astrology, on the other hand, that's where things get interesting."

"Do you vant me to move on the next vone?" asked Bartleby.

"Skip ahead a bit," said Nicoleta. She pointed to a shelf full of ledgers that looked exactly like the hundreds of other ledgers in the building. It was like an entire library held hostage by a single bookbinder.

"Once you know where the stars are going," she continued, "you can start to see what's going to happen next. I imagine that's why Myrtle sent us here, but it would have been nice if she could have been more specific. I don't even know what I'm ... wait a minute ..."

"What," asked Sloot, "did you find something?"

"I did," said Nicoleta, "but about five hundred years too late. You remember the Delightful Uprising?"

"I read about it in history," said Sloot. "I was always confused about the name."

"History is written by the vinners," said Bartleby. "It vas delightful for them."

"Delightful for *him*," Nicoleta said. "The Domnitor was the only winner in that bloody mess."

"Long may he reign," said Sloot.

"Honestly, vhen are you going to stop doing that?" Bartleby flipped another page for Nicoleta.

"Stop doing what?"

"Bowing and scraping to the Domnitor."

"Long may he reign."

"There it is again! Are you just doing it out of habit?"

"Doing what?"

"Wait!" shouted Nicoleta.

"Vhat?"

"Go back a page."

Bartleby turned back a page and Nicoleta gave the book a good staring-down. Sloot looked over her shoulder, or rather, through it. It looked a lot like the hundreds of other pages they'd reviewed that night, though this one had far more notes in the margins than most.

"Vicked," said Bartleby.

"What do they say?" asked Sloot, who didn't recognize the language of the notes.

"No idea," said Bartleby, "but they look really cool."

"It's Goblish," said Nicoleta. "Don't tell me you can't read Goblish!"

"I never bothered learning. I didn't know the letters looked so creepy, or I'd have done a long time ago!"

"Goblish," said Sloot. "As in ... " He mouthed the word "goblins" instead of saying it aloud.

"Of course," said Nicoleta. "Am I the only one here who knows Goblish?"

"How?" Sloot was aghast at the thought of learning to speak to so vile a species. "Why?"

"Why not? There's no such thing as bad knowledge, you know. Well, except for everything in the Anathemic Library of Ulfhaven. And the locked shelf in my tower. Oh, how I miss my tower!"

"Ooh, I can play this vone! I buried a book in the desert about three hundred years ago. I couldn't read a vord of it, but it nearly drove me to madness anyvay."

"What was it called?" asked Nicoleta.

"I can't pronounce it," said Bartleby, "but it's an ancient svear vord that means 'the quivering satisfaction of just having peeled your face off and gift-wrapped it for the supernatural horror who's about to consume you.'"

"Oh, I think that's—"

"Please don't," implored Sloot, who did a nervous little dance. He had no desire to add such a word to his vocabulary. He was already having enough trouble coming to grips with the idea that goblins' chattering was actually speech, not just a spirit of general excitement at the prospect of making rude intestinal noises.

"It's a new constellation," said Nicoleta.

"What is?"

"The notes! They're describing a constellation that's never appeared in the sky. Wait. No, it was there a long time ago. Thousands of years ago, and then it came down to ... oh, dear."

Despite the negative connotation, Sloot liked "oh, dear." It was a good phrase. You always knew where you stood with it. He took a moment to appreciate the fact that he knew better than to get his hopes up, and girded himself for the panic that was soon to come.

"I think the Serpents of the Earth are going to put it back."

"Put vhat back?"

"The Serpent of the Sky."

Like an old, familiar friend who'd stopped by to remind him that everything was horribly wrong, a panic rose up in Sloot. It was too bad he no longer slept, as this one seemed ready and able to keep him awake for days on end. A lot of wasted potential there.

"A flying snake?" he asked, his voice quavering for fear of both snakes and heights.

"Worse," said Nicoleta. "The Serpent of the Sky is a constellation, a source of great power for the Serpents of the Earth if they're able to harness its power."

❧⚶❧⚶❧⚶❧⚶

"That's villains for you," said Myrtle. "They don't *do* anything with their power. They just hoard it like those big beer mugs that they sell for Overdrinkerfest every year."

Myrtle had been waiting in the parlor when they returned from the Royal Astronomical Society. It was quiet. As close to pleasant in the house as it had ever been, in Sloot's reckoning. Nan was hiding in the basement from Constantin, who was doddering upstairs. He'd gotten very good at doddering of late, as though he'd been taking lessons. It was good that he was keeping busy, Sloot thought.

They kept getting up to check on Willie because he was so quiet. Suspiciously quiet. Children who've gotten into mommy's cosmetics quiet. But every time they looked, he was sitting in the circle, grinning like a fox eating peanut butter from a wire brush. That was unsettling, but not nearly as much as the giggling. It was bursting with treachery. It was the sort of giggle you did when you knew something everyone else didn't, and they were all going to hate it when they found out.

Fortunately for Sloot, his over-developed capacity for denial wasn't going to let something as silly as the imminent unleashing of evil prevent him from enjoying an otherwise pleasant conversation. Even if it *was* about the impending doom threatening the world at the hands of the Serpents of the Earth.

"I don't know," said Bartleby. "I've seen this sort of thing before. A lot of dark magic goes into putting evil stars in the sky. It's vicked cool."

"Cool as it may be," said Nicoleta, who'd given up on reprimanding Bartleby's praising evil for its style, "it's got to be dangerous. Like Myrtle said, villains like to hoard power. They wouldn't spend it unless there was a big payoff."

"Well, let's think through it logically," said Myrtle. "What does Mrs. Knife want?"

"Probably world domination," scoffed Nicoleta. "Honestly, villains are so predictable. It's always world domination."

"Willie might know," said Myrtle. "He seems to know an awful lot he's not telling."

"Directions to Carpathia," said Sloot.

"Vhat? *Go north.* That's it."

"I know," said Sloot, "it doesn't make sense. Just don't bring it up around her! She tried to stab me last time."

"You're dead, Sloot." Nicoleta had never seemed very impressed with Sloot, and evidently wasn't interested in starting just then.

"Hang on a minute," said Myrtle. "You asked her why she wanted directions to Carpathia and she tried to stab you?"

"Pretty much."

"Pretty much?"

"Well, she started raving about the Dark before that."

Myrtle rolled her eyes. "Honestly, you didn't consider *why* she might have been trying to stab you?"

He hadn't, in fact. In Sloot's estimation, crazed villains' motivations for attempted stabbing were far less important than the deed having gotten underway.

He shrugged.

"And just to be clear, you said the Dark, right? Not just the dark?"

"Right," said Sloot, "like proper *Dark.* Her eyes went all crazy villain and her knife came out. Rave, rave, rave. Stab, stab, stab."

"What could that mean?" pondered Myrtle. "The *Dark.*"

"Vell," said Bartleby, "it might be too obvious, but she could be talking about ... the Dark."

Of course, Bartleby would know. He lived for that kind of stuff. Perhaps *lived* was the wrong word to apply to a necromancer. Sloot thought of Gregor, who looked like little more than a flaky pastry crust baked onto an old skeleton. *Was* Bartleby alive? Given that he could cross the veil between the Narrative and the Hereafter at will, Sloot had doubts.

Bartleby explained at length—because he kept getting excited about anecdotes that led him down tangents about other "vicked" dark things—that the Dark was a very real place. Well, not *very* real. It was a sort of ethereal pocket that didn't so much exist between the proper planes of existence as lurk among them. It seemed to have formed of its own volition a very long time ago.

Luckily for all of the prehistoric entities floating around in the ether back then, the demons were aware of the Dark forming, and decided to keep an eye on it. The most important bit of information to arise from the passage of countless aeons of vigilance was that nothing ever came forth from it. It really didn't pay to be a low-level demon back then, especially if you'd gotten into the job for the excitement.

The dwarves who live under the mountains in Svartalfheim—which was technically within the borders of Nordheim, though one would do well to avoid bringing that up around them—were one of the first mortal races to learn about the Dark. The dwarves were curious and inventive, two traits that turned out to be very detrimental to the goblins, who would fight just about anybody back then. They fought a years-long war with the dwarves, which the dwarves won.

The problem with goblins ... well, there wasn't just one. Goblins were essentially the result that one would expect from a mad scientist being handed trickery, deceit, and a handful of razor-sharp teeth, and then expected to *not* use them to create something monstrous and capable of destroying all of existence. But the particular problem that the dwarves faced when they defeated them was that goblins didn't so much live in places as infest them. Any respectable race of mortals would define boundaries, build cities, and implement municipal tax codes to give people a reason to threaten to vote for the other guy next time. The goblins didn't have any of that.

There were certain things you were supposed to do when you lost a war. First and foremost, you cleared out of your opponent's country. Then you probably lost a good deal of your own. It descended into repatriation and politics from there, but the dwarves found themselves in the unfortunate position of being lucky to get past step one. They were a wise and magnanimous bunch, and knew that simply casting them out of the mountain would mean leaving them to infest the other nations of the world. Eventually, they'd just have to fight them all over again, quite possibly in greater numbers.

"So they cast them into the Dark," said Nicoleta, her voice barely more than a whisper as she watched Bartleby with a rapt expression.

Bartleby scoffed. "Really? You let me tell the whole story, then svoop in and give avay the ending?"

"Sorry," said Nicoleta.

"Anyvay," said Bartleby very pointedly, "the dvarves cast the goblins into the Dark, vhere they vere trapped for centuries."

"And then, what?" Sloot puzzled. "They mysteriously started turning up in the Old Country?"

Bartleby fixed Sloot with a disgusted look, shaking his head slowly. "You people are the vorst!" he shouted. "Can I not have a single dramatic revelation in my own story?"

"Sorry," said Sloot.

"We're sorry," said Nicoleta.

"Vhatever," said Bartleby. He burst into a puff of black smoke, and a few bats flew off in different directions. All things considered, it was far more impressive than Willie's tried-and-true arms-crossed-and-frowning start to a sulk.

"Where did he go?" asked Myrtle.

"Off to pout somewhere," said Nicoleta. "I've seen him do it. I know what you're thinking, but it's actually quite impressive. He's a brooder, that one."

"So the goblins were all cast into the Dark," said Sloot. "Nothing ever came out of the Dark, but then they started showing up in the Old Country."

"They must have found a way out of the Dark," said Nicoleta.

"A way that only leads into the Old Country?"

"Apparently."

That was where it started to get really interesting. Or, more accurately, terrifying. Goblins only ever turned up in the Old Country, and as far as any of them were aware, none of them had ever left. One could reason that the effects of mischief did more damage there than anywhere else, draconian dictatorships being less resistant to shenanigans than more sensibly governed nations; however, one of the few scientific studies to have been performed on goblins had revealed that their love of mischief was rivaled only by their love of revenge.

"They'd never forgive and forget with the dwarves," said Myrtle. "Once a sizable host had made it out of the Dark, they'd march straight for Svartalfheim."

"And there are thousands of goblins in Salzstadt alone," said Sloot. He thought back to the Fall of Salzstadt. He'd shouted some of the worst swear words known to humanity—well, known to him, anyway—and must have brought several hundred over from the Dark himself that day.

"It only makes sense if they can't leave the Old Country," said Nicoleta. "They're trapped there."

"They must know that Svartalfheim is in Nordheim," said Sloot, "and that Nordheim is on the other side of Carpathia. That means they'd just have to—"

"Find out how to get into Carpathia," said Bartleby, popping up from behind the couch and startling them all. "That's vhat it feels like to have your anecdote stolen out from under you!"

"I said I was sorry," said Sloot.

"That's why Mrs. Knife needs directions to Carpathia," said Myrtle, her eyes going wide. "She's a … goblin?"

It made absolutely no sense, but nothing else did either. There were other things that didn't add up as well.

"The border guards," said Sloot. "They couldn't see across the border either. It was like … in their eyes, the universe ceased to exist across that line. I stepped over into Carpathia and they couldn't see me anymore."

"Vere the guards goblins?"

"No, human. Well, formerly."

Bartleby furrowed his brow and stroked his chin with his long, black fingernails.

"Goblins have no magic," said Bartleby. "Othervise, I'd say that a goblin vizard probably reanimated them. That vould account for their blindness to Carpathia."

"It was probably Gregor who reanimated them," said Nicoleta. "Is he a goblin too, then?"

"I doubt it," said Bartleby. "That is to say, he vasn't a goblin the last time I saw him."

"The last …" Myrtle opted to end her sentence with a quizzical look instead of words, which can be tedious in this sort of situation.

"Ve change bodies every so often. Necromancers, I mean. Vhen they vear out, ve just take over another."

"That's awful!" said Nicoleta.

"That's life." Bartleby shrugged.

"No, it isn't! It's exactly the opposite!"

"If it's any consolation, I only take over the bodies of really bad people. This guy vas a serial arsonist," he said, thumping his chest.

"It's still not great," said Nicoleta with a grimace.

"Tell that to all the people whose houses he never burned down."

Sloot could see an uncomfortable silence coming from a mile away. Farther, even. It was really too bad there was no money in it. He'd have profited handsomely from this one.

"It doesn't matter," said Myrtle after a while. "For now, it's imperative that we warn Vlad."

"Warn Vlad?" asked Nicoleta.

"Unless a new hole opens in the Dark, there's only one way for the goblins to cross into Carpathia. Vlad has to invite them in."

"I thought that vas vampires."

"Same principle," said Myrtle, "only vampires aren't as smart as goblins."

"Vampires are cool," said Bartleby reproachfully.

"It doesn't matter," said Nicoleta. "Oh!"

"Vhat?"

"I've just figured something out."

"Vhat?"

"The Serpent of the Sky," said Nicoleta. "Constellations are used for navigation!"

Sloot gasped. "If the goblins control their own constellation, they might not need an invitation!"

Nicoleta began pacing around the room. "We need to get to Carpathia to warn Vlad! What's the fastest way?"

"I don't have to walk again, do I?" asked Sloot.

"No," said Myrtle. "I just have to stop hiding you."

"Hiding me? What do you—"

"There," said Myrtle, making a gesture that could be considered obscene if it didn't have the flourish on the end. "That should do it. Everyone hold hands, it shouldn't be long now."

⤞⤞LUCILLE⤝⤝

S loot figured that he should get used to Myrtle being right about everything. Demons who could foretell the future generally were, and she was his girlfriend to boot.

"Where have you been?" asked Roman. He was brandishing Sloot's shrunken head at him, an off-putting maneuver that could hardly have been made more disconcerting. Unless perhaps Roman had glued doll eyes over Sloot's stitched-up sockets. Sloot silently chided himself for allowing that idea to pop into his head, and was thankful that the dead didn't dream.

"He's been with me," said Myrtle.

"We needed him here," said Roman.

"He was needed at home as well," Myrtle spat. "Where do you get off summoning him every five minutes?"

"I'm his spymaster," said Roman. "And what gives you the right to keep him from his duty to Carpathia?"

"I'm his girlfriend!"

"Since vhen is Sloot a spy?" asked Bartleby.

"Silence!" boomed Vlad, in the way that only a warrior of her stature can.

"Your Dominance!" shouted Nicoleta, who prostrated herself in an incredibly uncomfortable-looking curtsy.

The sheer amount of courage that it would have taken to refer to

Vlad's visage as "haggard" could not reasonably be housed within any single person. Unless perhaps that single person happened to be a horde of screaming berserkers who'd been zoned as a single person, for rent control purposes—a request which no landlord would likely be brave enough to refuse. It was safer to say that Vlad obviously hadn't slept in quite a while, and that the work she'd been putting into her scowl was really paying off. She sat, as was her custom, in her armor on her dragon throne, her massive sword resting on her lap.

No, not resting. Biding its time.

"You're looking, er," said Sloot, desperately wishing he'd chosen any other words to start that sentence, "formidable, your Dominance."

"Enough flattery," said Vlad, her voice echoing throughout the throne room. "Tell me everything you know about this Domnitor."

"Long may he reign," said Sloot.

What erupted from Vlad was not a mere roar of fury. It was the distillation of mortal danger to anything or anyone within sword's reach. The frighteningly sharp steel, which probably had a name like Gutcleaver or Lungpopper or Lucille, passed through Sloot in a way that—were he still of the corporeal persuasion—would have left him to quiver for half a minute or so, before one half of him slid from the other. His blood would have puddled impressively on the floor, no doubt.

"Ow!" shouted Bartleby. A chunk of stone exploded from the floor beneath Sloot when Lucille struck it. It careened off Bartleby's head, leaving a hole behind his ear you could've used for carrying lunch money for five or six people. A thick coagulation of very old black blood began lazily pooling in the wound.

"You dare praise another lord in my hall?" bellowed Vlad.

Sloot apologized, or at least had every intention of doing so. His voice, it seemed, was too terrified to abandon the safety of his insubstantial throat.

"If it pleases Your Dominance," said Roman, "this is Sloot Peril, or rather the ghost of he who formerly was. He was Your Dominance's deepest spy within the borders of the Old Country, and no doubt cannot restrain himself from regurgitating the praise of the southern despot, no more than he could have restrained himself in life from breathing in his sleep."

Vlad considered Sloot, her wide-eyed fury refusing to abate before it had slaughtered something.

"Blaspheme again in my hall," shouted Vlad, no doubt fully aware that she had not relented an iota of fury, "and I will find a way to murder you further, wretched ghost!"

"Er, ahem, yes, Your Dominance," Sloot stammered.

"I'm sure it could be done," said Nicoleta, her analytical nature running rough-shod over any shred of pity she might have felt for Sloot just then. "I imagine the Lebendervlad could drag him through one of the Black Smilers and—"

"Thank you, Nicoleta," said Roman, a tinge of nervousness in the chuckle that followed. "We'd prefer *not* to see Sloot obliterated by Vlad's spectral ancestors, I think?"

The Lebendervlad were the thirty-six Vlads the Invader to come before the current one. They were all quite dead, but by use of a system of horrific icons known as Black Smilers—skulls of fallen enemies stuffed with demonic larva—they were able to take on semi-corporeal forms and fight with the living Vlad. That was how they passed along their extreme martial prowess, thus making Vlad the Invader the most deadly warrior anywhere in the world.

"It could be done, that's all." Nicoleta's upper lip cornered in a sneer and her eyes bulged in Roman's direction. "Pardon my simple scientific curiosity," the look seemed to say, though with far more sarcasm than necessary.

Once Sloot was convinced that he was in no imminent danger of being ripped apart by former heads of the Carpathian state, he found himself eagerly reporting everything that he knew about the Domnitor, long may he ... well. You know.

It wasn't until he'd been droning at length about the subversion of the Domnitor's taxable interest in the Three Bells Shipping Company—which, as all in attendance were aware to some degree, was operated primarily to the benefit of the Serpents of the Earth—that he had a revelation. He stopped mid-sentence.

"It doesn't make sense," said Sloot.

"Of course it doesn't make sense," said Roman. "Why anybody in their right mind would thank the Domnitor for a ninety-percent-across-the-board tax rate defies all logic."

"No, not that," said Sloot, although hearing Roman phrase it like that *did* make it seem a bit excessive. "I meant the plot to kidnap the Domnitor."

"Of course it makes sense," said Roman. "You've obviously not spent a lot of time thinking about the intricacies of global domination! Anyone who had their blade to the throat of the Domnitor, may he live long enough to fall into Her Dominance's clutches, would control the Old Country, and with it most of the shipping routes on this side of the world."

"True," said Sloot, "but not for Mrs. Knife. She already controls the Old Country."

"Not entirely," said Roman. "Controlling the Domnitor would solidify her claim."

"But she doesn't care about that," said Sloot. "She only wants to come here, and she can't. She needs directions."

"That's the weird part," said Nicoleta. "The only thing that makes any sense—despite the fact that it makes no sense at all—is that Mrs. Knife is a goblin."

"What?" Roman guffawed, a bit too forcefully in a way that seemed suspicious. "That's ridiculous!"

"Ve thought so too," said Bartleby, "but vhy else vould she need directions to leave the Old Country? It only makes sense if her sight vas cloaked by the Dark, like the goblins."

"How do you know so much about the Dark?" asked Roman, his face a morass of panic and incredulity.

"I'm a very old necromancer," said Bartleby. "Well, not *very* old. For a necromancer." He preened. A large glob of coagulated blood dripped from his head wound and went *splat* on the floor.

"Do you need to have that looked at?" asked Nicoleta.

"It vill be fine."

"It looks like it took out a chunk of your brain."

"I'm not really using it," said Bartleby with a shrug. "Necromancy's a lot like possession that vay."

Roman turned a questioning glance to Vlad. She returned a nearly imperceptible nod, the sort that was all the rage with stoics, according to Arthur.

Roman sighed. "To be clear, I wasn't happy about keeping you in the dark for as long as we have. No pun intended."

"That figures," said Myrtle. "Roman's been working an angle! Pardon me while I drag my complete and utter lack of surprise out to Obvious Street. They're having a parade for it."

"It's *top secret information*," Roman declared in an over-enunciated sort of way.

"Top secret, eh? Wave at the parade as it goes by, will you? Or would you like to be the grand marshal?"

"Are you quite finished?" asked Roman, his hands resting on his hips.

"You shouldn't wait for that," said Myrtle. "There's a brass band coming, and they're trumpeting a new arrangement about how you've always got some double-dealing in the works. Honestly, have you ever dealt fairly with us?"

"Silence," said Vlad. She didn't shout this time, but her hand moved to Lucille in a not-so-subtle, just-give-me-a-reason way.

"Sorry, Your Dominance." Myrtle had the look of a demon who wasn't quite positive she couldn't be slain by this particular mortal's sword. "Enlighten us, spymaster."

"Thank you," said Roman, sparing no sanctimony. "Thousands of years ago, before Carpathia was unified by Vlad the First, or the Old Country was called by its proper name, there was a war between the goblins and the dwarves."

"Ve know," said Bartleby. "The dvarves von and cast the goblins into the Dark."

"That wasn't all they cast into the Dark," said Roman, apparently having reserved a measure of smarm for such an eventuality. "Do you know *why* the dwarves waged war on the goblins?"

"Vouldn't you?"

Roman started to unfold a lesser-known tidbit of early history that most of the historians of their time, being human, turned a blind eye toward. Before humans came along and developed advanced concepts of ownership, replete with complicated real estate commission structures and tiered marketing scams, the mortal races all got along fairly well. Part of the reason for the widespread harmony was the fairies, who outnumbered everyone else combined.

"I know about fairies," said Nicoleta. "Carpathia's full of them, though you can't often see them. They pout a lot."

"That's because life's not fair," said Roman.

"All of the fairies are perpetually pouting because life isn't fair?" asked Sloot.

"That's why they call them fairies," said Roman. "May I continue? The rest of the mortal races gave peace with humans a try, and it would have worked out well, if it weren't for humanity's darkest secret."

"Which is?"

"Most humans are easy-going and reasonable," said Roman. "But a few of them—a few of *us*, rather—are right villains. They'll do anything in the name of amassing power and wealth, even if it's at the expense of everyone else."

Roman went on to explain that although the fairies outnumbered everyone else, some of the more cunning humans figured out that they could use alliances to get what they wanted. The dwarves, being wise, declined the humans' attempts to woo them. The goblins, on the other hand, were itching to get up to whatever mischief presented itself.

They were also quite literally itching, as hygiene had never caught on among the goblins. Fleas, therefore, had.

To seal the deal, a human king married his daughter to a goblin prince. Goblins have no princes, so they drew lots and the shortest straw had to pretend to be one.

The human/goblin alliance went after the fairies, teasing them mercilessly and running them out of the business of maintaining the balance. The fairies took their metaphorical ball and went home, disappearing into the woodlands to play by themselves, where they could treat each other fairly in all things. The dwarves saw the writing on the wall and holed themselves up in their mountain.

The alliance between the goblins and the villainous humans came to an end in large part because goblins aren't very smart. But they are smart enough to know when they're not getting their fair share. The humans had profited immensely from their combined mischief, while the goblins fought over scraps. The humans, treacherous villains that they were, refused to help the goblins go after the dwarves to secure wealth and power of their own, so there was a schism. The princess who married the goblin prince—who was now the goblin king—and several humans in her court had become saturated with goblin mischief, so they stayed with the goblins. Likewise, there were many goblins who stayed with the humans. Humans were particularly skilled in the subtle arts of getting fat and lazy, two conditions prized very highly among goblinkind.

The goblins waged war on the dwarves, who had been stockpiling weapons since they locked themselves away in their mountain. When the dwarves inevitably won the war, they killed the goblin king and banished the rest to the Dark. The princess, being human and therefore most ambitious among them, solidified her power as queen of the goblins, has ruled over them ever since. She decided to age until she was no longer young and fair, gnarling to a satisfactory point before staring time itself in the face and giving notice that she'd not be aging any further.

"You can't be saying what I think you're saying," said Nicoleta.

"If you think I'm saying everyone lived happily ever after, then you're right."

"I think you're saying that ... Mrs. Knife is the queen of the goblins."

"That she is," said Vlad.

"How long have you known?" asked Myrtle.

"Not long," said Roman. "I'd have told you sooner, had Sloot not been avoiding my summons."

"We get it," Myrtle sighed. "But how did you find all of this out?"

"Thanks to her, mostly." Roman gestured toward Franka, who was walking into the room at that very moment, as if they'd planned it that way.

"Who's this?" asked Myrtle.

"This is Franka," said Sloot. "She's with the Skeleton Key Circle. They keep track of the earthly remains of the Souls of the Serpent. After they're dead, of course."

"They're not remains until they're dead," said Myrtle. "And you trust her?"

"You should too," said Franka. "It will save a lot of time."

"The Skeleton Key Circle isn't part of the Serpents of the Earth," said Roman, "but the two go back a long way together. Nearly to the beginning. The Circle has been keeping some interesting records."

"We can't trust her," said Myrtle. "She's in cahoots with the Serpents of the Earth! For all we know, she could be spying for Mrs. Knife."

"She's not," said Roman. "They've killed most of the other members of the Circle, and they're after the rest to translate the Keepers' journals. The Circle keeps them encoded for exactly this sort of thing."

"Oh, all right," said Myrtle. "So she belongs to a secret order that works for another secret order hiding body parts, and now—surprise, surprise—one has decided to betray the other. I have to say, this has 'trustworthy' written all over it."

"You are right to be suspicious," said Franka. "I would be."

"Then how can we trust you?"

"Because of this."

Franka held up a package that was neatly wrapped in black velvet and tied with silver cord.

"And what is that?"

"Constantin Hapsgalt."

Sloot gasped. Even after all the time he'd spent as a ghost, being this close to a dead body gave him the creeps.

"Vicked," said Bartleby. A nicely wrapped pile of human remains was just the sort of thing he'd go in for. He also seemed very excited about Vlad's throne room, with all of its fiery braziers and looming

gargoyles. His enthusiasm wasn't dampened in the slightest by the oozing wound on the back of his head.

"It's a lovely gesture," said Sloot, "though I'm not sure what it's got
to do with trust."

"Everything," said Nicoleta. "The remains of a Soul of the Serpent
are powerful artifacts! We can use them to foil the Serpents."

"How?"

"I'm not sure yet. Bartleby, take that and come with me. We're going
to the tower!" Nicoleta squealed with glee, like she and her girlfriends
were going to try on prom dresses, or some other equally sexist comparison that has no place in modern social commentary. "Come on, there's
no time to lose!"

Bartleby cautiously approached Franka and took the package from
her, watching her with a wary expression in case she was only kidding
about being trustworthy.

"No harm shall come to them," said Franka, "or I'll visit the same
upon you. Understand?"

Bartleby nodded. He took the package and scampered away after
Nicoleta.

"Is that proof enough?" asked Franka.

"For now," said Myrtle. "But if I may ask, why are you here?"

"That was my idea," said Roman. "She needs to keep her gruesome
charges away from Mrs. Knife, right? Where would they be further from
her reach than outside the Old Country?"

"I see," said Myrtle. "Clever."

"It looks like you have everything in hand here, spymaster," said
Vlad. "I should go."

"Where are you going?" asked Myrtle. "Er, Your Dominance?"

"To Stagralla."

"Wait, you're not—"

"I am."

She was going to kidnap the Domnitor!

"Wait!" cried Sloot. "Er, if it pleases Your Dominance?"

"Why?"

"It's a ruse," said Sloot, suddenly connecting several seemingly incongruous dots. "It has to be! Mrs. Knife doesn't care about ruling the Old Country, she told me herself! She's just trying to throw us off her scent so she can put her constellation in the sky. If Nicoleta was right, she can use it to march all the way to Svartalfheim without your invitation across the border!"

"Nicoleta is working on that now," said Vlad. "She will stop it. In the meantime, I still need to ransom Greta back."

"Your fastest ship awaits, Your Dominance," said Roman. "Swift winds at your back, blood and honor!"

"Blood and honor," said Vlad. Her fist punched the air, and she turned again to walk away.

"But what if they do the thing with the stars before you return?" Sloot pleaded. "What if we can't stop it? We need your help!"

Vlad stopped in her tracks, wheeled on Sloot and marched toward him with all the fervor of a butcher with one more cow to process before he goes on holiday.

"You will not fail," said Vlad, her finger literally in Sloot's face. Then, without another word, she left.

"Well," said Roman, "you heard Her Dominance."

"I did," said Sloot. "She's got a lot of confidence in us, though I'm not sure it's reasonable to expect that we can—"

"It was an order, Peril, not a vote of confidence!"

"Oh," said Sloot. He really shouldn't have been surprised. Starting with Vasily Pritygud's disastrous report crossing his desk, his life—and subsequent lack thereof—had been a never-ending sequence of impossible tasks set before him, each more capable than the last of skewering him with dreadful consequences. Why should this be any different?

"What happens if the goblins make it into Carpathia?" asked Myrtle. "Even Vlad can only slaughter so many of them on her own."

"I've thought of that," said Roman. He rubbed his hands together and grinned. "Peril, you're being promoted."

"Promoted?" All of the excitement that should have been evident in Sloot's voice yielded the floor to despair, no doubt saving its strength for some really bad news which, statistically speaking, should be just around the corner.

"Try not to sound so excited," said Roman caustically.

"The last time I was promoted, they made me Willie's financier."

"Which led to a life of adventure!"

"Exactly." Sloot was sure there was a word for two people making the same point to opposite ends, but he was far too invested in lamenting his condition to try and remember what it might have been.

"Fine, then you'll have to suck it up. I need you to go and talk to the fairies."

"You said they were dangerous!" If there was one thing Sloot could remember at will, it was things he had been warned to avoid. He was still fairly certain that all fruit was covered in poison until rinsed.

On their first trip to Carpathia, they'd snuck through a garden, and Roman had warned him: *Be quiet through the garden. Fairies live in nearly all of the gardens in the city, and they can be more dangerous than the goblins in Salzstadt.*

"You'd do well to listen to me on that one," said Roman.

"I don't mind if I do."

"Oh, not now! You're already dead, they can't do anything to you. Sloot Peril, you are hereby promoted to Agent Third Class and authorized to undertake clandestine conversations with would-be allies of the realm."

"I don't suppose Agents Third Class receive a salary?"

"They do not," said Roman. "Now, I imagine you can find a garden somewhere in Ulfhaven without assistance?"

"Yes." Sloot sighed. "What would you have me do?"

"Go and find a fairy," said Roman. "Tell them you want to speak with their fairest flower."

"And then what?"

"Rally them to our banners! Honestly, Sloot, you're going to need to start making more of an effort if you ever want another promotion."

"I didn't want—"

Myrtle gasped. She stared at Roman in bewilderment.

"What?" asked Roman, responding to Myrtle's look with a surprised one of his own.

Realization crept into Myrtle's expression, but the bewilderment wouldn't be unseated so easily. They made a hasty peace and lived together in harmony for a moment, until she shook her head and turned to Sloot.

"You go on," she said to him.

"What? You don't mean that I should—"

"It will turn out fine," said Myrtle. "In fact, it will be better than fine. We really need you to do this. Do you trust me?"

He did. He really, really did. Somewhere within him was a voice that was screaming at him that you couldn't trust a demon, but it was sure to be stuffed into a locker and told to shut up by a roaming gang of teenagers any minute now. Besides, it was probably living people who shouldn't trust demons. Being dead blurred the lines, not to mention the fact that this particular demon was his girlfriend, a fact that he gleefully pointed out at every opportunity.

He nodded.

"Off you go then," said Myrtle with a smile and a wink. "I'm going to have a very serious chat with Roman while you're at it."

⤜⤟ABATTOIR PARK⤞⤝

The gardens of Carpathia were as lush and verdant as any that one might find elsewhere in the world. They were also terrifying. There were more plants in an average Carpathian garden that could kill you than those that couldn't, and only a few of them required that you eat, smell, or even look at them to do so. The Reticulated Stranglethorn, for example, had a collection of barbed roots that would grapple around anything that moved within a few feet of it. The Murmuring Thistle constantly emitted a note so low that anyone within hearing distance would spontaneously start bleeding from the ears and eyes.

The Malignant Blossom was harmless in its own right, but it was well-connected in the criminal underworld and extremely paranoid. Its victims were innumerable because it was very good at covering its tracks.

"I'm already dead," Sloot repeated to himself as he floated through the obviously deadly but strangely beautiful gardens in Abattoir Park. He tried fathoming why anyone would leave a place like this lying around in the middle of a city, where anyone could stumble into it and casually mingle with their own grisly death, but quickly gave up. Why bother fathoming why Carpathians do anything? Best just to steer clear of cannibals, if you don't want to get eaten.

Before he was able to return his focus to the terrifying flora that would love nothing more than to eviscerate the corporeal form he'd neglected to bring along, Sloot was filled with an altogether different sense of lurking dread. It was the quiescent knowledge, with no proof but the undeniable feeling, that he was being watched.

These things tend to go one of two ways: either the feeling passes without incident, leaving the afflicted to go on about their business feeling slightly rattled; or it is proven valid when the watcher decides that he—or she, or it—has lurked long enough, and that the time for assailing victims with unequivocal malevolence is at hand.

It should come as no surprise that Sloot, being one of the single least fortunate persons ever to have lived, died, and been forced to keep going to work nonetheless, has never had a feeling of being watched end in the former, more mundane fashion; therefore, said lack of surprise should apply by extension to what happened next.

"Halt!" cried a tiny voice.

"Don't kill me!" Sloot's eyes slammed shut, and his limbs contorted into the classic Craven Bulwark position, which seemingly everyone who's never been in a fight believes—wrongly—is capable of guarding them against harm.

"You're already dead," said the tiny voice.

Sloot opened his eyes so he could use them to assess the situation, which was smart. Smart and terrifying, because he was surrounded. Well, sort of.

"What business do you have in the forest, please?" said one of several dozen roughly ankle-high people, who were not so much menacing him with spears as leaning against walking sticks and staring at him with rapt curiosity, but it was all the same to Sloot.

"I've come to talk to the fairies," said Sloot. "Er, specifically, to your fairest flower."

"Have you?" asked the tiny and particularly hairy man, whose gossamer wings fluttered in agitation. "And why do you get to do that, please?"

Sloot hadn't been prepared for that. If he were being completely honest, he hadn't prepared for anything at all, so it really shouldn't have come as a surprise. In fact, his entire death up to that point had been a long series of events forcing him into action without the opportunity to prepare. Very different from the greater part of his life, during which he'd maintained solid financial projections well into his doddering octogenarian years, though those were now moot. He made a mental note to spend some time seriously lamenting the fact that he'd never get to update those again, as soon as the opportunity for some deep and painful brooding presented itself.

"I," said Sloot, hoping something eloquent would fall from his mouth if he gave it a gentle push. It didn't. "Er, please?"

"That's better," said the tiny man. "But please *what*, please?"

"I'm sorry?"

"That's all right."

"Please forgive me," said Sloot, feeling infinitesimally more confident now that he was on his own self-abasing turf, "but I really don't understand."

"I forgive you," said the tiny man with all the pomposity that one generally reserves for receiving awards, despite his lack of tuxedo. "It is to say that ghosts do not ever visit the fairies, so why is it that you get to do it? Please."

"Er, I don't know," said Sloot. "I can't really speak for other ghosts. We're not unionized or anything. I just want to speak with your fairest flower on this occasion in particular." He paused, then seeing a scowl start to form on the tiny man's face, hastened to add "Please?"

The tiny man's face narrowly managed the turn-off, and relaxed. "I just don't see how it would be fair, if you please."

Fairies. Sloot generally avoided picking up on things too quickly, preferring to wait and see if it caused problems for more reckless people before he followed suit. He decided to make an exception this time.

"Well, it would be," Sloot replied, "provided that every ghost who *asked* to speak with the fairies was permitted to do so. If you please."

The tiny man appeared to consider this from within his obscene wealth of body hair, which he could have obscured with more than a simple loincloth like all of the other—surprisingly sartorial—fairies.

Then again, the phrase "if you've got it, flaunt it" wasn't coined so it could gather dust.

"You make an interesting point," he said at last. "Would you excuse us for a moment, please?"

"I'd be happy to," said Sloot, who was more than a bit relieved to quit the center of their attention. They gathered in a tiny huddle which, as huddles are wont to do, erupted into a tiny sussurus.

The reprieve gave Sloot a moment to shrink in terror from the Caliginous Palm, which was leaning precariously close to him and ... sniffing.

"It's just trying to work out whether you'd make a decent meal," said the tiny, hairy spokesman of the fairies, as though that were no cause for alarm.

"Would you mind telling it that I wouldn't, please?"

"Sorry, but unfortunately, I *would* make a decent meal, so I can't get that close. It will figure it out shortly, so just try to ignore it until then, please."

"Oh. Er, thank you."

"You're welcome. Anyway, we've taken a vote, and we've decided that it would be fair to grant you an audience."

"There were dissenting opinions!" shouted a fairy who was obviously in his tailor's good favor.

"Duly noted," said the tiny hairy man, who introduced himself as Lilacs. He went on to explain, in fairness to the dissenters, that there was some concern among the fairies that the ruling would open up the veritable floodgates to hordes of ghosts who'd been biding their time, and suddenly the fairies would have to spend all day talking to ghosts.

"It's not that we dislike ghosts or anything," said Lilacs, "but we've got other things to be getting on with in our day, if you please."

"Of course," said Sloot, who knew all too well what it was like to be summoned away by one wizard or another, mid-conversation and without asking whether it was convenient just then. "If it helps, I only know a few ghosts, and I'd be happy to refrain from talking about this with them."

"There's a good lad," said Lilacs with a wink. "Now then, what would you like to talk about, please?"

"Thank you for asking," said Sloot, figuring that it couldn't hurt. "Well, er, there's some trouble brewing in the Old Country, and—"

"Oh, the Old Country," said Lilacs, who had apparently just come into enough haughtiness to qualify as a fortune, and was keen on spending it. "Poor sods down there. It really isn't fair, the way they're the only ones who have to put up with the goblins, you know."

"It's funny you should mention that," said Sloot. He explained the looming threat from the south to Lilacs, who was none too pleased about the idea of goblins in Carpathia, but grudgingly admitted that it would make things fair. He simply preferred the sort of fairness that sent all of the goblins back to the Dark so no one had to deal with them, and the goblins got the whole Dark to themselves. That just seemed fair all around.

There was another tiny huddle, another tiny sussurus.

"We're going to have to talk to Dandelion," said Lilacs, once they'd come to an agreement by show of tiny hands.

"I'm afraid I don't know who that is," said Sloot.

"Well, you didn't know who *I* was," said Lilacs, with warbling incredulity, "I don't imagine you'd know the General either, would you? That wouldn't be fair, if you please."

"Of course," said Sloot. "And where is Dandelion? Er, please?"

"He's on his way, thank you."

"Oh, that's nice of him," said Sloot, who wasn't altogether comfortable with the idea of people coming to him. It usually worked the other way around, in his experience.

"It's only fair," said Lilacs. "After all, you came all the way here, didn't you?"

"I suppose so."

"Besides, this garden has much better acoustics for a public hearing, if you please."

"A public hearing?"

"A public hearing!" shouted the chorus of fairies in unison, causing

Sloot to fear for a moment that he'd accidentally wandered into a musical number. He tolerated musical numbers to the degree that the Salzstadt Ministry of the Arts deemed appropriate, he just didn't know any of his lines. This was a lot less common than his dream about being naked in the counting house, which made it slightly more disconcerting.

"We can't be expected to make any decisions about a pending goblin menace without having a public hearing," said Lilacs. "It wouldn't be fair."

"No," said Sloot, "I don't suppose it would."

The fairies all worked together to coax some of the less horrifically deadly vines and creepers into a sort of arena for the hearing. The whole thing was about the size of Sloot's first apartment, or the foyer to Willie's last closet. It was ample for the fairies, and nearly long enough in one direction for Sloot to lie down. They left the roof off so Sloot could watch from outside. Most of the carnivorous vegetation had figured out that he wasn't edible by the time Dandelion arrived.

"The assembly will come to order, please!" shouted a tall-for-a-fairy fairy in a frock coat that didn't skimp on the shoulder pads. "Pray attend as his majesty, King Lilacs, welcomes General Dandelion to the Western Gardens!"

There was a round of polite applause, during which Sloot wondered why Lilacs hadn't introduced himself as *King* Lilacs before. It seemed like a relevant detail, and an odd one to overlook. He further wondered why the king would be the only fairy not in a fabulous suit.

Sloot also tried to join in the applause, only to discover that one required hands to make the sound of two hands clapping, to say nothing of the philosophical implications of halving that. He went through the motions anyway, for the appearance of civility.

"Hail, General Dandelion," said Lilacs, "if you please. Welcome to our gardens, where you are welcome to stay as long as you like."

"Thank you, Your Majesty," said Dandelion. Like the king, he wore only a loincloth. He was also squat and hairy, possibly more so on both counts than King Lilacs. Using his natural sense of accountancy, Sloot surmised that it would be possible to produce an accurate accounting on that score, the only barrier being the fact that he firmly didn't want to.

Given that Sloot couldn't possibly have gone into bystanding at a fairy public hearing with any expectations, one of the infinite number of things that he hadn't expected was for King Lilacs and General Dandelion to thrice shake a fist at each other. This resulted in Dandelion holding out two fingers slightly apart, while Lilacs hand lay flat.

"We have performed the rite of ancient and honorable combat," said Lilacs, "and General Dandelion has bested me! The floor is yours, General."

"Thank you, Your Majesty. Did you know that I am undefeated in ancient and honorable combat?"

"Undefeated! Ever?"

"Never."

"Well, that hardly seemed fair, if you please."

A murmur of general agreement wafted up from the assembly.

"I wholeheartedly agree," said Dandelion. "That's why I never eat honey."

"Never?"

"Never ever."

Lilacs scrunched his face in consideration.

"I think that about balances out," said Lilacs. There was a gentle round of applause. "Proceed, please."

"Thank you. Good time of day, fairies of the Western Gardens!"

"Good time of day, General Dandelion!" they echoed in response. The canopy of foliage was so dense that it was hard to tell what time it was, so Sloot assumed this was a generic greeting among the fairies.

"I'd like to bring you good greetings from the Southern Gardens, if you please." He paused, and the assembly applauded. "Thank you. Good greetings to all of you. Now then, since I am here at His Majesty's invitation, I would like to yield the floor, please and thank you."

"We return good greetings to you, General Dandelion," said Lilacs as the polite applause died down. "It is also fair that we should temper this lovely exchange of greetings with some bad news."

"Bad news?" asked Dandelion. "Oh well, I suppose that's fair. What is the bad news, please? Oh, and point of order, did you know that there's an enormous ghost watching us right now?"

"Goblins," said Lilacs. "And yes, thank you. The ghost brought us the news about the goblins."

"And you granted him an audience anyway?"

"To be fair, we granted him an audience before we knew about the goblins thing."

"Oh," said Dandelion. "Bad luck, that."

"Quite."

"So what about the goblins, please?"

"Well, in short, they're coming."

"Coming? Here? Are you sure, please?"

"Not entirely, thank you for asking. Ahem. Hello there, Mr. Ghost!"

"Er, it's Peril," said Sloot. "Sloot Peril. If you please."

"Ah, *Peril*," said Lilacs. "A fine Carpathian name! Well then, Mr. Peril, what's the likelihood of the goblins coming to Carpathia, please?"

"Well," said Sloot, who hadn't done a proper *a priori* forecast or even reviewed the empirical probabilities surrounding the matter like a good accountant would have done, "high."

"Hello." Dandelion waved.

"Er, yes," said Sloot, waving back. "Furthermore, there is a high likelihood that the goblins will invade Carpathia."

"When, please?"

"Soon."

"How soon, please?"

"I couldn't say," said Sloot. "The passage of time isn't the forte of the dead, I'm afraid."

"I see," said Lilacs. "Well, I assume there's going to be a war council."

It wasn't a question *per se*, but Sloot got the distinct impression that he was meant to answer it. Several hundred distinct impressions, actually, as all eyes were now upon him.

"Er, that sounds like the sort of thing that Vlad would go in for."

There was a collective gasp from the assembled fairies at the mention of the Invader.

"You never mentioned that you were here on *her* behalf," said

Dandelion with gravity nearly sufficient to pull any nearby stars into him.

"Didn't I? I mean, I didn't. That is to say, I'm not technically—"

"Well, that's wonderful news, isn't it?"

The round of applause that rippled up coaxed Sloot into silence. He wasn't an official emissary or anything, and had no idea if he was authorized to convene a war council. Wasn't that when the leaders of armies met to plan a war? Vlad didn't have an army! He wouldn't have thought of a host of intensely fashionable fairies as an army either, but they weren't much smaller than the goblins. Besides, when it comes to wars, a small army stands a better chance than no army at all, which can only win if the other side gets bored and decides to run off and become a sports team instead.

"I knew she'd come around eventually," said Dandelion.

"Come around?" asked Sloot.

"Do you think she'll apologize to both of us at once, or individually?" asked Dandelion.

Sloot cringed. He'd never known Vlad to apologize to anyone for anything.

"It's hard to say," said Lilacs. "On the one hand, she and I are both rulers of the people."

"True," said Dandelion, "but on the other hand, she and I are both generals of our respective armies."

"Only she doesn't have an army."

"I wouldn't bring that up, if you please."

"Oh, you're right. After all, it was her grandfather that killed Ashkar and brought the curse down on them, wasn't it?"

Dandelion gave a solemn nod. Sloot didn't know whether he should be surprised to learn that the fairies knew about the doom that Vlad the 35th had brought upon the Carpathian army by slaying the old necromancer. As Ashkar burned alive, he spat a curse declaring that not one soldier would join the ranks of the Carpathian army, so long as there was a Defenestratia at the head of it. What the fairies probably didn't know was that Gregor, who was Mrs. Knife's right-hand creepy necromancer, was almost certainly Ashkar in a new—albeit rotting and decrepit—form.

"Indeed," said Dandelion. "Not very fair to her, was it?"

"No, I don't think it was."

The deliberations went on for a while after that, interspersed liberally with the further exchange of pleasantries, and including a bunch of unrelated business that Sloot largely failed to understand. But he was too polite to duck out. He felt that the giant ghost looming over the proceedings might be conspicuous if he were suddenly absent.

It wasn't an entire waste of his time, though. He learned quite a bit about fairy culture and the intricate compensational model that was the basis of their economy. It wasn't fair, for example, that Dandelion and Lilacs held exalted titles that no one else could claim; therefore, they eschewed the exquisite raiments made available to the rest of the fairies. He also learned that fairy tailors were unmatched for skill among all the people of the world. It was a good thing that there were a lot of them, because it simply wouldn't be fair if some of the fairies had a really nice wardrobe while others didn't—Dandelion and Lilacs aside, of course.

Sloot found himself wishing that he'd known about the complex fairy economical model when he was alive, so he could have studied it; then again, he was fairly certain he'd never have survived the Carpathian flora in the attempt.

⊱⊰INFERNAL BUREAUCRATIC FULFILLMENT⊱⊰

A nd you didn't think it necessary to ask any further questions?" Necessary? Well, that was debatable. Probable, in fact. But Myrtle wasn't allowing for the fact that it would've been up to Sloot to do the asking, and "why should Vlad have to apologize to you?" wasn't a very Sloot Peril thing to say. "Oh, er, all right," was as close as he'd gotten.

"Sorry," said Sloot. No matter how often he said it, the pained look on his face was the proof that he meant it every time.

He'd returned to Castle Ulfhaven to find Myrtle, Nicoleta, and Bartleby in one of the undercrofts. They were used for storing weapons, armor, taxidermied beasts, or decorative implements that were not presently on fire in some grander part of the castle. Myrtle and Bartleby were digging through crates.

"It was probably something that happened a very long time ago," said Nicoleta. "I don't think a fairy has talked to one of the Vlads since King Lilacs got drunk with Vlad the Twenty-Eighth."

"The same King Lilacs?" asked Sloot. He wasn't well-versed in Carpathian history, but imagined that the span of nine Vlads the Invader must be quite a long time.

"I wasn't around back then," retorted Nicoleta, "nor was I with you when you spoke to the present King Lilacs."

"Oh," said Sloot, failing to think of anything useful he might have said instead.

"It could be, though," Nicoleta continued. "According to what I've read, fairies live a really, really long time."

"I vas in a bar a long time ago," said Bartleby. "Three fairies valked in and asked the bartender for a bottle of gin."

"That sounds like the setup to a really bad joke," said Myrtle.

"Vhy does everybody say that? Anyvay, they vere really nice, and ve vound up drinking gin until the sun came up."

"How is that relevant?"

"I thought ve vere just talking about fairies." Bartleby rolled his eyes. "Hey, is this it?" He held up a small, blackened iron brazier shaped like a pile of skulls that had been in a very serious argument with a pile of bony hands over a pile of spikes.

"No," said Nicoleta, "but I'm pretty sure I packed that one away around the same time. This has to be the right undercroft, I can feel it!"

"How about this one?" asked Myrtle.

"Nope, no bat wings."

"This vone?"

"That's it!"

Bartleby grinned in a very unsettling way, but not nearly as unsettling as the brazier he was struggling to hold aloft.

"I'm just not sure how we're going to get it back up to the tower," said Nicoleta.

"A shrinking spell vould probably—"

"I'm afraid not," Nicoleta interrupted, "It's a particularly magic-resistant brazier, has to be in order to do its job. Last time, I had to catapult it through the tower's retractable roof."

"Your tower has a retractable roof?"

"The contractors said it would be pointless," Nicoleta sneered, "but I insisted. Shows how much they know about unshrinkable braziers."

"Couldn't you just do the ... whatever it is you do with scary-looking braziers down here?" asked Sloot.

"Shows how much you know about wizarding," Nicoleta scoffed. "You can't honestly think that I became court wizard by summoning the spirit of living fire to obliterate my competitors, just so I could cast my flashiest spells from the undercroft."

Not only was Sloot's original question severely unanswered, it was now part of a tour group that had thousands of other questions about wizarding, not the least of which being "is lunch included in the price of the tour?"

"Leave it to me," said Myrtle.

"How are you going to—"

"I'm a demon, remember? You said the tower has a retractable roof?"

Nicoleta nodded.

"I'll meet you up there."

In response to the blank stares that buzzed around her like flies, Myrtle sighed and a pair of scaly black wings unfurled from her back. She seemed embarrassed about it, regardless of how "vicked" Bartleby assured her they were.

"Please just go," said Myrtle, staring at the ground in embarrassment. Nicoleta and Bartleby shuffled off without another word, though Bartleby looked back a couple of times with apparent envy.

"Should I ..." Sloot jerked a thumb toward the door through which the others had fled. He desperately wanted to follow suit, but got the impression that this might have been one of those moments where boyfriends were expected to stick around, despite what their girlfriends had said.

"Please," she said weakly. She continued to stare at the floor, clearly chagrined.

By the time Sloot made it up to the tower and past the door—which had given him a dressing-down for passing through it without having bought it a drink first, as magically-infused doors are wont to do—Myrtle had flown the brazier in through the roof, and Nicoleta was talking Bartleby through some agitated finger-waggling.

"No, no," Nicoleta groused, "it's three times around and *then* the wrist flick! What are you trying to do, infest the tower with toads?"

"You really don't have to vorry about me this time," said Bartleby.

"Using fiendish implements of fire to scry vith the bones of a blackened soul is right up my alley."

"Says the man going straight from three-fingered claw to wrist flick like he'd never studied basic anthracomancy."

"I skimmed it."

"You don't skim anthracomancy!"

"I did."

They ultimately got the thing lit, but not without sufficient arguing to make decent use of the classic comparison with old married couples. Sloot wandered off when they started yelling at each other over which codex they should use to interpret a series of runes. As far as he was concerned, there was only one valid interpretation for fiery runes belching forth from the blue-green flames in a nefarious-looking brazier: things were soon to get very, very messy.

Of all the people in the world who might have enjoyed wandering among the shelves in the wizard's tower, none of them were Sloot Peril. All of the books—even the ones that weren't moving of their own accord, or trying to lure him in with sickly-sweet *here, ghostie, ghostie* calls—were utterly terrifying. Any fool could tell that every one of them was chock full of danger. He was especially mistrustful of the ones that just sat there, pretending to be harmless. They were the worst sort of evil: the patient sort.

One of the books sighed. No, not a book, Myrtle. She was slumped against a shelf, staring off into space.

"What are you doing down there?" asked Sloot.

"Oh, I'm …" she sighed again. "Wallowing, I suppose."

"In what?"

Myrtle failed to suppress a wan smile. Sloot knew that feeling all too well, the one where you really wanted to be depressed for a while, but you couldn't even get that right.

"Why did this have to happen to me?"

"It happens to everybody," said Sloot. "From time to time."

"Everybody doesn't become a demon when they're murdered by a necromancer."

"Oh, that."

"Yes, *that*. What did you think I was talking about?"

"Er, never mind," said Sloot. Perhaps it *was* just him who truly understood the simple pleasures of a nice, self-pitying wallow.

Myrtle drew in a breath. It was more than a life-sustaining reflex, which Sloot suddenly wondered if demons needed to do. It was the prelude to a monologue. A buoy for the soul, a brace for the will, a buttress for the resolve. Her eyes turned up to meet his. She started a sentence with the words "I just," when a scream and a crash interrupted her.

"Vhat dc you think you're doing?" Bartleby shouted. Myrtle wasted no time thinking before charging headlong toward the commotion, which Sloot remarked as incredibly brave. His instinct had been to give the whole thing the old hot soup treatment, and give it a few minutes to cool before having anything to do with it.

"Put him down!" shouted Myrtle.

"I warned him," said Franka, who was holding Bartleby over her head with apparent ease. "No harm shall come to Constantin's bones, or I'll visit the same upon you. I believe I was very clear about that."

"There's not a scratch on them!" shouted Nicoleta.

"He threw them into the fire!"

"It's *magical* fire," said Nicoleta. "It's not burning them, I swear it!"

"Prove it."

"I can," said Bartleby, "if you'll just put me down!"

"You can trust them," said Roman, failing to suppress a chuckle.

"Vhat's so funny?" Bartleby demanded. "Put me down, voman!"

"Fine," said Franka. She rolled her eyes and dropped Bartleby unceremoniously to the stone floor. Her annoyance turned to shock when, rather than crumpling into a heap of pallid necromancer, Bartleby exploded into a colony of bats, which flew off in all directions.

"Foolish mortal," Bartleby's voice echoed through the tower, "you vill pay for your insolence!" The bats began to coalesce back into a shadowy humanoid form. "You vill feel the wrath of—ow!"

Franka's fist shot into the flapping cluster of bats, drawing the illusion abruptly to a close and sending Bartleby sprawling to the floor.

"By doze!"

"That's where you should've ended up the first time," said Franka.

"Vhat did you do to by doze? Foolish bortal, you—haig odd."

Bartleby drew his wand out from within the folds of his robes, pointed it at his face, and gave it a wiggle.

"Grrrnk!" Bartleby blinked several times and shook his head.

"That looked like it hurt," said Nicoleta.

"You have no idea," said Bartleby.

"You barely flinched when Vlad took a chunk out of your cranium!"

"I can see vhy that vould be confusing," said Bartleby, "but ve have more pressing matters than necromantic physiology at the moment."

"Oh, no," Sloot moaned.

"He said *physiology*," whispered Myrtle, "and Arthur isn't here."

"Are you sure?"

"He was in my head for a couple of decades. I've always got a sense of where he is."

Having neither been possessed by a philosopher nor turned into a demon, Sloot was at a loss to discern why Myrtle and Arthur were still linked. Then again, Myrtle had experienced both of those phenomena, and may not have understood the link either. It didn't really matter. Whatever the explanation, Myrtle clearly wasn't holding the clean end of the stick.

The *shinggg* of a blade being drawn from its sheath drew Sloot's attention to the fact that Franka was still vexed about Constantin's bones. The violent crackling that resulted from Bartleby tipping his head to one side expressed his continued displeasure in the same matter.

"I'll pull your still-beating heart from your chest," Franka sneered.

"I'd be truly impressed if you could," Bartleby hissed.

"Stop it, the both of you!" growled Myrtle. She was visibly straining with the effort of keeping her teeth from going all pointy, snarly, dog-who'd-seen-another-dog-it-hadn't-met. Strangely, it didn't make Sloot any less attracted to her. He found *that* deeply troubling, but then again, he would.

In the moment of awkward silence that followed, a winged imp shot out of the flaming brazier with a ferocity that left no doubt who had the right-of-way just then. It collided with a shelf, which wobbled a bit.

"Careful," grumbled one of the books on the shelf. It gave a little stretch, repositioned itself, and went back to sleep.

"Sorry," said the imp. He picked himself up, straightened his glasses, and started leafing through some papers from his satchel. "Right then, which of you is at least a seventh-level Black Knight, a Ceremonial Warlock, or a subscriber to the Soft Cheese of the Month Club?"

Sloot took comfort in the fact that, for once, he wasn't the only one staring at everybody else in the room without a clue as to what was happening.

"Hmmm," said the imp. He pulled a clay tablet from his pocket that had angry-looking sigils all over it, and studied it over the tops of his glasses. "This *is* the Upper Level of the Wizard's Tower, Castle Ulfhaven, Ulfhaven, Carpathia, is it not?"

"Yes," said Nicoleta.

The imp consulted a glowing rune on his wrist. "Right time, right place. And you are members in good standing with the Serpents of the Earth, are you not?"

"Not exactly," said Roman.

"Not exactly?"

"It's a gentler way of saying 'no.'"

"Ah," said the imp. His face went all wrinkly with the effort of thought. "Bit of a pickle, I'm afraid. I've been sent with certain information that can only be divulged to a seventh-level Black Knight, a Ceremonial Warlock, or a subscriber to the Soft Cheese of the Month Club."

"I'm a Keeper in the Skeleton Key Circle," Franka said.

"Oh, all right," said the imp. He produced a little leather-bound book from his satchel and consulted it. He frowned. "It says here you're equivalent to a fifth-level Black Knight. Close, but no cigar."

"We receive complimentary Christmas baskets from the Soft Cheese of the Month Club."

"Every year?"

Franka nodded. "Our union negotiated it about thirty years ago."

The imp consulted the clay tablet again and frowned. "Sorry, not quite good enough. It does specify *monthly* subscriber, right here on the ticket." He pointed to a squiggle on the tablet that looked to Sloot like a dagger who'd been taught to smile, and had to assume that the imp was reading it correctly.

"Hang on a second," said Myrtle, shaking her head. "Who are you? What's this all about?"

The imp gave Myrtle a quizzical look, pointed to the blue-green flames erupting from the brazier, and then shrugged in lieu of saying "duh."

"What sort of spell were you casting with that thing?" asked Myrtle of Bartleby.

"Good qvestion." Bartleby turned to Nicoleta.

"We were trying to find out whatever we can about the Serpent of the Sky," said Nicoleta. "I wasn't sure what sort of answer we were going to get."

"A redacted one," said the imp. He patted his satchel. "It's all in here, but the legal representatives for the Serpents of the Earth are accomplished lobbyists in the realm of metaphysical informational exchange. If your request had been pertinent to anybody else, my office probably would have given it the old rubber stamp and sent it along to fulfillment."

"Fulfillment?"

"Fulfillment. It's generally up to them whether this sort of thing returns as a cryptic riddle, a puzzle to be solved, some beast or another that must be defeated before its treasure may be unlocked ... you get the idea. However, since the *alleged* Serpent of the Sky falls under the auspices of the Crankley-Lavamurder Act of the 457,692,113th Infernal Legislative Session, the delivery had to be notarized."

"And that's why they sent you," said Sloot.

"Naturally," said the imp. "I am a notary, after all."

He really didn't need to add that last bit. All Infernal imps are notaries. Everybody knows it.

"There's got to be a way to work this out," said Nicoleta. "We put forth the proper request, don't we have rights or something?"

The imp rolled on the floor, laughing until he wept. Having no other recourse, everyone else in the room waited with varying degrees of patience until he'd finished.

"Thanks," he wheezed at last, "I needed that. Oh, boy! You managed to squeeze 'proper request,' 'we've got rights,' and 'there's got to be a way' into the same breath! That's going to put me way ahead in the office pool!"

"I'm glad you're amused," said Nicoleta, who clearly wasn't. "What about bribery? I'm sure we can do some bribery."

"As an agent of the Infernal Bureaucracy, I am strictly forbidden to refuse a suitable bribe. Do you have any kittens? I'm famished."

"No!" shouted Nicoleta. In life, an inordinate number of her wizard's robes had kittens on them. She loved kittens. As far as she was concerned, feeding kittens to a notary was right out.

"Oh." The imp grimaced and rubbed his stomach. "Look, if you've got nothing I want, I'm afraid—"

"Bartleby, do the last bit of the incantation, would you?"

Bartleby muttered a few words in conjunction with a bit of wand-waving, and the blue-green flames sputtered abruptly and died out. True to Nicoleta's word, Constantin's bones were still in excellent condition. Well, excellent for a pile of old, bleached bones, anyway.

"If bribery won't work," said Nicoleta, "how are you with threats of violence?"

"I admire your spirit," said the imp, who then winced at having said that to a ghost. "Oh, sorry. Anyway, I'm afraid you've misread the situation. I don't need the flame portal, I'll just teleport out the old-fashioned way. Ta ta!"

The imp stood there, or rather continued to hover in mid-air, occasionally flapping his wings. He quickly adopted an expression of incredulity.

"Ahem. Ta ta!"

Nothing.

"Perhaps you didn't notice that this is a wizard's tower," said Nicoleta. "You think you can teleport in and out of a wizard's tower without a portal?"

⊱⊶THE SERPENT OF THE SKY⊷⊰

D o your worst," the imp had said.

There was an uncomfortable moment. Uncomfortable for everyone but Franka, who rather seemed to enjoy it. That made the moment even less comfortable for everyone else in attendance. But there occasionally comes a time when threats of physical violence must be made good, or no one will take you seriously when you threaten to torture someone. That was the sales tactic taught to Little Loyalists before they went door-to-door selling cookies, possibly where Franka had learned it.

There was further discomfort when it became debatable who was enjoying it more: Franka, or the imp.

It turned out that the imp was very well-versed in the art of sarcasm and trash-talking. "Oh, well, if anything's going to get me to talk, you'll not find it between those ribs. Honestly, did your granny teach you torturing?"

Eventually, the imp relented. It wasn't clear to Sloot whether he did so because he could no longer withstand the torture, or if some requisite amount of time had lapsed. Evil beings that they were, imps were sticklers for the rules. In any case, he told them that the Serpents of the Earth were converging at the Carpathian border to summon the Serpent of the Sky at the new moon.

"I've got a fairly good idea where they'll do it," said Sloot.

"Don't worry yourself, Sloot," said Nicoleta. "It shouldn't be too hard to work out the location. They'll need to form a very wide circle around an altar."

"There's one near the castle that Mrs. Knife's guards are keeping near the border. I've seen it!"

"What? There's no castle near the border."

"Well, not in the proper sense," Sloot admitted, "but that's what they called it. It's actually more a pile of rocks where a bunch of zombies are milling about."

"There vas a place just like that vhere I used to hang out vhen I vas a kid," said Bartleby. "Our parents vere alvays vorried ve vere up to no good."

"And look at you now," said Roman with a smirk.

"It could be anywhere, really," said Nicoleta. "Well, anywhere in the Old Country, if our theory about Mrs. Knife is correct."

"Er, pardon me," said Sloot, "but I'm fairly certain I know where it is."

"Really?"

"I can't see why I'd want to lie about something like that."

"No, it's just ... well, to put it plainly, you haven't been very ... useful of late."

"Oh."

"No offense."

No offense was the thing that people said when they knew very well they'd just said something offensive, but they didn't want to come off as the sort of person who was in the business of hurting other people's feelings. It was a very eat-your-cake-and-have-it-too thing to say, and it almost never had the desired effect of leaving the target unoffended.

"Just because you haven't seen what he's been up to," said Myrtle, winding up for a good telling off, "doesn't mean that he's not been useful! Sloot's got a great deal more on his plate than you do. What was it you were doing before he arranged for Bartleby to help you with your magic?"

"You can't talk to me like that in my own tower!"

That was just the beginning of a veritable vortex of unkind words, drawing everyone into it and arming them with vitriol. Tipsy uncles running off at the mouth with ill-informed political opinions at holiday dinners rarely manage to divide people so efficiently. It was a good thing that there were no amateur historians on hand, not only because this was a dark chapter best lost to the ages, but because amateur historians inexplicably feel qualified to extol the merits and follies of anything happening in the past, present, or future. It would have been fuel for the fire in this case. Amateur historians should always be encouraged to stick to commentating on the past, and even then, only among themselves.

"Enough," said Roman. "As cathartic as all of this might be, we may be short on time here. Does the new moon happen soon?"

"Tonight," said Bartleby. "Ve should hurry."

The speed of Bartleby's reply sent several quizzical stares in his direction.

"Vhat? I alvays know the lunar cycles. Every good verevolf vatcher does."

"You're a werewolf watcher?" asked Myrtle.

"Vhat, I can't have a hobby?"

"All the more reason you should trust me," said Sloot. "Really, I've seen the place you're describing! I thought they were going to have a bonfire or something, but this makes more sense! Well, not *sense*, exactly. It suits the purpose, though."

Theories abounded regarding how they could make it there in time. Myrtle could teleport there, but she couldn't summon anybody else; and while her demonic powers gave her an edge, the general consensus was that the greater assembly of Serpents of the Earth would have the upper hand. Sure, she could summon Sloot if Roman would loan her his skull, but he'd be roughly as useful as a bag of wet hair if it came to a fight, which it most certainly would.

To be fair, bags of wet hair are not entirely useless. Just ask the Arts Council of Salzstadt, or rather, the zombies now holding seats on the board thereof. At least a quarter of the modern art exhibits in the

Museum of Ministry of Propaganda Approved Art have included, or consisted entirely of, bags of wet hair.

They ultimately decided on a portal. The challenge there was that it was up to Bartleby to open it, given that there were living people among them who wanted to remain such when they arrived. Nicoleta was still agitated the entire time that she was talking Bartleby through the incantations, which Sloot felt may have had an effect on the outcome.

"It's three hundred feet off the ground!" shouted Nicoleta. The space beyond the shimmering hole in the air gave the tower a view that any realtor worth her salt could have sold for a fortune.

"*Ve're* three hundred feet off the ground," said Bartleby. He made a face that said "duh" in the inflection of one of the cool kids who never let you sit with them.

"Flaptybum's Eleventh Geographical Rune was specifically designed to—"

Boom! Whiz! Bang! Whatever Flaptybum's Eleventh Geographical Rune had been specifically designed to do, Nicoleta's lecture about it seemed less important in the moment than ducking out of the path of a volley of smoking yellow bolts of noxious energy that flew in from the portal. Most of them splattered harmlessly upon the walls and ceiling of the tower, but one smashed a pedestal that had a particularly nasty-looking book chained to it. The book hit the floor and started wriggling out from beneath the detritus that landed atop it.

"No!" shouted Nicoleta. "The Tetrapocrypha! Don't let it open!"

Roman, in a burst of unexpected work-in-lieu-of-delegation, threw himself atop the book.

"You'll have to try harder than that!" shouted Bartleby. He returned fire through the portal, smoky purple screaming skulls blasting forth from the tip of his wand. He erupted into a fit of villainous laughter that could only have been the product of a lifetime of rehearsal.

While it was possible that the magic being fired into the tower would have no effect on the dead, Sloot didn't want to break his heretofore unblemished record of staunch risk aversion. He dropped to the floor and tried to make himself as flat as possible. He might have even tried sinking into it a bit, had years of exposure to magic not seeped into the stones and made the floor resist that sort of thing.

"It's like they were ready for us," said Nicoleta. She was standing directly in the line of fire, and a series of glowing red projectiles passed straight through her with no effect.

Sloot kept his head down anyway. Despite their lack of effect on Nicoleta, he didn't know for sure that the red ones wouldn't hurt him. Then there were the yellow ones. And Bartleby's purple ones. Some green ones started appearing as well. As time went on, a veritable rainbow of magical projectiles pummeled the inside of the tower.

Sloot wished that he could help. Not with the problem at hand, mind you, that was far beyond his comfort zone. Instead, he kept his head down and lamented the fact that there were no ledgers that he could save the day by balancing. What else could he do, other than get shot up by potentially dangerous magic?

"We've got to do something," Myrtle shouted over the din of magical warfare.

"Got my hands full at the moment," shouted Roman, who was barely able to keep the pages of the Tetrapocrypha together.

"They're coming!" shouted Nicoleta.

"What? Who's coming?"

"Goblins!"

Sloot crept forward. While the prospect of getting shot by a magical projectile was scary, an advancing congress of goblins was scarier still, to say nothing of an advancing congress of goblins that he couldn't see. Sneaking a peek, in this case, was a calculated risk that could serve as an incremental reduction in Sloot's overall level of terror.

Sloot's calculations could not have been more wrong. Even considering the occasion of his own violent demise, He'd never seen a congress of goblins so nightmarishly huge. They were piling on top of each other, a putrid, unwashed mass of miscreations swarming upward toward the portal.

"Stand aside," growled a voice from behind them. It cleared a path with the efficacy of a magic spell, though it was not spoken by a wizard.

"Vlad!"

"I told you to stop the Serpent of the Sky!" She lumbered forward in her red steel armor, crouched behind a tower shield that was nearly as tall as her. If Sloot wasn't mistaken, it was the same armor and shield she'd used at the Fall of Salzstadt. The shield had only blocked arrows that day, but now the magical projectiles were bouncing off of it as well.

"That's what we were trying to do," said Nicoleta. "The plan has gone awry!"

"So it has." Vlad stood at the portal, bracing her shield against her shoulder and looking down on the swarming congress of goblins rising up toward her.

"Wait a minute," said Sloot, to no one in particular. "If Vlad is here, then that must mean that … oh, dear."

"What are we going to do?" asked Myrtle.

Vlad said nothing, just waited. She was mouthing something silently to herself. Most people might not have picked up on it, but Sloot's mastery of numbers left him in no doubt that she was counting down, though he couldn't have guessed why.

"Spymaster!" Vlad shouted.

"Yes, Your Dominance?"

"Do something about our guest in the dungeon."

Roman answered through gritted teeth as he wrestled with the Tetrapocrypha. "Yes, Your Dominance."

The Domnitor! Long may he reign. She'd done it! She'd gone to Stagralla and kidnapped him. Sloot had known about the plot! He was tangentially involved in the abduction of his liege! And not even with the particular plot that had been launched by his fellow salts in Uncle. Sloot harbored serious doubts that this would end well.

Vlad turned then to Nicoleta. "Stop the stars."

"I will, Your Dominance."

Vlad nodded, and then she jumped.

That was unexpected, though mathematically speaking, Sloot should have seen it coming. Heroic types like Vlad seldom approached danger in a way that he found sensible.

Sloot threw caution to the wind and craned his neck through the portal just in time to see Vlad land shield-first on the topmost goblin in the pile, sending the whole swaying structure collapsing inward on itself.

"Vhat is she doing?" shouted Bartleby from behind a shelf. He fired a few more blasts from his wand through the portal.

"What she does best," said Nicoleta. "Come on, we've got to help her!"

"How?" asked Sloot.

"Wait for the wizards to stop shooting into the portal," said Myrtle. Her eyes went black and her leathery wings unfolded. "When they're focused on Vlad, I'll slip in behind them."

"Take me with you," said Franka, before Sloot had an opportunity to raise any objections. She crouched on the stone floor in front of Myrtle, sword in one hand and wand in the other. Myrtle shrugged and placed her hands on Franka's shoulders.

What could Sloot do? He was keen to be useful, in some auxiliary capacity, of course. He couldn't make coffee for everyone, so that was out. How about the minutes? Were minutes usually recorded for battles? How would anybody know what happened otherwise? He'd heard lots of stories about valiant warriors who committed acts of what might have turned out to be stupidity, only they worked out well, so they were reported as acts of bravery instead. He supposed that was what bravery was, in the end. Risks that turned out well.

"Now!" shouted Nicoleta. The magical bombardment had ceased, and she was watching all of the Serpents of the Earth's wizards directing their fire into the towering pile of goblins, trying to hit Vlad.

That's low, thought Sloot. Weren't the goblins and the evil wizards supposed to be on the same side? Evil *and* indecent. Not respectable evil, like murderers who only go after people who smugly say "I could have told you that."

It quickly dawned on Sloot that only *most* of the wizards were shooting at Vlad. A few of them, one of whom had to be Gregor, were lurking in the ring of stones behind the border "castle." Sloot only had a moment to enjoy having been right about the location when it occurred to him what was happening. The pile of goblins and the wizards firing wands at them were a distraction! They were probably very close to completing the ritual for the Serpent of the Sky.

"Wait," said Sloot, just as Franka and Myrtle leaped through the portal. They banked together into the dark of night, circling around to sneak up on the distracted wizards.

"Wait for what?" asked Nicoleta.

"Vait until they see vhat I can blast them vith, now that I've got a moment to prepare," said Bartleby.

"Later," shouted Roman. "Come help me shut the clasp on the Tetrapocrypha, will you?"

"The wizards," said Sloot, "and the goblins. It's all a ruse! Look over there, at the castle!"

"I'm not seeing any castle," said Nicoleta, squinting along the horizon.

"It's not a—oh, the pile rocks!"

"What are they ... oh, no," said Nicoleta. "Sloot, you've got to warn them!"

"Me? How can I possibly—"

"Just float down there and do it," Nicoleta snapped. "I've got to deal with things up here! You two, the binding strap has to wrap around the Tetrapocrypha the other way. No, the *other* way!"

I really wish I could do something useful, Sloot had thought before. That had been foolish. The forces that control the universe are always listening, and they're very good at catching people lying to themselves. For Sloot, wishing that he could do something useful was his subconscious' way of saying "I really want to hide behind something and wait this out, but I don't want to feel cowardly about it."

Stupid forces that control the universe, Sloot thought. *This is what my aspirations to a slightly lower grade of faintheartedness have done for me. Why couldn't I have simply enjoyed a cold oblivion devoid of existence after death?*

"Get going!" Nicoleta shouted.

Sloot closed his eyes and propelled himself forward. He was

pleasantly disappointed, upon opening one eye, to see that he was not plummeting toward the ground as he'd expected, but floating gently toward it. His disappointment turned unpleasant when he opened the other eye and turned to look at the swarming congress of goblins.

You never forget how you died. Well, Sloot had been dead for a while now, and he hadn't forgotten how he died. It hadn't yet been forever, but the feeling of being crushed to death under a congress of goblins was still very vivid in his mind. He tried to take some small comfort in the fact that there were no undead mixed in this time, but it was no good. His mind simply couldn't count absence of the undead in a teeming pile of violence as a bright side.

Vlad was in there. She needed to know that she was fighting the wrong fight, which meant that Sloot was going to have to tell her. All of the logic that applied to disembodied spirits—if you could really call it logic—told him that he'd come to absolutely no harm by wading into the fray, but it didn't help. He could still feel their weight on his chest, crushing the life from him.

He looked back up to the portal, hoping against hope to see Nicoleta floating down, having finished dealing with the Tetrapocrypha. No such luck.

Nothing left to do but dive in, then. He gave brief consideration to the possibility that it might be fun. He shook his head. Nope, he wouldn't be fooling himself that way. Educational, perhaps? Slightly more convincing than "fun," but it still wasn't helping. As expertise in piles of goblins went, Sloot felt that he already knew everything he needed.

Duty, then. That was something Sloot understood. He was a true salt of the Old Country, through and through. Never mind that he was doing his duty to the Carpathian sovereign. If there was one thing that every salt knew, it was duty.

He firmed up his resolve to simply march into the swarming throng, and nearly followed through with it before stopping just at its edge.

A toe. Why not just a toe? Sloot was well aware that time was running short, but what if he was wrong? What if he *could* get hurt? He wouldn't be any good to anyone dead. Deader? No matter. He slowly pushed one foot toward a pair of goblins who seemed to be trying to dig their way into the pile, and the worst possible thing that could have happened did: they noticed him.

A pair of broad, needle-toothed grins turned themselves on Sloot. They crouched and started reaching slowly, gently toward him, as though he were a deer in a petting zoo. One which they were very keen to eat.

"Er, hello," said Sloot with a nervous smile. "Lovely night for a brawl, isn't it? How do you think it's going so far?"

One of the goblins lunged forward and grabbed at Sloot's waist, to Sloot's high-pitched, screaming terror; however, predictably, the goblin fell through him and ended up face-first in the dirt.

"Terribly sorry," said Sloot, before he was able to stop himself. "Are you all right?"

The goblin was on its feet and snarling. It wheeled and jumped through Sloot again, landing claws-first on its comrade, and either oblivious or indifferent to the fact that it was rending the guts of its kin.

Considering all of the factors, Sloot could not in good conscience avoid the inevitable any longer. He steeled his nerves as best he could, which was hardly at all, and floated into the quagmire. Had he not been so deeply invested in the compounded trauma that was now piling onto his psyche, he might have thought it interesting to see what it looked like inside one of these. In the tightest, load-bearing parts of the structure, most of the goblins were just sort of wriggling helplessly or passed out altogether. Sloot kept moving in the direction that must have been toward the center, where Vlad would undoubtedly be.

He was only off by a dozen yards or so, but he'd heard Vlad's battle cries often enough to know them when he heard them. He shifted his course and ended up in what he could only describe as a constantly collapsing dome of shadowy smoke surrounding Vlad. She turned constantly, bashing forward with her shield, swinging wide with her hammer, kicking out with her spiked steel boots, and dispatching goblins by the score in puffs of smoke.

"Your Dominance!" shouted Sloot.

"Peril, isn't it?"

"It is, Your Dominance."

"Speak quickly, I'm busy."

"Er, yes, Your Dominance. Sorry, Your Dominance."

With a minimal amount of stammering and apologies, Sloot told Vlad about the castle and the ruse. After a trip up to the top of the pile and back down again, he got Vlad turned in the direction of the circle of stones behind the castle. She fought her way slowly, inexorably through the goblin horde in that direction.

"Tell me, Peril," said Vlad.

"Yes, Your Dominance?"

"Have you ever seen this many goblins in one place?"

"I can't say that I have, Your Dominance." That was true. Until that day, the most goblins he'd ever seen at once had been at the Fall of Salzstadt. While that had been a large enough congress to demand swear words to describe it, it paled in comparison to this one. This was, in no uncertain terms, an *expletive redacted* load of goblins.

"That's ... troubling."

"Indeed," said Sloot, who was nearly as troubled by the fact that Vlad didn't appear winded. He was exhausted just watching her.

All of a sudden, she was through. The stars of the night sky appeared through the dissipating cloud of hammered goblins. Sloot floated out into the clearing, but Vlad turned and stood her ground against the goblins that were still swarming all around her.

"The wizards!" shouted Sloot, wheeling around in search of imminent danger.

"What wizards?"

"The ones firing up at the portal," cried Sloot. "They turned on you when you jumped, surely they're—"

"Dead," said Franka. She was completely drenched in blood, kneeling on the ground a few feet away. At least she had the courtesy to seem winded from the effort.

"Well, that's a relief," said Sloot, who didn't generally approve of mass murder, but perhaps being dead himself had diluted the associated horror. "Wait, where's Myrtle?"

Franka pointed up toward the portal. The congress of goblins was still climbing atop each other, forming a horrid sort of mountain, its peak reaching for the entrance to the tower. Myrtle flapped her wings just above the peak, her razor-sharp claws dispatching goblins with every swipe.

"Your Dominance," shouted Franka, "we have to hurry! The goblins will not stray from the pile, you may disengage in safety!"

"Never!" shouted Vlad. "Retreat is for cowards and weaklings! I have never stooped so low, and I shall not start now!"

Sloot said a swear word, reasoning that one more goblin wasn't going to amount to much bother in the aggregate.

"It's not retreating," said Sloot, pointing toward the ring of stones. "That's the real fight, over there! The more powerful enemy!"

"You make a good point," said Vlad, "but I can't turn my back on the enemy in front of me. It could take half an hour or more to dispatch this horde!"

"Half an hour?"

"Forty-five minutes, perhaps."

As impressive as Vlad's estimate was, it didn't account for the fact that they were dispatching goblins by the score, but the pile didn't seem to get any smaller. Sloot couldn't see where they were all coming from, but assumed there was an elite cadre of linguists hidden away nearby, swearing up a storm. They probably even knew the correct pronunciation of "cadre" without having to think about it.

Sloot looked over to the ring of stones and the sickly green glow that cast from within it. He heard a cackling that chilled him to his very core, one that required the years of practice that only a necromancer would have time to put in.

Gregor.

Vlad was still close enough to the pile that a few goblins would charge her at a time, effectively preventing her from getting on with things that desperately needed getting on with.

Franka's fists shook in frustration. "Do something!"

Sloot sighed. He didn't question that she was talking to him. He had an innate sense that told him to assume orders barked in his presence were meant for him. He cringed as he floated in front of Vlad, shouting "here, goblins! Come listen to all of the worst swear words I know!"

He shouted the one that starts with a "W" and calls one's least favorite uncle's hygiene into question. Then he yelled out a sentence that used the noun, adjective, and verb forms of the one that starts with a "J." That one really got the goblins' attention. They seemed to forget about Vlad altogether and start chasing after Sloot, who floated off in the opposite direction as quickly as he could, shouting the one that rhymes with "custard" over and over again, even though it made absolutely no sense in context.

It worked! Sloot hazarded a glance over his shoulder, and beyond the bloodthirsty congressional committee that was hot on his heels, he saw Vlad and Franka sprinting toward the circle of stones. He only hoped they'd get there in time.

Well, that wasn't exactly true. While he did hope for that, he applied most of his hope of finding some means of losing his pursuers before they caught up with him. His level of panic was too high in the moment to allow any brutally obvious revelations past the velvet rope of realization.

He eventually managed it by turning and plunging into the greater congressional pile. He didn't bother checking, but assumed that his pursuers followed along and re-assimilated into the mass. The feeling of relief from having plunged himself, once again, into the teeming mass of goblins quickly wore off. He floated upward and exited through the top of the pile, not far from Myrtle.

"Myrtle!" he shouted.

"Sloot! What's happened to Vlad?"

"She and Franka are going to deal with the castle."

"That's good," she said, then grunted with the effort of dispatching another pair of goblins with her wicked claws. "I can't keep this up forever. We're going to have to close the portal!"

"I thought the goblins couldn't leave the Old Country!"

"Not usually," said Myrtle, "but Nicoleta thinks portals might be an exception. Take that!" Another three goblins vanished in puffs of smoke. "I really wish I had my broom right now." Her claws were doing an impressive job, but nothing ripped through goblins like a well-made broom.

"Things aren't going well down there," shouted Roman. He was leaning through the portal, watching the castle through an old brass spyglass. "I don't know if Vlad will be able to get to Gregor before he finishes the spell!"

"There's still a chance," shouted Nicoleta. "Bartleby, open the Astrogrammaton to the chapter on inescapable blackness. I think there's a spell in there you could manage. Hurry, we only have a few minutes!"

"Less than that," yelled Myrtle. Her claws reduced another goblin to shadow. She was ripping through them with ferocious efficiency, but it wasn't enough. The goblins just kept coming. There were far more than Myrtle, Roman, and Bartleby combined could ever overcome, even if they wielded two brooms apiece.

"We're going to have to close the portal!" shouted Myrtle.

"Sloot!" yelled Nicoleta. "If Vlad kills Gregor in time, the ritual might fizzle out. You have to tell her!"

"But what if—"

"Go! If we have to close the portal before Bartleby finishes this spell, we'll lose our only chance!"

Sloot spared a glance at Myrtle as he turned, but she was far too busy slaughtering goblins to meet it. Of all the things that could have interfered with his romantic endeavors, Sloot couldn't have foreseen this one in particular. If Myrtle had, she hadn't told him about it.

He floated as quickly as he could over the carnage of the battlefield, past the colossal goblin congress piling itself ever skyward, the corpses of the wizards that Myrtle and Franka had killed, and coming at last to what seemed to be an enormous magical shield surrounding the circle of stones.

"Curse their magic," bellowed Vlad. "Cowards! Dispel this shield and meet me with honor!"

"You're wasting your time," said Franka. She sat patiently on the ground, legs folded and back straight. Sloot had seen Bartleby do that before, when he was trying to teach Willie meditation. It looked terribly uncomfortable. Then again, he'd never bothered with the pursuit of good posture. In accounting, bad posture was the mark of a man who'd slaved over his ledgers properly.

"Can you pass through it?"

"Who, me?" asked Sloot.

"Of course, you!" Vlad growled with all of the fury and adrenaline that one would expect of a warrior who trained for combat from dawn to dusk. "Get in there and possess that necromancer!"

"I wouldn't know how to—"

"Go!"

Given the choice of charging headlong through a magical shield that may or may not be harmful to disembodied spirits, or further vexing the most skilled warrior that history has ever seen, Sloot enthusiastically opted for the former. As luck would have it, the shield neither impeded nor obliterated him. It did leave him with the psychic equivalent of a headache, which was worrisome, but only a bit. There had been a time, before misfortune got Sloot promoted out of the counting house, when "only a bit worrisome" would have eventually risen to the top of his queue of things needing fretting over. These days, it didn't stand a chance.

There were half a dozen wizards in black hoods with their backs to Sloot, chanting toward the stone altar where Nipsy sat, surrounded by piles of bleached bones. Sloot recognized the bindings on the piles because Constantin's had the same treatment.

"They're Soul remains," Sloot said to himself. "There must be dozens of them!"

"Hi Sloot," said Willie. He lounged fabulously just above the ground, smiling guilelessly upward at Sloot.

"Willie! What are you doing here?"

"I don't know." Willie grinned. He didn't seem confused about it at all. It was as though not knowing things was such a large part of his being that he'd simply embraced it. "Mrs. Knife told me to come. She said there would be a man doing magic, but I guess she meant Gregor. I thought she meant something cool, like balloon animals."

"You're too late, Peril!" Gregor had a mad gleam in his eye. It was just the sort of gleam one would expect to see a few inches above the bloodthirsty sneer he was also wearing.

"What does that mean?" Willie whined. "It can't be finished already. You haven't done any tricks or anything! It's not fair!"

"Quiet, Willie! Oh, we're nearly finished with a saucy bit of magic now." He cackled with rabid delight.

Gregor waggled a wand at Nipsy. Sickly yellow tendrils of thick wet smoke flowed from the wand's tip, meandering among the remains of the Souls like pickpockets at a street fair. His other hand was gesturing thaumaturgically at Willie. Sloot noticed that he looked withered, drained; as though he'd just sat through his grandfather's old war story for the umpteenth time, having long ago given up on convincing him that you couldn't use certain words for foreigners nowadays.

"What's he doing to you?"

"Don't worry," yawned Willie, "I'm sure it's all part of the trick. I once saw a man in a top hat cut a lady in half, but she was back together by the end of it."

There was a banging sound from behind Sloot that resembled glass cracking. He turned around to see Vlad slamming her warhammer against the magical shield.

"Do something!" she shouted, her voice muffled by the shield. "Possess that necromancer!"

Sloot didn't have the foggiest idea how he might go about possessing someone, especially given that Gregor had most likely possessed that particular body while it had still been alive.

"Think, Peril, *think!*" he shouted to himself, as though it were a voice-activated process.

"I hope he finishes soon," said Willie. He yawned. "I feel so sleepy."

"Sleepy?" Sloot hadn't felt sleepy since before he was crushed to death. He noticed smoky white pulses of light that were flowing from Willie to the half dozen wizards facing the other way.

"The wizards," said Sloot, "they're draining Willie's vitality!"

Sloot drank in the horrifying realization. Wizards could, in fact, harm the spirits of the dead! The only thing standing between him and an oh-so-sweet "I told you so" was the technicality that he'd not, in fact, told anyone anything of the sort. At least he still felt the fiery shot of a full-scale panic rise up within him. Never let it be said that Sloot Peril ever insulted an inducement to terror with anything less than the full brunt of his discomposure.

"No, no, no, no, no, no, no!" Sloot whimpered as he floated as quickly as he could away from danger. That was difficult to do, partially due to the sheer number of things that counted as "dangerous" by Sloot's measure, but mostly thanks to Gregor.

"Don't let Peril escape!" he shouted. A couple of wands turned in his direction, and he felt a jolt. What was it? It wasn't painful. It was something he hadn't felt in a long time, and it took him a moment to place it.

Tired. Yes, that was it. He felt like he could sleep for a week. He turned and saw steamy little wisps of his essence pulling away from him, floating toward Gregor and his cadre of wizards.

Is Willie still alive? Sloot wondered. Oh, he knew what he meant. Still deceased in the ambulatory sense. He thought back to Constantin's lawyer telling him about the blood economy. They'd only covered vitality going into a ghost, not a word regarding withdrawals. He wondered how quickly they could drain a ghost entirely. Could this be the end for Sloot Peril? Er, again?

"I'm afraid so," came a disembodied voice. It sounded even more timid than Sloot's typical inflection, more wretched even than the one he used when imploring mercy from muggers, by which he meant children selling cookies.

"You're not Gregor," said Sloot. The voice seemed to be coming from somewhere within the crusty old sack of bones, but it definitely wasn't him.

"No," wheedled the voice, "I'm just the wretched fool he possessed nearly a century ago. You wouldn't happen to know how to kill a necromancer who's lived for over a thousand years, would you?"

"I'm afraid not."

"Oh, well. Thanks anyway. Gosh, but I'm on tenterhooks for the sweet release of oblivion."

Sloot was horrified. Anyone with an inkling of humanity would be, not just a career worrier with a flawless record. At least when Myrtle was possessed by Arthur, she was still largely running the show. This poor fool had apparently been relegated to silent partner, a passenger within his own mind.

"What's your name?" asked Sloot, hoping the conversation would help him stay awake.

"I don't remember. Lawrence, maybe?"

"And what did you do before you were possessed?"

"Nothing good, I'm afraid. I mostly beat people up, as I recall. I was a big fellow."

"Not that big anymore," said Sloot. He was right. Gregor was an emaciated walking corpse. He looked like someone had wrapped pancetta around a pile of kindling and taught it to sneer.

All of a sudden, the connection was broken. There was an explosion of light, and Nipsy started howling.

"Hey," shouted Willie, "what are you doing to my dog?"

"The Serpent!" shouted Gregor. "The Serpent of the Sky! Rise up, horrid stars! Rise!"

Nipsy and the remains of the Souls gathered around him flamed and sparkled. They rose up into the air, coalescing into the shape of a gargantuan, coiled serpent. The serpent hissed and rumbled, its great maw opening as it shot toward the heavens.

Despite the overwhelming feeling of dread, Sloot had to fight to keep his eyes open. Even Franka running through him to collide sword-first with one of the wizards wasn't enough to give him a surge of whatever passed for adrenaline with the dearly departed. Neither was the roar from Vlad as she charged toward Gregor, his bolts of magic bouncing harmlessly off her enchanted armor.

Distracted by his overwhelming desire to have a lie-down, Sloot was having trouble focusing. He watched the Serpent of the Sky rising up into the heavens, flaming, sparkling—and suddenly, it winked out.

Gregor screamed in fury. "Where is it? Curses upon all of you, where is it?"

Gregor received no answer but his own screaming, as Vlad tore his wand arm from its socket.

"Villain!" she shouted at him.

"Curse you," he spat back at her. "You're the villain! I'll have my revenge, I swear it!"

"Not without a body to possess, you won't!"

Sloot looked around. Vlad was right! Franka had already killed all of the other wizards with ruthless efficiency, not that Sloot needed any more reasons to be afraid of her. Furthermore, she seemed to have disappeared. There wasn't a living human nearby. Not one *not* wearing enchanted armor, anyway. No one for Gregor to possess. This could mean the end of the curse! Vlad could raise her army again!

She lifted her hammer high.

Gregor said a particularly vile swear word.

A goblin went *pop!*

Crunch.

At least Lawrence must have found some peace. Well, Sloot hoped for that, in any case. He hated to think of anyone trapped silently within their own mind, especially when his head had been reduced to the consistency of uncooked eggs with the shells mixed in.

"It is done!" shouted Vlad.

"Not quite," croaked the goblin that had just blinked in.

Sloot's jaw went slack with disbelief. "Gregor?"

"Peril," sneered the goblin in an all-too-familiar way.

"Gregor!" said Sloot, the horror plain on his face. He wouldn't have thought it possible, though he had to admit he knew nothing about magic. Perhaps possessing the bodies of goblins was a very humdrum practice for necromancers.

Gregor said a swear word. "I've never had to be a goblin before. This is going to take some getting used to." He flinched, and said another swear word. "I bit my tongue! Curse all of these pointy teeth, why are there so many?"

There was a great rumbling noise from behind them. Sloot turned to see the enormous pile of goblins collapsing in on itself. They must have decided to give up on reaching the portal, since it was no longer there.

"Myrtle!" shouted Sloot. She'd stayed on this side of the portal, no doubt to hold the goblins off for as long as possible while Nicoleta and Bartleby did … whatever it was that they did to stop the Serpent of the Sky. Myrtle flapped her powerful wings and headed in Sloot's direction.

Vlad bellowed in fury. The sound was terrible on its own, which was good, because the maneuver seemed to be missing something.

Blood, thought Sloot, with a nod to himself. Goblins dissipate into shadow when they're cut down, so Vlad didn't have a drop on her. It was the first time that Sloot had ever thought, "you know what's missing here? Copious amounts of blood and gore," and it had very nearly made him feel like a proper Carpathian. It would have done, if that thought hadn't been immediately followed by some sincere fretting over who was going to clean the battlefield up, and whether they'd manage it before the Domnitor returned, long may he reign.

Gregor cackled with delight. Wait, perhaps not delight. He might have been mid-going-mad, coming to grips with the fact that he was now in the goblin possession game. It could have been both. It seemed perfectly reasonable to Sloot that necromancers might be delighted by their own descents into madness. But even if he'd wanted to consider the matter further, the congress of goblins charging toward them moved said consideration to next quarter's business.

"Oh, no," said Sloot. "This is going to be bad."

"You're telling me," said Willie with a yawn. "Nan said if I'm to have a puppy, I mustn't let him out of my sight. Oh, well, I'm sure one of the servants is looking after him. What's for dinner?"

"No," said Sloot, " I mean—"

"Any last words, Invader?" Gregor's cackling had gained the accompaniment of some properly villainous hand-wringing.

"I should ask you the same," growled Vlad.

"Go ahead," Gregor spat. "If you strike me down, I will only—"

Vlad's hammer passed frighteningly swiftly through the space that had, until then, been occupied by the newly minted goblish necromancer. Had Gregor been permitted to finish his sentence, he might have said "I will only dissipate into a cackling shadow and escape to most likely turn up and thwart you at some later date." Unlike Myrtle, Sloot couldn't see into the future, so he could only validate the first part of that with any certainty.

"Now for the rest of them." In true heroic fashion, Vlad turned toward the oncoming congressional horde like it was just another day at the office.

"Sloot!" shouted Myrtle, who was hurtling swiftly toward him. "Wait for me!"

"Wait for you? Before what—"

And suddenly, Sloot wasn't there anymore.

❧⟶IN DISGRACE❧⟶

H e's had ample opportunity," said Hans.

"True," said Geralt, "but he never really got the training, did he?"

Sloot was still very sleepy. He remembered Hans and Geralt from when he'd first arrived in the Hereafter. Geralt Schlangenkessel was financier to the late Constantin Hapsgalt, and Hans Schweinegesicht was financier to Constantin's mother, Otthilda. They each spared a sidelong glance in his direction, but obviously preferred talking about him like he wasn't there. That was the fashionable thing to do in cases where the subject had fallen out of favor, and was probably in a lot of trouble.

Oh, thought Sloot, with a sinking feeling. He was still very, very tired. How much of his vitality had Gregor and his cronies drained away? Sloot didn't particularly enjoy being a disembodied spirit, but reasoned that it was probably better than *not* being a disembodied spirit, which—according to the philosophers—might or might not mean being nothing at all.

"Training or no," said Grumley, "he conspired with the enemies of the Serpents of the Earth, and that is not something that we can forgive willy-nilly."

Something was different about the dining room, but in Sloot's listless state, he couldn't figure out what. The wall that Willie's body had melted to summon Nipsy had been repaired, but that wasn't it. The table that could easily have seated and entire orchestra, second chairs and all, was gone. That much was obvious, but there was something else.

He shook his head and immediately regretted it. It did what it was intended to do, snapping him out of half-sleep and giving him a moment of clarity; but in light of the discovery it afforded him, he'd much rather have continued drifting in his haze of confusion. The difference was the floor. Instead of the psychic approximation of carpet over stone that he'd expected, it was now a swirling morass of grey spiritual energy, composed of innumerable tormented souls writhing in agony.

"The Well of the Void," Sloot said aloud, his voice quavering.

Sloot was chained to the wall by his wrists. The others were hovering above the Well by the chandelier, looking warily downward on occasion, as though worried they might fall in.

"Quite," said Grumley with a prim sneer, his moustaches bristling with a righteous I-told-you-so. "You've been given ample opportunity to get the affairs of the Soul in order, Peril. I've tried to give you enough rope to hang yourself, but you couldn't even manage that. And then you turn up in the company of none other than Vlad the Invader! What are we supposed to make of that, hmmm?"

At the best of times, Sloot would have been hard-pressed to come up with a satisfactory lie. The truth came as easily to him as exaggeration to a snake oil salesman. So prodigious with the truth he was, he could have been an anti-politician, had that but been a career.

Fortunately for Sloot, he was also as groggy as a sailor the morning after a lost wager. He was as hard-pressed to remain coherent long enough for the truth to unrumple itself and stumble out into the light.

"Bah!" said Hans. "This is intolerable! Why do we have to wait for him to give account of his actions? Let's just toss him into the Well and be done with it. I don't have all eternity, you know."

"No one does," said Grumley, "but rules are rules."

"You keep the Well of the Void under the floor in the dining room?" asked Geralt, who'd only been dead as long as Sloot had.

"No, no," Grumley chuckled. "The Well isn't stuck to a particular place. It comes and goes as needed. Convenient, eh?"

"Quite," said Geralt with an approving nod.

"Get on with it," Hans growled, his upturned nose giving a porky snort. "You're accused of being in league with Vlad the Invader! What do you have to say for yourself? Do you deny the charges?"

"And you call yourself a loyal subject of the Domnitor," scoffed Geralt, "long may he reign."

"Long may he reign," Sloot blurted.

"Don't you dare!" Geralt squawked. "Traitors shall not mock the reign of the Domnitor, long may he reign!"

"Long may he reign."

"Stop it! It's against the law for traitors to—"

"It's against the law to be a traitor," Grumley snapped. "But you forget, sir, yet again, that the laws of the Old Country do not apply here! Would you please focus on the matter at hand so that we can conclude our business?"

A scowl that could have dissuaded crows from bothering crops took up residence on Geralt's face. His chest puffed up to bursting. Sloot knew what he must have been feeling, and would have felt the same himself, had someone told him to stop defending the good name of the Domnitor, long may he reign. In fact, Sloot had half a mind to jump to Geralt's defense in the matter. Not only was it the right thing for a true salt of the Old Country to do, it might buy him more time to think of a way out of his predicament.

"He's obviously guilty," said Hans. "The Book of Black Law was very carefully written to *not* require a stenographer at these proceedings, specifically so we could cherry-pick the most convenient rules and get the results we're after. Let's just dispense with his testimony and get on with chucking him into the Well."

"The Book of Black Law doesn't require stenographers because they were very expensive when it was written," said Grumley. "I don't think—"

"Now, don't you go thinking too deeply about the Book of Black Law!" Hans floated menacingly close to Grumley and waggled a finger under his moustaches. "It's not subject to interpretation! It is the guiding body of law—"

"Everything is subject to interpretation," Grumley waggled back. "If the Prime Evils had been able to conceive of every possible—"

"The will of the Prime Evils isn't subject to interpretation either!"

"Gentlemen, please!" shouted Geralt, with all the audacity of a junior clerk running on pluck and coffee alone. "We just need to hear his testimony. Can we leave the interpretation of the Book of Black Law for another time? We'll be here forever if we get into a philosophical debate."

In the moment of silence that followed, the room trembled. It was almost imperceptible, leaving Sloot to question whether it had actually happened, or if he was simply paying homage to the old trope of a dog sleeping by the hearth, raising his head suddenly at the sound of nothing.

It wasn't nothing. It was footsteps. The hurried, agitated sprinting of one very perturbed for having been called upon without an appointment.

"Who said philosophy?" demanded Arthur, who was suddenly in the center of the room, fists turned upward in front of him. "Debate me, you cowards! One at a time or all at once, I'll have the lot of you!"

"Who the devil are you?" asked Hans.

"Who are any of us?" Arthur howled. "Identity is nothing more than the continuity of self as perceived by the ego!" It had obviously been a very long time since he'd gotten to debate philosophy with anyone. He had a lot of pent-up vitriol and was eager to spew it wherever it might land, regardless of what damage might result, like a fire hose in a china shop.

They went around in circles for what felt like hours to Sloot, though he had no way of knowing. Even if the concept of time were properly perceptible in the Hereafter, he couldn't shake the feeling of drowsiness. His thoughts kept drifting off into the nonsensical, causing him to wonder things like whether five toes per foot was really the optimal arrangement.

"There you are," said Myrtle, who suddenly appeared in the room. "I told you to wait for me!"

"Did you?" Sloot tried to remember, but it was no good. He yawned. "Sorry, not sure I had much choice in the matter."

"Never mind, what's going on here?"

"We've very nearly come to an accord on the moral relativism inherent in any financial transaction," said Arthur. "It really only makes sense if you've heard all of the arguments. I'll start from the beginning. Let's say you have a partial monopoly on the production of liquor in a religious separatist society, and—"

"Never mind that too," said Myrtle. "Release Sloot at once, and we'll be on our way."

"I think not," said Grumley. "He has committed crimes against the—wait, does she know about the ... ?"

"The Serpents of the Earth?" hazarded Myrtle.

"Right," said Grumley. "We just need to hear his testimony before we can cast him into the Well of the Void, which I'm just now realizing has nothing to do with the conversation we've been having for the last ... however long. Who are you, anyway?"

"And we're back to identity!" shouted Arthur. "Fine, I'll recap. Separating the id from the ego—"

"Enough!" shouted Myrtle. "You'll not be casting Sloot's soul into that Well under any circumstances."

"Oh, no?" scoffed Grumley. "And who are you to make demands here, young lady?"

"Don't *young lady* me, you old git! But to answer your question, I am the rightful owner of Sloot Peril's soul."

"What?"

"Don't make me repeat myself. I can have a notary verify it if necessary."

"Can you?" asked Grumley with a smirk. "I've heard you lot are on the outs with the notaries at the moment, owing to some particularly brutal torture?"

"He wouldn't stand for anything less," said Myrtle. "Anyway, I have special dispensation."

Myrtle snapped her fingers and three documents appeared, scrolls hanging in midair before Grumley.

"What are these?" he demanded, searching each of his pockets before finding his reading glasses atop his head.

"Certification of Demonic Jurisdiction," said Myrtle, pointing to one of the documents. "That one's the Binding Soul Transfer for Sloot Peril, and the one you're reading now is a standard waiver of all rights to argue with me on the matter, to which agreement is only contingent upon having read it."

"What? That's diabolical!"

"Technically, it's Infernal," said Myrtle, "but I take your meaning."

Grumley fumed. He opened his mouth as if to scathe her with a retort, but he must have known that the penalties for breach of an Infernal waiver were painfully severe.

"Very well," said Grumley, "he's free to go."

The shackles suddenly disappeared from Sloot's wrists, and he fell. Fortunately, before he fell into the Well of the Void where he would suffer for eternity, it disappeared as well. Sloot collided with the stone floor which, according to the Agreement, warranted an "ouch!"

"You can't be serious," cried Hans, his jowls waggling under the force of his consternation. He was the sort of person who defined "justice" as persons other than himself receiving the most gruesome possible punishment available to them for any reason, regardless of insignificant details like "innocence" or "guilt."

"I wish I wasn't," Grumley scowled, "but her paperwork is in order. Sloot Peril is released from duty *in disgrace*, but he shan't be remanded to the Well of the Void."

Myrtle put a finger to her chin thoughtfully. "I'd fire him in disgrace *in verso perpetuity*, if I were you."

"What?" As pleased as Sloot was to have escaped the Well of the Void, he'd never been fired from anything. He'd further never been fired in disgrace, and he'd certainly never been fired in verso perpetuity, whatever that meant.

"She makes a good point," said Hans. "Firing him in disgrace in verso perpetuity puts a tidy bow on the whole affair, doesn't it?"

"It does," said Geralt, "but I thought she was on Peril's side."

"As did I," Sloot mumbled weakly.

"Fine," said Myrtle, "if you'd like to provide him a reference for his next employer."

"Out of the question!" Grumley's moustaches flared. "Peril is free to go, but he must leave this place! He is no longer employed by Lord Hapsgalt, having been fired in disgrace in verso perpetuity!"

Suddenly, Sloot found himself slumped against a tree just outside the house.

"Well, that was quick," said Myrtle. She was sitting on the ground beside him.

"What just happened?" asked Sloot, stifling a yawn.

"You were released from Willie's service," said Myrtle with a satisfied smirk.

The contract! Sloot had nearly forgotten. In exchange for his soul, Myrtle said she'd help him break the bonds of his entanglements. He no longer had to work for Willie or the Serpents of the Earth! That just left Uncle, Carpathian Intelligence, and Winking Bob.

"Thanks," said Sloot. "But what's 'in verso perpetuity,' and why'd you tell me to fire me in it? It sounded mean."

"You'll know soon enough. Now, you sit tight for a moment, we're expected in Castle Ulfhaven."

⋙THE CARPATHIAN AGREEMENT⋘

It just seems like a waste." Myrtle's gaze swept back and forth around the cavernous war chamber of Castle Ulfhaven. Her voice echoed in the darkness.

"It would be more wasteful not to use it at all," Roman mused.

There wasn't a spot of dust to be found in the circular room because the servants of Castle Ulfhaven weren't fools. They knew the penalty for sloppy work, or rather they didn't, and were keen to keep it that way. The only sign that anyone had ever been in the room at all were the innumerable gouges and bloodstains on the stone floor, the evidence of centuries-old disagreements that had been settled the old-fashioned way.

Bloodstains left on stone didn't count as sloppy work. They were a warning.

Only a few torches had been lit along one section of the wall, and chairs had been brought in.

"How's the Domnitor getting on?" asked Myrtle. "That was who Vlad had left in the dungeons before the big dust-up with the pile of goblins, wasn't it?"

Long may he reign, Sloot thought. He was here! In this very castle, at this very moment!

"It was," whispered Roman. "I've moved him to more comfortable accommodations, but don't tell Vlad. She vastly overestimates what it takes to intimidate a pubescent boy."

Sloot looked at Vlad, who was gripping the arms of her chair hard enough to splinter them.

"Chairs." Vlad grimaced and ground her teeth.

According to Roman, this would mark the first war council in Carpathian history where the attendees would remain seated, and their blades would remain sheathed. It was a very sensible request made by the fairies, though it had put Vlad in a very dark mood. Not that Vlad was ever *not* in a dark mood. Darker than usual, then.

There were chairs beside Vlad's throne for Myrtle, Roman, and Bartleby. Vlad didn't see the point in providing chairs to ghosts. Sloot normally wouldn't have either, but he was still so deeply weary, Gregor having drained so much of his vitality away.

"Stop slouching," Nicoleta hissed. She didn't seem to mind the no-chairs-for-ghosts thing.

"I can't help it," Sloot yawned.

"That's bad," said Bartleby, giving Sloot a worried look. It differed very little from his haunted ennui look. Sloot could only tell the difference because Bartleby was looking at him. The haunted ennui look always seemed to be directed toward something very far away, or possibly not there at all.

Nicoleta waved him off. "He's just tired," she said.

"And vhen vas the last time you vere tired?"

Nicoleta's squint of remembrance gave way to wide-eyed realization. "That's *really* bad, isn't it?"

Bartleby nodded.

"Hmmm?" Sloot only asked because he noticed the pair of them staring at him in a very something-is-terribly-wrong way. Sloot was used to things being terribly wrong, but was only alarmed when everyone else noticed it too.

The fairies were taking their sweet time filing ceremoniously into the war chamber. There were quite a lot of them in attendance. Even so, the door was wide enough that they all could have entered at once. The fact that they didn't had set Vlad's teeth on edge.

"Can't you do anything?" Myrtle asked.

"I'm not really supposed to," Bartleby whispered. He glanced at Vlad, who had already shot one annoyed look in his direction. With Vlads the Invader, one was generally all it took.

"Supposed to?" Nicoleta was aghast, a description which may or may not have counted as offensive to the dead. "Look at him! He's fading away!"

She was right. Since becoming a ghost, Sloot had taken on a certain translucence. Now, though, he practically had to move around to keep from fading into the background.

"Don't tell me *this* is where you draw the line in meddling with dark forces beyond mortal comprehension." Nicoleta's tone had shifted into mockery beginning with the word "meddling."

"Ugh, fine," said Bartleby. He looked around, though for what, Sloot couldn't fathom. He appeared to find it, whatever it was. Then he locked onto Vlad with a nervous stare and produced his wand as surreptitiously as possible. He gave it a couple of flicks with his wrist, and a gasp went up from the fairies that had made it into the room so far.

"What's wrong?" asked the voice that had come out of Sloot, when he noticed that everyone was looking at him in horror.

"Vicked!"

"Something's not right." The voice that had come out of Sloot was far too low and menacing. He felt off-balance. A bit more alert, but still not quite right. He looked down to see that his long, jagged claws had returned to their standard level of translucence, but he was positive that they'd been hands before.

"That's what Willie looked like before," said Myrtle.

Sloot's claws went to his forehead, then felt their way up a pair of double recurved horns. He started to panic.

At least Vlad wasn't looking at him. That's not to say that she hadn't noticed. A lifetime of fighting with the ghosts of her ancestors had imbued Vlad with an uncanny awareness of everything happening around her at all times. But she was still fixed on the fairies in a classic display of intimidation.

Vlad wasn't simply not looking at Sloot, she was *pointedly* not looking at Sloot. The intensity of her absence of regard for him was like having rented prime advertising space to declare that she didn't consider Sloot a threat. Sloot was positive that he looked menacing, but definitely not to the degree that Vlad would be seen taking notice.

"What did you do?" Nicoleta whispered as loudly as she could.

"There's blood everyvhere," whispered Bartleby, gesturing around the room. "I didn't think anyone vould mind if I used a bit to perk Sloot up."

Nicoleta rolled her eyes. "You mean the centuries-old blood of generals staining the ancient stones of the Ulfhaven war chamber?"

"Oh, right!" Bartleby laughed a very villainous laugh. You had to take lessons to have a laugh that sinister, Sloot was sure of it.

"That's not permanent, is it?" Myrtle regarded Sloot askance.

"I vouldn't think so," said Bartleby. "Just a bit too much savagery in the blood. It should vear off after a vhile."

"A vile what?" asked Roman.

"A *while*," said Nicoleta.

"Ah." Roman nodded.

"Silence!" Vlad snarled over her shoulder. Then she turned back to the fairies. "Proceed."

By the time they were all in, there were enough fairies in to encircle the room. They didn't though, as their voices would have been impossible to hear at such a distance. They used a bit of sorcery to construct a tiny amphitheater like the one they'd used in Abbatoir Park, set just outside the Invader's easy reach. They could have gotten a bit closer, but they were smarter than that.

"Thank you very much for inviting us into Castle Ulfhaven," said King Lilacs, hovering at Vlad's eye level on his fluttering gossamer wings. "You have a lovely home."

"Enough with the pleasantries," Vlad barked. "We are assembled today to take up arms against the looming threat—"

"Excuse me, please." Lilacs raised an index finger. "Point of order, but could we observe parliamentary procedure, please? Proper salutations will go a long way toward mending fences, General Defenestratia."

"Parliamentary procedure?" Vlad grimaced as though she'd just been fed a pile of manure that had somehow managed to go bad. "In Carpathia? Never! My ancestors never would have borne such an affront to their sovereignty, and neither shall I!"

"But what about my sovereignty, if you please? I'm a king too, you know."

"I have no use for kings," said Vlad. "Bags of guts who festoon their brows with gold. Your crown will not keep your head on your shoulders here, fairy!"

The tiny amphitheater erupted in a din of well-tailored outrage. A sea of angry faces shouted at Vlad to "watch your tongue, please!" and "take that back, please!"

"That's enough, please!" Lilacs' voice rose above the din, thanks to his tall—for a fairy's—crown's secondary purpose as a megaphone.

Convenient and economical, thought Sloot. He also wondered what King Lilacs' guts would taste like under the light of a blood moon. He flinched and hoped that the side effects of his necromantic transfusion would wear off soon.

"I haven't spoken to a Carpathian ruler in nine generations." Lilacs set the crown back onto his head. "Your great-great-great-great-great-great-great-grandmother was just as quick to anger, but only after several hours and as many cups of Carpathian Blood Brandy."

Sloot remembered the Blood Brandy. It was made from bear's blood and fermented in hollowed oak trees. According to Carpathian sommeliers, it wasn't fit to drink until the tree slumped over dead.

"Point of order, if you please." General Dandelion stood. "Technically speaking, wouldn't that make Vlad the Twenty-Eighth less quick to anger?"

"I suppose it would," said Lilacs. "Thank you for the clarification, General."

"You're welcome, Your Majesty."

There was a round of polite applause from the amphitheater.

"This is intolerable," grumbled Vlad.

Roman leaned in to whisper to Vlad. "Yet it must be tolerated, Your

Dominance. Even if Ashkar—or Gregor, or whatever else he decides to call himself—had properly perished when your hammer made a stain of him, it would still take years to amass a new army. We don't have that long!"

"There's got to be another way." Vlad pounded the arm of her throne with a mailed fist. "What would my forebears say if they found out I made peace in the war chamber?"

"They won't," said Nicoleta. She and Bartleby had placed a ward on the Black Smiler just outside the chamber door that would keep the Lebendervlad from entering. Black Smilers, Sloot recalled, were made from the charred skulls of vanquished enemies, stuffed with demonic larva, mounted on spears and enchanted so that they glowed a sickly yellow. They were the magical totems that permitted the spirits of the thirty-six former Vlads the Invader to roam about the castle in their ghostly forms, don suits of armor to share their martial knowledge with the current Vlad, and occasionally forget that they were dead and challenge her for the throne.

Vlad the Thirteenth did that on a regular basis. He'd taken one too many hammer blows to the helmet in his day.

"We will happily join forces with you to keep the goblins out of Carpathia," said Lilacs. "These lands are our home as well, and we would hate to see them overrun by the congresses in the Dark."

"That settles it then," said Vlad.

"However," Lilacs continued, "we need a concession from you before we have an alliance."

"How dare you?" shouted Vlad, leaning forward in her throne. "I am Vlad Defenestratia, I concede nothing! My ancestors quelled this land, and have ruled it since—"

"I remember," shouted Lilacs, using his crown as a megaphone again, so that he could match Vlad's impressive volume. "I have watched the line of Defenestratia since the first of you threw that fellow out of his tower. That wasn't very nice, even if he did have it coming, but I don't hold that against you personally."

Vlad drew in a hot and ragged breath, the sort that was destined to result in a tirade of swear words so vulgar they could make steel blush. Before said tirade could trumpet its charge with a disparaging word about Lilacs' mother, Roman place a hand gingerly on her forearm.

"Forgive me, Your Dominance," he whispered, "but perhaps you'd consider hearing them out? They're *fairies*, after all. It's unlikely they'll ask for anything too grand."

"Wouldn't they?"

"No, Your Dominance. It wouldn't be fair."

It was unnerving, watching Vlad swallow her tirade. It was apparent to Sloot that she had very little practice with that sort of thing. He thought that if he'd been born into the greatest line of warriors that the world had ever seen, he'd probably not be very good at holding back his anger either. Of course, the amount of conjecture that Sloot had to put into that assumption was unnerving on its own. Sloot was as far from being the greatest warrior that the world had ever seen as Vlad was from wishing the Domnitor a long reign.

"Very well," said Vlad from between clenched teeth. "What are your demands?"

"Oh, we have no demands," said Lilacs. "That would be very rude. Very rude, indeed!"

There was a chorus of agreement from the amphitheater. All of the fairies in attendance nodded.

"As you prefer," growled Vlad, her teeth grinding together. "What are your *concessions*, then?"

"There is only one, and it is the source of the silence between Our Majesties since my last conversation with Vlad the Twenty-Eighth." One of Lilacs' eyebrows went up, and his eyes danced an enticing arc around the room. He evidently hoped to pique everyone's interest, but predictably ended up only piquing more of Vlad's irritation. Little credit should be extended to Lilacs for this, as it was exceedingly easy to manage.

Vlad's stony silence convinced any excitement that might have otherwise buzzed into the room that it would do well to remain silent.

"Recognition," Lilacs said at last.

Vlad said nothing, but maintained her icy stare.

Roman cleared his throat. "Recognition, King Lilacs?" he asked on Vlad's behalf.

"We have dwelled in the forests of Carpathia since long before you lot started chucking people out of windows," said Lilacs. "We are as much a part of this land as the humans who call themselves 'Carpathians,' if not more so. We would like to hear you say so, please."

"Carpathians are Carpathians," said Vlad. "Fairies are fairies. We do not ask for recognition among your people, why should you want it from us?"

"Because we got left out!" The air went *whump* when Lilacs stomped his dainty little foot in midair. Of course, Vlad couldn't have been seen to be impressed by this tiny marvel of physics, so it was left to Sloot to give a wide-eyed look that was half wonder and half terror. Who knew what else that dainty little foot was capable of doing?

"You got left out," Vlad repeated. Her eyes narrowed. They were narrow before, so it was a wonder that they were not now shut altogether.

"Vlad the First united all of the warlords in the land against the Plutocrat," said General Dandelion. "Why didn't he come and talk to me, please? I'd met the Plutocrat before. He was a real jerk. Why didn't Vlad ask me to bring our army into it, please?"

Vlad turned to Roman, giving him a blank look. Roman cleared his throat, giving the appearance that this was something they'd planned before everyone else arrived.

"Er, well," Roman began, "if the Carpathian history books are to be believed, Vlad the First had amassed a great host. The greatest that the land had ever seen, in fact. Perhaps he already had all the soldiers he needed."

"Oh, the history books may indeed be believed," said Dandelion. "It was a mighty host, far larger than any assembled before, and none have rivaled it since. But he could have stopped far short of that and gotten the job done. Why did he keep recruiting, please? There's only one logical explanation, thank you: to show off."

"To show off?"

"To strike terror into the hearts of your enemies," Dandelion continued. "If Vlad the First had asked us to take the field with him on that fateful day, we'd have nearly doubled the size of his host."

"Doubled?" marveled Nicoleta.

"Indeed," said Dandelion with a wink. "In fact, we'd fully expected him to do so. We'd gotten our armor polished up and everything, so we'd be ready when Vlad came to call on us. We were still standing in formation and waiting when we heard that Vlad had thrown the Plutocrat from his window, and they were forming a new nation! How do you think that made us feel, please?"

"Left out," said Lilacs.

"Left out!" said Dandelion. "Thank you, your Majesty."

"You're welcome, General."

"All we're asking is that you kindly correct an oversight. Recognize the fairies as Carpathians, please, and we can get on with it."

If Sloot had been granted a wish in that particular moment, he'd have squandered it. It would have made sense to wish to avert the impending goblin war, or remove the stain of the Serpents of the Earth from history, or possibly even wind back the clock and put himself blissfully back into his cramped apartment above the butcher shop. He'd have given up any measure of adventure for a return to his halcyon days, hunched over his little desk in the Three Bells' counting house, sweating through his wool suit in the stale air, breathing in the sweet smell of moldering ledgers.

Even considering all of that, Sloot found himself desperately wishing for something—anything—to break the uncomfortable silence that had fallen over the room. He'd seen Vlad on the battlefield, and had been filled with dread at hearing her bloodthirsty roar. Well, *roars* would be more accurate. There's the one she bellows before cleaving two people in half with a single stroke of her longsword, the one she thunders when her hammer pushes her foe's head down inside his chest, the one she howls when her dagger causes an arterial spray to coat half of her face in a very theatrical way ... the list goes on, but suffice it to say that even though Sloot was terrified to his core by each and every one that he'd ever heard, he'd have taken a dozen of them directly in his face if it meant not having to listen to this particular silence for another instant.

It was the sort of silence that eroded mountains. Even with hundreds of fairies in the little amphitheater, the absence of sound in the room was so potent that idioms about pins being dropped were far too nervous to get on with themselves. A thousand years of fairy angst was plain on as many fairy faces as they watched Vlad, willing her to agree.

"No," said Vlad.

"No, please?" Lilacs' voice quivered, his question the very soul of disappointment. It was accompanied by the sound of the dreams of a thousand fairies deflating in unison. Just the sort of thing that could ruin the rest of one's Saturday, though a Tuesday would be unaffected. Tuesdays are the worst.

"No," Vlad repeated. A further silence hanged itself in the air between her Dominance and the fairies, flailing and kicking in the breeze.

"Well," Dandelion sighed, "good luck fighting the goblins without—"

"There's more to it," Roman interjected. "If I may, your Dominance?"

Vlad gave a barely perceptible nod, one rife with loathing for the idea of further explaining a "no." Vlads the Invader were accustomed to being obeyed, or at least openly challenged with sharpened bits of steel. Explanations were for people who wore spectacles and never got blood on them.

"Your request for recognition is more than reasonable," said Roman.

"Thank you," said Lilacs.

"You're welcome. However, there's too much at stake for her Dominance to simply acquiesce. Namely, the curse."

"We've considered that," said Lilacs. "We're sure that it doesn't apply to our army. We asked lawyers and everything."

"Fairy lawyers?"

"Of course! We've got quite a few of them. They all specialize in mediation and equity."

"It's a pity that none of them specialize in Carpathian law," said Roman. "Then they might have known that Vlad's recognition would make all of you eligible for service in the Carpathian army."

"There would have to be an exception," Dandelion interjected. "Every fairy serves in the fairy army, and—"

"There are no exceptions." Vlad's voice rumbled like a bear just waking from its long winter slumber, and her tone invited as much scrutiny as said hungry bear would apply to any morsel it deemed edible.

"Do you know much about curses?" Roman asked.

"I should think so," said Lilacs, puffing up his chest. Then his head tilted a bit, and his brow wrinkled. "Well, perhaps not me personally, but several of my kinsmen have studied them at university."

A few hands shot up in the little amphitheatre. It probably wasn't often that that sort of experience became relevant to a conversation, a fact that said fairies' parents had no doubt pointed out to them when they'd decided on their majors.

"Oh, that's good. They could probably have told your lawyers that curses cannot be circumvented by legal means."

"I'm afraid I don't follow."

"Curses are intricately detailed constructs of Infernal law," Roman began. "When a wizard casts one, an Infernal legal team gets to work, cataloging every law and precedent of every tangentially relevant system, to define the scope of the curse in a maddeningly precise level of detail."

"Meaning, if you please?"

"Meaning that Vlad couldn't carve out an exemption for fairy service in the Carpathian army, even if she wanted to. Had that exemption existed before the curse had been uttered, you'd be all set. However, since it was not, it can't be changed now. Carpathians serve in the Carpathian army, human or otherwise."

Dandelion's hands flew to his hips, and he rounded on Lilacs. "I told you we should've had some curse experts working with the lawyers on that one!"

"That would have made sense," Lilacs replied, "but I wasn't about to dictate that sort of thing. Wouldn't have been fair to the lawyers."

Hundreds of tiny fairy heads nodded in agreement.

"So if I follow," Lilacs continued, "if Vlad recognizes us as Carpathians, we would be compelled to disband our army and join hers, and then ... what, please? Metaphysics would intervene and, I dunno, turn us all into conscientious objectors or something?"

"Well," said Roman, "Carpathian law does not allow for objections to military service, conscientious or otherwise, but something like that."

The assembly descended into a sussurus, as everyone suddenly became a legal expert and started whispering their opinions to the person sitting next to them. Any of the actual lawyers could have explained that it doesn't work that way, but they doubted that anyone was interested in paying their premium rates for the privilege.

"Enough," Vlad boomed, her brooding posture no longer content to be mistaken for patience. "The goblins will find their way into Carpathia soon, and no one will be safe unless we fight them together. Will you fight with me or not?"

"Just a moment, please," said Lilacs. "We understand that recognition as Carpathians is a fraught subject, but we've been overlooked for a thousand years! You can't just say, 'sorry, it's complicated,' and expect us to say, 'oh, all right then.' It wouldn't be fair!"

"I didn't apologize," Vlad seethed.

"Do it the other way," blurted Sloot. His voice had started to climb back up to its proper octave, which was a relief.

"What?" asked Vlad's expression, though no words crossed her lips.

It was an interesting problem. So interesting, in fact, that Sloot had neglected to tremble for the fates of his two nations for a moment while he considered it. If ever there were a place for the ghost of Sloot Peril in international politics, this was it. It wasn't balancing numbers in columns, but it wasn't far off. Two parties in a dispute over titular rights in a matter of controlling interest. International politics? Humbug. This was accounting.

"It's too problematic to acknowledge the fairies as Carpathians," said Sloot, "so why don't you become a fairy?"

The air sizzled. Sloot was already dead, but he wilted away from the heat of Vlad's death stare out of respect. That was what you were supposed to do when fearsome warlords glared at you, even if they couldn't make you any deader than you already were. It was expected.

Vlad rose slowly, deliberately from her throne. The seething fury in her eyes managed to intensify and fix itself on Sloot. "I am a Carpathian. I am Carpathia!"

Sloot cringed. He was very good at it. "Forgive me, your Dominance, but so am I. Er, so *was* I."

"Ha!" Vlad spat. "Barely."

"Perhaps," Sloot continued, only mildly wounded, "but I was *also* a true salt of the Old Country, and a loyal subject of the Domnitor, long may he reign."

"That was just your cover." A nervous laugh floundered out of Roman with all the grace of a drunk whose shoelaces had been tied together. "No need to lay it on so thick, eh?"

"Well, yes," said Sloot, "but, in another way ... in a more confusing, but also accurate way ... one in which, if you look at it objectively, setting aside blind patriotism ... that is to say, pragmatically speaking—"

"Would you mind getting on with it, please?" asked Dandelion.

"Well, I'm both, aren't I? A salt and a Carpathian."

"You can't be serious," said Myrtle. "After coming to Carpathia and experiencing real freedom? You still defend the Domnitor—don't you *dare* say it—after feeling the weight of his boot lifted from your neck?"

Long may he reign, thought Sloot to himself. Myrtle hadn't asked in a way that invited him to a conversation about the subject. It was more like a magician swinging a watch in front of his nose and asking whether he was sleepy, or whether his assistant should knock his head in. Either way, he was going to end up on the floor.

"It's not a perfect analogy," said Sloot, dodging Myrtle's baleful glare as best he could. "What I mean to say is why couldn't Vlad be a Carpathian—*Carpathia,* for that matter—and a fairy at the same time?"

"Unthinkable!" Vlad splintered the arm of a chair with a well-placed kick. "Out of the question!"

"Why not, please?" Dandelion fixed Vlad with a squint, looking at her askance.

"Indeed," said Lilacs. "What's so unthinkable about being a fairy, please?"

"Now, now," said Roman, his nervous laugh returning for the most awkward encore in Carpathian history. "I'm sure that her Dominance didn't mean to imply that—"

"Implications are where cowards go to cry," Vlad snarled. "I said what I meant, and I'll slay everyone in this room if—"

"Incorporate!"

All eyes were on Sloot. That was horrible in its own right, but at least no one was shouting death threats. Yet.

"I used to run the numbers for incorporations at the Three Bells all the time," Sloot continued. "Two separate entities merge into one corporation, for a period of time, to work together toward a common goal."

"Carpathia is a sovereign nation," Vlad sneered, "not a shipping company."

"Well, that's true, but you're the sovereign, aren't you? Er, your Dominance?"

Vlad went back to brooding. Sloot began to wonder if that was just her face's resting position. But before he was able to consider it further, or reach any sort of conclusion, bad timing reared its ugly head and he found himself elsewhere.

⚜WINK AND A BOB⚜

Winking Bob's sitting room was a lavish, airy affair. Impressive, especially given that it was most likely situated in an unused sewer tunnel, like every other place associated with Bob's black market. It had nothing on the views that Sloot had seen in places like Whitewood and Gildedhearth, the resplendent mansions of the late Lords Hapsgalt, but views were notoriously difficult to come by underground, where they almost certainly were. Pristine white upholstery was likewise impressive in such a filthy place.

Bob was wearing her reaping smirk. The last time she'd spoken to Sloot, she'd made it clear that unless he was able to help her kidnap the Domnitor, long may he reign, she'd attach the disastrous financial report that was the source of all of Sloot's tribulations to the blank piece of paper he'd signed. She could use that to drive financial markets into utter chaos and ruin, leaving her the only person to turn a profit.

Sloot hadn't delivered, of course. Moreover, the Domnitor had been kidnapped by Vlad the Invader, and Bob's penetrating stare made it clear that she knew Sloot had something to do with it.

"I don't need any proof," said Bob with a wry smile. "I'm holding all of the cards! I'm a woman of my word, and I told you I'd collect from you one way or the other."

"All aforementioned references to concepts of proof and promises shall be interpreted in theoretical contexts," said Edmund, "no evidence being available that said references ever took place."

Sloot trembled for the fate of the global economy.

Fortunately for the global economy, Myrtle was getting the hang of tagging along with Sloot when he was unexpectedly summoned away. Perks of being a demon who knew a thing or two about the future.

"Careful," Myrtle sneered. "That's a demon's boyfriend you're threatening."

Bob smiled in the unsettling way that every gran in Salzstadt knows how to do. It would not be entirely unbelievable to learn that they'd all gone to school for it, so subtle was its execution. Originally designed as a response to "I'm not eating these vegetables, and you can't make me," it worked surprisingly well in conversations with demons, too.

"It's a pity you don't want to be friends anymore," said Bob, a hint of a pout creeping across her face like a burglar with a sack full of silverware. "How quickly we forget who it was who brought us up from nothing. Edmund?"

"Statements pertaining to the alleged past associations between parties allegedly engaged in conversation at this or any other point in time shall not be admissible in any deliberation regarding the enterprise thereof, owing to the degree of speculation that may or may not have been involved therein."

"Blow it out your ears," Myrtle spat. "We're not friends, we're not associates, and if you continue threatening Sloot, I'll stop withholding my demonic compulsion to do some impromptu quilting with your skin."

Sloot whimpered. It was in the running for recognition as his signature move. Myrtle might have been making up the whole "compulsory flesh quilting" thing, but he didn't want to ask and find out that she wasn't.

"Your threats have been entered into the official record," said Edmund, scribbling furiously in a little notebook.

"And Bob's threats to Sloot?"

"You're a demon," said Edmund, shooting her a grin that was far too smug for the occasion. "You know perfectly well that you should've brought your own stenographer if you wanted anything beneficial to you in the official record." He paused, then added, "which may or may not exist."

Myrtle sighed and rolled her eyes. Edmund had a keen legal mind, and she obviously knew that he was right.

"It doesn't matter," said Myrtle. "Just say what you have to say so that we can get back to things that matter."

"Pity," said Bob, plainly relishing the upper hand. "I don't *want* the global economy to dive into a death spiral from which it will never recover, you know."

"Noted," said Edmund as he scribbled in his notebook, no doubt rephrasing Bob a bit to make that sentiment seem far more magnanimous than its true context would allow.

"But you leave me little choice," Bob continued. "All I asked was that you act in good faith in the acquisition of the Domnitor, for use as my puppet."

"Long may he reign," said Sloot.

"In a manner of speaking," Bob replied with a wave of her hand. "However, you've obviously done quite the opposite, and delivered him into the hands of a foreign despot who, as far as we know, plans to use him as a puppet to seize control of the Old Country government for herself!"

"*You* planned to use him as a puppet to seize control of the Old Country government for *yourself*," Myrtle pointed out.

"Not according to the official record," said Edmund, who pointedly wasn't writing any of that down.

"Inasmuch," Bob continued, "what sort of businesswoman would I be if I failed to levy the penalties that I clearly stated would result from this very thing?"

Edmund drew in a breath. "Attestations with regard to businesses owned, operated, or avowed to exist, or ever having existed in, or tangentially related to the interests of any person or persons who may have just attested thusly shall not be construed as pertaining to specific or non-specific entities, officially incorporated or otherwise."

"You've left me no other recourse," said Bob, her demeanor a reasonably accurate parody of sympathy. "I'm going to have to release this uncorrected financial document bearing your signature. The markets will burst into flames, and the Three Bells will crumble under the weight of your abject incompetence, and the name of Wilhelm Hapsgalt will be forever linked to the concept of bad financial management."

Sloot released a mournful wail, the sort one has to be dead to manage. He was sure that he'd have to haunt something for whatever portion of eternity remained to him. Perhaps the charred ruins of the counting house? That would be fitting.

"Go ahead," said Myrtle, far more casually than Sloot would ever have dreamt to do. "Sloot is no longer in the employ of the Three Bells or Wilhelm Hapsgalt."

"Because he's dead," said Bob, "I get it. No matter. He *was* in their employ, and this document—"

"Not so fast!" Myrtle smirked with the satisfaction of someone who'd always wanted to say that. "The lawyers for the Three Bells and the Serpents of the Earth—all the same people, in fact—will have already redacted every scrap of paper with Sloot's name on it. You'll not find a single shred of evidence that he'd ever worked for them."

Bob shifted uncomfortably in her chair. "Edmund?"

"It's possible," said Edmund, "but only if Peril had very recently been—"

"Fired in verso perpetuity," said Myrtle. "I saw to it myself."

Sloot gasped. Everyone else should have, but you just can't rely on villains for playing into a proper suspense narrative.

"What?" Bob shook her head in confusion. "In verso ..."

"In verso perpetuity," said Edmund. "The same as 'in perpetuity,' only going the other way."

"Backward in time?"

Edmund nodded, the veins in his neck bulging at the effort. "It's a colossal load of paperwork, but if you've got as many clerks as the Three Bells, you could manage it in a couple of days."

Sloot looked at Myrtle, and the corners of his mouth turned upward. "You saw it coming," he said.

Myrtle shrugged. "It's what I do."

"Well, that's just wonderful," Bob groused. "Your signature is worthless then, is it?"

"Er, sorry," said Sloot. He wasn't, really, aside from the polite way that anyone who'd spent eight summers at etiquette camp knew they should be. Sloot could have claimed bragging rights for having won the Best Tea Pourer trophy six times in a row, but he'd never dream of it, having spent eight summers at etiquette camp.

Winking Bob cracked her knuckles and sighed. "You owe me far more than an apology, Peril."

The scowl she wore now could not have been more different from the saucy smirk she'd affected when Sloot had first arrived.

"He doesn't, actually," said Myrtle. She'd found Bob's saucy smirk and was trying it on.

"My dear," Bob began with practiced condescension, "spare me whatever technicality you think is going to turn this minor setback in your favor. Edmund?"

Edmund banged his fist twice on a steel door behind him, then fished around in his leather satchel long enough for Sloot to wonder whether he and Bob share some sort of psychic connection, or if they'd just spent so much time in devious legal maneuvering that Edmund knew what was going to happen next. A moment later, the door opened and a wizard wearing a black robe with the hood pulled up entered the room.

"Sloot Peril," said Edmund, holding out a stack of papers at arm's length while the wizard engaged in some complex wand-waving, "you are hereby served with an Infernal Injunction, and shall cease and desist all dealings with parties known or unknown to the person or persons present here, if indeed such a place as might be described as 'here' exists, until such time as matters pertaining to aforesigned documents—blank or otherwise—have been resolved to the satisfaction of their bearers."

"*Alleged* bearers," Bob corrected him.

"Right. Alleged bearers."

"Ow," said Sloot.

Myrtle's brow wrinkled in concern. "Ow?"

"The papers," said Sloot, squinting and half turning away from Edmund. "They're making my head hurt."

Edmund and Bob exchanged a wary glance.

"What've you done to him?" Myrtle demanded.

"It's an Infernal Injunction," said Bob. "He's supposed to be bound to the spot, writhing in agony until it's lifted."

"That's horrible!"

Bob's head tilted from side to side. "I suppose," she acknowledged, "but it doesn't seem to be working very well."

"It might have something to do with the fact that Sloot's soul is my property," said Myrtle. "You'd need an Infernal Writ of Seizure to enforce that Injunction, and you're not likely to get one against a Demon in Odious Standing without cause."

"Ow."

"Oh, stop looking at it!"

"I can't." There were sigils crawling around on the page in an irresistible pattern, like thousands of stinging insects forming the shape of a goat eating its young. It was utterly revolting, yet there was something about it. Something that made Sloot want to plant himself on that spot and writhe in agony for a while.

"I'm not interested in his soul," said Bob, glowering at Myrtle, "but I never walk away from equity. The circumstances that led to Peril's signature becoming worthless were beyond my control. I demand to be compensated!"

"Ow."

"Fluctuations in the market," said Myrtle.

Bob gave a dismissive wave. "That's the sort of thing that I tell regular people when one of my underlings fails to smuggle a crate of quarantined silk worms off a dock. Edmund?"

"Prior statements involving the existence of laborers involved in illicit commerce shall be understood to have been intended in jest, and do not reflect the practices or policies of any person or persons who may or may not be in attendance at this meeting, which may or may not be happening."

While Edmund was droning disclaimers, Myrtle's eyes went dark. Not in a simple angry glower, but rather in a disappear-into-pits-of-smoking-shadow sort of way. Her claws and wings came out.

"Was I regular people, then?" asked Myrtle, in a pair of octaves. "Was I regular people when you told me that I'd have to clean out Whitewood entirely, if I wanted out of my contract with you?"

Bob rolled her eyes. "Yes, my dear, you were. And yes, I can see that you're clearly not regular people now, but neither am I, so let's be civil, why don't we?"

Edmund didn't seem nervous, which made Sloot nervous enough for the both of them. Sure, he was the largest person in the room by far, his shoulders nearly as broad as Myrtle's wing span; but Myrtle was threatening Bob! Shouldn't he have felt beholden to do some posturing or something? Sloot thought that was what tough guys were for.

"Civil," Myrtle sneered. "You mean docile. You prefer it when your opponents don't fight back, is that it?"

"Well, yes," said Bob, turning an incredulous look toward Edmund. "That's easier for me, you understand."

Edmund nodded.

"Anyway," said Bob, "I've got an idea. A little service that you can provide for me, and I'll wipe out your property's debt."

"Forget it," said Myrtle. "Just draw a line through this one in your ledger."

Sloot winced. "Actually, you'll want to add a line in red under—"

"Not the time, Sloot!"

"Right. Sorry. Ow."

"Sloot never owed you anything," Myrtle continued, "you just had leverage against him. That's dried up, so no more blackmail. We're leaving."

"Just sit down for a moment," said Bob. "I'm sure that it will—"

Myrtle waved a clawed hand toward the stout wooden door and it exploded, leaving nothing but a pair of iron bands swinging from the hinges.

"Come on, Sloot."

"Er, thanks for having us," Sloot said, demands of etiquette and all. He turned to follow Myrtle, giving one last, longing glance at Edmund's injunction. "Ow."

"This is your last chance," said Bob. She brandished a little envelope between two fingers. "Do you know what I have here?"

"No," said Myrtle without turning around, "and I don't care."

⚡GOBLINS MARCHING⚡

Myrtle looked down on the massive congress as she and Sloot flew overhead. "I don't know about you, but that's definitely the most goblins I've ever seen at once."

Sloot nodded. There were easily twice as many as had piled up toward the portal the other night, and that number had dwarfed the congress that had trampled him at the Fall of Salzstadt.

That was a strategy that had ended badly. "Swear," Roman had shouted, "swear like the wind!" Or something like that. They'd tried to attract as many goblins as possible to stave off the horde of undead, and Sloot had been crushed beneath the ensuing chaos. He tried not to think too hard about whether it counted as suicide, but might have been relieved to know that "having been trampled as a result of one's own bad idea" was considered less gruesome by comparison. In fact, in certain remote villages where marriage between cousins was less frowned-upon than it should be, it was the leading cause of death behind sampling too deeply from one's uncle's still.

"I didn't know goblins had siege weapons," said Sloot, casting a worried look over the enormous catapults, siege towers, and battering rams that they were dragging along the main road. "Does Vlad have siege weapons?"

"Do you know another Vlad that I haven't met?"

"You're right. Silly question."

"Not one of your best."

Sloot's brow wrinkled in thought. "I don't think I've ever seen any around Castle Ulfhaven."

"I don't think you bring them out unless you're besieging someone."

"Doesn't that hurt?"

"What, being besieged?"

"Sure," said Sloot, "that too. But I meant the arrow in your leg."

"What?" Myrtle looked down. As sure as children can be convinced to behave when they think holiday mascots are watching, there was a black arrow shaft stuck in her leg. She reached down and yanked it out. Sloot flinched.

Myrtle shrugged, and dropped the arrow. "Not really."

An arrow passed through Sloot.

"Hey!" he shouted down at the goblins, though with less of the stern "you watch it with that thing" than anyone else might have, and more of the pleading "I'd rather you didn't" that ensured they definitely would.

Myrtle expelled an exasperated breath. "Would you come on?"

"Sorry," replied Sloot, his eyes shut tight as he wished the constant stream of arrows would stop going *thwip, thwip, thwip* through him. Panic had gripped him. He simply couldn't move.

Myrtle said a swear word in frustration. A goblin went *pop* right next to her, cackled once, and then screamed as it plunged to its inevitable demise.

The *thwip, thwip, thwip* of arrows stopped, and was replaced by a dull *thwap, thwap, thwap* beneath him. He opened an eye and looked down.

Myrtle was hovering on her back, flapping her wings lazily and looking up at him. "Can we please move this along?"

"Are you ... ?"

Myrtle nodded.

Sloot felt ridiculous. The arrows might not be hurting Myrtle, but they'd still have to be picked out at some point. It was times like these that he wished he'd been made of slightly sterner stuff. Not so stern as to give him the urge to charge off to foreign places and engage in heroics, but stern enough to give him the resolve to keep moving forward with his eyes open, on occasions when he was in no danger whatsoever.

Myrtle cleared her throat.

"Right. Sorry."

They hurried along the main road, surveying the seemingly endless goblin horde as it marched toward the Carpathian border.

"There are no dead," Sloot mused aloud.

"I'm not sure they ever die," said Myrtle, pulling a handful of arrows from her shoulder as she flew. "I think they just *poof* back into the Dark or something. But if it'll make you feel better …"

She said a swear word, which was followed by a *pop*, a cackle, and a receding scream.

The rebuke caught in Sloot's throat and was beaten into submission, arresting its mad dash toward Sloot's teeth. He'd met Goblins' Rights types before, and they all sounded as crazy as people who waited until the last minute to do their taxes.

"I meant dead *people*," said Sloot. "The walking sort. I thought Gregor was in control of them. Don't you think he'd have brought them along?"

Myrtle shrugged, causing her to bob up and down a bit as she flew. "Maybe he's got a bit less control, now that he's a goblin. Or maybe he left them to do his bidding in Salzstadt."

They flew past the front of the congress. Sloot pointed down at Mrs. Knife. Myrtle banked slightly to fly directly above her, then unleashed a torrent of swearing so vile that Sloot had a flashback to his first—and last—trip to the dockside market on fish cleaning day.

All of Myrtle's screaming projectiles missed. She grinned anyway, as Mrs. Knife shook an angry fist up at her. A dozen or so arrows were sent in retaliation, three of which found her foot, arm, and stomach respectively.

"Worth it," she said, plucking them out as though they were flowers, and she a hill. A hill that could fly, see into the future, and collect souls in exchange for services rendered. Hills like that usually had great rings of stones atop them that were traditionally misunderstood.

"That seriously doesn't hurt?"

"Sort of," Myrtle replied, her head bobbing from side to side, "but I know that they can't really do anything to me. Makes it almost ... disappointing."

"You're *disappointed* at not being cut down in a hail of arrows."

"Of course not. It's more like ..." Myrtle paused and blushed. "Well, you know how I defected to Carpathia after the whole robbing-Willie-blind thing?"

"Yeah," said Sloot, who would have considered that metaphor apt if "blind" meant "took only one eye," and Willie was understood to be some sort of fly god with thousands to spare. Hapsgalt wealth didn't come with limits, as Sloot's corrected version of that fateful financial statement clearly showed.

"Well, I read as much as I could about Carpathian culture. It was confusing at first, then fascinating, and then ... well, I *get* it."

"Get what?" asked Sloot, who now understood why Myrtle had a book on Carpathian Invasion Theory when he'd gone to visit her, all hopped up on hero's potion.

"The excitement of battle! I mean, I don't want to take up professional soldiering or anything, but I can see why someone would want to. The other night, when I was fighting off a tower of goblins—I'm glad you were there, that would take some explaining—I got this sort of *rush*. But it went away, because I knew they couldn't really hurt me. I dunno, it's silly, I guess, but knowing that you can't be hurt just sort of makes it seem boring."

"That's not my idea of boredom," said Sloot, whose idea of boredom had yet to present itself. If his Quarterly Inventory of Buttons Needing Sewn Back On hadn't done the trick, it was unlikely that anything ever would.

"I know." Myrtle winked. She didn't seem disappointed, not that that prevented Sloot from worrying that she was for the rest of the flight.

Just as the "castle"—which was actually just a pile of boulders on the Old Country side of the border—came into view, so did Vlad. She was standing just on the Carpathian side of the border. Sloot could make out Roman, Nicoleta, Bartleby, and someone else standing with her. It wasn't until they got close enough to see a couple of fairies near them as well that Sloot recognized the "someone else" who was standing there, with his hands bound in front of him.

"It's the Domnitor," Sloot gasped. "Long may he reign!"

"Long may he—stop that," said Myrtle. "He's not ruling much of anything now, is he?"

"Myrtle!"

"What? He's not. Besides, we're about to throw in with Vlad the Invader against those who hold sway over Salzstadt right now, so perhaps rote recitations of allegiance are less than appropriate at the moment?"

To Sloot's horror, he saw Myrtle's point. He'd never have shouted "blood and honor" if someone mentioned Vlad in his regular pub, the one where you had to put a pint under your stool for every one you had yourself, so the goblins wouldn't steal said stool from beneath you.

Sloot missed that place. He missed Salzstadt. He missed slapping himself across the face every morning after reciting the Loyalist Oath toward the tattered paper facsimile of the Old Country's flag pinned to the door of his tiny apartment. It seemed so long since he'd been comfortably nestled in the trappings of the life he thought he'd lead for the rest of his days, "trap" never seeming like the operative word, and now it was all gone. Salzstadt would never be the same as it was, and he would never be the man that his quarterly projections left little doubt he was meant to be. He was dead. A dead man clinging to an old phrase he'd said so many times he no longer thought about its meaning.

"It's hard letting it go," said Myrtle. "Believe me, I know. But how old do you think the Domnitor is? Don't say it."

Long may he reign, Sloot thought, allowing it to rumble in the back of his throat.

"Ten," said Sloot. "Perhaps twelve. Maybe you could ask him? I'm too nervous."

"It's not important," said Myrtle. "Do you remember a time before we had a ... you-know-who?"

"No, I don't."

"And when did they announce that the old one had died, or stepped down, and that the new one had taken the throne?"

"I don't believe they did."

"You were, what, forty when you died? That can't be the same person who ruled the Old Country when you were a kid."

"Of course not."

"Why place all of your faith and loyalty in someone you've never seen before?"

"I have seen him," said Sloot. "Twice. Once on the wall before the Fall of Salzstadt, and right now."

"True, but you never saw the old one."

Sloot said nothing.

"Or old *ones*."

Sloot said even less. Even if she was right—*especially* if she was right—if it made no sense to swear fealty to someone you'd never seen, to pledge your loyalty to a position that could have been held by a person or persons who may have never even existed, it meant that the central purpose of Sloot's life had been a lie. It was pointless! Forget the oath and the slapping, why had he even bothered getting out of bed every morning for forty years?

Sloot shook his head. There was too much going on. The impending battle, the fact that he wasn't haunting anything just then, whether he and Myrtle would get to have another go at … you know. He simply didn't have the strength in that moment to consider whether his entire life had been pointless.

Myrtle must have seen all of those worries playing out across Sloot's face, as though it had loaned itself out to a community theater troupe who were interested in nothing more than upstaging one another. She mercifully said nothing more about it.

"Welcome back," said Roman. "You should consider your priorities before you allow yourself to be summoned away. We were in the war council, if you hadn't noticed!"

"Sorry," said Sloot. He strongly considered pointing out the irony in that rebuke, and would have had little trouble, given Sloot's shrunken head swinging morbidly from Roman's belt. But upon reading the collective mood, he decided that it might not be as important as all that. Not right now, anyway.

"Humans don't live that long," Dandelion was saying to Nicoleta. "I'm sure I've read that somewhere."

"She's not entirely human anymore," Nicoleta replied. "She's part goblin now."

"That doesn't make any sense! You don't change into a different race just because you got married."

"It didn't make sense to me either, but that's fairy tales for you."

"That's ... what, please?"

"Fairy tales. You know, stories they tell to children, when ... oh."

Dandelion's hands rested firmly on his hips. "So *fairy* tales are just children's stories, are they, please?"

"No, no," said Nicoleta, her hands raising slowly in a placating gesture. "That's not what I meant! Please don't—"

"Posies!"

"Yes?" shouted a sing-songy voice from somewhere within the host of armored fairies hovering in mid-air in an impressive formation.

"Could you come here, please?"

"I'm really sorry," said Nicoleta, "do you think that we could just—"

Dandelion was aghast. "I can't just circumvent the rules, that wouldn't be fair!"

"No, it wouldn't," said Posies, who was virtually indistinguishable from all of the other fairies, though Sloot got the distinct impression that it would be contrary to his best interests to lend his voice to that observation.

"Posies," Dandelion began, "as my official HFR representative, I would like for you to take down my complaint, please."

"HFR?" Sloot wondered aloud.

"Human-Fairy Resources," Roman whispered. "Got to have a department when you incorporate."

"I didn't mean to offend anybody," said Nicoleta, "that's just what you call them!"

"That's what *you* call them," Dandelion retorted. "We'd reserve 'fairy tales' for our epics, like the Ten-Mile Sojourn of the Fellblossom Twins, or the Year We Weren't on Speaking Terms with the Bees, or Apple Cobbler Sundays."

"Duly noted," said Posies, who was scratching away at a tiny journal with a long-tailed feather pen. "The matter has been recorded, and will be brought up at the next opportunity to schedule mandatory sensitivity training for all employees."

"What's sensitivity training?" asked Sloot.

"Touchy-feely stuff," Roman scoffed. "Nobody's allowed to offend anybody else, now that we've incorporated. We wouldn't have gone in for this sort of thing in my day, I can tell you that much."

"Right," said Sloot, who secretly liked the idea of sensitivity training. He casually wondered if he could get his mother to attend, and then felt a pang of guilt for not having done more to find out what had happened to her.

"I want to go home," said the Domnitor. He was crossing his arms hard enough to cut off his circulation, Sloot was sure of it.

It is worth pointing out that Vlad said nothing, if only to mark how emphatically she didn't.

"I *want* to go *home*." There was a perplexed look on the Domnitor's face, making it apparent that he was unaccustomed to having to repeat himself.

"Your home is overrun by the valking dead," said Bartleby, a bit too gleefully.

"Then I want to go back to Stagralla." He made a face that said, in no uncertain terms, that ignoring his demands any further would result in a stomp of his foot, so they'd all just better watch it.

"You might," Vlad growled, "if you're lucky. Here they come."

The cackling congress of goblins got down to the business of ruining the view of the otherwise perfectly lovely Old Country landscape. It was like a sea of razor-sharp teeth slowly pouring itself over a hill, the occasional hand rising from the mass in a rude gesture. It was nothing like the orderly ranks of the fairy soldiers, who showed no signs of dread as their enemy gathered in a seemingly endless swarm at the border. If there had been any doubt that Sloot wouldn't have qualified for enlistment in the fairy army, that would have cleared it up.

"Good," said Myrtle.

"Good?" Sloot had never looked at Myrtle with that level of incredulity before, but given the circumstances, there simply wasn't any holding it back. He pointed at the vile congress amassing mere feet before them. "What about any of this could possibly be misconstrued as good?"

Myrtle shook her head. "Nothing individually, but everything is going according to plan."

"What plan?"

"I told you I'd free you from all of your entanglements. I never said it would be easy. Anyway, I've got to go."

"What? Go? Go where? There's a war on!"

Myrtle took Sloot's face in her hands and kissed him. "I can't explain. I wish I could, but it would reveal too much. The future must unveil itself in due course, or everything that we're going to work for will fall apart."

"I don't understand," who might have done if he'd stopped to think about it for a moment. In truth, he just didn't want Myrtle to leave; however, coming to grips with that would have meant introspection, and they don't teach you that at the University of Salzstadt.

"You will. Soon enough." Myrtle opened her mouth to say something else, but looking around at everything that was about to happen somehow convinced her to let it go.

"I love you, Sloot," she said instead. "You're a better dancer than you give yourself credit for."

"What?"

"Remember our arrangement," she said to Roman.

Roman nodded.

What? thought Sloot, unable to force the word out of his mouth for all the confusion in the way. Since when did Myrtle and Roman have an arrangement? What is this arrangement, exactly? Does it exist for the sole purpose of keeping Sloot in the dark? Perhaps a scientific experiment to determine whether ghosts can get ulcers from worry?

"Tell me you love me."

"I love you."

Myrtle smiled, then disappeared in a puff of smoke.

"Where has she gone?" asked Nicoleta, who appeared to be understandably nervous at the departure of the second-highest-scoring goblin dispatcher from the last time they'd faced a congressional pile-up.

Vlad's head tilted to one side, her neck making the sound of a tree falling in the woods. "No doubt, she has her reasons."

"I wish I had her confidence," Nicoleta murmured to Sloot. "Then again, Vlad's always like this before a battle."

"Trusting?"

"Focused. There's nothing but the enemy before her."

Sloot nodded. He knew the feeling. Well, sort of. The closer it drew to taxes being due, the less he was concerned with anything but his ledgers. It was a different sort of carnage, red ink in lieu of blood, but the nightmares never ended. Tax season … never changes.

The swarming congress of goblins lurched to a halt not far from the border. They parted like a bad haircut and three figures emerged.

First was Greta, her hands bound at her back—which was doing wonders for her posture, if one were searching for a silver lining—and gagged with a filthy rag. She looked as though she'd seen neither the sun nor a washtub in a month.

Next, by less than an inch, was Mrs. Knife. She was using Greta as a shield, her blade held to her hostage's throat, her eyes darting in all directions with the sort of crazed paranoia that a joint venture of caffeine and insomnia must have taken months to perfect.

Finally came a goblin wearing black tatters, who could only have been Gregor. He looked much like the rest of the goblins, but thinner, paler, and wearing his trademark sneer in favor of the standard goblin crazed leer. His blood star floated above his clawed left hand, which was upturned in a gesture that Sloot didn't specifically recognize, but he was sure it was offensive enough to start a fight at a boulderchuck match. Then again, very little offense was required to start fights at boulderchuck matches.

They stood there, a dozen yards from the border, the vast congress of goblins writhing behind them.

"Come forth, Invader!" The pitch of Mrs. Knife's voice had risen considerably, both in pitch and in fury. "I'm thin on patience, and your girlfriend is running out of life!"

Vlad's jaw clenched. Sloot thought he heard a tooth crack.

"Shall we go, then?" asked Roman.

"Not yet," Vlad choked. It was the first time Sloot heard an emotion other than anger had made it past her steely facade, and Sloot had trouble identifying it right away. At first, he was fairly certain that it was some new expression of anger that he'd have known all about, had he grown up in Carpathia; however, as the moment drew itself out into a particularly tense eternity, he recognized it for the intensely complicated tincture that it was.

It was passion, for sure, but there was far more to it. There was the longing for the love that she'd been worrying over for so long. Sloot was a practiced hand at worry, and recognized it when he saw it. There was also trepidation, not for herself, but for Greta. Hope and despair were wrestling for the single chair remaining after the music had stopped.

Lurking behind all of that was rage. Not anger, anger was too simple. This was calculated, bottomless.

Vlad nodded once with practiced authority. Her deliberations were finished. She strode forth, and her retinue followed.

Mrs. Knife's eyes were already wide with a confluence of manic glee and jittery panic, but upon seeing Vlad, they managed to go just a bit wider. She licked her lips and bared her teeth in a way that reminded Sloot of the old grans at the farmer's market, when the farmers would bring out their most pungent onions. They'd look at each other the way that Mrs. Knife was looking at Vlad: like she'd find out how salty the Invader's blood was, if she got too close.

"Bring me the boy," said Vlad, her eyes locked on Mrs. Knife's. Roman guided the Domnitor gently to stand next to Vlad, about two feet away. Vlad's hand rested on the hilt of her sword, but it stayed in its sheath. There was no doubt in anyone's mind that the immediate danger to the Domnitor was no less than what Greta faced in that moment, with the tip of Mrs. Knife's blade poking gently against her throat.

"Our quarrel isn't with you, Invader," Mrs. Knife sneered. "We want out of this place. We want revenge against the dwarves. We must go north through Carpathia, and you must invite us."

"That's where you're wrong," Vlad growled. "When you pointed that knife at my beloved, you put war with me before all else. I offer you one chance at terms."

Gregor drew a noisy breath in through his razor-sharp teeth.

"Not yet," Mrs. Knife hissed toward him. She turned back to Vlad. "Here are the only terms I will offer. Invite us in. Show us Carpathia, and you will have her back."

"You will never enter Carpathia," said Vlad. She gestured toward the Domnitor. "The only terms that I will offer are—"

"Just a moment, please," said Lilacs who, up until now, had politely been waiting for an opportunity to get a word in edgewise. "I hate to interrupt, but we agreed to do the negotiations together, Vlad."

"He's right, you know," said Dandelion. "As managing partners in the United Coalition of Carpathian Monarchies Incorporated, we've got just as much say in the terms we offer as you do, Vlad."

Vlad's eyes closed tightly, and her jaw clenched.

"That's an improvement," Roman whispered to Sloot. "The HFR department has been on Vlad for her temper. She's one incident away from sensitivity training."

"Fine," barked Vlad. "What terms should we offer, then, and why couldn't you have brought this up before we were standing in front of the enemy?"

"Point of order," said Lilacs, his index finger aloft, "they are not yet the enemy, and may not officially become so until after the negotiations have concluded. Periwinkle, would you kindly strike that reference from the official record, please?"

"We'll have to hold a vote later," said Periwinkle, referring to a little book that she produced from her pocket. "Amending the minutes requires a simple majority vote by senior management, and a quorum must be present."

"We have a quorum now," said Dandelion. "All in favor, please?"

Lilacs and Dandelion raised their hands. Vlad glowered at Mrs. Knife.

"Two to one for," said Periwinkle, her tone indicating a small measure of disapproval for the haphazardness of the vote. "So redacted."

"Good," said Lilacs with a nod. "Now then, Mrs. Knife, would you be so kind as to give us a moment to confer with regard to the terms we are willing to extend, please?"

"You've heard the terms," said Mrs. Knife.

"You can have the Domnitor," said Vlad.

"What?"

"This boy is all you need to secure your control over the Old Country," said Vlad. "For Greta, I will give you the Domnitor, and I will ... " she paused, as though trying to remember how to pronounce a word in a foreign language that she barely spoke, " ... *forgive* you for taking her hostage."

"Vlad, please," said Dandelion, "this is entirely—"

Sloot had never heard Mrs. Knife laugh before, and would have sacrificed every penny of his retirement fund to go back to a time when that had still been the case. It was the very definition of shrill, the auditory experience of being stabbed in the stomach, in slow motion, forever.

"Your forgiveness means nothing," Mrs. Knife howled. "The boy means nothing! I already rule the Old Country! You will invite us into Carpathia, and then you will take us to the dwarves."

"Never," said Vlad. She gave Greta a forlorn look, which Greta returned with stoic silence. Sloot never saw what they had in common before, but he saw it now. "My duty is to my country. You will never be welcome in Carpathia."

"There she goes again," Dandelion said to Lilacs. "Vlad, you're getting very close to an official censure. Would you consult with us before making any further official decisions, please?"

"I second that," said Lilacs. "Shouldn't we hear from Greta, please?

I mean, she has a lot at stake here, and you made it a point to include her among the managing partners so it wouldn't be two against one all the time. That was more than fair, I thought."

Dandelion nodded. Periwinkle scribbled furiously to get all of this into the official record.

"Mrs. Knife," Lilacs continued, "would you remove that cloth from Greta's mouth, please? We'd like to get her vote for the official record. Please."

Mrs. Knife shook her head slowly from side to side. "My hostage. You choose."

Dandelion rolled his eyes and scoffed. "*Well.* You warned us that they were ill-tempered, Vlad! I owe you an apology for underestimating that."

"Is the gentleman officially apologizing, please?" asked Periwinkle.

"I suppose there's no time like the present," Dandelion replied. "*Ahem.* For the official record, as it pertains to the matter of my incredulity toward Vlad Defenestratia's assertions regarding the remarkable lack of politeness on the part of—"

"Enough!" shouted Vlad. "Release Greta, take the boy, and go back behind your great wall! We will put this behind us, though I am sure we shall be at war soon enough."

"I vote that we keep the Domnitor," said Lilacs.

"What?" Vlad bellowed.

"We've got more than enough fairy soldiers to keep the goblins in line," Lilacs continued. "I say we invite them in, they'll release Greta, and we can monitor them while they're passing through on the way to Svartalfheim to make sure they don't wreck up the place."

"That sounds fair," said Dandelion. "They'll want to keep their host as large as possible for their war with the dwarves, won't they? They wouldn't risk losing their strength fighting us. We're not their primary target, are we, please?"

"Agreed," said Lilacs.

"No!" shouted Sloot.

"Well, you're not a managing partner," said Lilacs, "so you don't get a vote."

"Wait, please," said Sloot.

"Oh, all right."

"Really?"

"Well, you said *please*."

"Oh. Well, thank you."

"You're welcome."

"Out with it!" shouted Vlad.

"She's going to kill Greta either way," said Sloot. "She said so in the dungeons!"

Vlad's head whipped around to look at Greta with wide eyes.

"I heard her myself," Sloot went on. "I thought there was a chance to save her sooner, but—"

"I love you," Vlad said.

A single tear ran down Greta's face. She nodded softly, coaxing a thin trickle of her blood onto Mrs. Knife's blade.

"But that's not fair," said Lilacs, barely above a whisper.

"Last chance," growled Mrs. Knife.

"Uh oh," said Roman. "I know that look."

For the second time, Sloot saw something in Vlad other than anger: hope. Mad, romantic hope. He knew it as well, because it's exactly the same thing that he'd have done in Vlad's shoes, if that were Myrtle on the end of Mrs. Knife's namesake. Nothing could ever have stood in its way.

"You are welcome in Carpathia," said Vlad.

It was plain on the faces of Mrs. Knife and Gregor, and in the stillness that suddenly came over the writhing congress of goblins behind them, that the deed was done. They stared in naked fascination at the hills of Carpathia that rose behind Vlad.

A hush descended upon all of them. A calm before the storm. It was all too brief. The soft splatter of Greta's blood spraying over the grass brought it abruptly to an end, and then the whole world erupted in war.

⊱⇒FOG OF WAR⇐⊰

O f all the people that Sloot hadn't expected to see on the battlefield … actually, there was a very long list. It's hard to say who'd have been at the top of it, so it may as well have been Willie.

"Hey, Sloot," he said, with the sort of impromptu joviality that people often employed when failing to avoid him at a party. He was actually about fifty feet above the battlefield, not on it.

"Willie! What are you doing up here?"

"Oh, good," said Willie. "I'm not sure either! I thought I was the only one. But why are you all the way over there?"

It wasn't uncommon that details escaped Willie's attention, but Sloot felt that the swirling, sickly yellow energy field around him should have been obvious enough that even he wouldn't have been able to overlook it. The last time Sloot had stood too close to Willie, he'd been drained of a good deal of vitality. He opted to keep Willie's energy field at arm's length.

"Really good view of the battle from up here." True to form, Willie had moved on to his next observation instead of waiting for an answer. He wasn't wrong about the view. The roiling horde of goblins was much smaller than the army of fairies. The fairies were holding their own, though, and Vlad was cutting a smoky swath through the bulk of them. Sloot didn't doubt for a moment that she was hunting for Mrs. Knife, though he couldn't see where she'd disappeared to. Lurking among her forces while letting them do her dirty work, no doubt.

At least the goblins weren't piling up toward them this time. Sloot still got the occasional shiver of dread when he thought about that tottering pile of goblins clambering up toward their portal.

"Willie!" shouted Nicoleta, floating up to join them. "What are you doing here?"

"It's a big secret," said Willie. "I don't know if—"

He froze, a look of realization dawning on his goonish face. He smiled.

"It's not a surprise if I know about it before," said Willie.

"Oh, no," said Sloot. "Not this again."

"You really got me," said Willie, waggling a finger at Sloot. "I didn't even realize that today was my birthday!"

"It's not," said Sloot, "and I assure you—"

Willie laughed. He slapped his knee and struck a pose that looked like a heron preparing to strike at a fish.

"This is even better than a man doing magic! Especially if it's Gregor doing the magic. His stuff's all black and boring. No rabbits or colored handkerchiefs or anything."

"Oh, Gregor's doing magic, all right!"

Sloot looked down to where Nicoleta was pointing. The chaotic mass of goblins had cleared a perfect circle just beneath them, around Gregor and a dozen or so blood wizards, who were sending streams of eldritch power up at Willie, hence the sickly yellow energy field around him.

"Did Nipsy set all of this up?" asked Willie, who was talking much faster than usual. "Is he dead? That would be sad. But then he could come have a sleepover! Not that I sleep anymore. Gosh, I feel like I'll never have to sleep again!"

"They're energizing him," said Nicoleta.

"Why?" asked Sloot.

"No idea, but whatever's happening, it can't end well."

For lack of a better idea, Sloot fidgeted. He was out of his depth here.

"What do we do?"

Nicoleta snapped her fingers. "Bartleby!"

"What?"

Nicoleta made a very mopey face and set herself to making a series of hopeless-looking gestures, the sort that one might make in conjunction with phrases like "oh, I give up," or "it's pointless, anyway."

There was an explosion of bats, and Bartleby hovered within a shroud of dark grey clouds. The clouds had their own thunder.

"Foolish mortals! Vhy have you summoned ... oh, hi."

"It's Gregor!" said Nicoleta, pointing frantically downward. "I don't know what they're doing to Willie, but it can't be good!"

"Hi Bartleby!" Willie waved with the ferocity of a kid who'd eaten an entire bag of sugar. His eyes went wide, then wider, until there were three glowing red pairs of them, each the size of dinner plates. His enormous, razor-sharp grin filled Sloot with a further sense of dread, though he'd thought he was already full-up. He somehow found room for more, like when pies come out after holiday meals.

"Er, hi, Villie." Bartleby gave a little wave. His expression didn't know whether to be impressed with Willie's wicked cool new look, or concerned with the few-and-terrible possible outcomes.

Nicoleta clapped her hands in front of Bartleby's face. "You have to stop him!"

"That sounds like fun," said Bartleby, his grin overflowing with malice. "That little tverp has it coming!"

He disappeared in a puff of smoke and bats, only to reappear in a similar one right behind Gregor. After a few seconds, some of Gregor's tatters burst into flames.

"What about the other wizards?" Sloot wondered aloud.

"Leave them be," said Willie's voice, at least in triplicate, one of which was speaking backward. "The power ... the power!"

"It looks like a modified empowerment," said Nicoleta. "Oh, dear."

Sloot gave into the futile hope that that was an "oh, dear" of sympathy for the wizards, and that they'd somehow bungled it and their spell was about to fizzle out.

"I think they've taken the safety off," said Nicoleta.

"Is that what happens right before everybody yells 'surprise!' and they bring out the cake?" asked a dozen of Willie's voices.

Orange bolts of energy screamed past Sloot. He looked down to see that they were coming from Gregor's wand, which he was doing a very poor job of controlling. A bright red line arced from Bartleby's wand to Gregor's posterior, and Gregor's free hand was slapping him in the face.

"Vhy are you hitting yourself?" Bartleby shouted, cackling.

"The time is upon us," came a deafening choir from Willie's mouth. It was as though he was speaking with every voice that had ever been his, from the bumbling idiot who was obsessed with his birthday, to the boyhood predecessor to that idiot—for whom birthday obsession would have been more expected—to the demonic thing he'd become on so many occasions, and had been joined by a multitude of unseen horrors that Sloot was just positive he'd never be able to pretend didn't exist.

On a stroke of stupendously bad luck, one of Gregor's orange bolts pierced Willie's energy field, stabbed through him, and froze. It wavered there, like a spear of sunset that had gotten stuck. It wriggled and writhed, trying to break free. When it decided it couldn't, it turned black and took Willie with it.

"I don't feel so good," said a single, guileless Willie. Then he started to rumble.

"Run!" shouted Nicoleta, and Sloot did just that. He sped off in the direction he was already facing, adjusting slightly to miss getting involved with Willie's nasty-looking sphere, arms and legs flailing in a way that he knew in his very core was deeply embarrassing, but he was far too terrified to care.

It all went dark. There was an explosion, Sloot was fairly certain, and then everything was black.

No, not black, not dark … Dark. He'd never seen it before, but he knew enough about the Dark to know what it was when he saw it, and this was it.

Somehow, he'd been transported to the Dark. Where was everyone? He could hear them, all sounding very far away.

"Hello?" he shouted, and was immediately sorry that he did. The sound that reverberated back to him sounded an awful lot like his voice, but only if he'd taken up a new career haunting the dreams of children. He resolved never to speak again.

He started to wander around, or thought that he did, anyway. Everything was so absolutely black that there were no frames of reference, no way to tell if he'd actually floated away from the spot where he'd been.

Was there even a spot from which to float? He wasn't sure. He wouldn't have gone so far as to wish that he still had a physical form to help him figure that out, as he had no idea what the Dark might have been doing to it. Best to sit and wait it out, he decided.

How long ago had that been? More evidence that he was in the Dark. Like in the Hereafter, he surmised that the passage of time was imperceptible in the Dark. He didn't know what else he could do but sit and wait it out, and he had no way of knowing whether he was sitting or not. So he waited.

⋟⋞ TIDYING UP ⋟⋞

"N ame?"

"Peril."

"And how are you feeling, Peril?"

"Sloot."

"Sorry?"

"That's my name. Sloot."

"That's not what I have here," said the perfectly average-looking man in the grey suit. He had a clipboard in his left hand, and was scanning it with a fury to rival most of the bureaucrats that Sloot had ever met in his life.

"My name is Sloot Peril."

The man's smile was calm and collected, but the way that he made eye contact with Sloot gave the impression that there was a rage just beneath his surface, and it was only a matter of time before it breached. His smile said "how may I assist you," but his eyes said "prepare to have the absolute *expletive redacted* assisted out of you, and do not even consider resisting."

"You've had a trying day," the man said politely, nodding in agreement with himself on Sloot's behalf. "Any other names rattling around in there that you'd like to make me aware of? Take your time."

His voice was patient. The bulging vein in his forehead was not.

"Er, my middle name's Gefahr."

The man's smile tightened. Sloot looked away awkwardly. It was then that he noticed that he apparently hadn't left the field of battle, though all trace of the battle had. It didn't seem like much of anything had ever taken place there, actually. Even the road was gone. The stones that had been piled into something the undead would accept as a castle were still there, but not in a piled sort of way.

The man scribbled on his clipboard, then let out a slow, soothing breath. "Now, then, Sloot Gefahr Peril, How are you feeling?"

"Well, I'm dead."

The man's eyes narrowed, and all of the erstwhile indications that he was on the verge of frenzy evaporated into curiosity.

"Are you sure?"

"Quite," said Sloot, nodding to agree with himself, subconsciously taking a page from the stranger's book. "I was trampled during the Fall of Salzstadt."

"Hmm," the man said. He tore the top page off his clipboard and let it fall to the ground. "Well, that would explain why you're not on this list. Excuse me a moment, won't you?"

He maintained profound eye contact with Sloot.

"Er, of course," said Sloot.

The man rifled through the pages of his clipboard, ripping a few more out and casting them blithely aside.

"Ah," he said, with a satisfied smile. He pulled a page from near the bottom and clipped it to the top.

"Name?"

"I'm sorry?"

"It's for the form."

"Oh, well, it's still Sloot ... er ... Sloot Gefahr Peril."

The man waited a moment after Sloot finished speaking, perhaps providing a moment for any last-minute corrections, before writing it at the top of the form.

"Thank you," he said. "Now then, Sloot Gefahr Peril, would you please account for your absence from the list?"

"What list?"

"I'm sorry, what?" Much to Sloot's chagrin, the man had returned to his prior mixture of unabated calm with an undercurrent of roiling savagery.

"Er, I beg your pardon," said Sloot, suddenly very glad that he had no life for this psychopath to take, "I just don't know … to what list you're referring."

Perhaps it was Sloot's panicked demeanor. Perhaps it was the great lengths he'd just taken to avoid ending a sentence with a preposition. Either way, the man's intensity seemed to deflate a bit. He smiled.

"The list of the dead involved in the incident," said the man.

"Incident?"

The man's smile didn't change for the duration of an uncomfortably long pause. "Look, this should only take a moment to clear up. Why don't you stay exactly where you are?"

"Er, okay."

The man turned abruptly away from Sloot and walked down the hill. He approached a trio of older people all wearing white, and gave them a curt nod. Sloot looked around to see that there were at least a dozen other people in grey suits milling about, measuring things, and taking notes on clipboards. He didn't recognize any of them. He felt a bit un-balanced, but he was sure that he'd known everyone but the armies of goblins and fairies before … before Willie exploded.

Willie exploded! He hadn't actually seen it since he was fleeing as fast as he could, but that was what had happened, wasn't it? Willie ex-ploded, and then everything went black.

No. It went Dark.

Sloot looked up. There was the Dark. There was sunshine all over the place, but the Dark loomed above them, stretching off into infinity in every direction. Where was the sunshine coming from?

"Sloot Gefahr Peril!" shouted the clipboard-wielding maniac. He was waving Sloot over. He and the three people in white were looking at him impassively. Sloot hadn't a clue as to what was about to happen, but then again, that had been the case for a very long time.

They stood there, watching him as he approached. The figures in white were older, though not quite old. There was a tall, gaunt man, a shorter and paunchier man, and a woman with wild, unkempt hair that was black, white, and every shade of grey in between.

"Sloot Gefahr Peril," said the man who'd interviewed him before, "allow me to introduce the Coolest."

The three figures in white all smiled and nodded in a very self-satisfied way.

"The ... Coolest?"

"Oh, you've heard of us," said the shorter man in a voice that threatened to leap into a musical number at any moment. He put an arm around Sloot's shoulder and started walking with him in no direction in particular. "What's truly strange is that we've never heard of you."

"And not strange in the fun, kooky mysticism kind of way," said the woman. "It's just strange. We know everybody."

"Well, I kept to myself a lot."

"It wasn't hyperbole," said the tall man. "We know everybody."

"I don't see how that's possible."

"Why, Elroy told you," said the short man, "we're the Coolest!"

"Er, right," said Sloot. This whole thing was unsettling. They were obviously lunatics, but Sloot was more accustomed to the waving-a-dagger-in-your-face types. He knew where he stood with them. "You all look very cool in your white suits. Very ... dashing."

"No, not *cool*," said the short man, finally starting to raise his voice like a proper lunatic, "the Coolest! You see, Lucia? I told you your idiot nephew knows as much about marketing as a loaf of bread!"

"He's my sister's kid, Donovan," said Lucia, "you know how she gets."

"He graduated from marketing school and asked us for a job," Donovan mumbled to Sloot conspiratorially. "It was supposed to be an internship, but before I knew it we were all head-to-toe white linen and 're-branded'—whatever that means—with new stationery and everything. The Coolest! Have you ever heard anything more ostentatious?"

"No," said the tall man. He lit a cigarette.

Lucia drew herself up with an indignation that Sloot had only seen in mothers when middle names were about to get thrown around. "Marco! You said you'd quit!"

"And I will," said Marco, blowing a cloud of smoke in Lucia's direction. "Not today, though. I'm too stressed out."

"That's understandable," said Donovan. "None of this was supposed to happen."

"Er, I'm sorry," said Sloot, falling gracefully into his favorite way to enter a conversation, "but could you tell me what's going on, please?"

"We were hoping you might be able to shed a little light on that, Sloot Gefahr Peril. Do you mind if I call you Sloot?"

"Please."

"Thank you. Sloot, until a few minutes ago, we thought we knew everyone and everything, but none of us saw this coming, and we have no idea who you are."

"Are you ... gods?"

"Hardly," laughed Lucia. "We're inter-cosmic—"

"We're gods," Donovan interjected. "Please, Lucia, can we get some answers out of him before we obliterate his mind with truths beyond his capacity to understand?"

"Oh, fine."

"Everything was going fine, Sloot, until the Dark started spilling out into the Narrative. We had to scramble a crew to clean it up, there's a literal mountain of paperwork that's going to have to be filed about this—a *literal* mountain, Sloot—and the only thing we can't account for is you."

"We should cut him open," said Marco, lighting a new cigarette off the end of his last one.

"He's a ghost," said Lucia.

"I'm sure we've got a knife for that."

"And *I'm* sure there's an easier way to sort this out than giving Sloot the old ghost knife treatment," said Donovan.

Marco made a dismissive gesture, then looked really cool smoking his cigarette. Sloot thought the only way he could have looked any cooler was if he wasn't smoking.

"You're not wrong," said Lucia. "And yes, I can read your mind."

"Active thoughts only," Donovan clarified. "So tell us, Sloot—or just think it out loud, if you prefer—who are you, and how did you spill the Dark into the Narrative?"

"Me? I didn't do this!"

"He certainly believes it," said Lucia.

"Oh, well," said Donovan, "I suppose it would have been too easy if we got to just blame everything on the oddity and call it a day."

"The oddity?"

"You," said Marco. He put his hand in his pocket in a way that left little doubt that he had a knife in there.

"Oh."

"So tell me, Sloot," said Donovan, "where did you come from?"

"Salzstadt," said Sloot. "Well, my mother was Carpathian—*is* Carpathian—oh, I'm not sure if she's still alive! That must make me the worst son ever."

"Doubtful," said Lucia. "There's Marco, right there."

Marco made a gesture so insanely vulgar that it gave Sloot the spiritual equivalent of a migraine headache. His ears started ringing, and the grass briefly turned a color he hadn't known existed.

"Ignore them," said Donovan. "What else?"

"Not much to tell, really," Sloot shouted over the ringing. "I grew up, went to work in the Three Bells counting house, corrected a report, was promoted to Willie Hapsgalt's financier—"

"Oh," said Donovan. "There it is."

"Sorry, there what is?"

"We were wondering why the Hapsgalts were still so rich! I swear, it's like you turn your head for a *second* and the richest family in all the known universe is wreaking havoc with the natural order of reality."

"Yes," said Lucia. "It's just like that."

"Er, pardon me," said Sloot, "but did you say you were wondering why the Hapsgalts were *still* so rich?"

Donovan nodded. "The matter kept getting away from us. The last time I checked, a fellow named Vasily Pritygud was supposed to have written a report to fix it."

The report. *The* report! The one that Sloot corrected! The one that started all of this mess! But how? If that report was the will of the Coolest, how did it come to Sloot for corrections?

"Anyway," Donovan continued, "that's where everything went awry. Can we get them all together so we can get rid of it?"

"Get rid of ... it?"

"Yes," said Lucia. "All of it, I'm afraid."

"All of what?"

"It. Everything. Well, not *everything*. The Old Country, Carpathia, a few patches of the Hereafter ... it'll be a lot of work, but it'll be a heck of a lot easier than trying to fix it."

"This is the worst," said Marco. He flicked the butt of his cigarette away, littering with more ferocity than Sloot had ever seen. He reached instinctively for his whistle, then recalled that he was a ghost. In any case, he doubted that the Ministry of Sanitation had jurisdiction to "rehabilitate" inter-cosmic gods in white suits.

"It's embarrassing," said Donovan, "that's for sure."

"Wait," said Sloot, more panicked than he'd ever been before, "why don't we—"

"Just a moment, Sloot," said Donovan. He snapped his fingers, and suddenly everyone was there. They were in the full exertion of war, as though nothing had happened.

"Wait a minute!" Donovan yelled above the din of war between the goblins and the fairies. "Not you."

He snapped his fingers again, and the two armies disappeared. A handful of people remained, Vlad being the only one among them who seemed disappointed to no longer be in the thick of battle.

"That's right," shouted Constantin, "and keep running! You lack the mettle to trifle with a Hapsgalt man, sirs!"

"That's better," said Donovan. He looked around, mild confusion commingling with annoyance on his face. "Is this everybody?"

"Hardly," said Willie. "I wouldn't turn up to this party. Not before I hit a bunch of better parties first, so I could rub everyone's noses in it." His smile turned to chagrin. "Hey, I exploded!"

"You weren't supposed to," said Gregor. "You were supposed to absorb enough energy to defeat our foes, but that idiot Bartleby thinks everything is a game!"

"Don't blame me, you vere the one who vouldn't stop hitting yourself."

"Quiet," said Donovan, "all of you. There's still someone missing, but I can't put my finger on who."

"Whom," said Sloot.

Donovan shot him a look that asked, "really?"

Greta had been brought back, though her throat was still open and gushing with blood. Vlad was undeterred by the arterial spray, and the two of them took the opportunity to make out like teenagers trying to prove they'd done this sort of thing before, and you were a real nerd if you hadn't. Mrs. Knife grimaced, backing away and waving her knife at anyone who moved. Arthur lounged in mid-air, contemplating the Dark above. Nan hid from Constantin behind a nearby tree, Dandelion and Lilacs hovered nearby, and Nicoleta tried not to be too obvious about sneaking glances at Vlad and Greta. She grinned.

Roman laughed. He was grinning from ear to ear. "I didn't imagine that the Coolest would be here at the end. Oh, that's rich!"

"Wait a minute," said Donovan, "I know you."

"Of course, you do," said Lucia. "We know everybody." She shrugged at Sloot.

"You're ..." Donovan snapped his fingers a couple of times while looking skyward, ostensibly hoping it would jar his memory. "Oh, right. You don't have a name, do you?"

"I've gone by many. They all know me as Roman."

"Your name's not really Roman?" asked Sloot.

"It may as well be," Roman replied. "I was never given a proper one. Hang on a minute."

Roman flexed his shoulders. A look of relief came over him as a pair of leathery wings unfolded from his back.

"You're a demon!" Sloot was thunderstruck. He'd been palling around with a demon this whole time! No wonder things kept getting worse. Had his mother known?

"An enigma demon, to be precise." Roman smiled, and then to Sloot's bewildered look said, "We keep secrets."

"More than that," said Nicoleta. "You *are* secrets."

"Right you are, love," said Roman. "Every enigma has a secret at his or her core, sort of like an initial investment to get the business off the ground. Only I don't know what my core secret is."

"That's a fun bit of paradox," said Arthur, who was suddenly interested in the conversation. Philosophers are very fond of paradoxes, given their utility in avoiding real work.

"Fun for you," said Roman, "but irritating for me. I don't get to know my secret, just everyone else's. Tragic, really."

"Right," said Donovan. "I'm sure you're to blame for all of this, and I'll work it out soon enough. I still have to find out who else is missing, though."

Roman's hands started to glow as he started working through a series of contorted gestures. "While you're working that out, I'd like to get what's coming to me, if you don't mind."

A portal appeared on the ground in the midst of all assembled, and twinkling lights arose from it like embers from a fire. The embers increased in number like bubbles in a boiling pot, and before the metaphor had an opportunity to get any further out of hand, they coalesced into an intensely beautiful woman.

"What the—" she began.

"Hello, Gwen," said Roman.

"Gwen!" said Marco, dropping his too-cool-to-care-about-anything facade for the first time since Sloot had met him, and grinning like a love-struck schoolboy.

"You know each other?" asked Donovan.

"We know everybody," said Lucia for what seemed like the dozenth time, based on her level of irritation.

"Roman," said Gwen curtly, and then her demeanor shifted to sultry. "Marco." She blew him a kiss.

All eyes were on Gwen, and most of the mouths below said eyes were hanging open.

"Careful," Roman warned, "Gwen is a love demon."

Sloot caught himself staring and panicked. He had a girlfriend! He was no good at lying about things, and was sure that he'd end up getting caught, regardless of the fact that Myrtle wasn't there. From what Sloot had heard, girlfriends didn't have to be able to read the future in order to figure out those sorts of things.

"A love demon who was in the middle of something," said Gwen. "I assume I've been summoned because someone would rather use sorcery than talk to someone they find attractive? That's usually what happens."

"Not this time," said Roman. "It's time for me to collect."

Gwen fixed Roman with a blank look, which slowly reworked itself into terrified realization. "You don't mean—"

"Oh, I definitely do."

Gwen looked up at the Dark. The curve of her neck made Sloot wish he'd taken music lessons so he could write an opera about it.

"Oh," said Gwen. Her naturally rosy cheeks went pale. "Oh, no, Roman. What have you done?"

"I'd say I've proven my point."

Gwen looked up at the Dark again. "Oh, this is bad."

"Yes," said Roman, "it is. Now pay up."

"I can't! Roman, you can't possibly expect—"

"I can, and I do." Roman was calm, a giddy smile on his face. That made Sloot all the more nervous.

"But *look* at this!" Gwen pointed up to the Dark. "I'd forgotten about that stupid wager. I never thought you'd actually go through with it!"

Roman laughed. "You of all people should know better than to underestimate a demon in a wager."

"Against a mortal, sure. But that wasn't serious! We were drunk!"

"I'm never more serious than when I'm drunk."

That sounds about right, Sloot thought.

"If it was an official wager, there will be a contract," said Donovan. "Allistair?"

An imp appeared in a puff of black smoke. "Yes, m'lord?"

"That was fast," said Sloot.

"He's on retainer," said Donovan. He pointed at Roman and Gwen. "Allistair, be a dear and find me the contract for a wager between these two demons?"

"As you wish," said Allistair. He disappeared in a very similar puff of black smoke.

"Now then," Donovan continued, "while he's working on that, why don't you explain this little wager for us? I don't know anything about it, which is disconcerting."

"Very well," said Roman.

❧ ROMAN'S WAGER ❧

The tale that Roman wove for them was set long ago in the Old Country, when it had been called whatever it had been called before. It probably wouldn't have made much difference at that point if Roman had told them, but he was an enigma demon. They didn't let go of secrets easily.

He and Gwen were lying atop a hill that would one day become a very affluent neighborhood, looking up at the stars and sharing a bottle of wine. The last of several that they'd shared that night, in fact.

To hear Roman tell it, Gwen had been giggling incessantly, and wouldn't stop going on about how grand love was. Roman had recently gone through a mutually agreed-upon breakup with an efreet—which wasn't the way that Gwen remembered it, but who was telling the story?—and, in any case, disagreed on the point of love's grandeur.

Roman made a number of dashing and charismatic good points, but Gwen was in no mood to listen to reason. They argued until sunrise, at which point Roman suggested a wager.

Enigma demons don't know their own essential secret, but they are able to divulge them at will. Doing so will cause them to unravel in a fashion that Roman had been assured is quite literal. It's like pushing a button that causes their hearts to leap out of their chests. "Oh, that's what that looks like," they might just have time to think before they keel over dead.

Perhaps Roman was tired, or perhaps Gwen was being so objectively insufferable about the amazing power of love that he was driven to the end of his wits. In either case, he made a wager with Gwen, insisting that he could prove that love was the greatest evil in the universe. If he was wrong, he'd divulge his essential secret to her and do his best to smile while she watched him unravel. However, if he won, she would have to reveal to him the greatest secret that she knew: the exact number of Unknowable Secrets.

"There's only one way that she could possibly know that," said Donovan, glaring at Marco.

"Marco!" shouted Lucia.

"What? Look at her!" He made some wavy hand motions that approximated Gwen's curvature. She batted her eyelashes.

"You told her an Unknowable Secret because she's pretty?"

"No," said Marco. "I told her how many Unknowable Secrets there are, because of what she can do with all of that ..." he made the wavy hand motions again.

Donovan closed his eyes and pinched the bridge of his nose. "The number of Unknowable Secrets *is* an Unknowable Secret, you imbecile!"

"How was I supposed to know?"

"You're one of the Coolest!"

Marco laughed and ran a hand through his hair. "Yeah, I am."

"Idiot."

"Anyway," said Roman, pointing up at the Dark, "there's my proof. Pay up."

"How is that proof?" asked Gwen.

"That was the result of a war that Vlad fought because of her love for Greta."

"Excuse me, please," said Lilacs, "but we fought that war to keep the goblins out of Carpathia."

"If you wanted to keep the goblins out of Carpathia so badly, why did Vlad invite them in?"

"And you think that proves that love is the greatest evil in the universe?"

"Of course it does," said Roman. "If it wasn't for her love for Greta, Vlad would have left the goblins to rot in the Old Country without a second thought! She wouldn't have convened a war council with the fairies, and she certainly wouldn't have opened the border to Mrs. Knife."

"I still don't see how that makes love the root of all evil."

"Look around! War! Death! The Dark is literally trying to crush the life out of reality, and is doing such a good job that the Coolest themselves had to intervene! All for love. If you're not willing to concede this one, I'm going to have to call for a legal intervention."

There was a puff of black smoke, and Allistair re-appeared.

"Here you are, m'lord," said Allistair. He handed a file to Donovan.

"Thank you," said Donovan, who must have taken a speed reading course. He flipped through the pages so quickly that Sloot cringed, sure that he'd tear one eventually. "Well, this just can't be! This appears to be a completely valid wager, but it shouldn't have been possible! We've gone to great lengths to ensure that enigma demons aren't capable of gambling with their essential secrets or the Unknowable Secrets under any circumstances."

"Not the older models," said Roman.

"Oh," said Lucia, managing to make the word seem more ominous than any Sloot had heard before. "You don't mean—"

"Yes, yes," said Roman testily, "I'm an Unknowable Enigma! Can we please just assume that I mean what you think I mean from now on? It's becoming tiresome, hearing 'you don't mean' all the time."

Back in the days before mortals had started walking upright and thinking less of each other for not wearing more fashionable shoes, the Coolest—whatever it was they'd been called back then—had a number of Unknowable Secrets lying around. This was during their golden age of innovation, and the complete lack of regulations left them free to create whatever they wanted using whatever materials they had at their disposal. There's considerable disagreement among the Coolest over which of them suggested putting the Unknowable Secrets into demons, as it turned out to be the single most problematic creation in their portfolio.

Lesser enigma demons are created every time a really good secret is successfully kept until death. Like Unknowable Enigmas, they don't know what those secrets are. Unknowable Enigmas further don't know that their essential secrets are Unknowable. As far as they're concerned, like lesser enigmas, they were powered by someone having witnessed a murder, an affair, or some really horrid dancing-like-no-one's-watching, then promised never to tell a soul and kept their word.

The trouble started when an Unknowable Enigma lost a bet and divulged his essential secret. It didn't just unravel him, it started the entire universe unraveling from that point outward. It took centuries for the Coolest to reverse all of the damage, which largely consisted of wiping out enormous swaths of afflicted reality and starting them over. One region of several million square miles completely wiped out an advanced civilization who had invented, among other things, perpetual energy generators, a cure for cancer, and shoelaces that never untied by accident.

Much to their chagrin, the Coolest discovered that they couldn't find a way to destroy the remaining Unknowable Enigmas without a worrisome level of unraveling reality. They tried locking them away in a vault, but that didn't end well. The rumor mill that they spun up among themselves spread like wildfire, empowering each of them with so many secrets that they neared critical mass. In the end, they had to settle for wiping their memories and dropping them off at very different places in the universe, where they had very little chance of running into each other.

Through no small amount of subterfuge, a great deal of conniving, and a few trips to his local library, Roman discovered that he was an Unknowable Enigma. He spent centuries quietly looking high and low, following whispers, portends, and rumors, anything that he thought might lead him to learn his own essential secret without having to divulge it.

"So you've been manipulating us from the beginning," said Sloot, his brow furrowing with the shattered disappointment of a child who'd just been told that Santa Claus wasn't real. Of course, that's not factually accurate. It's just something people say when they feel like being mean to children.

"Oh, long before that," said Roman. He gave a sheepish grin that indicated he must have felt a little bit bad about it, but probably not so bad that if he were given a chance to do it all again, he wouldn't have done it the exact same way. "Now that it's all coming to its conclusion, I don't mind telling you that every piece of this has required a great deal of finesse."

"Vasily's financial report," said Sloot. "I wasn't supposed to correct it. That was your doing."

"Well reckoned." Roman beamed with pride. "I've taught you well! You'll make a fine intelligence man someday. But that was a small matter. I don't mind telling you that I managed far more clever plots than that one."

"You can say that again," said Donovan.

"What's that you're reading?" asked Lucia.

"It's Roman's file. Wow, it's like we were on vacation for the last few centuries! How did we miss all of this? Did you know that he poked a hole in the Dark?"

Sloot's blood ran cold, and not in the refreshing way that vampires like it in the summer.

"The Old Country," he said, barely above a whisper. Then subsequent realizations elbowed their way in, and he started shouting. "The goblins! That's how they found their way in!"

Roman cringed, throwing Sloot a trepidated grin. Sloot knew that look. He'd worn it himself often enough to have exhausted it and need to purchase a new one. He wasn't accustomed to being on the receiving end of one, though. He imagined that it should have felt empowering. Perhaps if he'd been born someone else.

"I can explain," said Roman.

"It wasn't the mumbling men with the ginger beards," said Sloot, "it was you! I mean, their horrendous swearing caused a lot of trouble, but the goblins would never have found their way in if you hadn't poked a hole in the Dark. My country … our whole way of life … it could have been so much easier if it weren't for you and your stupid wager!"

"Well, yes," said Roman, "but ... come on ..." He made placating gestures with his hands, as though to say "we can just put centuries of mischief aside and pretend I haven't been toying with the fates of nations for generations, right?"

Sloot was aghast. To be clear, he was not *a ghast*, which is a bestial sort of ghost who looks like it's spent all its time in an Infernal gymnasium, lifting the heaviest things it can find, like that was the most interesting thing it could have done with its time. Sloot was sure that he'd be laughed out of places like that by the bigger boys, and if invited to one could produce a reasonable excuse with minimal effort.

"You're a monster," said Sloot.

"Technically, yes. Demons are a subspecies of monster. Ghosts are too, in fact."

"Oh, I didn't know. I suppose I should—hey, don't change the subject! You created a massive upset in the natural order of things! Everything's all messed up, and now the Coolest are going to ... what are you going to do, exactly?"

Marco lit another cigarette. "We'll need to take out all of the Old Country and Carpathia, from sky to bedrock, and then pull everything inward to close the gap."

Sloot wrestled with the enormity of what he was saying. Try as his now-tenuous grasp on reality might to reject it, he simply couldn't. Accountants deal in facts, and denial on that scale required the sort of imagination that he lacked entirely.

"There's going to be a lot of new oceanfront property in Nordheim," Roman mused aloud. "I'm just going to nip up there and make some investments, if you don't mind. I don't suppose that will count as insider trading?"

"Oh, you're not going anywhere," said Donovan, "and theoretical financial crimes are the least of your worries. We're going to have to get rid of you as well."

Roman grinned. "Good luck with that. I'm an Unknowable Enigma, remember?"

"Just because we couldn't unmake you in the old days doesn't mean it's not possible now."

"Yeah," said Marco, "we've got a lot of new knives that didn't exist back then."

"I'll believe it when I see it."

"Yeah, you will."

"I will. That's what I said."

"And you will, too."

Marco glared at Roman. Roman gave a bored sigh.

"What about me?" asked Gwen, who was cringing in a way that implied she was afraid to ask, but also featured some of her physical attributes in a very flattering light.

"You'll be fine," said Marco with a wink so greasy it dribbled onto his shoe.

"No," said Donovan, "she'll have to go as well. Everything that had anything to do with this mess could have been the defect that brought it all to this." He waved blithely up at the Dark.

"The goblins are going to be the really hard part," he continued. "They've been around for millennia, antagonists in countless sagas. We'll have to rewrite a lot of dwarfish history."

"Big deal," said Marco, a precariously long pillar of ash refusing to drop from the end of his cigarette. "We rewrite a few books."

"We have to do more than that," said Lucia. "What if we get audited? Auditors can go back in time, you know. We'll have to do the whole thing down to the smallest details."

"Your work ethic is boring."

"And your lack of one is galling!"

"Anyway," said Donovan, loudly enough to end the rapidly-digressing conversation between his colleagues, "it's all going to have to get done, so we may as well get started. Marco, since you enjoy razing so much, would you like to do the honors?"

Marco smiled with enough malice that it required an extra couple of rows of teeth. "With pleasure."

"Hang on a minute," said Myrtle, as she descended on leathery wings with Flavia in one hand and a bedraggled wizard in the other.

"Myrtle!" shouted Sloot. "Wait, how do you know Flavia?"

"I'm a causality demon. I know lots of stuff."

Donovan and Lucia breathed huge sighs of relief. Marco frowned.

"I knew someone was missing." Donovan slapped his knee. "A causality demon! Oh, man, I thought we were in it deep! I don't remember putting a causality demon here, was it one of you?"

Lucia shook her head. "It wasn't Marco, either."

"You don't know," said Marco, lighting another cigarette. "It could have been me."

"It could have been," admitted Lucia, "but was it?"

Marco paused, took a long drag off his cigarette, and coughed. "No."

"I thought not."

"We can review the files later," said Donovan. "Myrtle, was it?"

Myrtle nodded. Flavia and the wizard cowered in her grip, their feet not quite touching the ground.

"Myrtle," Donovan cooed, his mouth turned up in a toothy grin, "I'll bet if I delegate this to you, you can sort it all out, can't you?"

"No."

"No?" Donovan made a confused face that Sloot had seen before, mostly on Willie. He obviously wasn't used to being told "no" either.

"I can't," said Myrtle. She set her charges down and pointed to Sloot. "He can."

"What? Me?"

"Yes, you," said Myrtle. "I have foreseen it. It shall come to pass."

"No need to be so dramatic," said Lucia.

"Says the lady in the white linen uniform."

"Watch it."

"Sorry," said Myrtle. She nodded to Roman. "I see I've missed your big reveal."

Roman gave a little quasi-formal bow, like he'd just finished his first round of juggling and it was time to set the pins on fire.

Sloot's gawking meandered from Roman to Myrtle and back again several times. "I don't … where did you … how long have you … I don't know where to begin!"

"Out of the question," said Donovan.

Myrtle's face rearranged itself in a stunned expression. She'd obviously expected that to go another way.

"What? Why not?"

Donovan arranged his hands on his hips in a way that suggested a "because I said so" was on its way, but then he paused as though he'd remembered something.

"Well, he's just a ghost, for starters."

"That can be remedied," said Myrtle. "It is foretold."

Donovan sighed. "Stupid causality. Allistair?"

Allistair handed Donovan a file. "The file on the oddity, m'lord."

"Allistair, you are a treasure. What would I do without you?"

"Make another imp exactly like me, I imagine." He disappeared in a puff of black smoke.

"So literal, these imps," said Donovan, rifling through the papers in Sloot's file. "All right, yes, we can clear up the whole 'ghost' thing, but what about all of his entanglements? According to this, he's on everyone's side! It would be quicker to come up with a list of everyone who *didn't* have their hooks in the boy!"

"That was true not long ago," said Myrtle, "but we've closed out most of them. The only ones that remain now are the Old Country and Carpathian Intelligence services, and we can clear those up right now."

There were two puffs of black smoke, between which Allistair took the file from Donovan's hand and replaced it with a new one. Donovan perused the new file.

"Ah, there are updates," said Donovan. "We've really got to upgrade our personal timelines to include those ... things ... you know, everyone in the Grimmest Future's always staring at them? Fits in their pockets?"

"I wish," said Lucia, "but we'd never get this one to put it down." She jerked a thumb in Marco's direction, but he didn't notice. He was too busy fiddling with a spring-loaded knife he'd produced from his pocket.

Myrtle nudged Flavia with her foot. "It's time."

"W-what?"

"Go on, get on with it."

"No," said Flavia flatly. "It's some sort of trick. You're going to pull my head off at the last second or something!"

"I promise you, I won't."

"You're a demon! You can't be trusted."

"Demons can't break promises," said Roman. "I mean, we can *effectively* break promises, but it's really hard. Got to find the long way around, if you know what I mean."

"You're not helping," said Myrtle. "Look, for all of us to go on ever having existed, you have to do the thing that Winking Bob asked you to do with my blood."

"Cryptic much?" asked Lucia.

"Causality demon." Myrtle shrugged.

"Hold on a minute," said Sloot.

"I need you to trust me, Sloot." Myrtle walked over to Sloot and embraced him. "Don't worry. It'll take a long time, but this will all work out in the end."

The wizard opened the envelope and produced a piece of paper with a red spot in the middle.

"That was what Bob was holding," said Sloot. "That's your blood!"

Myrtle nodded. "She took it when I first started thieving for her, a long time ago. I didn't know why she wanted it at the time, but now I can see where it fits in with everything. Everything will make sense in time, I promise."

Sloot didn't know what to say, so he nodded and said nothing.

"Get on with it," Myrtle said to Flavia.

"I don't want to."

"Ugh," Myrtle groaned, balling her fists in frustration. "Fine. I don't like threatening people, but either you get on with it or I'll pull one of your arms off and watch you bleed to death."

"This just got interesting," said Marco.

"Oh," said Flavia, "okay. Walter?"

"It's Walter the Undying," said the wizard in an obviously false baritone that he had trouble maintaining. Sloot knew from experience that tenors have trouble sounding tough and/or mysterious.

"Not now, Walter," Flavia hissed.

"Oh, come on," groaned Walter the Undying, "if not now, when? It appears we're either going to be pulled apart by demons or erased from existence in a minute."

"Fine, Walter the Undying. Get on with it."

"Beseech me."

"What?"

"Look, my contract guarantees me certain perks due to my wizarding credentials! If you can't be bothered to properly beseech me by my full credentials in the final moments of existence, then what is any of it for? I may as well put my feet up and welcome the impending oblivion in peace."

Flavia sighed and drew in a breath. "I do humbly beseech you, Walter the Undying, master of the arcane and keeper of eldritch knowledge, employ thy art to this essence of blood, and consign this demon to the lowest circle of the Inferno for eternity!"

"There," said Walter the Undying, "was that so hard?"

"What?" Sloot gasped. "No!"

"It's all right, Sloot," said Myrtle. "Just trust me, okay?"

Trust her? He wanted to, but how? Consignment to the lowest circles of the Inferno for eternity didn't sound like the sort of thing that minor setbacks were made of. That sounded like a severe impediment to their relationship, to say the very least. Unless the lowest circles of the Inferno had accommodations for couples, but even then …

Sloot fretted fervently as Walter the Undying made a series of bent-finger gestures over the bloody paper. Even if he were brave enough to try and stop whatever Walter the Undying was up to, he didn't have the sort of corporeality that would lend itself to heroics.

All he could do was look at Myrtle one last time. Her eyes locked on his, and she smiled.

"Promise you'll take me dancing?" she said. Before Sloot had a chance to answer, Walter the Undying finished his finger waggling, and Myrtle was gone.

Sloot moaned. It was a properly ghostly sound, one that started in the dark of some ethereal pit of eternal sadness, and rattled his psyche like a nice pair of chains.

Everyone was silent. Flavia and Walter the Undying looked around at Sloot, Roman, and the Coolest, waiting for some metaphorical axe to drop.

"Well," said Donovan, "I'm not sure what that was meant to accomplish."

"Um, yes," said Flavia, attempting a bright smile but letting too much sick desperation put it together. "Would it be all right if Walter— the Undying—and I were off, then?"

Donovan shrugged. "I don't see why not."

"Wait," said Sloot. "Myrtle wanted to free me from my entanglements! I don't suppose you'd release me from my service to Uncle now, would you?"

"Well, it's not really up to me," said Flavia, "but it's already done."

"What?"

"Well, our leverage to keep you working for us was that we'd hurt Myrtle if you didn't," said Flavia. "I think consignment to the lowest circles of the Inferno covers that. We've made good on our threat, so it stands to reason that you no longer work for us."

"Oh," said Sloot. He looked to Roman.

"Sorry," said Roman. "You're not getting out of Carpathian Intelligence that easily."

"Wha— *easily*? Two nations' worth of reality are about to be removed from existence! Wait a minute, are you even still spymaster, given the circumstances?"

"Of course I am," said Roman. "If being a demon precluded me from service, I'd never have gotten the job in the first place."

"I doubt Vlad knew you were a demon when she assigned you the post."

"That's beside the point."

"No, it isn't!"

"This is taking forever," said Marco. "Can I start razing now?"

"Hang on," said Donovan. He snapped his fingers and Vlad and

Greta were rolling around on the ground in from of him, blushing and out of breath. Greta was still spraying blood from her artery. Sloot was fairly certain it was the first time he'd seen Vlad blush.

"What is going on here?" Vlad demanded, jumping to her feet in a protective stance over Greta. Her hand moved to her hip, but found no sword. She simply raised her fists, showing not a shred of doubt that her lack of a weapon would not even remotely hinder her ability to defeat anyone who came at her.

"It's a long story," said Roman.

"Roman's a demon," blurted Sloot. "He's caused a conundrum that's going to unmake reality, but I can try and stop it if you release me from service to Carpathian Intelligence."

Vlad looked around, seeming to notice the white linen suits on the Coolest for the first time. She shrugged.

"Fine," she said. "You are released from service."

"Thank you, your Dominance."

"You weren't much of a spy anyway."

"Okay, not really necessary."

"Do a better job as a reality repairman, or whatever."

"Yes, your Dominance."

Vlad pulled Greta up into her arms and ran off for the cover of a nearby shrubbery. Sloot marveled at her sure footing in the bloody grass, but reasoned that not slipping in pools of blood was a minor skill for a warrior of her renown.

"Well, that's all of your entanglements," he said. "But I'm not sure you're cut out to handle this."

"I am," said Lucia.

"What? How?"

Lucia rounded on Donovan with an incredulous look. She pointed up at the Dark. "Are you really so eager to deal with this yourself?"

"I think you mean 'ourselves.'"

"Oh, no, I don't! I want to give the kid a shot. What's he going to do, destabilize this chunk of reality even more, with an even greater paradox?"

"He could," said Donovan. "He's an oddity, remember?"

"He was tapped by a causality demon, remember?" Lucia shoved a finger in Donovan's chest. "If you're so keen to fix this without any help from me or Marco—don't say a word, Marco, I'll find you something to raze—then be my guest. Otherwise, I suggest you make a demon of the oddity and give him enough rope to hang himself."

Sloot hoped that Lucia was speaking metaphorically about the rope, but he wasn't willing to bet on it.

"I suppose you're right. Whether we raze this bit of reality now or later, when it's a bit more ruined, doesn't really matter. Plus, I haven't known many causality demons to be wrong."

"Many?" asked Sloot, warily.

"Well, they're not infallible," said Lucia, "but they usually know what they're talking about."

"So we're *not* going to raze the land," grumbled Marco.

"Oh, lighten up," said Donovan. "There are plenty of dead stars that you can feed to the Horrors from the Void, if you're bored."

❧⟶NEW DIGS❧⟶

B eing corporeal again was weirder than Sloot had thought it would be. He'd assumed that it would be like riding a bicycle, only Sloot had never learned. Too risky, in his view.

He did have prior experience with corporeality, though. After a few weeks of practice, he was sure he'd stop smacking himself in the face with his own hands and tripping over his feet when he walked. Well, maybe only as often as he had when he'd been alive.

He steeled himself for the paperwork. The intricacies of Central Bureaucracy had taken his breath away once. If that metaphor had been applied proportionally to Infernal Bureaucracy, he'd have been left standing there with his lungs hanging inside-out from his mouth, and that would just have been the line outside the building.

"What I wouldn't give for a pair of Blinzwalders right now," said Sloot. The best shoes in the world for standing in line were handcrafted in Salzstadt, at Blinzwalder's on Bittestrasse. He'd already decided that once he actually got down to the business of fixing reality, Blinzwalder's would need to be put back exactly as it had been.

He was intuitively aware that no actual time had passed, not in the Narrative, anyway. He'd been fitted with an Infernal clock—and no, they hadn't meant *internal*, though that would have been at least partially correct as well—when he'd been made a demon. Infernal time was brutally efficient, packing eons into proverbial blinks of a mortal eye. He'd been standing there for the better part of a week in Infernal time, during which the line hadn't moved one iota. Thus far, it was colossally difficult to be a demon.

Demon 100th Class, to be precise. According to the Coolest, if Sloot's solution to the crisis of reality that Roman's wager had caused was to be reviewed with any credibility, they couldn't show him any favoritism. Sloot had also learned—and almost wished he hadn't—that the classes of demons corresponded to the levels of the Inferno, of which there were 99. There was no doubt that the Coolest were taking the whole "no favoritism" thing entirely seriously.

Over the course of the week that followed, Sloot was sure that he saw the line move ahead of him. His mind may have played tricks on him once or twice, but there were definitely at least half a dozen times that he saw a single step ripple forward in the distance, but the ripples never seemed to make their way back to him.

Finally, after about a month, he worked up the gumption to ask the worm-ridden rot demon in front of him what was going on, and learned that demons below 98th class stood in line to stand in line, and that the "lucky" wretch at the front usually held that spot for a decade or so before being invited to stand in the back of the proper line.

That would have driven most people, demons, or just about anyone else to the depths of utter despair, but not Sloot. Sloot was driven to the depths of despair *and* madness over the next few centuries by Infernal reckoning, during which he made up his own language and taught it to a race of imaginary figments who worshiped him as a god. They gradually lost confidence in Sloot, and he was overthrown for a democratically elected god who granted wishes and didn't wring his hands so much.

Finally, he stepped to the back of the proper line. Fortunately for Sloot, the relative grandeur and mild reduction in the smell of brimstone soothed his nerves just enough to pull him back from the brink, just close enough to sanity to remember who he was and why he was there.

There was some real queuing happening in the proper line. Never mind that Sloot knew nothing about the Inferno beyond the oppressive red sky, black clouds, and uncomfortable synthetic fabric of the initiate robes they'd given him to wear. He was entirely within his element here. If anyone had been counting, they'd have known that Sloot made it all the way to the front of the line—with only a single detour that ended him at the back again to start all over—in a mere 1700 years, when 1703 was the average. It was still more than enough time to return to his deific delusions by the time he reached the front of the line.

"Name?" demanded the listless Demon 99th Class at the teller-style window in a bored monotone.

"I Am He Who Has Always Been," boomed Sloot, or rather tried to boom, but demonhood hadn't equipped him with anything more menacing than the tinny squeak box he'd been born with the first time. "Tremble Before My Visage, And—"

"That'll be the line talking," sighed the demon behind the window, with the sort of agitated indifference of a wedding guest who was allergic to both chicken and fish, but chose one just to move things along. "You're not a god, you're a demon. Think on it a moment, I'll wait."

Time unwound. Innumerable planets and constellations of Sloot's concoction unmade themselves over the course of a few months, allowing him to retrace the enormity of it all to a single explosion at its galactic center. He pressed on through the void before the birth of it all, and found the meek, nascent demon who'd gone just a bit loony while standing in line.

"Peril," he said at last. "Sloot Peril."

The bureaucracy demon rifled through a stack of papers, pausing occasionally to read a bit.

"Not in this one," it said, reaching for another stack. It rifled through that one as well, probably unaware that it was doing so to the silent accompaniment of Sloot's complete lack of confidence that that would be the right stack either.

"Not in this one either," it said, to Sloot's complete lack of surprise. "Hang on a minute."

Sloot watched as the bureaucracy demon slid off its chair and ambled down a long hallway behind it. He took a moment to appreciate

the acuity of demonic vision. Even at his pathetically low level, he could make out every boil and pustule on the bureaucracy demon's hairy back, and had plenty of time to wonder whether this acuity was a blessing or a curse. The demon opened a door at the end of the very long hallway, and Sloot saw an impossibly vast room beyond it. There were enormous bookcases overflowing with papers. The demon picked up a slender stack like the two it had reviewed already and made the long trek back to its seat.

"Now then," it said, taking a very long moment to re-situate itself in the chair, "let's have a look at this one."

Sloot sighed as it rifled through the stack of papers and, finding nothing pertinent, got up and started walking back toward the hallway.

Sloot threw himself against the barred window. "Er, please, there's a good chance I'm not on any of the lists! I've got an extenuating circumstance!"

A hush fell over the room, allowing Sloot to notice for the first time the buzz of black flies that served as an undertone to everything else. It seemed as though the entirety of Infernal Bureaucracy had taken the opportunity to pause, which wasn't as rare an occurrence as one might assume.

"An extenuating circumstance, eh?" The demon licked its lips with a warty tongue. "Do tell."

"Well, the Dark sort of ruptured into a big chunk of reality," said Sloot. "The Coolest got involved, and they made me a demon so I could sort it out."

"Uh huh," said the bureaucracy demon, in a way that one does to acknowledge that someone had begun to tell a story. Unfortunately for Sloot, he'd already finished.

"They said I was an oddity," he struggled to continue. "A man named Elroy had a list. I wasn't on that one either."

The bureaucracy demon—and everyone else within earshot, which was a lot of demons, thanks to the acuity of demonic hearing—stared at him blankly for a very, very long time. When he failed to continue, everyone went back to what they'd been doing before.

"I don't know any Elroy," said the demon, and back he went to the room at the end of the long hallway, returning eventually with another slender stack of papers. This continued over the course of the next several years, which Sloot declined to count. He reasoned that if Infernal Bureaucracy bore even a passing resemblance to Salzstadt's Central Bureaucracy, pitching a fit would lead him nowhere but the end of the line; and in his case, "the end of the line" most likely meant the end of the line to get into the line.

No, thank you. Sloot had come this far. In life, he'd prided himself on his ability to navigate Central Bureaucracy, and he fully intended to pride himself on the same sort of thing in his ... well, *post-afterlife* would have to do for now.

Once the bureaucracy demon had rifled through every stack of papers and determined that Sloot wasn't to be found in any of them, it took the better part of an ice age putting all of the stacks of paper away in the enormous room at the end of the long hall.

"That's that then," it said, after working its way into the perfect position on its chair. It picked up the form that was blank with the exception of Sloot's name, and checked the "No" box next to the word "Listed."

Sloot did everything in his power to avoid descending once again into madness. He was fairly sure he'd succeeded, but reasoned that he probably wouldn't have known if he hadn't.

"Now then, what can I do for you, Sloot Peril?"

That took Sloot aback. Donovan had snapped his fingers, and Sloot was suddenly a demon 100th class standing in a pre-line.

"Er, the usual," said Sloot.

"What?"

"The usual?" he repeated, turning it into not so much a question as a plea. "Sorry, but I'm not entirely sure how this works."

"This is the requests counter," said the bureaucracy demon, his voice a frigid expanse of failing patience, every inch of which rested against the edge of ranting. "You wait in the line, you make a request, and we start processing the form."

"Oh," said Sloot. "What sort of things can I request?"

"Just about anything. Your chances of having the request rejected are the same as your demonic class, which is...?"

Sloot sighed. "100th."

The demon tsked. "I wouldn't have wasted my time in the line, if I were you. Still, you may as well make a request, since you're here."

"Why bother? It's got a 100 percent chance of rejection!"

"You said yourself, you're an oddity."

Perhaps more than anything else, that was the thing that worried Sloot the most. Predictability and order had been the only things that had ever provided him any real comfort. Being told by a divine being in a linen suit that his essential nature was the very opposite of those things was the stuff of existential crises.

Think, Peril, he demanded silently of himself. The way he saw it, there were two options. The first was to resist, which every impulse within him was screaming for him to do. There were still caves in the world, weren't there? Giant rocks under which he might fling himself, withdraw from the world and count himself the king of neatly ordered rows of smaller rocks, arranged by size and/or color? There was order to be found in everything, he was sure of it!

The other option was to lean in. It almost seemed reasonable, given that going along with his instincts had never actually worked out. He wasn't entirely sure he even had any instincts, for that matter.

No, wait! That wasn't true. He had one.

One.

He'd said it himself, just now, when he was on the precipice of a chasm of self-pity, about to resign himself to it and throw himself a party. Myrtle must have seen it too. Why else would she have gone to such lengths to place him here, in the center of all this chaos and uncertainty?

Sloot Peril had an instinct for order. He could find it anywhere, in anything. If he could make a sensible ledger for Willie's lifetime footwear purchases based on rumors and innuendos about cobblers who'd long since gone into hiding, unraveling a paradoxical conundrum crafted by an ancient demon over thousands of years should be ... well, quite difficult. Still, if anyone could do it, why not Sloot?

That was it, then. Sloot had two options, and he was going to take them both. He'd resist the mounting chaos by embracing it, and ask it nicely to stand in orderly lines.

Sloot drew up all of the resolve that he could muster and said, "I'd like to be a better dancer."

Squinting, the bureaucracy demon raised an eyebrow. "Really? That's it?"

Doubt, overly-familiar harlot that she was, nestled herself seductively against Sloot and nibbled his earlobe. It took all of his resolve to rebuff her, but rebuff he did. That was what Myrtle had said, wasn't it? *You're a better dancer than you think?* Sloot knew far too much about probability to believe that such a cryptic statement was just gibberish, especially from someone who could see into the future.

"Please and thank you," said Sloot with more certainty than he knew was within him. His voice nearly dropped into an upper baritone register there. It felt good, but in a terrifying sort of way.

⚡️ENTER THE BARD⚡️

Sloot had seen dwarves in the history books, though there was no telling whether those sketches were even remotely accurate. Given the goblin problem in the Old Country and the fact that the dwarves had defeated them before, Sloot didn't imagine that the Domnitor, long may he—he really *did* need to stop doing that now, didn't he?—that the *government* would have any reason to encourage dwarfish discrimination or anything.

In point of fact, if they'd made any attempt to vilify the dwarves, they'd done a horrible job. Dwarves were always portrayed as cheerful fellows with rosy cheeks, long beards, and strong work ethics to be admired by all salts.

Igor was not a dwarf, and looked nothing like the rosy-cheeked, industrious sketches that Sloot had seen in his youth. He was closer to that than anything else though, so it was a good enough place for Sloot to begin his comparison.

Igor's cheeks were not rosy. They were as grey as the rest of him. Neither was his beard long, but rather patchy, filthy, and mysteriously singed in a few places. He seemed hunched over with the effort of lugging the crooked scowl on his face, and his serpentine yellow eyes were nearly as threatening as the stench rising off him.

"Everything's in order," Igor croaked, "you just need to sign."

Sloot was unsuited to demonhood in a multitude of ways, from his fear of demons to his unwillingness to indulge in anything remotely craven. Still, he wasn't about to sign anything without reading it thoroughly, in part because he'd connected with his internal desire to con other beings into signing up for unfavorable conditions of his own. He was wrestling idly with his feelings about that compulsion as he read the contract that Igor had handed him, and resolved to give that train of thought his full attention when the opportunity presented itself.

"You're missing citations," said Sloot.

"Which ones?"

"All of them," said Sloot. "Any of them! This doesn't make any sense at all. Why would I be required to contract with a bard?"

"Hard to have songs and poems written about your exploits of you don't," Igor shrugged. "Look, I don't make the rules. They assigned me as your bard, and you're supposed to sign the contract."

"Who's 'they?'"

"Who isn't?"

"I'm sorry, I don't go in for rhetoric."

"I don't know the names of every stinking demon who had a hand in the legislative process! I'm just a lowly denizen of the system like yourself. Now, I'm sure I've got a pen here somewhere."

Igor went rummaging in a filthy sack that looks like it may once have been made from burlap, but that had been eaten away by an accumulation of filth so tenacious that it should have evaporated ages ago. Sloot surmised that it was only being held together by the filth's refusal to go silently into the night.

"You're lying," said Sloot. He held the contract out for Igor to take it.

"I assure you, I'm not."

Sloot sighed. "You've written notes to yourself in the margins. This says, 'See if the mark will go in for letting me have the top bunk, if we find ourselves staying somewhere that has bunk beds. Also convince him that the government—or whoever—requires the mark to feed his bard food without rocks in it, as my teeth are killing me.'"

Igor flashed a sheepish grin like a shattered window. "Oh, come on, everyone's going to want to be your bard once they find out what you're about! You're working for the Coolest, right? Secret mission, and that?"

"How did you—"

"Never mind," said Igor. "Look, I'll do a good job with the barding and all. I'll strike the bit about feeding me rocks, if you want. I don't mind them that much, honest!"

Sloot searched his mind for a way to brush Igor off, but he came up empty. He didn't want to be rude, and none of his limited social tools seemed capable of getting him out of this otherwise.

"I suppose I could give you a tryout or something," Sloot relented. "What instruments do you play?"

That wasn't the sort of question that Sloot imagined would send a bard into fits of nervous stammering, yet there they were. A nervous stammerer himself, Sloot recognized it when it happened.

"You don't play any instruments, do you?"

"What?" croaked Igor, a bit more emphatically than would have been believable. "That's just ... oh, you're lucky I'm not easily offended!"

Sloot blinked. Anything else might have distracted from his frown of incredulity, which he felt he might have been pulling off for the first time.

"I've got..." Igor dug furiously into his filth bag, eventually drawing out a length of wire. "This?"

"That's not an instrument."

"Oh, a music critic, are you? Seen every musical instrument in the universe already?"

Doubt sidled up to him again, purring and eager for another go. Sloot blushed.

"All right then," he said, his voice cracking once. "Play it."

Another frightened stare from Igor. Sloot still wasn't sure what to do with those, rarely ever having been on the receiving end.

In a fit of unrehearsed brilliance—if one were to remove all meaning from the word—Igor gripped the ends of the wire with both hands and pulled in a rhythmic sort of way that lacked any rhythm at all. The result was the sort of twangy fumbling that Sloot might expect to hear from a barn in the deep woods of Carpathia during the world's most awkward family reunion.

"Oh, come off it," said Sloot, no longer able to wear the facade of patient humor. "You're not a bard at all! This certainly isn't a valid contract. I'm going now, and I'd strongly prefer if you didn't follow me, please and thank you! I'm sorry if that's harsh, but—"

"All right," moaned Igor, "I'm sorry! I didn't want to do it like this, but do you have any idea how hard it is for a gremlin to break into barding?"

"A gremlin?"

"We break things," he explained with a caustic little grin, and a palms-up gesture of appeasement. "I mean, I'm good at it and all, but I'm tired of it. I've always wanted to be a bard, and the only way I get to do that is if I land a gig. Please, can I be your bard?"

Sloot vacillated, as he was wont to do. On the one hand, he didn't believe that anyone should be forced into any occupation that they didn't want to do, with the obvious exception of tax evaders being assigned to sewer-scrubbing details. On the other hand, a gremlin bard—gremlish bard?—just sounded like it had "disaster" written all over it, especially given that this particular one didn't even know how to play the non-instrument that it had, or rather, didn't.

"I'm sorry," he said at last, "I just don't think it's a good idea."

Igor sighed. His dejected look quickly turned angry. "What if I threaten you?"

"What?"

"You know, promise to do you harm."

"I know what threats are," said Sloot, who was all too familiar, "I was trying to express shock."

"Oh, right. Look, if I'm not a bard I'm just a gremlin, and I'm honor-bound to continue doing my job. Big task like the one you've got ahead of you? A lot of things that could go wrong there, I imagine. It would be a shame if you had a gremlin mucking about in it."

"It would," admitted Sloot. "There's a contract for that sort of thing though, right? Wouldn't I have to sign off on that?"

"No such luck," Igor grinned, clearly pleased with this turn of sentiment in the conversation. "We gremlins are old-school. No unions, no contract negotiations, just an instinct for mischief and nothing to lose."

Sloot felt defeated. At least he knew where he stood with defeat.

"I'm not signing that contract," he said.

"Please?"

Sloot shook his head. He was awash with fear for the potential consequences of having anything to do with Igor, but nothing could have convinced him to sign such a poorly written document.

"Look, you get yourself a proper instrument and learn to play it, and I'll consider drawing up a proper contract to make you my bard, all right?"

"Agreed!" Igor smiled broadly, showing Sloot the horrible things that slithered among what appeared to be coral reefs growing on his back teeth. "So, where are we off to?"

"No, no," said Sloot. "You come and find me once you've worked out the instrument thing. Don't come following me!"

"It'll be easier to find you if I just come along now."

"I'd really rather you didn't."

"I'm a gremlin. You'd be surprised how often I hear that."

Coming Home

Erstwhile bard at his heels, Sloot teleported for the very first time back to the site of the battle, where the Coolest had made him a demon. Another of the perks of being a demon was his innate sense of time, which told him that the few millennia he'd spent in Infernal Bureaucracy had amounted to little more than a moment in the Narrative. He'd expected to see everyone still milling about, but there was no one and nothing.

"This is where it all happened," mused Igor. "The Coolest were right here! Wow."

"Just the sort of thing a bard would sing about," said Sloot.

Igor put a finger to his chin thoughtfully, then shrugged. "I guess so."

"You guess so?"

Igor nodded. Sloot thought about pointing out that gods—or something approximating gods—standing around in the Narrative, casually discussing the fates of entire nations' worth of reality was exactly the sort of thing that proper bards would kill to have at the ready, but he didn't want to be mistaken for encouraging Igor.

"That's that, then." Sloot folded his arms and looked out over the empty plain that gave the Old Country-Carpathian border a place to be. The Dark roiled overhead, a turbulent shadow held at bay by some unseen force from devouring everything around it. It was his to sort out, but more than that, it was his only job. No other obligations, just the work in front of him.

Freedom! Horrible freedom.

Sloot couldn't remember ever having been left to his own devices to this degree, and the enormity of it made it impossible to catch his breath. Breath! He'd gotten used to not having to do that anymore. Why would they make it so demons had to breathe? Whoever "they" were. The Coolest, probably.

"You should try to breathe," offered Igor.

"That's all I'm doing!"

"Oh. Good job, then."

Sloot's sense of panic threatened to force him back to the resting rate of anxiety that had been a constant for most of his life. The first one, that is. There had to be more, something other than a single job that would place some constraints on his life.

Well, there was Myrtle, for starters. She was still alive, wasn't she? Working in the lowest level of the Inferno had to be simply awful. He needed to rescue her! That was something. He avoided thinking about the sheer enormity of that task, denial being a powerful weapon in his arsenal. One panic at a time.

He had his friends to think of, too. He didn't know where any of them were at the moment, though they'd certainly turn up in the course of fixing the whole "Dark threatening to plunge both the Old Country and Carpathia into eternal night if he were to fail at his task" thing.

Sloot started hyperventilating. He'd come full circle! There had to be something else. His mother had always been good at talking him out of his worry, what would she—

Of course, thought Sloot, *that's it!* He hadn't seen his mother since long before the Fall of Salzstadt, when she'd revealed that she was a Carpathian spy and he'd agreed to take her place. He'd done his best to avoid thinking that she'd died during the time between then and now, which was fairly easy to do. His mother was old, but when he'd seen her last she'd been stronger than most people half her age. Stronger than Sloot, for sure. He wouldn't have wanted to fight her, mostly because she was his mother, partly because he was a coward, and at least a bit because he'd heard on the streets that she was a biter.

"Hang on a minute," said Sloot. There was something happening in his mind. It was like a new sense was opening up. All of a sudden, there was no doubt in his mind that she was alive and kicking, the latter in a very literal sense that very moment. He could sense precisely where she was, on a big stony field outside a little Carpathian town called Kadaverstraag.

※ ☆ ※ ☆ ※ ☆ ※ ☆

"About time you came to see your poor old mother," said Sladia Peril, leaning back in her rocking chair and holding a jack-booted foot up in Sloot's direction. "Help us off with this, will you?"

"I only just learned where you were," said Sloot, squinting against the feeble light in her little cottage as he fumbled with the laces, but not because he had trouble seeing. His demon eyes were sharp enough to have shown him all he needed to see in perfect darkness. He surmised that he must have been squinting out of habit.

"How?" Sladia demanded. "Who talked? I'll gut them like a rat on goulash day!"

"Nobody," said Sloot, while silently swearing off goulash for the rest of his life. "It just sort of … came to me." He sighed. "Mother, there's something that I need to tell you."

"You're a demon?"

"How did you know?"

"It makes sense," said Sladia, far less fearlessly than Sloot imagined she should have. "I heard you'd died in the Fall of Salzstadt. If I'm being completely honest, I didn't think you had it in you."

"You thought I lacked the capacity to die?"

"To die *for your country*," Sladia corrected him. "I thought I'd done too good a job, raising you to be a true salt, lacking any trace of a killer instinct. If I were a betting woman—which I am, but not on the fates of my kin—I'd have wagered you'd live a long and boring life, never to be called upon by Roman at all."

"He's a demon too, you know."

"That makes sense, too. He was always one step ahead of everybody. Once is lucky, twice is well-prepared, but he got us out of dozens of impossible situations over the years."

"When you say us …"

Sladia winced. "You were there for a couple of them."

"Mother!"

"What? You didn't die, did you? You were perfectly fine. I always took excellent care of you."

As much as he wanted to argue, he simply couldn't find an adequate retort. Moreover, he found himself thinking that perhaps he didn't want to argue after all. Sure, Sladia hadn't been the perfect parent, but she'd loved him. He had no doubt about that. In the end, wasn't that all that really mattered?

"I love you, Mother."

Sladia's eyes narrowed. "What have you done?"

"Nothing! I just wanted to tell you I love you, that's all."

She watched him for a long moment. "All right then. Back at you. But don't think that means your gremlin friend can come into my house! I'll garrote him with that bit of wire he keeps plucking."

Sloot looked out the window and saw Igor sitting there. He was looking out over the little town, plucking at his sad excuse for an instrument.

"He's not my friend."

"Workplace associates," Igor said over his shoulder.

"Not that either!"

"Now that's hurtful," said Igor. "Just because I tried to con you into signing an eternal contract for services I'm presently incapable of adequately rendering?"

"Yes. That's exactly why."

"You've got a lot to learn about being a demon," Igor scoffed. "Honestly, if you can't con people into signing fraudulent contracts, you're not going to get very far with this whole 'repairing reality' thing."

"Does that have anything to do with the Dark looming over everything?" asked Sladia.

"It does," said Sloot. "How do you know about the Dark?"

"I was in the intelligence game for decades," said Sladia, who then went very still, as though realizing she'd given away too much. "Or was I?"

"You told me as much before," said Sloot. "That was the last time I saw you before … well, everything. What happened to you?"

"Retirement," said Sladia. "I wasn't sure if I'd ever get to see Carpathia again, so I snuck out of Salzstadt the first chance I got. I was born here in Kadaverstraag, so I came here first. As luck would have it, the Corpse Grinders had just lost their coach in a freak boulder accident."

Sladia was talking about the Kadaverstraag Corpse Grinders, of course. They were her hometown's boulderchuck team. Boulderchuck, the official national sport of Carpathia, was nearly elegant in its simplicity. The rules were really no more complicated than the name of the game.

"Can being crushed to death by a boulder at a boulderchuck match really be called a 'freak accident?'"

"No, but it wasn't at a match. Happened in his kitchen."

"That's unexpected."

Sladia shrugged. "You know what they say: you play with boulders, you'll inevitably be crushed by one. Anyway, they needed a coach, and I wasn't about to be one of those people who retires and doesn't have a job."

"That's what retirement *is*."

Sladia shook her head. "Like I said, I did too well in raising you like a salt."

They sat there in silence for a while, broken occasionally by the pathetic twanging of Igor's bit of wire.

"How are you going to do it?" asked Sladia.

"Do what?"

"Fix everything. The Dark and all."

"I have no idea." Sloot didn't even know what 'fixed' meant in this sense. Did he just have to repair the Dark, tuck it back away into the ether? Doubtful. Well, he probably did have to do that, but there was also the matter of the paradox that Roman had opened up. The consequences of an Unknowable Secret being revealed were supposed to be catastrophic.

The question that really chilled him wasn't how he was going to fix it, but whether he *should*. If he were to calculate the odds, which was the one task he was qualified to undertake, he had little doubt that the safe bet for the larger part of reality would be to simply do away with Carpathia and the Old Country before any more damage could be done.

But how could he? His mother was sitting right there in front of him! And what about Myrtle? She'd gone to an awful lot of trouble to earn him this chance at setting everything to rights. He couldn't very well just say "no thanks," and "tra la la la la" as he skipped off into some carefree delusion in which everything would simply "be all right."

"Good," said Sladia, who was studying Sloot's face with the same intensity that a dog stares at a hamburger in a child's flailing hand. "It looks like you've worked out your resolve. That was always the hardest part for you, wasn't it?"

Sloot nodded idly, then thought about what she'd said, and realized that she was right. He'd always been loath to make tough decisions, even when he knew the right thing to do. Of course, he was going to try and sort it out. He wasn't going to let his mother be swept up in the wholesale annihilation of targeted swaths of reality, he wasn't going to let Myrtle spend eternity doing whatever ghastly chores the lowest circle of Inferno had in store for her, and he certainly wasn't going to listen to that wretched twanging for one more minute.

"Igor!" shouted Sloot.

"Yeah, boss?"

"Stop playing that wire, would you please? And I'm not your boss."

"Sure thing, boss."

Sloot sighed. At least the twanging had stopped.

He walked out into the yard, looking south toward the looming cloud of the Dark against the pink and orange sunset.

"There you are," he said to the Dark. "And here I am."

Stories were always full of heroes. Everything that Sloot knew about them screamed that this was just the sort of setting where a clever warning would come across as witty and cool. "You just watch it," they'd say, and look particularly dashing doing it. Unfortunately for Sloot, witty and cool were not tools in his repertoire. He settled instead for a stoic silence, one that he managed to maintain for nearly a full minute before his instinct for panic took over, and he ended up curled in a ball on his mother's doorstep.

Sladia must have seen that coming, because she appeared in the doorway a moment later with a cup of warm milk and a blanket. Sloot took the cup. Sladia draped the blanket over his shoulders and led him gently inside to the sofa.

"Have a good night's sleep, son. It'll all look better in the morning."

Sloot wished that she were right. Unfortunately, he couldn't think of a single occasion when he'd awoken even minutely less panicked than when he'd gone to bed. But despite all of that, as he sipped his milk, he felt comforted. Secure. He was a far cry from sure that everything was going to turn out for the best, but as long as everyone he cared about was depending on him, what could he do but try?

"Should I include this bit in the song?" asked Igor.

"What, the hero boldly drinking warm milk and trying not to cry himself to sleep?"

Igor shrugged. "Nowhere to go from there but up."

ACKNOWLEDGMENTS

It's no small amount of work that goes into making novels of my silly stories. While I'd love to take all of the credit ... well, no, I wouldn't. It's bad enough that my name has to be on the cover. Time to share some of the blame--er, *credit*--around.

To Lian Croft, Najla Qamber, and Rebecca Poole for the illustration, cover, and layout, respectively.

To my publisher, Lindy Ryan, for the copious and *only-mildly-threatening* reminders that deadlines are not suggestions.

To my family, Shelly and Jack, the best reasons I could ever have for doing anything (also for reminding me to eat on occasion).

Thanks also to Shelly for being my first reader. She does all of my readers a service by pointing out the best (and not-so-best) parts of the initial draft.

And last, but far from least, to the readers. I'd be utterly remiss in failing to acknowledge those who take the time to read and review my work. Even when they disagree with me on the overall level of literary genius in my work, their ratings and reviews are my life's blood. Not literally, but literarily. Thank you for caring enough to grace the internet with your feedback, for better or for worse.

ABOUT THE AUTHOR

Sam Hooker writes darkly humorous fantasy novels. He lives in California with his wife and son, who he hopes are secretly amused by his howling at the moon with the dog at all hours of the night.

Read more about Sam at http://shooker.co.